When We Were Friends

Nancy Yeager

---

1. http://StreetlightGraphics.com

For the sister of my heart; I miss you every day

CHAPTER ONE
2016

Frannie Willets drove north on Indiana State Road 3, hoping for a sinkhole, a spring flood, a twenty-car pileup, anything to keep her from the reunion with her ex-best friend. No such luck as highway signs and her phone's GPS directed her to the exit ramp, toward the address Lexi had given her. Still, Frannie blew right past the diner where her former partner in crime waited. She parked two blocks down on Main Street and climbed out of her beat-up white Camry into the clean air of Licking, Indiana, population 2,432—if you believed the interstate billboard. She locked the car, probably unlike anyone else here, but four years behind bars had made her suspicious.

Eyes forward, shoulders back, hands down by her sides—courtesy of the guards' strict training—she followed the incline of the sidewalk, up the tree- and shop-lined street that said *welcome* in a plain-spoken Midwestern accent. Lexi probably loved it here. Probably felt safe.

Frannie felt like making a run for it.

She passed a few pedestrians going about the business of life. One old man gave her side-eye, probably seeing at a glance what she really was. *Eyes forward. Steady.* Soon this ill-advised meeting would be over, and she would be back at the halfway house, in a medium-size town just fifteen miles from the tiny spot on the map where she and Lexi had grown up. Not that she would be staying there much longer.

The closer Frannie got to the diner, the more her hands shook. She chose not to focus on that, chose to focus on staying alert instead. And she failed. She didn't see the wispy blond kid, who couldn't be much older than six, step into her path until it was too late. Frannie jumped out of the way and slammed her shoulder against a steel lamp post. She clenched her teeth and fists, ready to absorb a blow or at least a few inventive curse words.

Then she collected herself. Straightened her jacket. Calmed the hell down.

This was a kid, outside on a perfect spring day. Not an inmate with a bad attitude and something to prove.

The kid wasn't alone. She clutched a bright-pink leash, at the end of which was the saddest sack of fur Frannie had ever seen, with a matted black coat, one weepy eye, and four mud-caked paws. For the life of her, Frannie couldn't tell what breeds had gone into making the mutt, and she was pretty sure she had seen pictures of nearly every breed there was. But oh, that face. Long black muzzle and liquid brown eyes. A face like that could melt her heart.

Kid and mutt both stared at Frannie.

"You must be Lexi's friend," the girl said.

Wow, this town really is small. "And you must be a Who from Whoville."

The kid twisted her pale face into a scowl.

"Like in *The Grinch*," Frannie explained.

"Not funny."

Frannie shrugged one shoulder. "Not trying to be."

"Mission accomplished."

Frannie rethought her assessment of the kid's attitude. She glanced away from the girl with the sad blue eyes, round pink cheeks, and down-turned lips. A face like that could break her heart.

As Frannie watched the mutt—maybe it had some poodle in its family tree, now that she thought about it—he raised a back leg and took aim at the lamppost. And missed.

"Oh, shit!" Frannie barely sidestepped out of the way as the dog sent a stream of pee arcing in her direction.

"Language! There's a *child* present." The words came out of the pale little person in front of her, but they sounded like they could have been channeled from the woman waiting for Frannie in the diner.

"How'd you know I'm here to see Lexi?" Frannie asked.

Without answering, the kid walked away and tugged her mangy mutt along behind her. They trudged off into the alley between what looked like an old motel and the greasy spoon that held Frannie's fate. With her scraped elbows and muddy sneakers, the girl looked as much like a stray as the dog. Frannie shook her head. A town full of strays. This really was Lexi's kind of place, and Frannie should know, since she had been the first misfit her ex-best friend had ever tried to rescue.

By the time she reached the front door of Patty's Diner, with its blue-and-white-striped awning over the Plexiglas front window with the name stenciled on it, Frannie was calmer. She stepped through the front door. As it swung shut behind her, a bell jingled. Her eyes adjusted to the dimmer light. She took in the red leather booths and blue Formica tables along the wall of windows to her right, square blue tables surrounded by white chairs down the middle strip of space, and the long white counter to the left. The smell of thousands of fried-eggs-and-bacon breakfasts hung in the air. A mellow pop-rock tune hummed out of tinny speakers in the drop ceiling.

Shit.

It was enough like the diner where she and Lexi had their first jobs to make her lean against the door to collect herself. *Eyes forward. Breathe. Focus.*

Maybe Lexi had thought meeting in a familiar-looking place would set Frannie at ease. That just showed how little Lexi knew about her now. God, how she needed to be somewhere, *any*where else.

Behind the counter that she could imagine packed with regulars for breakfast and lunch each day, coffeepots percolated, and day-old pastries aged. Two middle-aged women, one a Black woman in a dark-blue pantsuit with a white blouse, the other a white woman in a navy-blue skirt covered by a light-blue apron, stood at the far end of the counter. When Frannie caught the Black woman's eye, she nudged her companion, and they disappeared into the kitchen, leaving Frannie alone in the midst of the mid-afternoon lull.

Almost alone.

Lexi slid out of the booth at the far end of the room. Her dark, curly hair was longer now and hung down over one shoulder. The baby fat on her cheeks had completely melted, taking her from the cute kid she had been to the beautiful woman Frannie had known she would be, even that first day in third grade. Lexi had walked into the classroom, the new kid in school, carrying a light-blue binder and a Goosebumps book. Lexi Harris had been seated in the second row beside Clarissa James, the most popular girl in the class, while Frannie sat in the back between Jeremy Thompson and Zane Zimmer. Frannie hated Clarissa more than ever in that moment, although she couldn't exactly say why.

Now Lexi, wearing a pink-and-blue floral sundress and navy flats, stood to greet her. Strange, Frannie had forgotten how tall Lexi was, but when she reached the table and Lexi stepped forward, the top of Frannie's head only reached her chin. Frannie stiffened when Lexi hugged her, which made her ex-friend drop her arms and motion for Frannie to sit.

"You look great." Lexi slid into her own side of the booth and put her hands in her lap. "Your hair is so pretty. It's been a long time since I've seen your natural color. It looked almost red in the sun."

It had been so long since Frannie had dyed her hair, she had forgotten it had been pitch-black the last time Lexi had seen her, and for four years before that. She had also forgotten, until just that moment, that she had been wearing these same ripped jeans and leather coat the last time they had seen each other, when Frannie had left Lexi, broken and bleeding, in a run-down motel. Frannie's stupid plan had led them there, and Lexi had been too fragile to pay for their crime, so it was only right that Frannie was the one who should pay for it alone. She had driven two hours away before calling the state police to turn herself in.

From all appearances, Frannie's last-ditch effort to right her wrong had worked. As much as she had resisted this meeting, it was what she needed after all. Seeing Lexi's new life assured her there was nothing more Frannie could do for her, nothing Lexi needed. No obligations and no regrets when Frannie left it all behind her. And no chance she would nearly ruin Lexi's life again.

Lexi nodded toward one of two mugs on the table. "I ordered tea for us. Earl Grey."

"Thanks."

Frannie didn't mention she no longer drank hot tea. Hadn't since she had gone inside and found the tea service to be lacking, to say the least. She shifted in her seat to try to get comfortable, but it didn't help. The truth was, she would never be comfortable until this place and all the places like it, all the places where the small-towners could spot wrong-side-of-the-tracks trash like Frannie from a block away, were in the Camry's rearview mirror.

"Look, Lexi, I'm not going to lie. There's only one reason I agreed to see you." She was already lying. Maybe in her new life, she would do better. Not talk about the past, but not lie about it either.

Frannie glanced around the empty diner but still lowered her voice to a whisper. "I need my share of the money. My parole's up in six weeks, and as soon as the state of Indiana is through with me, I need to be through with *it*. I need to move somewhere else and start over."

"Move where? How far away?"

As far as I can go on my share of the hundred grand. But she couldn't tell Lexi that any more than she could tell her she wasn't just moving. She was disappearing. "I haven't worked out the details. But I'll need cash to get a new start."

Lexi cupped her hands around her mug and stared down into it. It took her a minute to respond. "First, tell me how you're doing. I mean, you do look great. But four years of your life, Frannie. Jeez Louise." Tears welled in Lexi's eyes.

"Don't do that!" Frannie hadn't meant to shout.

The woman in the pantsuit popped her head out through the kitchen door.

Lexi waved at her. "Everything's fine, Patrice."

The woman gave Frannie a hard look but receded into the back again.

"Sorry," Frannie said, "but it's been almost a year since I got out, and I try not to think about it any more than I have to."

"I just want to know that you're okay. That you're going to be okay. After what you did for me."

Frannie handed her a paper napkin. "I'm fine. I did exactly what my lawyer told me to do. I kept my head down and my mouth shut, didn't make enemies. I worked in the library for a year then got into the training program for cosmetology. Paid for by your tax dollars, so at least I don't have to spend any more money on school."

"Not quite what you'd planned though." When Frannie didn't respond, Lexi filled in the silence. "Your mom told me you're working at a salon."

"You've talked to my mother?"

Lexi shrugged one shoulder. "Just every now and then. She told me you're cutting hair."

Frannie shook her head. "I'm shampooing hair and sweeping and cleaning up the place. It's a living. Well, not really. It won't be enough."

She toyed with telling Lexi she needed the cash to fund her very own witness protection kind of escape to someplace where no one knew her. She would start by getting lost in the city crowds of Chicago until she could figure out a way to slip across the Canadian border and use her stolen nest egg to set herself up in a new life. In a place where no one in the aisles of Walmart and Rite Aid recognized her and pushed their kids behind them while they asked Frannie awkward questions. Where the salon owners didn't remember just enough about her past to tell her they didn't hire criminals. Where there weren't people who had suspected she was no good her entire life, staring down their noses with half smiles that said they had finally been proven right.

Where she couldn't screw up again and ruin the lives of everyone she cared about.

But if Lexi knew the truth, she would waste her time and Frannie's trying to stop her.

"Just tell me where it is," Frannie said. "I'll go get it myself. You don't have to get your hands dirty again."

"Let's just take a minute and catch up. I got married, you know." Lexi wiggled her left hand to show her small diamond ring and simple wedding band.

"I heard. My mother said it was in the local paper back home."

"It was a small wedding. Really small."

Frannie touched Lexi's hand. The contact that used to be so easy and natural was almost painful now that they were nearly strangers, but she forced a smile. "It's okay. You don't have to explain. I wasn't waiting for my invitation in the mail. It's not like the warden was going to give me a day pass for a wedding."

"It felt wrong not to have my best friend standing up with me."

Frannie pulled back her hand. "We both did what we had to do." She leaned forward and dropped her voice again. "And now I have to protect myself. Lex, if I don't get that money, I won't be safe. The police and the state think the money I had in the car when they arrested me, plus the little bit my mother scraped together for me, was restitution. But Jack Greene knows he's still out nearly a hundred grand. He's not going to let that go."

"What makes you so sure?" Lexi's hands twitched as they hovered over her tea mug. "You haven't heard from him, have you?"

"He wouldn't be that stupid. Between my parole officer and the managers of the halfway house, I'm still more Indiana's property than not. But when my parole is over, Greene will come for me."

Frannie understood Jack Greene now more than ever, having served time with white-collar criminals who had gotten away with their crimes for decades. She knew how their minds worked, how important it was to them to send a message when anyone crossed them. Lowlifes like Frannie who had swindled masters of the universe had to be punished. That made Frannie worse than useless to anyone from her old life. It made her dangerous.

"He can't come after you without admitting he was hiding a lot of cash. And he's too smart to do something to the woman who went to prison for stealing from him. People would figure it out and might start looking at him too closely."

Lexi must have put a lot of thought into this. Unfortunately, she was nearly as naïve as she had been when they were kids, when she had believed lighting candles and reciting mantras and wishing on stars could change their lives.

Frannie traced the handle of her own mug of the tea she wouldn't drink because it was a vestige of the person she used to be and had nothing to do with who she was now. "He stopped by the drugstore where my mom works."

Lexi widened her eyes. "In Smithton? What was he doing all the way down there?"

"Telling her he has no hard feelings toward me. Which we both know is bullshit."

"You think he's threatening you by proxy?"

Frannie nodded.

"So, when your parole is up, you plan to take the money and do what? Just disappear?"

Maybe Lexi wasn't so naïve, after all.

"I'm still working out the details," Frannie said. "It's for the best. And I haven't told my mom, so please don't say anything to her. I just need my share of the money to make a new start."

Lexi frowned down at her empty tea mug. "You can have all of it."

"All of what?"

"All of the money. After what you went through... And my life here is good. I'm happy. I have a family and a job I love at a day care. I don't need anything that belonged to that man."

A bubble of happiness formed in Frannie's throat for the first time in longer than she could remember. "That's... That would be a big help. Thank you."

"Under one condition."

The bubble burst.

Lexi reached across the table and squeezed Frannie's hand. "You said you have—what was it—six weeks left on parole? Move here. Spend time with me. Meet my husband and my stepdaughter and—"

Frannie yanked her hand out of Lexi's grasp. "And what? Pick up where we left off? Pretend nothing ever happened? That's a terrible idea, Lexi."

Lexi sat up straight and made herself look as imposing as a day-care teacher in a floral print dress could. "Terrible or not, that's my condition. Six weeks, and it's all yours. Or you can walk away today. With nothing."

Frannie ground her teeth together. Of all the times for Lexi to grow a spine. How could her ex-friend not see that Frannie was toxic? And it wasn't like she could fly under the radar in a town this small. If Jack Greene looked hard enough, he could find her. And then he would find Lexi, and he would get suspicious that Frannie hadn't acted alone.

Frannie shifted tactics. "I can't just move. There are terms of my parole. I have to have a job, a place to live."

"Done and done." Lexi turned toward the kitchen. "Patrice, can you come out for a minute?" She turned back to Frannie. "Patrice owns the diner and a few other businesses in town."

"So Patty is Patrice," Frannie said.

Lexi shook her head. "Patty is Patrice's daughter."

The woman in the pantsuit reappeared, carrying a pot of coffee and an empty mug. "My Patty is all grown up and a big-shot lawyer now." She set down the mug on the table. "Nice to meet you, Frannie. I noticed you didn't touch your tea. Thought you might like to try my coffee. Best in the state."

"I would. Thanks." Frannie took a sip of hot black coffee that melted over her tongue. "That's amazing."

"I've already told Patrice you worked at the diner back home for a few years and then were the head server at that nice Italian restaurant," Lexi said. "She needs the help, and she'll be a good boss." She lowered her voice to a stage whisper. "And she responds well to flattery."

Patrice grinned. "No need for flattery. If Lexi vouches for you, you're good people."

The woman was sweet. Kind. Likely not a person who would want an ex-con working in her diner. Which could work to Frannie's advantage.

"Lexi said you're willing to give me a job," Frannie said, "but I think you should know, I just got out of prison last summer. I'm still on parole."

Patrice frowned. "Did you think I wouldn't know that? My daughter is an attorney. She'd have a fit if I hired anyone without doing a background check. And Lexi told me herself. Vouched for you too. That's good enough for me."

Leave it to Lexi to find a town full of people with hearts of gold. Or more likely, people willing to do anything for Lexi. She had that effect on people. And she actually deserved it, she was that sweet. If Patrice expected more of the same from Frannie, she was in for a rude surprise.

"You start tomorrow," Patrice continued as though it were a done deal. "We start serving breakfast at seven, and it's usually packed, which means you have to be here at six to set up."

"Six a.m.?"

Patrice glanced at Lexi. "She does know breakfast is in the a.m., right?"

Lexi grinned. "Yes, ma'am. And she'll be here. Right, Frannie?" Her pale-blue eyes held a hint of defiance. Behind those eyes was the only person who knew where Frannie's money was.

Frannie sighed and turned to Patrice. "You'll have to talk to my parole officer after I tell her you're hiring me. And I hope the tips are good because I'll need to rent a room."

Patrice pulled a business card from her apron pocket and handed it to Frannie. "Here's my information. I'll also tell her I'm your landlord. I own the apartment building next door. Nothing fancy, but you get your own parking spot and an outside entrance with a terrace."

The place Frannie thought was an old motel. Outside terrace just meant a cement walkway with an iron railing. But even that was probably too rich for her blood. One of the best things about the halfway house, besides the protection it provided from Jack Greene, was that it was dirt cheap.

"How much?" Frannie asked.

"I'll float it to you for the first month, take it out of your wages. You'll keep all your tips. Utilities are included, and you can eat here before and after your shifts."

Frannie looked at Lexi and Patrice, pretty sure they'd had this whole conversation long before she had arrived. It might be a done deal, but she wasn't giving up without some negotiation. "I'll stay one month."

Lexi pressed her lips together.

"Take it or leave it," Frannie said, pushing her luck.

The hard defiance in Lexi's gaze flexed a bit. "Fine. One month. Then if you want to leave, you can go with my blessing."

By blessing, Lexi meant money, all hundred grand of it. Frannie stuck out her hand, and they shook on it.

Patrice pointed out the window. "Here comes Miss Bettina, dragging that sad thing behind her."

Frannie looked out the window at the pale blond kid and her mangy mutt. Of course. "Your stepdaughter."

"And her dog, Max. We just got him last week. She picked him herself at the shelter." Lexi's face beamed with pride and love as she spoke. She slid out of the booth. "Come on. You can get to know them on the walk home. You're coming to our house for dinner."

Frannie swigged down more of the coffee and stood to follow Lexi. "That really is great," she told Patrice, her new boss and land-lord who looked at her with neither pity nor disdain. "Has anyone ever told you blue is your color?"

Patrice smiled. "We're gonna get along just fine."

Lexi was already out the door and kneeling on the sidewalk to hug the kid and pet the mutt. When Frannie joined them, Lexi would have just what she wanted: a full complement of strays.

One month. Just thirty days. Then Frannie would get her money, and a couple of weeks after that, Indiana would cut her loose. Freedom, real freedom from everyone who had ever known her, pegged her for a loser, and been proven right, was almost in her grasp. And then the people she had disappointed the most could get on with their lives without her.

One month, she repeated like a silent mantra as she stepped outside the diner and into Lexi's life. One long, god-awful month.

CHAPTER TWO

The kid kept things close to the vest, Frannie had to give her that. She could respect that.

Not that Frannie particularly enjoyed sitting in a lawn chair on the back patio, untouched glass of sweet tea in front of her, while the wispy thing and her mangy dog sat in the middle of the large diamond of freshly cut lawn and stared at her.

"Shouldn't you climb one of those trees or something?" Frannie knew from Bettina's half smirk that Frannie had just lost a game she hadn't known they had been playing.

"The weeping willow won't hold my weight, and the low branches of the other trees are too high. Daddy has to give me a boost. Besides, Max doesn't like that game. He can't climb." Bettina laid her hand on the dog's head, and with his tongue lolling out of the side of his mouth, it was quite possible that Max smiled at her.

Frannie took a sip of tea—very sweet with just a hint of lemon because of course Lexi remembered how she liked it—and stood. Through the open kitchen window, she heard Lexi stirring and chopping and rattling pans. Which meant Lexi could probably hear her too. So she moved onto the lawn and sat on Max's other side.

She plucked a piece of short, smooth grass and rubbed it between her fingers, trying to remember how to make a duck call with it. Remembering Lexi had taught her that, she dropped the blade.

"I noticed you kept a close eye on me the whole walk home," Frannie said.

Bettina leaned forward to peer around Max. "My home, not yours."

Frannie nodded. "I'm just passing through town."

"I thought you were staying."

Frannie shrugged. "For a short while. Visiting, I guess. I'll be staying in the apartment building next to the diner."

"What aren't they telling me about you?"

"They?"

"The adults."

Frannie glanced at the child. Her big blue eyes were intense and penetrating, demanding absolute honesty. Frannie couldn't do absolute, but she could come pretty close to honest. She stared up at the clear evening sky, but even without an orange jumpsuit, barbed wire, and armed guards, she was still trapped. Penned into a box she would never escape, at least not as long as she was somewhere anyone knew her.

"I was in jail."

Bettina's eyes widened, and she leaned her shoulder into Max, who licked the girl's cheek and bore her weight gracefully. "Jail is where bad people go."

"Sometimes." Frannie selected another blade of grass, this one longer. The perfect-looking lawn wasn't so perfect after all. Neither were descriptions of people. Good or bad. Smart or stupid. Redeemable or lost cause. The worst person she had known on the inside had never committed a violent act or held a weapon, but she had destroyed lives and would destroy more when she had the chance.

"Sometimes," Frannie continued, "a good person does a bad thing."

"Is that what happened to you?"

She sighed. This kid was too smart for Frannie's own good. "I don't know how good most people would say I am, but what I did—I stole some money—I did for a good reason. Someone really needed my help, and it was the only thing I could think of to do. But I got caught, so I had to go to jail and pay my debt to society."

Max shifted and lay down on the grass, pushing his side against Frannie's leg. She scratched his ears. Bettina watched the interaction closely then focused her unwavering gaze back on Frannie.

"Did it work? Did it help the person who really needed help?" the girl asked.

Frannie looked around the big backyard and the sizeable two-story brick house, which had a wide porch with a swing on the front, plain but sturdy furniture inside, and a kitchen full of bright-white cabinets and sleek gray granite counters. When she had first arrived here, Frannie had considered whether Lexi would have the money hidden here. For about thirty seconds. Lexi believed more in dreams than in logic, but even dreamers know how to protect their loved ones. Lexi loved her new family. She would never put them at risk with a stash of stolen money hidden under their noses.

Frannie taking the rap for their crime had given Lexi a chance. Lexi had taken that chance and made a new life for herself, just like Frannie had intended.

"It worked." She rubbed the coarse fur between Max's ears, and he settled his head in her lap. "Better than I imagined it would."

Bettina watched Frannie petting Max then plucked a blade of grass the way Frannie had. "I sometimes do something bad." She kept her head lowered but raised her gaze to look at Frannie. "There's a box under Daddy and Lexi's bed. It's mine, kind of. There's an old dress in there and a bracelet I'll get when I graduate high school. And pictures."

A hard, tight lump gathered in Frannie's throat. "Pictures of your mom."

Frannie's mother had told her Lexi had married a widower with a little girl. But the reality of a motherless daughter was so much harder to bear than an abstract idea of a widower's child.

"Daddy and me look at them together sometimes, but I'm not supposed to go into the box by myself," Bettina said. "Sometimes I do though."

That seemed odd, out of character for Lexi. At least the Lexi she used to know. That Lexi would want a child to know about her own mother.

Frannie forced a smile that she hoped was encouraging. "Maybe if you asked them to take out the pictures more often—"

"No." Bettina threw her blade of grass. "I want to look at them by myself."

Frannie rubbed an imaginary knot under her rib cage. Something about the kid's puckered frown and Cindy Lou Who eyes made her want to tell her about a fatherless child who had never even known the man who had spawned her. But like so many other things, that was in the past and was better off staying buried there.

"It's okay if you want some time by yourself to remember your mom," Frannie said.

Bettina wiped her cheek and leaned against Max. "It's not that I'm remembering her. It's that I *don't* remember her."

Frannie didn't realize how tightly she had been gripping Max until he pulled his head away and shook it, sending his ears flopping wildly. Then he settled his nose back on her leg. "Sorry about that, buddy. He's a very good dog, you know."

"I know," Bettina said. "That's why I picked him. I knew right away he'd be my best friend. I'm going to take him to show-and-tell someday, and Jenny and Bella will love him."

"Are those your friends?"

Bettina focused very hard on a small clover she had picked out of the lawn. "Not yet."

Well, hell. To anyone else, those two words would have sounded innocent. But Frannie recognized the song of an outsider when she heard one. She took deep gulps of air to keep breathing because her throat kept trying to close. First, she had made the kid talk about her mother then about not having friends. Lexi would kill her if she returned her stepdaughter to her in a puddle of tears.

"I'm sure it'll be fine." Frannie wasn't sure of that at all. She hadn't made a friend until third grade when Lexi had moved to town. Lexi had told her Bettina was only in the latter half of kindergarten.

"I think it'll be better when they stop calling me Teeny. Short for Bettina."

The name Pantsless flashed in Frannie's memory. "Nicknames can suck. Frannie's a nickname, you know."

"It is? Short for what?"

"Francesca."

"That's prettier than Frannie. Why don't you go by Francesca?"

No one had ever asked her that. "I don't know, really. I've just been Frannie for so long, it's hard to think of myself as anything else. You, on the other hand, have only been Teeny for what, the school year?"

Bettina shook her head. "My whole life. I think my daddy gave me the nickname."

"Is that why the kids call you that? They heard your dad and Lexi call you Teeny?"

"I guess so." The girl patted Max's head as she spoke. "It wasn't so bad in preschool, but now that we're in real school, I want the other kids to call me by my real name."

"You'll always be Bettina to me," Frannie promised. "And while I'm here—visiting—I'll do what I can to remind everyone else of that too."

It was something, a very small something, but still something Frannie could do to make herself useful. She was pretty sure she should hug the kid but could only bring herself to pat her on the shoulder.

Bettina's mouth twisted into something that might have been a smile. "You must be a good person after all. Max likes you, and he barely likes anyone, Francesca."

Frannie gave the dog's ears another scratch. "Why, thank you, Max. And thank you for pointing it out, Bettina."

"You're welcome, Francesca." She frowned as the dog walked over to an empty steel bowl on the patio. "He's out of water, but I'm supposed to stay with him when he's outside."

Frannie could take a hint. "I'll go inside and fill his bowl. Maybe I can even talk Lexi into sending out some biscuits for him."

Bettina grinned, jumped to her feet, and raced to the far end of the yard, prompting Max to spring up and lope behind her. So much energy. If she didn't know better, Frannie would say she had actually made the kid happy, a kid who, despite having a dad, a new stepmom, and a mutt who all loved her, was still missing enough in life to be lonely.

With a sigh, she pushed to her feet and grabbed Max's bowl on the way to the screen door. She paused when she heard a man's voice.

"Do you think it's okay for them to spend so much time alone together?" That must be Rob Martin, the widower-turned-new-husband.

"You don't trust Frannie with Teeny, after all she did for me?" Lexi asked. "Four years of her life, Rob, for *me*."

Frannie wondered if Lexi had told Rob everything about the burglary. Probably. Lexi hated to lie.

"I know. I just worry about my girls," he said.

Frannie's first reaction was to hate Rob and his implicit accusations. But he wasn't wrong, and that made it tough to hold a grudge, even for Frannie, who still carried around hard feelings about things that had happened to her in elementary school. Maybe some small part of her was still a good person, but she was also a danger to Lexi, and now her family. Lexi was someone's mom, or at least the closest thing that pale wisp of a thing had to it. Leaving Frannie only one option.

Tonight, she would make her excuses to skip dinner, which would be easy enough. She had a three-hour round-trip drive to collect her few belongings from the halfway house and had to get up at a god-awful hour for her first shift at the diner. After that, she would live up to the letter of the promise she had made to Lexi. She would stay here, but she would spend as little time as possible with her ex-friend. Frannie and Rob were of the same mind on that point, and they would probably both be counting the days until she could disappear.

CHAPTER THREE
September 2011

Everyone had told Lexi not to get her hopes up. At least everyone who knew she was keeping an eye on Frannie's case, which meant her parents and Frannie's mom. She couldn't give up hope though. It was the least she could do for Frannie—to keep the faith.

She sat in a booth by the window in the small family restaurant across from the county courthouse. She stared at the wide, automatic front doors, waiting to see Frannie emerge, her lawyer on one side of her and her mother on the other—triumphant, paroled. Free. Every time the doors slid open, Lexi held her breath and whispered her mantra. *She's going to be fine. She's going to be fine. She's going to be fine.* Lexi hadn't decided yet whether she was asking the universe or telling it. But after two hours of waiting, watching strangers emerge and disappear into vehicles and drive away, her whispered words sounded desperate even in her own head.

A new server stopped by her table. The one who had brought her a breakfast of eggs and toast, which she had barely touched, was now long gone. "Warm up your coffee, darlin'?"

"Actually, I'm drinking tea." Lexi's gaze slid sideways. She didn't want to miss seeing Frannie after waiting all this time.

The lady patted her shoulder, and Lexi thought she was probably far from the first person who had sat in this booth, waiting for word about a loved one's fate that was being decided across the street. "I'll bring a fresh tea bag and more hot water."

Lexi was on the verge of turning her head to thank her but caught a glimpse of a familiar form. Finally. The woman had a halo of red hair, but it was longer and a few shades lighter than Frannie's natural color, which no one had seen in a couple of years. Crystal, Frannie's mom. And she was alone. Lexi's heart leapt into her throat and nearly choked her. She reached for the waitress's arm, as much to grab on to something to anchor herself as to get the woman's attention.

"A friend is going to join me," she managed to say around the hard lump in her throat. "Could you bring a cup of coffee for her?"

"Sure thing, darlin'." Her voice was softer, sadder.

Lexi thought her teary reaction probably wasn't any more surprising to the server than her watchful waiting had been.

The woman had just set down fresh tea and was filling a coffee mug when Crystal came through the front door, squinting as her eyes adjusted to the lower light. When she spotted Lexi, she joined her without stopping at the hostess station.

"Thanks," Crystal said as the waitress withdrew.

She slid into the seat across from Lexi without removing her raincoat, which was covered with a sheen of moisture. She tore open two packs of sugar at once and dumped them into her coffee. She stirred slowly then took a long sip. She still hadn't looked Lexi in the eye.

The news must be very bad.

Still, Lexi couldn't ask. She couldn't say the words, and she hated herself for it. After what Frannie must have gone through that morning, standing in front of a judge, admitting her crime—*their* crime—without Lexi there, taking the blame for something that never would have happened if it hadn't been for Lexi's incident. How had this happened? How had any of it happened?

She burst into tears. Not a sob or wail. Just a steady stream down her cheeks and a runny nose, which she wiped with a rough paper napkin.

Crystal set down her cup and stared out the window. "Four years."

Lexi took a sip of tea, waiting for her to say more. When she didn't, Lexi found her voice. "That's a long time to be on probation, but..."

Crystal finally looked at her. She shook her head. "Four years in prison."

"Prison? For four years?" Lexi went numb. "There has to be a mistake."

"That's the minimum." Crystal stared down into her coffee cup. "That's the earliest she could be paroled, assuming good behavior."

Lexi needed to scream. To shriek and howl and clear the table with a sweep of her arm. But the rage was fading fast. Lexi tried to hold on to it because she knew underneath it was utter helplessness.

"There has to be something—"

Crystal shook her head. "It's done. That's the deal."

Lexi reached across the table and took her hand. "But she's a good person," Lexi said. "The best person I know." She should tell the whole story, right here and now, despite the promises Frannie had made her swear. This was Frannie's mother. She deserved to know the truth. And more importantly, Frannie deserved to have her mother believe in her.

"I know she's a good girl," Crystal said before Lexi found the nerve or the words to explain anything. "This was so out of character for her. But we let her down, didn't we?"

You let her down most of her life. Lexi couldn't say that to a woman whose only child, only family, was being ripped away from her for the next four years, but it was true. It wasn't so much that Frannie'd had to hold down jobs from the time she was fifteen to help pay the bills. She had also had to dig overdue notices out of her mother's nightstand and set up automatic payments from her own savings account after their water had been cut off once and their electricity service stopped twice. And not only that, Frannie had cooked most of their meals, biking to the store to buy groceries so they would have something other than Pop-Tarts and chips in the cupboard. And then there were the Sunday mornings when Frannie woke up wondering whether her mom was there, whether she had decided to come home or to stay overnight with her date du jour.

This mess wasn't on Crystal though. It was on Lexi. Still, Lexi blamed Crystal too. "Frannie had to grow up fast."

Crystal's mouth and shoulders tightened, and she aged ten years in front of Lexi's eyes.

"I m-mean," Lexi stammered. "I don't know what I mean. You're right. I wasn't there for her."

Crystal's shoulders dropped a little, but she didn't look any younger. She cleared her throat. "We didn't see that she was struggling. I knew she was lonely, but she'd been such a loner as a kid, before..."

Before she had met Lexi in the third grade. Before Lexi had barged into her life and insisted they become BFFs. Before Lexi had pretty much ditched Frannie for her new college friends, only to go running to her when she needed someone she could trust. Someone Lexi knew would do anything for her. Hide her secret for her. Break into a safe. Go to prison to keep Lexi out of it.

"She's going away for four years." For Lexi. She couldn't wrap her head around it. "What happened to the plea deal?"

"That *is* the plea deal. They dropped the grand larceny charge, and they went on the lower end of the burglary sentence."

"But not the lowest." That would have been two years. Lexi had been an idiot to think Frannie would get the minimum, let alone to believe she would be let go for time served plus probation. Frannie—*they*—had gone up against Jack Greene, for heaven's sake.

Crystal squeezed her hand. "She asked me to give you a message when we said goodbye."

"You've already said goodbye?" Lexi glanced at the courthouse door.

Crystal cleared her throat and blinked fast. "They take prisoners remanded into custody out the back door."

Lexi's stomach twisted, and she nearly vomited her few bites of breakfast on the table. She took deep breaths to collect herself.

"She asked me to remind you of your promise."

"My promise."

"She said you'd know what she meant," Crystal said.

Lexi did. But Frannie couldn't expect her to keep quiet and stay away now. She couldn't deny their friendship for four long years. She couldn't let her best friend hang alone.

"There are things... reasons..." She couldn't share them with Crystal. But... "I should tell someone. Maybe it would help."

"No." Crystal's voice was muted but firm. "She made me promise I'd hold you to whatever the two of you decided. It's the least I can do for her. It's all either of us can do now." A sob escaped her throat. "She'll miss her early twenties. Her first legal drink on her twenty-first birthday. Four birthdays, four Christmases. Dates. Nice young men. Maybe someone she would..."

Lexi slid into the booth beside Crystal and put her arm around her shoulder. The older woman sagged against her, heartbroken. How could Lexi live with the guilt? How could she let her best friend rot in prison while Lexi didn't take a bit of the blame? "If you knew the whole story," she started.

Crystal shook her head. "Frannie made a mistake, and now she's going to pay for it. If you want to do something for her, keep your promise. And go on with your life. Your mom told me you haven't picked your fall classes yet."

"I've decided not to go back to the university." Lexi pressed her lips together and stared down at the table, too embarrassed to tell Crystal she couldn't go back because she had flunked out. No surprise, since she had barely showed up for classes after the incident, and she had missed three of her final exams in the spring.

"That won't help Frannie," Crystal said. "Finish school and make something of yourself. Set a good example for her. Do something she can aspire to when she's free."

Lexi nodded. She couldn't go back to her old college or those friends or Brandon. God, Brandon. But she would figure out something. She would make Frannie proud.

"When can I visit her?" she asked.

"You can't. I'm sorry, Lexi, but Frannie has been very clear about that from the get-go. She does not want to see you. I'm sure she still loves you like a sister, but for now... I don't know. Maybe she's ashamed to have you see her this way."

Lexi was crying again. "But I have to be able to see her." To apologize. To thank her. To make it right. To figure out how to get her out of there.

"I'm sorry, sweetie, but she won't see you. At this point, I barely got her to agree to let me visit every Sunday."

A once-a-week visit. The smart and promising—even if other people didn't see it—young woman who was giving up her early twenties to protect Lexi would get a once-a-week visit with her mother as the only thing to sustain her for the next four years. Spots obscured Lexi's vision. She gasped but couldn't get a full breath. Her chest ached. It might explode. A fitting punishment.

Crystal patted her shoulder. "Breathe, sweetie. Come on. Slow, deep breaths. We have to be strong now, for Frannie's sake."

Lexi obeyed then sat up straight, relieved to see that no one in the nearly empty restaurant was staring at her while she made a spectacle of herself, made this day all about her. She was an ass. The worst friend ever. She didn't deserve Frannie. She never had.

"Whatever she needs, Crystal," Lexi said. "Please let me know if there's anything I can do for her. And let me know the minute she says she wants to see me. Until then, I'll come see you as often as possible to hear how she's doing."

Crystal frowned. "Why don't you call me instead?"

Lexi's heart ached as her last tie to Frannie was severed. "Sure. Of course." She moved back to her side of the booth.

Crystal stood and shook out her raincoat. "I have to get over to the lawyer's office. They have some papers for me to sign, and one of the paralegals is going to walk me through next steps. How to see her at the prison, things like that."

Lexi nodded, barely able to move because she was numb. Shock was setting in. "Thanks for telling me. And for being with her. And for everything."

"I'm her mother," she said. She turned and left without another word or look in Lexi's direction. Crystal must suspect this was Lexi's fault.

Lexi had botched her own life, and by dragging her best friend into it, had ruined Frannie's.

She would find some way to make amends. She would do everything Frannie had asked of her, including putting the pieces of her own wreck of a life back together. Then when Frannie did get out of prison, Lexi would be ready to help her rebuild hers.

CHAPTER FOUR
2016

Only three days into her job at the diner, Frannie was ready to toss the cheap black sneakers she had recently bought and invest in shoes she couldn't really afford for the sake of her arches. She gripped the edge of the serving counter for balance and rolled on to her toes. The suspicious old man she had passed on the sidewalk the day she had come to town sat on the other side of the counter, three stools down. He watched her out of the corner of his eye.

"Can I get you anything else, Mr. Connor?" she asked.

He didn't acknowledge her existence, just hunched farther over the afternoon print edition of the local newspaper. Because this damn town was quaint enough to still have such a thing.

Patrice bustled through the kitchen door and caught Frannie frowning at him. "Would you like some more coffee, Mr. Connor?"

He glanced at Patrice. "Sure would."

Patrice nodded at Frannie then walked past her toward the front door to tilt the blinds against the sun. Without a word, Frannie filled the old man's cup, leaving a half inch to the rim to accommodate the nice pour of skim milk he liked to add. When he still said nothing, she placed the pot back on the burner and walked into the kitchen, where she could lean against the tile wall and stretch her feet in peace while she waited for the clock to hit 4:00 p.m.

Patrice found her a minute later. "One more customer out there."

"I'm just about to punch out."

Patrice smiled. "You should've moved faster. Don't worry. He just needs a cup of coffee. He's here for a business meeting with me, but I need to make a call first. I'll be out in five."

"The things I do for you."

Frannie exited the kitchen and grabbed a pot of coffee off the burner. The customer sitting between her and the end of her shift was easy enough to spot since he was the only person in the place other than the old man who despised her. The dark-haired man sat at a booth with his head bent over a laptop and didn't look up when she approached.

Something about him—maybe the way he kept his spine straight as he leaned forward or the way he seemed aware of his surroundings even though he appeared absorbed in what was on his screen—made her think cop. Or prison guard. She fixed her own posture and kept her eyes straight ahead as she approached his table. She flipped over the white coffee mug, filled it, and laid two creamers on the table, only then realizing it was late afternoon and she hadn't brought the pot of decaf to give him a choice. He didn't seem inclined to notice her existence, and she didn't have the energy to endure a judgmental cop stare, so she silently backed away from the table.

She had already turned away from him and almost made her escape when he spoke to her without raising his head. "I take three creamers."

She pulled another packet from her apron pocket. She should have dropped it on the table, held her tongue, and gotten away unscathed. But his cop-like arrogance—no "please," no "thank you"—reminded her that while she might be property of the state of Indiana for another month plus, she was no longer incarcerated. She didn't have to toe the line. She could step right over it.

She dropped the creamer on the table with a thump. "It's your heart attack waiting to happen."

She waited for Mr. Arrogance's response with one hand wrapped around the coffeepot like a weapon she would never have the nerve to use, the other ready to block her face.

"You're still a smart-ass even if you do wear pants now." When he raised his head, he met her gaze with steel-gray eyes that narrowed as he grinned.

She would rather have seen a cop.

"Seth Collins. What the hell are you doing here?"

"Is this your normal table-side manner, or is this lovely persona reserved for old friends?"

"Neither. I call it my Seth Collins special." The words were out of her mouth before she realized he could misconstrue that. Maybe he had missed it.

"Nice to know I still rate."

So, yeah, he hadn't missed it.

He was still grinning. It made him look too much like the boy who had stood by her locker in the spring semester of her sophomore year in high school and asked if she would be at a party at some random jock's house that weekend. No name-calling, no sarcasm in his question. For a few hours that day, she had considered breaking her own rule about socializing with high school idiots and dragging Lexi to the party just to see what Seth would do if he saw her there. She had returned to her senses but spent the next week looking for him around random corners and observing him from across the lunchroom. Now that she was grown up and—she hoped—a little smarter, she could see she'd had a crush on him, even after the way he had teased her mercilessly in elementary school.

"You went into some special program after graduation, right?" she asked. "Police academy or something?"

"Police? Oh, the cop vibe. I get that sometimes. I'm not a cop. Four years at West Point, another five in the army. I get out this summer."

"Oh. Different uniform, bigger guns."

He shrugged. "Yes on the uniforms. On the guns... You don't watch the news much, do you?"

She knew she should just say no and walk away. But that day at her locker, she had wanted to ask him so many questions and hadn't been able to bring herself to. Other things she had wanted to do that day: brush his dark hair out of his eyes, run her hand over the teenage stubble on his jaw, kiss him right there in front of her locker and the prying eyes of her homeroom classmates.

"I, uh... I'm not up on much," she said.

There was no good way to say it, and if he knew Patrice, he would probably find out anyway.

"I just spent four years in prison," she said. "Well, almost eight months on parole now but four years before that."

He nodded. "I heard."

"Yeah, I should have guessed. Bad news travels fast." Especially bad news about screwups like Frannie.

"I didn't hear right away," he said. "I was halfway around the world when it happened. My mom told me when I got home almost a year later that you'd robbed some rich guy in South Bend."

"It was burglary, not robbery. Big difference."

"Which makes the sentence seem even more harsh. You were just a kid."

Was that pity she heard in his voice? Better than the contempt she was used to hearing when she ran into old classmates these days, but not much.

"I was old enough to know better and stupid enough to take a risk. One that didn't pay off." Not for her, anyway. "As evidenced by the fact I'm nearly twenty-five years old and back to working at a small-town diner. Not very impressive compared to a degree from West Point and years of serving your country."

He frowned. "I'm sure you had your reasons for what you did."

She waited for him to ask what those reasons had been. He didn't. She almost liked him for that.

"And you paid your debt to society, and you're making an honest living," he said.

And biding my time and jumping through hoops to get the rest of Jack Greene's ill-gotten gains and disappear into the wind. So much for honest.

"Patrice said you just needed coffee, and my shift is over, so..."

"Wait." He lightly touched her arm, and they both froze.

It occurred to Frannie this was the first time they had ever touched. In all those years of taunts, showdowns, and one very weird locker interlude, they had never made skin-to-skin contact.

"Don't leave on my account." His voice came out quieter.

She pulled her arm out of his reach. "I don't do anything on your account. Never have, never will."

"I picked the wrong nickname for you back in school. Lexi's was the right one: Fearless Frannie." He poured one of the creamers into his coffee and tore open a second one.

"But how could you have impressed Clarissa and the other shiny girls with that?"

He slopped creamer over the side of his mug. It splashed onto the table, and a few drops landed on one of the papers in front of him. She pulled a napkin out of the silver holder on the table and wiped up the spill before he could react. He watched her hands then met her gaze again.

"Is that what you thought, that I wanted to impress those girls?"

The coffeepot was getting heavier by the second. She set it down on the table. Not great waitress protocol, but if she was going to have it out with her elementary-school nemesis, she wasn't going to break her wrist while doing it.

"No. I'm sure impressing the rich girls by picking on the poor kid wasn't your motive at all."

He furrowed his brows, looking genuinely confused. "The poor kid? Frannie, I was a poor kid too. Most of us in the school were. Pretty much everyone who lived in our neighborhood."

It was a truth she hadn't realized until sometime in her late teens. The houses were small, mostly shabby, almost all rentals. Still, there was poor, and then there was *Willets* poor. "You made fun of me because my mother couldn't afford new pants when I outgrew the ones from Goodwill, and I had to wear skirts and torn tights for the rest of the school year."

Seth took a large gulp of his three-creamer coffee. His face hadn't lost its confused expression. He took his time responding. Frannie folded her arms over her chest. Whatever he had to say for himself, she could wait for it.

"I thought you wore the skirts to be a girly girl," he finally said. "I knew your tights were torn because you were also a tomboy and usually up to something a little dangerous, like climbing the biggest trees and the highest monkey bars. Or that time in kindergarten when you walked home through the woods all by yourself. Like Lexi used to say: fearless."

It was the second time he had mentioned Lexi. That thought collided with something in her brain and started forming a question she should ask him, but she was distracted by what he had just told her.

"If it wasn't about me being poor, why did you make fun of me?"

He set down his cup. "Because I did stupid things as a kid too. I wasn't trying to make fun of you. I was just trying to get your attention." His steel-gray eyes were intense. "A bad-ass tomboy in cute skirts. What boy in his right mind wouldn't be intrigued?"

"You were seven."

He shrugged. "And already incorrigible."

Frannie had no reason to believe anything Seth Collins said, and she refused to be swayed by some ridiculous, short-lived high school crush that never should have happened. Still, it was true he had never used the word poor in teasing her. Not once. Not ever. The shiny girls had done that. He had also never mentioned her missing father, her mother's multiple jobs, or the time her mother had forgotten to pick her up at school, precipitating that solo walk through the woods. The shiny girls were the ones who had shared those secrets far and wide.

The day her mother had forgotten to make arrangements for getting her kindergartner home from school, Frannie had sat in the cafeteria with the kids in the aftercare program, a program her mother couldn't afford, starving but sure she shouldn't take a snack because that would probably cost money. She longed to bury her anxiety by coloring but was terrified of opening one of the pristine coloring books for fear her mother would be charged for it. It was finally second-grader Seth Collins's taunts of Frannie Pantsless that made up her mind for her.

She tugged on harried Miss Smythe's skirt and swore she had seen her mother's van pull up outside. Her performance convinced the teacher to allow Frannie to go outside by herself, at which point she crossed the empty parking lot and slipped into the woods, looking for the shortcut she and her mother sometimes used to walk home. She arrived home eventually but not before being terrified she would be eaten by a fox, snatched by a stranger in an SUV, or lost so long she would starve to death. The stunt had gotten Frannie grounded from watching cartoons for months, her mother threatened with a call from Family and Social Services, and Miss Smythe brought before the school board and nearly fired.

But that was the day Frannie had learned she could only rely on herself.

"I'm sorry, Frannie," Seth said. "I really am."

Now he was here, grown-up and great looking and full of remorse. But what the hell was the point at this late date?

She waved her hand to brush away his apology. "Maybe I should thank you. Maybe you're the one who made me fearless." She sloshed some more coffee into his cup and turned away from him as her boss came out of the kitchen. "If you need anything else, ask Patrice."

"Wait, Frannie, I—"

"I see you two have met." Patrice beamed as she looked back and forth between Seth and Frannie.

"Actually," Seth said, "we're old—"

"Acquaintances," Frannie finished. "Seth grew up in the same town as Lexi and me."

"Oh, that's nice." Patrice gave Seth a side-eye then followed Frannie as far as the counter. "Speaking of Lexi, she just called. Something about that sad sack of a dog and a bath. There was crying in the background. I'm guessing that was Teeny."

"Bettina," Frannie corrected her boss.

Patrice raised an eyebrow but nodded. "Bettina."

Frannie sighed as she tugged off her apron. "The other night, I somehow let the kid talk me into promising to bathe the mangy mutt because he seems to like me. I don't know why they didn't wait for me."

"Hey, Frannie," Seth called as she pushed through the swinging doors into the kitchen.

She didn't even slow down. He had reminded her of something she could not allow herself to forget. He had gotten out of their stifling little town the right way: with a good education and hard work. She had gotten out by coming up with a terrible plan to help a friend and going to prison. This time, she would get the hell out of Dodge *before* she got caught with stolen money.

In the meantime, there was a kid out there who was almost as alone in the world as she had always been. That was one thing Frannie might be able to fix before she blew back out of town.

FRANNIE STEPPED INTO the backyard to find Lexi drenched and standing motionless on the patio with a garden hose, Max scrunching against the farthest corner of the fence, and Bettina kneeling beside the mutt, petting him.

Frannie took the hose from Lexi's clenched hand. "What happened? Why did you do this without me? I told you I'd help, and the dog likes me more than he likes you."

Lexi nodded. "I know. That's what I told Teeny. I told her to wait, that you'd promised to come Saturday to help with him. The next thing I knew, hose water was spraying in through the screen door, Bettina was screaming, Max was howling. I got out here, and they were both soaked and covered in mud. I got Teeny mostly rinsed off, but Max is a lost cause."

And probably too terrified to ever get near adults again, let alone one with a hose.

Frannie had never been allowed to have a dog, but since she had been about Bettina's age, she had wanted one more than anything in life. They couldn't afford another mouth to feed, even a canine one, so Frannie had done the next best thing and read everything she could about them. Her mother could deny her a pet, but she couldn't keep Frannie from learning everything she could about dogs. Breeds, personalities, behaviors, training. That had gotten her a part-time job at a vet's office to supplement her waitressing income when she was seventeen, enough so she could start saving money for vet tech school. That dream had crashed and burned along with all her others, but she had learned a few things that could come in handy now.

She took a deep breath and mentally reviewed her knowledge of all things dog. "Do you have something he really likes?"

Lexi pointed to a bag of bone-shaped dog treats on the patio table. "He'll look at me when I shake them, but he won't take a step in this direction."

"What about something else? People food, maybe. Something he loves but doesn't normally get."

Lexi tore her gaze away from the kid and the mutt and lowered her voice to a whisper even though Bettina was out of hearing range. "Frannie, it was awful. The screaming. She was shrieking and inconsolable. At first, I thought he'd bitten her, and I had these horrible visions of having him put down and needing to explain it to her. She's just starting to understand what death is and how it took her mother away from her, and I thought we were going to have to kill her dog."

"He didn't bite her, though, did he?"

"Not a scratch on her. Suddenly, washing Max was the most important thing in the world to her, and when it didn't work, she had a meltdown." Lexi's shoulders shook.

Now Frannie was the one who was paralyzed, unsure of what to do or say. She patted Lexi's shoulder. It was so foreign and strained. These two friends who used to sleep in the same bed at each other's houses, share clothes, tell each other about their secret crushes—well, most of their secret crushes—were now little more than strangers. Lexi's shaking turned into sobs.

Frannie gripped her shoulder. "Listen, what about lunch meat? Do you have some lunch meat? Can you go get some? I'll try to start coaxing the two of them in this direction. When I give you the signal, get ready with a small piece of meat for him."

Having a plan seemed to focus Lexi. She headed for the kitchen, and Frannie crossed the lawn. She stopped a few feet from Bettina and Max.

"Hey, kiddo. I hear it's been a rough day."

Bettina didn't speak, look in her direction, or in any way acknowledge her. Little did the kid know, Frannie was used to that.

"I wasn't lying, you know." Frannie continued as though Bettina were actually listening and really cared. "I said I'd come Saturday to help with Max. Your mom and dad will both be home, and with three adults—"

"No." Bettina jumped to her feet and put fisted hands on her hips. "No more adults. Adults scare Max. You're the only who doesn't. That's why you're the only one who can help."

Max, for his part, still hadn't acknowledged Frannie, and she wasn't sure they were on speaking or sniffing terms. Now she understood Lexi's helplessness. Even without shrieking and howling, these two were not to be trifled with. The dog was a mess, though, more matted than ever, with mud and grass shards caked on his fur and encasing his paws. His eyes looked weepier. His hangdog expression hung lower.

"We have to do something to help him, right?" Frannie asked.

Bettina glanced at him, her only friend in the world, and slowly nodded.

"Okay, here's what I'm thinking." Frannie spoke slowly because her brain was only a few words ahead of her mouth. "First, we do what we can to get him back to regular Max-ness. Lexi's over there with some lunch meat. You and I have to do what we can to convince Max to get within sniffing distance of it. Then we'll pet him, keep him as calm as we can, and very, very gently, I'll try to rinse him with the hose."

Bettina's eyes shone with tears. "He hates it."

Frannie stared at the huddled mass of black fur. "I suspect it's more that he fears it. We'll take it slow, try to convince him it won't hurt him. If we get him rinsed without incident, we'll try to add the shampoo then rinse that. Then maybe after he's dry, we can ease into brushing him. One step at a time."

She held out her hand for Bettina to shake. The girl tentatively grasped Frannie's fingers then whispered to her. "I want to take him to school with me *soon*."

The heartbreak in her voice resonated in Frannie's bones. The kid was in a bad way. Not everyone was cut out to be a loner.

"Let's take that one step at a time too. Get him used to more people than you and me. Nice and slow, so we don't scare him."

"Okay." Bettina looked up at Frannie. "How long though?"

It was mid-April. Frannie would be gone by mid-May. "The first week of May. I promise. Pinky swear."

She held out her pinky. Bettina stared at it.

"Come on," Frannie coaxed. "Your stepmom and I used to pinky swear all the time."

Bettina wrapped her pinky around Frannie's, and Frannie nodded in Lexi's direction.

It took fifteen minutes, but they managed to entice Max across the lawn with small pieces of ham and roast beef. With Lexi distracting him with shards of meat and Bettina holding his leash but staying a safe distance from his teeth, Frannie turned on the hose to a trickle and began rinsing him inch by inch. By the end of another fifteen minutes, she swore she had more mud on herself than the dog had at any point, but she had also managed to rub him with dog shampoo and re-rinse his fur. He was himself again.

Bettina ran into the house and returned with an armful of towels. Frannie could tell by Lexi's wince that they were good bath towels, but they didn't mention it to the kid. Instead, they each took a towel, and the three of them gently dried Max in unison. For his part, Max did his best to saturate all of them by vigorously shaking himself off every thirty seconds or so. When he was as dry as they were going to get him, which wasn't very, Frannie wiped some of the mud off herself while Lexi gathered the dirty towels into a pile and Bettina began discussing the impending brushing with Max.

Max tilted his head, listening intently. He sat on the patio and raised a back leg and scratched his ear. He scratched it harder. Then he scratched the top of his head, his cheek, and his chin. He bent to his other side and gnawed at his fur. Something about it was oddly familiar.

"Oh no," Frannie said.

She thought of Carla, a tall, broad woman with a long prison record and a bad haircut. She had shown up in the prison salon—a dark, dank room with an industrial sink for washing hair and one ancient hairdresser's chair—for a red dye job. An hour later, Carla's face and neck had turned as red as her hair.

As Frannie reached for the bottle of dog shampoo, Lexi lunged toward the dog.

"Max, stop!" Lexi cried.

But it was too late. He had dashed back into the wet yard, thrown himself onto his back, and rolled around in the mud before Lexi could get to him.

"What's he doing?" Bettina yelled. "Max!"

"He's allergic." Frannie held up the shampoo. "It has to be some ingredient in this stuff."

Her patience with the bath gone, Lexi found the strength to single-handedly drag the recalcitrant dog back to the patio. She handed the leash to Frannie. "Remember the chicken pox?"

Frannie nodded. Frannie had gotten it first and passed it on to Lexi. They had missed over a week of school, and Lexi's mom had taken care of them during the day while Frannie's mom worked. "Oatmeal baths."

"Hold on to him." Lexi dashed back into the house.

Max finally seemed to be losing energy for the fight.

Frannie patted the dog's head. "Bettina, drag that hose over here."

By the time Lexi returned with a box of colloidal oatmeal and another pile of towels, Frannie had the mutt thoroughly wet again. The three humans set back to work on one bedraggled dog, rubbing oatmeal into his skin then rinsing him thoroughly. This time, drying was a much quicker and less comprehensive task.

"I've set up towels and a space heater in the mudroom," Lexi said as she dragged the dripping dog into the kitchen and disappeared into another room.

Bettina sat down on the step to the back door and dropped her head into both hands. "My dog is 'lergic. Now what?"

This kid needed a win and soon. Frannie had been the one to research natural, hypoallergenic products for the unhappy and less-than-forgiving woman in the prison salon, with only ten minutes of Internet time per day and the limited resources of the prison commissary. How hard could it be to figure out how to wash one mangy mutt?

She sat down beside Bettina. "You're still on my calendar for Saturday. I'll do some research and figure out what we can use that won't make Max itchy, and we'll take care of this once and for all. Two days, okay?"

Bettina looked at her with narrowed eyes but nodded. She held out her pinky, and Frannie wrapped her own finger around it.

"Two days," Bettina agreed.

Lexi returned and squatted down in front of Bettina. "Hey, Max is all settled now. Do you want to keep him company until he's dry?"

Bettina nodded. "I think he needs me." She stood.

Lexi held out her hand. Bettina walked past without taking it. Frannie glanced at Lexi's face. Tears were in her eyes, but Lexi took a shaky breath and followed her stepdaughter into the house. Frannie stood, shoved her hands into her pockets, and wondered how much longer she should stay. She didn't want to cross a line and insert herself into Lexi's family business.

Before Frannie could decide whether to cut and run, the back door opened.

"Hey," Lexi said, approaching her with two glasses of iced tea. She held one out to Frannie. "I thought you could use this."

"Thanks." Frannie took one of the glasses and sipped the tea, stalling while her mind raced to think of something to say. "That was, um, intense."

Lexi's eyes watered again. "It's always intense." She blinked quickly. "I keep screwing things up. Getting a dog was supposed to be our thing, Teeny and me. But I'm in over my head and..." Her shoulders shook with silent sobs.

"Oh, Lex."

Frannie took Lexi's tea and set down both glasses on the picnic table. She laid a hand on Lexi's shoulder. Lexi threw herself into Frannie's arms and sobbed harder. Frannie stiffened, overwhelmed and unsure of how to respond. She patted Lexi's back until the crying subsided then pulled away.

"Sorry," Lexi said. She wiped away her tears. "I just... Sometimes it's so overwhelming. I work with little kids all day long. I get them, and they love me. And then I come home, and my stepdaughter doesn't even want to..." She took a deep breath and shook her head. "Sorry," she repeated.

Frannie shook her head. "Don't be sorry. It's a lot. She lost her mom so young, and here you are trying to..." Frannie stopped speaking before she could say 'replace her mom.' That was probably how Bettina felt, but that was unfair to Lexi, a woman who just wanted to love and be loved.

Lexi stared at her, waiting for something, some words of wisdom. Damn, she was looking to the wrong person for that.

"It just takes time," Frannie said. "With dogs, you know. Max needs time to adjust, to learn to trust." What was she saying? Why was she going on about the mutt when it was so obviously the kid breaking Lexi's heart? She was total shit at giving advice about something so important.

But Lexi nodded. "Yes, we all need time to adjust."

"There is one thing that might help," Frannie said. "I know it's not my business, but she told me she wants to be called Bettina, not Teeny."

Lexi frowned. "Rob gave her that nickname when she was a baby."

"But she's not anymore. I think that's her point." Frannie waited for a backlash. Who was she to tell Rob and Lexi how to raise their kid?

"No, she's not. Thanks for telling me that." She squeezed Frannie's hand.

Frannie had braced herself for an angry comeback, but she wasn't prepared for Lexi's gratitude. "You've got this now, and I have to run."

Far and fast and forever.

Lexi wasn't the only one in over her head. Family friend, kid helper, mutt tamer. It was all way beyond Frannie's capabilities. She was in the deep end and sinking fast. And her thirty days couldn't be over soon enough.

CHAPTER FIVE

Frannie stood in the middle of a narrow aisle in Patty's Grocery and Packet Store, a printout of her list in her hand. The prison commissary had been limited, but there had been a comfort in that. Now she stared at row after row of vinegar. How in god's name could there be a need for more than a dozen brands and half a dozen types of vinegar in a town with 2,432 people? She finally did the sensible thing and closed her eyes and grabbed a bottle off the apple cider shelf.

"Interesting selection technique." She jumped at the sound of a male voice behind her. "Very discerning."

"Seth Collins." She turned to face him, surprised to find him just a few feet away from her but relieved that she wasn't being tailed by store security as she had been more than a few times back in Madison, in the grocery store near her halfway house. "Are you following me?"

"No. Not that it's a bad idea."

Frannie slipped sideways and started walking—fast—in search of the next ingredient on her list. Apparently undeterred, Seth kept pace with her.

"I hope stalking me isn't going to become a habit for you. There are laws, you know." She glanced at him out of the corner of her eye. Then took a second look. He might be a pain in the ass, but he was a fine specimen of man.

The grin that widened on his face told her he hadn't missed her double take.

"This is purely coincidental," he said. "I swear. I'm picking up supplies. I'm staying at the motel for a few days to oversee the new integrated security system for Patrice's businesses."

"Army pay must not go very far."

"Army pay is fine, and they're pretty strict about moonlighting. I'm just doing Patrice a friendly favor."

Frannie turned down the next aisle and stopped in front of the baking soda. "There's a motel in this one-horse town? I must have missed it."

"Just outside the town limits, north off of State Road 3. Patty's Roadside Inn."

Frannie shook her head. "You've got to be kidding me. Is there a business in this town my boss doesn't own? And are they all named after her daughter?"

"Yes to the second question. As to the first, a few dentists' and doctors' offices. The pharmacy on Main. The two gas stations. Although she did threaten to open a car wash to compete with the Gas and Go if old man Wentworth didn't step up the detailing service."

"You sound like a local," Frannie said. "Why are you staying at a motel?"

"I live close to Camp Atterbury. My place is about an hour away, and I didn't feel like driving back and forth all weekend."

Seth pulled a box of baking soda from the shelf and dropped it into Frannie's shopping basket. She raised an eyebrow and glanced from the box to his face.

"It's point five cents cheaper per ounce than the other brands," he said then shrugged. "Can't be any worse than your very scientific selection technique."

"There's nothing wrong with my technique. You need to fixate less on it." She kept the box he had picked and moved along the aisle.

"I can't," he said as he kept pace with her. "I've been thinking about your technique since I saw you at the diner Thursday. Or at

least, what I imagine to be your technique. Blame my Y chromo-
some."

Frannie blushed. She couldn't remember the last time something
had embarrassed her enough to make that happen. "Yeah, see, this is
how you get labeled a stalker."

He pulled a box of high-protein granola cereal from the shelf as
they passed it, without missing a step in keeping up with her. Good
reflexes. Not that she was thinking about his reflexes. Or his technique. Except at the moment, she couldn't think of anything else.

"I'd prefer to be a suitor." He stopped walking, and despite herself, Frannie stopped with him. "Unless you're not interested. Seriously, Frannie, I'm not trying to be a creeper. But I would like to
make you dinner." He peered into her basket. "Especially now that I
see you're living on apple cider vinegar, baking soda, and aloe vera?"

"I leave the cooking to Oscar at the diner. This stuff is to make
shampoo." She ran a hand through her hair when he glanced at it.
"Not for me. For a dog. It's a long story."

"You can tell me over dinner. At your place. I don't have a
kitchen at the motel."

He was giving her that intense look with the half smile that he
had given her that day at her locker, when she had sworn he was on
the cusp of asking her out, and against her better judgment, she had
been on the verge of accepting. Then he had talked about a party instead, and the bell had rung, and they had gone off to their own classes, and a couple of months later he had graduated and left Smithton.
Now here they were, reconnecting, less than a week after she had reconnected with Lexi, in a small town a hundred miles from where
they had all grown up.

Frannie started walking again. She didn't want to look into his
eyes when he answered her questions. "You mentioned Lexi a few
times at the diner. Are you still in touch with her?"

"I've seen Lexi, yeah. I asked her about you, about how you were doing. I was surprised when she said you wouldn't see her."

Adrenaline made Frannie's hands shake. Fight-or-flight was kicking in, the way it had the first day she had walked down the street here and most days those first couple of weeks after she had been paroled. And the few times she had been cornered in prison, before she had agreed to pass along some messages for an embezzler, an arrangement that had bought Frannie some safety for the rest of her sentence.

"It's weird that you're both here in this tiny town," she said.

"Not so weird. I'm the reason Lexi is here."

Frannie stopped and stared at him, but he wasn't looking at her. They had arrived at the meat counter, and he began picking through packets of filet mignon. "Do you like steak, Frannie?"

Steak. The word made her mouth water. She hadn't had steak in years. There had occasionally been a grayish blob referred to as steak in the prison cafeteria, but she had learned to steer clear of that pretty fast. She had been living frugally since she had been paroled, saving every penny she earned as a shampoo lady that she didn't absolutely have to spend to survive. The money Lexi owed her was the real nest egg, but until Frannie had that in her possession, she wasn't taking anything for granted.

"I like steak." She was letting herself get distracted. "But what do you mean, you're the reason Lexi's here?"

"I told her about this place when I ran into her back home. It was about a month after I'd heard what happened to you." He glanced at her. "She said she couldn't stand to live there anymore, and she couldn't go back to college. An army buddy of mine grew up around here, and I'd visited him a few times. I told Lexi about it. I thought she might like it."

Frannie nodded. "This is a Lexi kind of place. I thought that the first minute I saw it."

Seth held a packet of steak over his shopping basket. "So, did I pass? Do I have permission to come over and cook for you?"

The steak looked tempting. The man holding it looked absolutely mouthwatering. There was no way in hell she should give in to the temptation of either of them, but she hadn't been on a date since before prison, and she hadn't ever had a man—other than diner cooks—make dinner for her. And there was that matter of the schoolgirl crush she'd had on this scholar/jock/dater-of-cheerleaders after that one charged conversation at her locker. What could it hurt to take a bite of the forbidden apple? She would be long gone before it could bite her back.

"Okay, dinner," she said.

"Tonight okay?"

Yes, yes, yes. She took a deep breath. "Well, maybe. I mean, I guess that will work for me."

He dropped the steak into his basket. "Good. Now all we have to decide is what vegetables I'll make and what time I can come over."

"As for vegetables, anything that's not boiled." She grimaced at the memory of four years of soggy green stuff. "As for time, that depends. Have you ever bathed a dog, Seth?"

He looked down at her basket. "That long story you were telling me about?"

"Yep."

"Bathing a dog is one thing I haven't done, but I'm a hella fast learner."

That comment shouldn't have made her pulse throb in her throat the way it did. At this rate, she would be biting into that apple before they even got to the dessert course. She flashed a smile and hoped her face didn't betray her lewd thoughts. "Then meet me in the yard behind the apartment building beside the diner in two hours."

He grinned. "The apartment building Patrice owns? I'll be there. Now get out of here while I find ingredients for dessert."

Maybe she had given away her secret thoughts with a stupid look on her face. She cleared her throat. "What am I getting for dessert?"

He dropped his gaze to her lips then looked into her eyes. The heat from his stare ran down every inch of her spine and the backs of her legs, into the tips of her toes. "Any damn thing you want, Frannie."

With another grin, he turned on his heel and left her drooling beside the refrigerated case of raw beef.

She almost called after him to tell him the dog they were washing belonged to Lexi's stepdaughter, but she stopped herself. Some instinct told her she should surprise him, should surprise him and Lexi both with their meeting that afternoon. Even with Seth's explanation of how he had introduced Lexi to Licking, something didn't sit right with her.

She was being paranoid, but paranoia had kept her senses sharp and her person relatively unharmed those years behind bars. Paranoia reminded her to keep her distance from people around her. Paranoia worked for Frannie. She wasn't about to give it up now.

LEXI PARKED HER MINIVAN across the street from Frannie's apartment building. It had been years since she had driven *over to Frannie's place.* And this time she was bringing Teeny and Max with her. Old life and new life, weaving together into a seamless tapestry, like the threads of the friendship bracelets she and Frannie had made a week after meeting each other.

"And this time it will be fine, Max. I promise." Teeny was stroking the dog's head as he lolled on the back seat beside her. "Francesca promised too."

Lexi smiled as she watched them in the rearview mirror. Today had been a good day, and Lexi had Frannie to thank for that. Teeny and possibly even Max already trusted her. They knew she would take care of them, just as Lexi had known when she had walked up to the most fearless girl she had ever seen, a girl fearless enough to sit alone in the cafeteria at lunchtime and read her Goosebumps book and not give a toss what anyone thought of it. Fearless enough to tell Seth's brother to back off when he had pulled Lexi's ponytail that first day. Fearless enough to take care of Lexi all those years, until that fateful night when Frannie had sent Lexi off to the hospital and continued on without her, until the police had caught up with Frannie in some backwater town in Kentucky and dragged her back to Indiana.

As she had already done multiple times that day, Lexi repeated her intention mantra she had set during her morning meditation. *Today, Frannie and I will take a step forward in our relationship.* She took a cleansing breath in through her nose and blew it out through her mouth.

"Hey, Teeny... I mean, Bettina. What would you and Max think of calling Frannie Aunt Frannie?"

Teeny glanced up and met Lexi's eyes in the rearview mirror. "Max doesn't talk."

"I know that." Lexi forced patience into her voice. "I guess I meant you could call her Aunt Frannie, and he'd know who you meant by that."

"Oh." She returned to petting Max's head. "But she's not my aunt," Teeny said. "Daddy and Mommy don't have sisters and brothers."

She didn't mean to be sharp, at least that was what Teeny's teacher and Rob both kept telling Lexi. But it still cut Lexi to the quick when the normally sweet girl, now *her daughter*, dismissed her ideas or affections. They had grown so close when Lexi was Bettina's preschool teacher and even in the early months of Lexi dating Rob. But by the time Lexi was in love with both of them, Bettina had distanced herself from Lexi.

Lexi swallowed the lump in her throat. "But Frannie's like a sister to me, and we're all a family now."

Bettina glanced up at the rearview mirror again. "I think Francesca and me would think that's weird."

With that, she unbuckled her seat belt and grabbed Max's pink leash. She opened the door and hopped out onto the sidewalk.

Lexi joined them and took Max's leash in one hand and Teeny's hand in the other. At least the girl still hung on tightly and smiled up at Lexi as she practically skipped across the street.

"You said Francesca told you she made dog shampoo. I told Max it would make him beautiful but not itchy. That's what will happen, right?"

God, Lexi hoped so. She squeezed Teeny's hand. "I'm sure of it. Come on, Max. You have to give it a try."

The dog got distracted by the fire hydrant in front of Frannie's building, although he seemed more interested in lying down next to it than in marking it. Lexi shook her head. Poor misfit mutt. He was the one she had hoped Teeny would pick, but even *she* sometimes had her doubts he would ever be a normal dog. And of all the kids in the world, Teeny needed something normal in her life.

They'd had to schedule his grooming at Frannie's place because he refused to set foot in the backyard at home since the fiasco of their last attempt to wash him. He seemed to be taking the same attitude about Frannie's yard, which was impossible since he had never been in it. It took a few more minutes to coax him to enter, with Lexi tugging at his leash and Bettina pushing him from behind. When they finally crossed the threshold of the wrought-iron gate into the yard, Frannie, who had been waiting there for them, closed it behind him. He whipped his head around and looked at Frannie.

"Yeah, I know how you feel, buddy." For just an instant, Frannie's expression was wistful, but she covered it fast with a smile and a tousle of Teeny's hair.

For at least the thousandth time, Lexi wished she could do something to change what had happened, to wipe out those years of gates and fences and prison walls that had closed in her best friend. But there were no magical spells or incense-fueled incantations to fix what Lexi had broken.

"Hey," Frannie said to Lexi in greeting. She pointed to Lexi's bright-blue rain boots. "Good choice. You probably should have worn your raincoat too."

Lexi moved forward to hug Frannie, but she had already turned away to follow Teeny and Max into the yard. Frannie laughed at something Teeny said as she pointed to Max, who barked and romped off to a distant corner of the fence, and then Teeny laughed too. Lexi laid her hand on her belly and blinked back tears. *This is good. They're bonding. This is what I wanted.* It wasn't a lie so much as it was a half-truth. The whole truth was that Lexi wanted to be invited inside their happy bubble with them.

"Hey." Frannie smiled at Lexi. "Come on, Lex. Let's teach you how to wash a dog the right way."

That was it, the invitation she had been waiting for. Now Lexi laughed, too, and walked with Frannie to join Teeny and Max by the fence.

The screen door squeaked behind them, and Frannie glanced over her shoulder. Her smile widened, which made Lexi turn, curious about who could make her friend beam that way. Lexi sucked in her breath in surprise.

"Seth!" Lexi called.

"Lexi!" He looked as shocked as she was.

Seth set down two glasses of iced tea on the wooden picnic table a few feet from the back of the building and crossed the yard. He held out his hand, and Lexi shook it instinctively, only wondering about the formality after she dropped his hand, which was cold and moist from the glasses. She glanced between him and Frannie, trying to figure out when and why they had reconnected.

Seth cleared his throat. When Lexi looked at him, he widened his eyes at her. "So, Lexi, Frannie tells me—"

"Wait." Lexi held up a hand. "I don't understand. What are you doing here? And why didn't you come by the house if you're in town?"

"The house?" Frannie turned and smiled at Bettina. "Hey, kid. You better take Max over to the patio before he digs a hole under Patrice's fence."

"Sure." Teeny dashed off across the yard, and Max loped behind her.

Frannie turned back to Lexi. "Seth told me the two of you had run into each other a few times since high school."

"Of course we have," Lexi said. "Seth is Rob's best friend. He introduced us."

Frannie, always pale, now went pure white. "Rob?" She shook her head then nodded as though she was just figuring out something. "An old army buddy. He didn't say it was Rob."

Lexi glanced between Seth and Frannie. "I don't understand."

"Were you in on it too?" Frannie's voice was low and quiet, the tone she took when she was dressing down a bully or protecting a friend. Now it was aimed at Lexi.

Lexi held up her hands in surrender. "I don't know what's going on, Frannie. I swear. Seth?"

Seth hadn't taken his eyes off Frannie since she had sent Teeny to the other end of the yard. "It's nothing really, Lex. Rob just wanted to make sure everything was on the up-and-up, and he knew I knew Frannie from way back."

"Oh god." Lexi staggered back a step. Frannie might be fearless, but she could also be merciless when someone betrayed her. By sending a spy into her midst, Rob had obliterated any hope of trust. From the way Frannie stared at her, Lexi knew Rob wasn't the only one she blamed. "Frannie, I swear I didn't know."

"Let's not get upset here." Seth took a slow step toward Frannie.

"Back off." With those two words, Frannie stopped Seth—decorated soldier and all-around tough guy—in his tracks.

"I'm such an idiot." Frannie picked up a glass of iced tea and clutched it until her fingers turned white. She glanced between the glass and the fence. Max barked, and Teeny laughed. Frannie exhaled between her teeth and slammed the glass back down on the table.

She wiped her hands on the front of her jeans, her shoulders rising and falling with deep breaths. When she looked at Lexi, her face was calm, almost serene. "Get out, both of you."

Seth opened his mouth, but Lexi spoke first. "But Teeny! You promised her you'd wash Max with her."

"And I will. And then I'll walk both of them back to your house. But you cannot stay here."

Seth grimaced as he looked at Lexi. "Frannie, it's not Lexi's fault. She didn't know. Rob asked me to keep it between us."

"It's true." Lexi had no qualms letting Seth take the heat off her. After all, he had been senseless enough to go along with Rob's misguided plan.

Frannie shrugged one shoulder and picked up the hose. "Doesn't matter. I didn't ask to be here. I didn't ask anyone to trust me. And I sure as hell didn't come here to be spied on by someone pretending to want to get to know me again."

"I wasn't pretending. I swear." Seth's voice was calm and level but a pitch higher than normal. "I wanted to see you again. Ever since Lexi said she was asking you to come here, I've been thinking about you, about what I'd say to you and—"

"And what you'd do to me, like flirt with me and lie to me and make me think you actually ever liked me?" Frannie squirted the hose at him.

He jumped. "Jesus, Frannie. That's cold!"

"You should be used to it. Snakes are cold-blooded, right?"

"Frannie," Lexi said then stopped.

Lexi meant to defend Seth. He was a good guy. His heart was in the right place. As much as she loved Rob, she had to admit her husband could be very persuasive and ridiculously overprotective—and not above using the interest Seth had expressed in Frannie to his own advantage. But when Frannie gave Lexi the same deadeye stare she had given Seth, it was every person for herself.

"Those two cooked this up themselves," Lexi said. "I had nothing to do with it. You have to know that."

"Get. Out." Frannie turned the hose in Lexi's direction.

Lexi glanced at Teeny and Max romping and laughing, oblivious to the crap show happening among the grown-ups. She couldn't bear to miss this chance to see the child truly happy and to watch her with Frannie. Suddenly, being on the outside of their little bubble looking in didn't seem so bad now that the alternative was no view at all. "Frannie, please."

Frannie squirted Lexi's boots then aimed the nozzle at her face.

"Okay." Seth took Lexi's arm. "We're going."

Lexi shook her head but couldn't think of anything to say that would make Frannie see reason. Fearless Frannie had a stubborn streak a mile wide and ten miles deep.

"Just make sure you hold Teeny's hand when you cross streets. And you have to hold on to Max's leash if there are cars around because he can get away from her, and..." Lexi stopped talking when tears gathered in her eyes.

She let Seth turn her around and walk her out of the yard. This time when the wrought-iron gate clanged closed, Lexi was the one trapped on the wrong side of it. She waited until they had crossed the street to her minivan, well out of Frannie's earshot, before she turned on Seth.

"What the heck were you thinking?" she asked. "Both of you. Do you see what you've done?"

"I didn't know you were the person coming with the dog. When did you get a dog? Rob didn't mention it."

"About two weeks ago, and of course he didn't mention it," Lexi said. "He's been a little preoccupied, accusing my best friend of being some sort of craven criminal. With your help. Why did you agree to this? You know he's overprotective."

"I was just trying to give him some peace of mind." Seth shoved his hands in his pockets. "Besides, I wanted to see Frannie again. For what it's worth, I don't think she's up to anything except trying to get out of this town, which has nothing to do with me, by the way."

Lexi sucked in her breath. "Are you saying my best friend wants to get away from me?"

"I'm saying she's not your best friend anymore, Lexi."

She slapped his cheek. Hard. Harder than she knew she could slap. His head snapped to his right, and he groaned as he touched his mouth and came away with a spot of blood.

"Christ! What was that for?" he asked.

Lexi jumped into the van and slammed the door closed. She struggled to think of a mantra, words to repeat to calm herself, words to send into the universe to calm Frannie, but her mind was a blank. Seth knocked on her window.

She rolled it down. "Step out of the road so I can drive away, please." She rolled it back up.

Seth put his hands on his hips and stared at her for a minute then threw his hands in the air and stepped out of her path.

She rolled down the window again. "One more thing, lover boy. You may not think Frannie is my friend anymore, but I still know her. I know you've had the hots for her since high school. And I know you just blew all of that today." She grinned now, the viciousness relieving the tight pressure that had gathered low in her belly. "After your little stunt, Frannie would let an actual snake in her bed before she'd sleep with you. And general fearlessness aside, she's phobic about snakes."

Lexi rolled up her window and gunned the engine. She didn't look in the rearview mirror to gauge Seth's reaction as she peeled away from the curb. She didn't need to witness the devastation on Seth's face to know how horrible she had been.

Seth was Rob's best friend, and his stupid maneuver had come from a good place, just as Rob's stupid idea had. And Seth was Lexi's friend too. She owed him a lot. For being a shoulder to cry on. For being the one other person who could remember Frannie with kind words. For introducing her to his best army buddy.

"Poor Seth. I'm sorry." *I'm sorry. I'm sorry. I'm sorry.*

She sent the words out into the universe but feared it was too late. She was pretty sure she had ruined everything with her selfishness. Again.

FRANNIE WALKED THE cleaner mutt and happier kid the ten blocks to Lexi's house. She waited on the sidewalk close to the street until Lexi opened the door and shepherded her strays inside the house, and then Frannie turned and marched back to her house without a backward glance. Two blocks from her apartment, she got a series of texts from Lexi, thanking her for taking care of Bettina and Max, apologizing again, lamenting the fact that Frannie hadn't given her the chance to invite her in for tea and a face-to-face apology.

Not that it's on you! Please call when you're ready to talk, the last one read.

Frannie's T-shirt and hair were nearly dry by the time she entered the large room that made up most of her apartment, but her jeans still clung wet and cold to her legs. She stepped out of them and hung them on the back of a kitchen chair. To her right was the kitchen and a fridge stocked with a few leftovers from the diner that could be cobbled together into a dinner. To her left was the siren song of a comfortable couch, inviting her to lie down and nap and forget about the shitty day. She ignored the pull of food and sleep and withdrew an unopened bottle of white wine from the fridge and a juice glass from the cupboard.

Technically, wine was contraband, not allowed under the terms of her parole, although her parole officer had told her just not to get drunk in public. But parole officers were notorious for setting up ex-cons to fail in the hopes of putting them back behind bars. Just what Frannie needed, one more person expecting her to crash and burn.

"Screw it," Frannie muttered. "Screw them all."

The minute she settled on the couch with her drink and the TV remote, her phone buzzed with a call. She cursed. Lexi had left it to Frannie to make the next move, but she was already going back on her word. Breaking Frannie's trust. Lexi and Collins were two peas in a self-serving pod. But when Frannie saw the number on the phone screen, she couldn't ignore the caller.

She took a swig of wine straight from the bottle, dropped onto the sofa, and pasted on a smile in the hope she would sound happier than she was. "Hi, Mom."

"Frannie! I wasn't sure I'd catch you at home."

"I'm not working tonight. But I have a double shift tomorrow."

Her mother sighed. "I know. I got your voicemail. I'm sorry we'll miss our Sunday dinner. I look forward to them."

Frannie almost choked on another sip of wine, this one from her glass. "I don't think you've ever said that."

"Of course I have. Haven't I? Anyway, sweetie, I wanted to catch you before I leave. I have a meeting tonight."

The hair prickled on the nape of Frannie's neck. "On a Saturday night?" *Meeting* must be the new code word for hot date.

"It's just a meeting," her mother said as if Frannie had scoffed out loud. "But I wanted to tell you, I got a call from the halfway house. They said they left a message for you, but you hadn't called them back. They need your room."

"So soon?" Frannie clutched the phone. Her hands shook with adrenaline. That room had been an escape hatch from this town. Now the hatch was closing. Frannie was trapped.

"Yes," her mother continued as if the walls weren't closing in. "They needed to move out the rest of your things. It was just a pile of books, that old jewelry case you lug everywhere, and some of your winter clothes. They're here at the house, in your bedroom."

Her childhood bedroom. At least she still had that. Strange that it didn't offer any sense of escape.

"And then I stopped by JoJo's to say hello and get a pedicure."

"You stopped by my salon?" Frannie took another swig of wine, polishing off the juice glass.

"Not anymore," her mother said. "You have a new job."

Frannie lurched forward on the couch. "Mom, you didn't tell them I wasn't coming back, did you?"

Her mother tsked and made some other noises to indicate she was offended, but Frannie remained silent. "I didn't have to tell them anything," her mother finally answered. "One of JoJo's nieces needed a job, so…"

Frannie rubbed her temples. One of JoJo's dozen or so nieces always needed a job. She was stupid to have told him she would be gone for a few weeks. She should have kept shifts there two days a week, the long drive be damned. Another escape hatch slammed shut.

"That doesn't matter now that you have a new job, right?" her mother asked. "How's that going? And how is Lexi? And that adorable family of hers?"

"They're fine. It's all fine." Nothing was fine. Everything was going to hell in a handbasket. A handbasket with no exit.

"I thought you'd be more enthusiastic after picking up stakes and moving across the state to be closer to her."

"It's not across the state, Mom." It was just another hour and a half farther from her mother's house. Okay, one point in Licking's favor. *Not fair. She's been here for me the past four and a half years.* The first twenty hadn't been so hot, but still. "Don't worry, Mom. Everything is good. And as soon as I get a regular schedule, we'll set up a weekly dinner. I promise."

"I'd like that, Frannie. I really would. But now I have to fly!"

"Right. Your meeting."

"Take care, sweetie."

"Thanks, Mom. You too."

Her mom hung up first. Frannie stared at the phone in her hand for a long minute, wondering what her mother would say if Frannie called her back. Then again, what would Frannie say? *It sucks here. Nobody trusts me. No one is really my friend.* Wah, wah, wah.

No. Enough of that bullshit. Frannie had come here for the money, not a friend.

With her hair salon job and room at the halfway house gone, she might be forced to stay here for the remainder of her parole. But she wouldn't get sucked into Lexi's life, even if it meant spending her free time alone. Hadn't she craved solitude when she had been stuck in a prison dorm for four years? Hadn't she done just fine without friends for the first eight years of her life until Lexi Harris had waltzed into the school cafeteria and changed everything?

And then there were the years between high school and prison, when Lexi had gone off to college in Indianapolis, and Frannie had moved in with three strangers in a crap apartment. Lexi's roomies had become Lexi's new besties, while Frannie's had made minimal overtures at including Frannie in weekly roommate dinner outings but stopped inviting her when she refused most of the time. She didn't tell them it was because she couldn't afford to eat out, and they didn't ask. The pain of being excluded had been swift and shocking. But it was good. It served a purpose. It reminded her of what she used to know but had forgotten.

Frannie Willets did not need anyone.

She got past her desperation. Kept her distance from everyone, including Lexi, except on the rare occasions when Lexi sought out her company. Frannie figured out how to be a loner again. Until Lexi showed up pregnant and desperate and alone herself.

Now five years later, Frannie had moved to Lexi's town and started to fall back under her spell. But in less than a week, Hurricane Frannie was already wreaking havoc. She had brought out the worst in Rob and Seth and had probably instigated a fight between Lexi and Rob. It had to stop. Frannie, so eager to be part of Lexi's life again five years ago, had almost ruined it. She wouldn't make that mistake twice.

CHAPTER SIX
August 2011

Lexi stumbled out of the shabby bathroom. She curled on top of the double bed in the cramped motel room that reeked of mold. Frannie tossed and turned on a threadbare green plaid sofa. The crappy accommodations didn't really matter. They were only staying a few more hours, long enough for Frannie to catch some more sleep before they drove across the state line into Ohio. They were headed to New York, for the distance from home as much as for the easy access to a clinic. It was early evening, and Frannie wanted to be on the road by dark.

Lexi closed her eyes.

She was home in her pink and frilly bedroom. Frannie was here, in torn overall jean shorts over a tie-dyed T-shirt. Her favorite summer outfit the year when they were ten. Frannie smiled and held out her hand. Lexi reached for it. Someone stabbed her. A hard, deep dagger to the gut. Lexi groaned, panted, punched at nothing and no one. Empty air. Another stab, sharper this time. She screamed.

"Lexi, what is it? What's wrong?"

Lexi surfaced from sleep, slowly realizing it had been a dream. A nightmare.

Another stab of pain jolted through her, and she screamed again, not able to contain it. Like a knife through her uterus. Like she was being torn apart.

"Hurts so much," she said, panting.

"We have to get to a hospital. I'll help you to the car."

"No." Lexi leaned into Frannie and slid off the bed. When she stood, there was so much pressure between her legs, she thought she would burst. "Help me to the bathroom."

Frannie slung Lexi's arm over her shoulders and half supported, half carried her to the bathroom. Inside the small tiled room, Lexi nudged Frannie away. "I just need a minute."

Frannie stepped out of the bathroom and closed the door. Lexi made it to the toilet by clinging to the wall, moving hand over hand with each small step, and finally settled on the seat. She heard Frannie's voice through the thin walls.

"She's in a lot of pain," she said, "and there's a lot of blood on the bed."

There was blood? Lexi glanced down at her sweatpants and underwear pooled around her ankles. They were covered in it. Her head swam. Another unbearable pain focused her. The pressure between her legs intensified. She wanted to scream, but sound carried through these walls. What if there was someone in the room next door?

"Lex," Frannie said. It sounded like she was in the room with Lexi now. She must be pressed up against the door. "I called a clinic, and they said you should go to the ER." Frannie pushed into the bathroom.

Lexi stood to push her back out the door, but the pressure in her abdomen overwhelmed her. A warm rivulet ran down her leg. She grabbed a thin towel from the rack and shoved it between her legs as a wave of fluid gushed out of her. She sank to her knees and leaned her forehead against the cool bathtub wall.

"Lex, can you hear me?" Frannie laid her hand on Lexi's neck. She was right next to Lexi, but it sounded like she was far away or underwater. Or maybe Lexi was. "The ambulance is on its way."

"It's too late." Lexi knew what was in the towel, knew it was more than blood. "The... It's gone."

"What are you saying, Lex? Can you open your eyes and tell me?"

It was only then that Lexi realized she had closed her eyes. The stabbing pain had subsided to a dull ache, and now she just wanted to sleep. "It's gone. It's over. The…"

She couldn't call it a baby. It had never been a baby to her. Not before now. She sobbed. So stupid. Everything they had done for the past week had been so Lexi wouldn't be pregnant anymore. But Lexi couldn't stop crying.

Frannie leaned over her, and the shower hissed to life. "Let's get you cleaned off. Do you think you can stand?"

Lexi nodded and let Frannie peel off her sweatshirt. She climbed into the warm spray by herself. Frannie left the room but kept the door ajar while Lexi lathered up as much as she could with the tiny bar of hotel soap. She had rinsed away most of the blood by the time Frannie returned with a pile of clean clothes. Lexi turned off the shower and raised one foot to step out of the tub, but spots danced in front of her eyes. Lexi dropped to her knees.

"I'm right here," Frannie said. "I've got you."

She helped Lexi climb out of the tub and scrub dry with thin hotel towels. Frannie handed Lexi a pad then gathered up bloody clothes into a plastic bag while Lexi dressed.

"Go lie down until the ambulance arrives," Frannie ordered.

Lexi shook her head. They both knew she couldn't go to a hospital.

"Lex, I think you lost a lot of blood. Let's just be safe. Let them take you to the hospital." She helped Lexi onto the bed. "You don't have to tell them your name, if you don't want. That's what the lady from the clinic told me. And here." She pulled a wad of bills out of her backpack. "Pay in cash. Or tell them you don't have insurance and can't pay. They still have to treat you."

Frannie was throwing out too much information, and Lexi couldn't process it. All she could think about was the ruined towel on the bathroom floor.

"It's for the best," Frannie was saying. "Now you can go home and recover, and it's all over."

That couldn't be right. It sounded wrong. "We still took the money." Lexi thought of the duffel bag stuffed into the bus station locker, full of stacks of hundreds, not tens like Frannie had thought when Frannie had grabbed it out of Jack Greene's safe. "He'll call the police, and they'll figure it out. He'll know. Brandon will know." Lexi was shaking and so, so cold. And the more she thought about how her secret would come out and her life would be over, the more she shook.

"They don't know," Frannie said. "They won't know. I'll take care of it, I promise. Just go to the hospital and let them give you blood and *do not die* on me."

Lexi saw a look on Frannie's face she had never seen there before. Fear. Abject terror.

"I must look like hell." Lexi tried to smile, but her teeth were chattering too hard. Frannie wrapped another blanket around her.

Sirens blared, and red lights flashed outside the thin curtains. The ambulance must be in the parking lot below them.

"I have to go now so they don't find us together," Frannie said. "I'll leave the door unlocked for the paramedics. Do not tell anyone anything about this. We were never together. You had no idea what I planned to do." Frannie kissed Lexi's cheek and whispered, "Best friends forever." And then she disappeared.

Lexi was freezing, probably in shock, possibly in real danger. But she didn't care about any of that because she knew Frannie was about to do something awful and terrible and irreparable and stupid and noble. She was going to admit to the burglary, claim she acted alone, and take the punishment for both of them.

CHAPTER SEVEN
2016

Two days after Max's disaster and Bettina's meltdown, Lexi and Bettina sat on the step outside the back door of their house. Max sprawled on the stone patio in front of them as they took turns reading pages of *Goodnight Moon*. Reading with her stepdaughter had become one of her favorite things because it caused Teeny to let down her guard and lean against Lexi's arm and laugh. Bettina used to do that a lot before the wedding.

There had been a glimmer of that bond returning when she and Rob had announced to Teeny that she was going to have a sibling. Then there had been a horrible night of blood and pain, and they'd had to tell her that she wasn't getting a little brother or sister after all.

Lexi's phone buzzed on the step beside her, and she jumped. She had left so many apology messages in the last twenty-four hours without a response, but now Frannie was finally calling her back.

"Sweetie, can you read the last few pages to Max? I have to take this call."

Teeny took the book from Lexi but frowned. "Okay, but Max is restless. I think he needs to pee."

The dog had been fidgeting, but they had walked him in the front yard just an hour earlier.

"I think he's okay. I'll just be a few minutes." Lexi crossed the patio and stepped barefoot into the cool grass. She glanced at the caller

ID then frowned as she answered the call. "Hi, Dee. Is everything okay?"

"I'm sorry to bother you at home," her boss said. "But we've both been so busy, and I wanted to let you know about the meeting I had with the parents of the brothers who can't seem to get along."

Lexi sighed. "The Stanleys."

She'd had Jamie Stanley in her class last year and had his younger brother, Dylan, this year. As the only teacher at the preschool who had taught both boys, Lexi was Dee's sounding board as she tried to navigate what had become a case of sibling rivalry on steroids.

A few minutes into the conversation, Teeny tugged on her long denim skirt, and Lexi turned around to see Max a few feet from them, at the edge of the patio.

"Max really has to pee, but he's still afraid of this grass," Teeny said in a stage whisper.

Lexi covered the phone and patted Teeny's head. "Just give me a few minutes."

Teeny glared at her then stomped back to Max's side.

Lexi turned around again. "I'm sorry. What did Mr. Stanley say about Jamie acting out on the playground?"

"Lexi!" Teeny's voice was a high-pitched wail.

Lexi turned toward Teeny just in time to see the last drops of pee coming out of Max and adding to the large pool underneath him. "Oh, shi... for heaven's sake."

Max slunk away from the puddle and pressed himself up against the wall of the house while Teeny's eyes shone with threatening tears. Again.

Lexi pulled her stepdaughter into a hug, which Teeny didn't return. "Dee, I'm sorry, but I really have to go. Can we finish this in the morning if I come in ten minutes early?"

"Sure thing. You go take care of your own little one."

"Thanks. See you in the morning." Lexi clicked off the call and stuffed the phone into her pocket then patted Teeny's back. The girl finally relaxed in the circle of Lexi's arms.

"It's okay, sweetie," Lexi said. "Max just scared himself. I want you to run inside and get one of his dog cookies for him, okay?"

"But he peed on the stones," Teeny said, edging close to a wail again. "And he might need a bath, and Frannie's not here."

No, Frannie was not. It was another knife in Lexi's heart. "He doesn't need a bath right now, and I promise Frannie will come back before he needs another one." Come hell or high water. "Now we just need to tell Max he's not in trouble. He did the only thing he knew to do."

As a twenty-five-year-old woman, she couldn't seem to get it together. How could she expect more from a one-year-old scared dog who hadn't yet learned he could trust his new family?

Teeny took off like a shot. Lexi took a few steps toward the shaking dog and bent down on her haunches, still giving him several feet of space.

"It's okay, boy," she whispered. "You're not in trouble."

His trembling subsided. Progress. More than she had made on any other front in days. But darn it, that wasn't good enough. She wanted to make progress with her friend. The friend who hadn't spoken to her in two days. It was time to put an end to that.

Teeny emerged from the house with two dog cookies.

"Coax him back over to the steps and feed him," Lexi said, "then finish reading your book to him. I'm going to have a quick word with Daddy, then I'll send him out to clean up the patio, okay?"

Teeny nodded, already focused on cooing and tempting Max. Lexi went into the house, knowing she had left that task in the best hands for the job. It was a lesson learned that she now needed to apply to the Frannie debacle.

Lexi crossed through the kitchen and entered the family room, where Rob sat in a recliner and Seth sat on the sofa watching a baseball game. She picked up the remote from the coffee table and clicked off the TV.

Seth sat forward. "Lex, he was just about to pitch a—"

"Seth." Rob's one word quieted his friend. "What's up, babe?"

"We've been going about this all wrong. My messages and apologies won't work." She pointed the remote at her husband. "It has to come from you. You broke it. You fix it."

Rob took a deep breath. "I take it we're talking about Frannie."

"About her trust," Lexi said.

Rob leaned forward and put his elbows on his knees. "It's not that I don't want to fix this, but maybe it's not meant to be. Or maybe it's just the wrong time. Give her a few more months. Or a year."

"No. You get to sit in here watching baseball with your best friend." She laid a hand on her belly and pointed the remote toward the kitchen, drawing a shaky breath and blinking back tears. "Meanwhile, I have a bag of unopened Oreos in my cupboard, waiting for *my* best friend to come visit *me*, to want to come to see *me*. I want to watch rom coms and true crime shows like we did for years, before everything went wrong. Not in a few months. Not in a year. *Now!*"

Rob jumped to his feet and wrapped Lexi in a hug. His bulk and warmth soothed her, but she refused to lean into him. Not unlike what Teeny had done to her.

He kissed the top of her head. "Where is she right now? The diner? The apartment?"

Lexi shook her head and pulled slightly away from him. He frowned, but his eyes showed concern, not unhappiness.

"She's probably just getting off work," Lexi said. "We'll have dinner and get Teeny—Bettina—ready for bed. That should give Frannie enough time to unwind with a bubble bath and some wine. With any luck, she'll be in a good enough mood that she won't slam the door in your face."

"Bubble bath and wine?" Seth jumped to his feet. "I could head over right now, apologize for all of us, make sure she doesn't slip in the tub."

"Sit down, Seth," Rob and Lexi said in unison.

Seth dropped back onto the sofa and scowled. "Just trying to help."

"Yes, yourself," Lexi said. "Do that on your own time, not mine."

Seth saluted. "Yes, ma'am."

Rob squeezed her hand. "Okay, so the schedule is dinner—pizza should be here in about ten minutes—then head over to the apartment and grovel at Frannie's door until she forgives me or throws a wine bottle at me."

Lexi worked hard not to curl up the corners of her lips but couldn't help herself. "Something like that."

"So, old man"—Rob turned toward Seth—"if Lexi lets us eat in front of the TV, we'll get to see about another half hour of the game. I'll record the rest."

"No more baseball tonight." Lexi pointed to the backyard. "Max had an accident. You'll need to clean off the patio."

Rob took the remote from Lexi and pressed the record button for the DVR. He handed the remote back to her and kissed her on the lips. "I'm on it, babe."

"Oh, and please send Bettina inside to help me make the salad," she called after him.

"Salad? With pizza?" Seth pushed himself to his feet. "Now I think I'm glad I'm being kicked out."

"Bettina likes salad, especially with roasted beets and goat cheese." Just like Frannie, she didn't add.

Seth wrinkled his nose. "Goat cheese? Now I *know* I'm glad I'm being kicked out."

She stepped into his path to stop him. She had hurt his feelings, first on Saturday at Frannie's, now again tonight. He had been Rob's best friend since they had met in the army, but he was her friend too. If it hadn't been for him, she never would have met the man she was building a life and family with. She wouldn't have gotten to be Bettina's stepmother. He was entitled to a pass on a mistake or two. Holding Rob's overprotectiveness and Frannie's defensiveness against Seth wasn't right. And she had to make things in her life just right.

"You're not going anywhere," Lexi said. "You were invited for dinner, and you're staying for dinner."

"I don't have to, if you're still upset."

She twisted her hands in front of her. "Which leads me to the next thing. I'm sorry about Saturday. I was horrible to you. And that slap. I don't even know what... You're a good guy, Seth. So is Rob, and I know you both meant well. If Frannie ever speaks to me again, I promise to put in a good word for you."

He held up his pinky. "Pinky swear, the way you and Frannie used to?"

She laughed. "You have a good memory." She wrapped her pinky around his.

"And I promise the same, to put in a good word for you when she speaks to me again."

"*When*, not *if*?"

Seth gave her a quick hug and a hard pat on the back. "You gotta have faith, Lex. Here comes Bettina. I'll go outside and supervise Rob with the patio cleanup."

Faith. She had plenty of faith. But she wasn't above throwing in morning mantras and promises to the universe to help faith along. That was how she had stopped her parents from divorcing when she was eight years old, hidden the truth from Brandon Greene, her first love, about what his father had done to her, and made a new life for herself after Frannie was gone. Now faith and mantras and promises to make everything right would bring Frannie back to her. And once Frannie was back in the fold, Lexi could heal emotionally and, eventually, physically.

She laid her hand over her empty womb and pictured a little sister for Teeny taking root there. Maybe someday.

Seth strode away, tousling Teeny's hair as he went, which made the girl smile. Frannie used to say he was arrogant, but Lexi wasn't so sure. Maybe he was just confident. God, to go through life with that much confidence, knowing you deserved good things and would get them. It must be liberating. It probably even allowed for a good night's sleep, a luxury Lexi barely remembered. Her shoulders sagged with exhaustion, but she smiled at Teeny and followed the girl into the kitchen.

Seth might find his way back to Frannie with swagger and self-confidence, but she had to find her way back to her best friend the only way she knew how: on a wing and a prayer.

FRANNIE'S DAY HAD GONE badly. Her mind raced with thoughts of the betrayal, and her fists clenched every time she considered Lexi's involvement in the whole mess.

But by the time Frannie finished her double shift at the diner, the welcome distraction of exhaustion set in. At 7:00 p.m., she returned to the small apartment that was her temporary home with a plan to push the distraction into full-blown numbness.

She pulled a glass out of her cupboard and the white wine out of her fridge. She stared at the half-empty bottle. She had polished off the first half in one sitting. For a woman who had never done much drinking and hadn't touched a drop in five years, that was a lot.

She shoved the bottle back into the fridge, drew herself a hot bath, and soaked in it until her muscles loosened and the water cooled. By the time she dressed in cut-off gray sweatpants and a worn-out red Ramones T-shirt, she was almost too tired to eat real food. She pulled open the cupboard and stared at a box of Pop-Tarts then slammed the door shut. It reminded her too much of the years when she had been too young to cook, and at least a few dinners a week had consisted mostly of sugar and had popped up out of a toaster.

Frannie opened the fridge and considered the small collection of Styrofoam boxes, leftovers of the meals Oscar, the diner's main cook, had prepared for her over the past week. The only thing that tempted her in the least was the damned wine.

A knock at the door made Frannie jump. She guiltily closed the fridge door and stood frozen in front of it. Who the hell would visit her on a Monday night? It could be her parole officer, which would be a pain in the ass. Or Lexi, which would be even worse. Frannie hadn't yet turned on lights in the catchall room, so she could pretend she wasn't home. She crept to the front window and shifted the closed curtains an inch to see who she was avoiding. A man stood there with his head down and his hands behind his back. Not Seth. That was good. Not Jack Greene, either, which was even better.

The man shifted, and the light from one of the streetlamps lit his face. Lexi's husband. Frannie squinted just to make sure it was him. He was the right height and build, maybe an inch taller than Seth and thin and broad-shouldered but not as solid and muscled as Seth. She dropped the curtain and cursed. When the hell had Seth Collins become the standard against which she measured other men?

She took a deep breath and shook out her hands and feet, braced herself, turned the dead bolt, and cracked the front door open an inch. "Yes?"

Rob smiled. It was the first time Frannie had seen that. Of course, she had only met him for a few minutes the first day she had arrived in this Podunk town.

"I'm glad you're home," he said. "I come bearing gifts—"

"I don't want them."

"And an apology. A really big, really sincere apology."

Frannie hesitated with one hand on the door, ready to slam it shut. She glanced out over the gravel parking lot in front of the building and the street beyond it. Being on the second floor made it easy to see far in all directions. No one else in the lot or the street. "Just you?"

"Just me. I screwed this up, Frannie. Please don't blame Lexi. She misses you." He pulled one arm out from behind his back and held out a Tupperware container.

"What's that?"

"Beet and goat cheese salad. Lexi said to make sure to tell you she figured out how to make it like that restaurant in Chicago. You can't use canned beets. You have to roast fresh ones."

Frannie stared at the plastic container as she remembered the restaurant in Chicago with the amazing view of the lake and the city lights. She had gone on family vacations with Lexi and her parents when she and Lexi were teenagers. Every year it was the same trip, first to a cottage on the southern tip of Lake Michigan for two weeks, then a few days' trip up to Chicago so Lexi's dad could attend his company's annual sales meeting. Every year, while he was at a corporate dinner, Lexi's mom took them to the fanciest place Frannie had ever seen, and Frannie ordered the strangest menu items she could find. She liked most of the food, hated some of it, but every time they went back, she ordered the beet and goat cheese salad.

Rob gently shook the container. "Please take it. Lexi will kill me if you don't."

Frannie took the container. "Thanks." She moved to close the door.

"There's more." Rob pulled out his other hand to show her a package of Oreos. Lexi was pulling out all the stops on this trip down memory lane. "Please, let me come in for a few minutes to explain myself."

She was about to tell him she could buy her own damn junk food, thank you very much, but he gave her a hangdog expression to rival Max's. With a sigh, she stepped back and pulled the door open a few feet. Rob stepped past her, moving fast, and handed her the cookies as he made a beeline for the kitchen table. He slung his light-weight coat over the back of a chair and sat down.

Frannie glanced down at the package of Oreos then closed the front door. "Make yourself at home, I guess." She set the cookies and salad on the counter and decided this conversation would require a different kind of sustenance. "Would you like a glass of wine?"

"Do you have any whiskey?"

"Just the wine. White. Take it or leave it."

"Wine, it is," he agreed.

"No wineglasses," she said as she poured their drinks into juice glasses. She set one down in front of him and took a seat across from him.

He gulped half the contents of his glass then sighed. "Frannie, I was an ass. I shouldn't have sicced Seth on you. Lexi thinks I'm over-protective."

Frannie raised an eyebrow.

Rob rubbed a hand over the stubble on his jaw. "And I probably am."

"You do remember I didn't ask to be in this town, right?"

"I remember. And I know I have no right to ask anything of you."

"True," she said. But it appeared he was going to ask anyway. Couldn't he see how used up and worthless she was? What did he possibly think she had to offer?

She took a swig of wine and braced herself for the ask.

"I'm worried about Lexi. She does this thing." He shook his head. "It's this odd way of thinking."

"Magical thinking. Candles, incantations."

Rob took a sip of wine. "Morning meditations, mantras."

"Well, lots of people meditate and light candles and pray."

"I have no problem with any of that." Rob set down his nearly empty glass and stared into it. "It's the fantastical thinking that worries me. She thinks she can fix all the world's problems by herself."

Frannie pushed her wineglass out of the way and propped her elbows on the table. "Did she ever tell you about the time her parents nearly got divorced?"

"Yeah. She said they fought a lot for a while then made up and decided to move to get a fresh start, and that's when she met you."

Frannie nodded. "Yes, but did she tell you how they made up?"

"These are my in-laws. Do I want to know?"

Frannie smiled. He had a quick, subtle sense of humor. He was definitely Lexi's type.

"Not that," she said. "Lexi told me the story a few weeks after we became friends. One night, shortly before they moved, her parents were fighting yet again, and she was desperate to keep them together. She'd been reading some kids' book about fairies or witches or something, so she got the bright idea to sneak into her mom's bathroom and steal a candle. She lit it and recited some rhymes and made wishes on stars. Everything she could think of.

"A few days later, her mom took her out for ice cream, and Lexi thought, 'This is it. They're going to tell me they're getting a divorce.' Then her dad showed up while they were eating ice cream. Her parents kissed each other, then they kissed her, and they told her they were moving to a new town for a fresh start."

Rob furrowed his brow. "Wait, you're not saying Lexi thinks lighting a candle and reciting some rhymes saved her parents' marriage, are you?"

"I don't know what she thinks now, but it's what she thought then. But if she still lights candles and recites mantras…" Frannie shrugged.

Rob rubbed the back of his neck. He looked as exhausted as Frannie felt. Damn it, she was not going to feel sorry for him. Or Lexi. Or Seth. Especially not Seth.

"Did she tell you about the miscarriage?" Rob asked.

Frannie's mind flashed back to the tiny bathroom in a seedy motel room. So much blood, in the toilet and on the tile floor. A pile of once-white, blood-covered towels. Her best friend ice-cold, shaking, as pale as death. She shivered. "I was there."

"The first one, I know. I'm talking about the second one, last year."

"You and Lexi?"

He nodded. "We were so excited. Too excited. When she was about eight weeks along, I convinced her we should tell Teeny. I thought she would be so happy, too, and I was right. She loved Lexi right from the start, but things got harder after the wedding. Then when she found out Lexi was bringing her a little sister or brother, Teeny looked at Lexi like she'd hung the moon." He put his hands over his face. "I was so stupid. It was all my fault, getting everyone's hopes up like that."

He hunched over like he was folding the pain into himself. Against her will, Frannie's cold, hard heart ached for the three of them.

"What happened?"

He let out a long sigh. "At about twelve weeks, Lexi started bleeding. It wouldn't stop. We rushed her to the hospital, but it was too late. She was a wreck, as you can imagine. And Teeny. I think Lexi wants to have a baby for Teeny as much as for us, maybe more."

No wonder Lexi was so desperate to have Frannie help make Bettina happy. And even less wonder that Lexi always looked so disappointed to be left out when Frannie and Bettina huddled together over Max. Lexi had never been a loner and never would be. Being cut off from someone she loved must be breaking her very big, very soft heart.

Looks like Rob's not the only one who's been an ass. Out loud she said, "That's twice now. The first time, she was under a lot of stress, and we were on the run. What happened the second time?"

"Lexi has something called APS. It's an autoimmune disease that causes blood clots. She's on blood thinners that keep her healthy, so she thinks next time she gets pregnant, she'll be able to carry it to term."

He stood and walked to the counter. He poured himself another juice glass of wine and took a sip of it. Frannie waited. He had something big to say, and a part of her wasn't sure she wanted to hear it.

He finally spoke. "Lots of women with APS have successful pregnancies. Lexi is sure she'll be one of them. But the condition puts her at high risk for preeclampsia, a deep vein blot clot, possibly even multiple-organ failure."

Frannie tried to wrap her mind around that. "Organ failure? She could actually die from pregnancy?"

He set down his glass, which was empty again. "After the miscarriage, she had a deep vein thrombosis. That's a blood clot that starts in the deep veins in your legs. They caught it in time because she was in the hospital, but if they hadn't..." He blew out a breath. "I thought I was going to lose her." He closed his eyes. "Shit. I was so fucking scared, I can't even describe it."

His hands shook as he ran them through his hair. He had lost his first wife and had nearly lost his second a few short years later.

"Thank you for telling me. I wish Lexi would have." She leaned back in her chair. "Then again, I haven't really given her a chance. The only times I've seen her have been to help with Bettina."

"You make Teeny happy, and Lexi would do anything to make her happy these days."

Once Frannie made someone happy, did their happiness become her responsibility? How the hell was that going to work when Frannie's days here were seriously numbered?

"Maybe I should stop by one day soon, check on the kid and the dog," she said.

"That would be nice." He took a deep breath. "Thank you." He fidgeted with his wineglass. "Any chance you're free tomorrow night?"

She shook her head. "I picked up double shifts at the diner. My next free night is Friday." Unless she could talk Patrice into putting her on the schedule that night, too, which would serve the dual purposes of earning her more cash and filling her empty social calendar.

"Lexi would love to have you come over for dinner," he said. "I have to warn you, though, Seth might be there. He has a standing invitation for Friday night dinners. Or I could disinvite him this week."

She threw back the rest of her wine then shook her head. Asking Rob to do that would mean she was holding a grudge, which might lead Seth Collins to think she gave a damn about his opinion of her. And she absolutely did not. "He can do what he wants. It's a free country."

"Does that mean you'll be there?" he asked. "It'll give us a chance to get to know each other. You might come to realize I'm not too much of an ass. And talking you into dinner would get me some serious husband points."

"You're not my in-laws, but I still don't want to know."

He grinned. "Can I take that as a yes?"

"You can take that as 'I'll think about it.' That's the best I can do right now."

"It's a start. Give Lexi a call when you're ready." He held out his hand.

She shook it.

"Thanks for letting me in. And for listening." He gathered his coat from the kitchen chair and headed to the door then turned back to face her. "One more thing about Seth. He's a really good guy. Don't let the fact that I talked him into doing something stupid for me get in the way of whatever you two are."

Frannie crossed her arms over her chest. "We're not anything. We used to know each other, that's it."

"Uh-huh." Rob leaned his back against the door. "You should ask Seth about a conversation we had about first loves when we were in the sandbox."

"The sandbox?"

Rob nodded. "Afghanistan. He talked about this fearless girl. Cute redhead. Small package, big attitude. He stupidly let her get away. I'm pretty sure he's going to try hard not to make the same mistake again."

Frannie tucked her hair behind her ear and tried to look calm on the outside while her heart hammered in her chest and images of the one fleeting moment they'd had in high school flashed through her mind. "I'll consider myself warned."

Rob laughed. "I can see he'll have a challenge on his hands." He pulled open the door, still smiling. "Be careful. Men like Seth live for the challenge."

TUESDAY AFTERNOON AT the diner, Frannie rubbed her lower spine and dreamed about the hot bath she would soak in when she got off work in half an hour. After that, she would have to think about calling Lexi, like she had promised Rob she would. Lexi was probably lighting candles and reciting mantras out the wazoo, entreating the universe to push Frannie into a decision. And the universe would give Lexi her way. Who was Frannie kidding? There was no way she was going to let down Lexi or Rob after hearing about what they had been through last year.

Pasting on the smile reserved for customers, she picked up the coffeepot and topped off Mr. Connor's cup. He glanced at her, almost as if he acknowledged her personhood.

"Ready for pie, Mr. Connor?" she asked. "No peach today, but we have cherry."

He made a grunt that could have gone either way, but she knew his habit. By the time he got to his second cup of coffee, he would want pie, and Patrice had taken a deposit to the bank, so he couldn't convey the message through her. But he would be sure to complain when Patrice returned if he hadn't gotten his dessert.

Frannie scooped up the pie for him, topping it with a small amount of whipped cream, exactly the way she had seen the other servers prepare it for him. When she set it in front of him, he scowled and scraped off the cream, but he took a bite of the pie and grunted again.

"Progress," she mumbled to herself as she slipped into the kitchen to check on the order for table three.

Oscar had just assured her it would only be a few more minutes when Beth came in through the swinging doors and made a beeline for Frannie.

"Tell me you didn't just seat another table for me," Frannie said.

"She requested you," Beth said.

"But I'm supposed to be off the clock soon."

"You will be. She just wants decaf coffee and pie." Beth smiled, looking way too happy about messing up Frannie's date with a tubful of bubbles and a big glass of wine from the bottle of red she had bought yesterday.

Frannie slouched and lumbered out of the kitchen. On her way past the coffee station, she grabbed the pot and straightened her posture before heading to the table, putting on her happy-to-serve-you smile again. From behind, she couldn't identify the woman who had asked for her. Long, dyed-blond hair, which meant, thank God, it wasn't Lexi. She hadn't shown up here yet, but if Frannie didn't call her soon, she probably would.

The mystery customer also didn't look like any of the regulars Frannie was already able to claim after less than two weeks at the diner. When she reached the side of the table, she turned over the coffee cup on its saucer.

"Beth tells me you'd like some pie today." As Frannie began pouring the coffee, she glanced at the woman's face. And stared.

Her mother grinned at her. "How do you like your old mom as a blonde, Frannie?"

"What are you doing here?"

Her mother pushed her chair back from the table. "Frannie, the coffee!"

"Oh, shit!" Frannie set down the pot on another table and grabbed a wad of napkins from the dispenser to wipe up the spill. "There. I'll wipe down the table with bleach later, but that should do for now."

"Frannie, you're so jumpy. What's wrong?"

"I just didn't expect you. Let me get rid of this." She carried the pot back to the warmer and threw away the paper towels.

Beth handed her a piece of pie. "For your mom," she said. She furrowed her brow. "Are you okay? You don't seem that happy about seeing her."

That was too complicated a discussion to have at work. Or anywhere, really. Frannie smiled. "It's just been a long day. Thanks for getting her pie."

She joined her mother at the table and slid the pie in front of her.

"So, Mom, what brings you here?"

"I wanted to say hi."

Saying hi was hardly a reason for a three-hour round-trip drive.

"And I should also say hello from Lexi's parents," her mother said. "They hope to see you soon. And from Jack Greene. He stopped by the pharmacy again."

"Jack Greene?" Frannie clasped her hands together to keep them from trembling. "As in I-stole-his-money Jack Greene? You didn't talk to him, did you?"

"Of course I did. I'm not going to be rude when he's so polite. I told you, he was very impressed that you paid back what you stole plus interest. He's genuinely concerned about you."

More likely, he was concerned about his hundred thousand dollars. He was shady as hell. There was no telling why he'd had that much cash in his house safe, and Frannie had been an idiot to think she could get away with keeping it.

"This pie is as amazing as Beth said it is," her mother said. "She's a doll. And this seems like a nice place to work." Her mother pointed her fork at Frannie. "But you look tired. Are you getting enough sleep?"

"Mom, I'm an adult. Don't worry so much."

"I'm your mother. I'm allowed to worry."

Her mother's angst over her well-being was a relatively new development. It might have been helpful if she'd had it when Frannie was a kid, but now it was just a pain in the ass. Frannie had survived prison, for Christ's sake, but reminding her mother of that would make her cry. Frannie had done that to her too many times in the past five years.

"You're right about being tired," Frannie said. "I need to get home and into sweatpants." She braced herself and forced a smile. "You're welcome to come over. The place isn't much to look at, but I have coffee, tea, red and white wine, although I don't think they're very good."

"That's sweet, but I'll see your apartment next time. I really did just want to stop in to say hello. And to show you my hair, which you haven't mentioned." Her mother ran her hand over her dye job and smiled. "I did it myself."

Frannie crossed her arms over her chest as she surveyed her mother's auburn roots. "You could have called me. I would have driven down on my day off to do that for you."

"You don't have time for that. Besides, you always talk me out of blond."

"I think it suits you," Beth said from a nearby table she was cleaning. "And I can see where Frannie gets her hairdressing skills."

"She was going to be a veterinarian," her mother told Beth. "She's better with animals than with people," she added in a fake whisper.

Frannie pressed her lips into a thin line. Beth and Ginny, her fellow waitresses, were always trying to learn more about her past. *"Not the prison part,"* Ginny always said. *"But before and after that."* Frannie never volunteered information and only answered their direct questions in the vaguest possible terms. Crystal's visit would give them enough gossip for the next month.

"Sorry to interrupt," Beth said. "I'll get back to my customers and let you two catch up."

Frannie leaned against the back of the booth while her mother dug into the pie. Despite her mother's love of sugar, a person should not live on pie or Pop-Tarts. "I know you said you're in a hurry, but I can bring you some real dinner to go with that. Anything on the menu. My treat."

"Thanks, honey, but I'm not hungry." Her mother took a big swig of coffee and another bite of pie.

"Don't you have Bible study on Tuesday nights?" Frannie asked. "What time does that start?"

She knew damn well it started in half an hour. Her mother would never make it back to Smithton in time, but Frannie couldn't come out and ask why her mother was here instead. The question she really wanted to ask was *What do you need from me?* But her mother would take offense. Keeping Crystal Willets on an even emotional keel was more exhausting than any double shift Frannie had ever pulled.

Her mother finished her last bite of pie then pushed away her plate. "I don't go to Bible study much anymore."

"Why not? You liked it so much."

Her mother had found the group of church ladies a year into Frannie's sentence, and they had seemed to be real friends to her, the first group of friends Frannie had ever seen her mother join. It had given her some peace of mind to know her mother had people to look after her while Frannie was gone. She was counting on them still being there for her mother when Frannie disappeared for good.

Her mother shrugged. "They're just so boring. Jodi's son is back in prison for another DWI, and Liz's daughter didn't get paroled. Too many fights or something."

Frannie furrowed her brow. "Wait, Mom, is this a support group for mothers of convicts?"

"No! No, it's a Bible study. But a lot of us have—or had—that in common. Not Alice Horsely, but she does have two kids—a daughter and a son—who've done stints in rehab."

"And the other—what, three or four?—do they all have kids in jail?"

Her mother nodded. "And it's all they talk about. I mean, other than whatever scripture we're studying that week. It's like they don't even want to hear things I have to say anymore."

Great. Her mother was back to having no one but Frannie for company. She would have no support system when Frannie was gone.

"So, that's why you drove all this way to see me on a Tuesday night?" Frannie asked. "I mean, it's nice. I was just surprised," she added to disarm a potential outburst.

"Actually, I was at a training course for work in Indianapolis, so I wasn't far away." Her mother took a deep breath. "And yes, I was a little worried. When I talked to you on Saturday, you were tipsy and upset."

"As you can see, I'm fine," Frannie said. "I have a nice boss who feeds me decent food. I have nice coworkers who stick their noses into my business on the regular. I only have to be here a little while longer." Frannie pressed her lips together. Her mother didn't know about the one-month deal with Lexi, and she wasn't going to find out now. She rushed to add, "And I'd only had a couple of glasses of wine, by the way."

"You're terrible at holding your liquor." Her mother sighed. "In that long list of good things, you didn't mention Lexi once. I know you're upset with her."

"When did I say I was upset with her?" Frannie didn't remember that. Maybe she really was crap at holding her booze.

"You didn't have to. A mother knows."

"I'm fine. Lexi's fine. Her family is fine. The mutt they got for the kid is… He's probably as close as he's ever going to get to fine."

Her mother's face lit up. "Oh, they got Teeny a dog. I know they talked about it for ages."

A jolt of outrage shot up Frannie's spine. A small, jealous animal gnawed at her gut. They'd had a whole life together, the whole lot of them, here on the outside, while she had kept her head down and her mind numb and her hands busy, day after day, to survive long enough to cross the four-year finish line.

"It sounds like you're all very close," Frannie said. "I suppose you're bosom buddies with Seth too."

Her mother set down her coffee cup as she furrowed her brow. "Seth? Is he the one who introduced Lexi and Rob? That Rob's a nice guy, isn't he? They're such a good match. Didn't Seth go to school with you? Polite boy. And such a nice mother."

"He was a few grades ahead of me. His brother was in my class. Kind of a jerk."

"I assume you've seen him—the polite one, not the jerk—since you mentioned him. How is he?"

"Polite or not, he's a rat bastard. Always has been, always will be."

Her mother smiled. "So, you've given this Seth person a lot of thought."

No. No, she hadn't. *He* was the one bothering *her*. Tricking her into liking him just in time to betray her. Sending flowers and apology cards for being an asshole. Sending repentant text messages to her phone. If she was thinking about him, it was because he was giving her no choice.

"I don't want to talk about him or Lexi," Frannie said. "So, about this Bible study prison-support group, maybe you should invite one or two of the ladies for coffee instead of going to the meeting. You could start with Alice Horsely." It sounded like that poor woman could use a friend.

"Oh, Frannie, now who's worrying?" She reached across the table and patted Frannie's hand. "As it happens, I have a coffee date with a new friend tomorrow."

The way she said it, with a crooked smile and dreamy look on her face, made Frannie's Spidey senses tingle in the worst possible way. Dreamily saying "new friend" was how her mother always announced there was a new man in her life. Luckily, she had rarely forced Frannie to suffer through meeting them, and none of the relationships, if they could be called that, had lasted long. But another short-term fling could leave her mother wrecked in about a month or so. Just about the time Frannie planned to do her disappearing act.

"How long have you been seeing him?"

"Who said anything about a him?" Her mother took a long drag of coffee then carefully set the cup down on its saucer.

Beth arrived at the table with the decaf pot in her hand. "Top you off, Crystal?"

Her mother covered the top of the cup with her hand. "No thanks. I have a long drive home ahead of me. I don't want to have to stop every ten minutes. You'll know how that is when you get to be my age." This to Beth, who easily had ten years on her mother.

Beth laughed and nudged her mother's arm. "Oh, Frannie, she's a keeper."

Frannie forced a smile. "Yeah, I've kept her for twenty-five years, so..."

Beth snort-laughed. "You two are adorable." She pointed to Frannie's mother. "Don't you be a stranger. Come visit us anytime."

Frannie glared at Beth's back as she walked away.

"She's sweet," her mother said. "Now I'll have two reasons to come here. Three, if you count the pie. But I really should get on the road. You know how I hate being on the highway after dark."

Frannie slid out of the booth and walked her to the front door. "Have fun on your date."

"You're the only one who's calling it a date." Her mother kissed her cheek. "Get some rest, Frannie. I'll call you Friday, and we can decide if you're driving down to visit me this weekend or I'm driving up to visit you."

Frannie would have preferred to keep it informal, the way they had when she had been at the halfway house fifteen miles from her mother's place. One more reason to hate staying in Licking: having to arrange formal dates with Mom. Then again, maybe it was a sign that her mother didn't expect the coffee date to become anything more significant, like Saturday-night-dinner-turned-sleepover.

"I don't want to interfere, though, if you're busy." Her mother's hangdog expression said otherwise.

Frannie pictured that same look on her mother's face when she heard the news that her daughter had disappeared, had slipped into the wind never to be heard from again. Before she could think too much about it, she touched her mother's shoulder. "I can probably do something Sunday after my brunch shift."

Her mother left and stopped outside the stenciled window for one last wave. When she was out of sight, Frannie sagged against the edge of an empty table. Maybe getting serious with a nice guy wouldn't be the worst thing in the world for her mother. Frannie added showing interest in her mother's love life to the growing list of crap she had to address before she could make a break for it. She hoped Mr. Coffee Date was, in Beth's words, a keeper.

CHAPTER EIGHT

Frannie stood on Lexi's doorstep on Friday at one minute to six. She adjusted her pale-blue short-sleeved blouse and glanced down at her new dark-wash jeans. Blue was a good color on her. It downplayed the ruddiness in her skin. She shook her head and rolled her shoulders. What the hell did it matter? It wasn't like this was a first date just because her palms were sweaty, and her mouth was dry.

The front door swung open before she knocked.

"Frannie." Lexi, wearing another floral-print dress, this one in shades of oranges and reds, stepped back and pulled the door open wide. "What are you doing, standing out here? Come in."

It was the second time Frannie had stepped onto the hardwood floor of the front entryway of Lexi's house, but this time she was more nervous than the first.

Lexi shifted from one foot to the other then leaned forward, and they shared an awkward hug. "I just want to say sorry again for Rob sending Seth to spy on you."

Frannie patted her back then gently pulled away. "It's fine. I over-reacted." She held up the paper bag she was carrying. "I brought wine. Something dry and red. Oscar picked it up for me. He said the guy at the liquor store recommended it. I'm hoping it's better than the crap I picked out myself earlier this week."

"You didn't have to do that, but thank you." Lexi took it from her and led her to the kitchen. "Rob loves dry and red."

"He strikes me as more of a whiskey guy," Frannie said.

Lexi smiled. "Only when he's stressed." She pointed to stools lined up along the kitchen island.

Frannie sat down as instructed. "I didn't know if you drink wine. We hadn't gotten much past keg parties and that crappy stuff, Mad Dog or whatever it was, before... you know."

Lexi smiled. "Mad Dog. Oh my god, how could I have forgotten about Mad Dog? One sip made me sick. Actually, I still don't really drink much."

Frannie felt like an idiot. Of course Lexi would drink less than ever after Greene had given her spiked whiskey. "I should have brought dessert."

"No, you shouldn't have. Dessert is covered. Besides, I have a glass of wine every now and then, on special occasions." Lexi pulled out four wineglasses and lined them up on the counter. "This is definitely a special occasion."

Frannie glanced out one of the wide kitchen windows into the backyard, where Rob hovered over a big hunk of meat on the grill. "Where are Bettina and Max hiding?"

"They're not here tonight. They got a better offer."

Frannie had begun to think she was the best offer in town as far as the kid and the mutt were concerned. Not that it mattered. Although she was a little disappointed she wouldn't see the two of them traipsing through the backyard.

"Her grandparents—her mom's folks, the Robinsons—own a farm outside of town, and they just got a new baby goat. As soon as Teeny... Bettina heard about it, she wanted to introduce it to Max. Something about getting him used to more people."

Frannie smiled.

Lexi dug around in a drawer and pulled out a wine opener. "I didn't have the heart to remind her goats aren't people. But she was sorry she was going to miss you."

"She's a good kid. And she loves that sad sack of fur." Frannie shook her head slowly. "I hate to break it to you, Lex, but I'm not sure that dog will ever be a normal pet."

"Agreed." Lexi picked at the foil on the wine bottle. "But I've been thinking about that. Maybe normal isn't what Bettina needs most after all. Maybe she needs someone that needs her back."

Frannie held out her hand. "Can I do that? I just need a sharp knife."

Lexi handed her the bottle, the opener, and a knife, which gave Frannie something to distract her from considering whether Lexi was really talking about Bettina and Max.

"How are you?" Frannie asked when she had finally removed the foil and twisted the cork out of the bottle. "Rob said things were bad last year. After the miscarriage."

"I'm fine. Getting better all the time." She gave Frannie a small, tight smile. "I don't really like to talk about what happened."

"But you have to."

"Hey, Lex." Rob appeared on the other side of the screen door. "The ribs will be done in ten minutes. You can start bringing out the rest of the stuff. Hey, Frannie. Good to see you."

It sounded like he meant it, which left Frannie not knowing what to say. "Hi. I brought wine."

"Sounds great!" He disappeared again.

Frannie turned to watch Lexi, who was pulling containers out of the fridge. "I made beet salad again. I hope you liked what I sent over with Rob."

"It was great. Thank you for that. But Lexi—"

"How are *you*, Frannie? Tell me the truth. You look great, Patrice says you fit right in at the diner, but that's you. You fit in everywhere."

"You're kidding, right?"

Lexi slid onto the counter stool beside her and took her hand. "I'm not." She took a long, unsteady breath. "Frannie, I know you don't want to talk about it, but are you really all right? Four years."

Frannie did not want to have this conversation. She *refused* to have this conversation. It was done. It was over. She was fine. And the tears pricking her eyes didn't mean a damn thing.

"Did anyone hurt you?"

Frannie shook her head. "You know me. Head down, nose clean, avoid trouble. Except for the occasional bungled burglary."

That made Lexi smile, but it didn't last long. "I've heard it's hard to avoid trouble all the time when you're in there."

"Don't believe everything you see on TV." Her light-hearted tone didn't seem to land with Lexi, who stared at her, waiting for the truth. "Okay, honestly, it was tough for a few months. I got targeted a few times. Not as much as most of the newbies, but a few times."

Lexi's hand, still covering Frannie's, twitched. "What happened after that?"

"I made a deal. Negotiated protection in exchange for passing along some messages." She didn't mention her protector's name. The less Lexi knew about that, the better.

"Sounds mysterious and intriguing."

Lexi had always liked real-life mysteries. It was why she had made Frannie watch so many true-crime shows. Too bad Frannie hadn't paid more attention. She might have been a more successful criminal.

"Not really."

Lexi lowered her voice. "Were the messages about something illegal?"

Frannie shrugged. "They were in code. I didn't ask for any details. Alliances in prison can be important, and the options for who to do business with are limited. I picked the least evil."

Lexi folded her hands together and leaned back in her seat. "That was smart. Shrewd. It's so... It's—"

"It's so Fearless Frannie."

Frannie jumped at the sound of the voice behind her.

"Hi, Seth." Lexi slid off the stool and crossed the kitchen to hug him. "Rob's in the backyard, finishing the ribs."

Seth held out a bakery box. "Dessert as ordered, ma'am."

Frannie turned in his direction. Her heart nearly stopped when she saw him in tan fatigues, with a shadow of stubble on his chin and a wide smile aimed right at her. She swallowed hard and hoped he couldn't hear it from several feet away. "Nice outfit."

He held his arms wide. "Glad you like it. That's why I wore it." He gave her a wolfish grin that made her want to wrap herself in a red riding hood and let him chase her. "That, and field exercises. Breaking communication systems in big tanks so we can teach soldiers how to fix them in the field." He glanced at Lexi. "The exercises ran late, so I didn't want to take the time to go home to change."

"You made the right choice." Lexi opened the box and took a whiff of the brownies it held. "Mmm. Double chocolate?"

"Triple."

"Triple! Here, Frannie, have one." Lexi held the container under her nose.

They did smell amazing. And tempting. Like the man who had brought them. Obviously, it was a setup orchestrated by Lexi, who knew of Frannie's undying love of all things chocolate. Deep, rich chocolate. Brought to her by a man who looked even tastier than those brownies smelled.

"It'll ruin my dinner," she said.

"Suit yourself." Lexi was still grinning as she set down the brownies and snatched up the containers she had pulled out of the fridge minutes earlier. "I'm going to take these out to the picnic table and check on Rob." She hightailed it out of the kitchen.

"She's subtle," Seth whispered.

Frannie sucked in her breath and held it as he slid into the chair beside her.

"Frannie, I'm sorry for screwing up last week." He propped his arms on the counter and met her gaze. "I should have been honest with you. I was just trying to help out my best friend. You know how that goes."

Boy howdy, did she. At least he had only screwed up a date. Frannie had screwed up four years of her life and put Lexi at risk. "I get it. Rob's overprotective." And Lexi wasn't listening to reason.

"Part of it's his nature, and part of it was losing his first wife."

Frannie nodded. "Bettina's mother. Did you know her?"

"I never got the pleasure of meeting her in person, but I photobombed Rob's Skype sessions a few times. We were in the desert when we got the news about her diagnosis."

"Lexi mentioned cancer."

Seth folded his arms and leaned forward on the counter. "Ovarian cancer. Stage 4, by the time they caught it. It took weeks to get Rob cleared to get home. They only got a few months together after that. It was quick and brutal. So you can understand why he overreacts. And then with the miscarriage and the APS."

"You know about that?"

He nodded. "And the first miscarriage too. And that you were there."

Frannie stared down into her wineglass, refusing to take his cue.

"Lexi told me you stole the money to help her, Frannie. The first time I saw her after you went to prison. She didn't tell me about Greene, but later, after she met Rob and told him, she told him he could confide in me."

"She shouldn't have told you," she said. "I wish she hadn't even told Rob." That was supposed to have been their secret, for Lexi's protection. "But I guess I couldn't expect to hide it from her husband."

He laid a finger against her jaw and gently turned her face back to his. "Friends share things, and she needed a friend. Also, she wanted me to think the best of you. And I do, by the way."

She held her blink closed for an extra beat as she savored his touch on her skin for the second time ever. She might have been able to get him to touch her this way once in high school, but she had let him walk away. She opened her eyes to find him watching her. She thought about moving out of his reach but decided it couldn't hurt to enjoy the warmth of his fingers for a minute longer.

"Don't worry. I won't tell anyone your secrets." He traced her jawline and brushed her cheek. "Remember a few minutes ago when I said finding a way to survive prison was the most Fearless-Frannie thing I'd ever heard? That's not quite true. What you did for Lexi was."

She would not entertain this conversation. Maybe she should distract him. And if she enjoyed the distraction herself, there was no harm in that. She leaned close to him. His eyes drifted half closed, and he cupped both sides of her face with his hands. When their lips met, she pressed against him and gripped his shoulders. He slid his fingers into her hair. Lips parted. Tongues touched. Hot blood raced. She couldn't stop her sigh of pleasure. They kissed harder and hungrier, but she still needed more.

He ended the kiss and leaned his forehead against hers, his fingers still wrapped in her hair. *Breathless.* Frannie remembered Lexi playing that stupidly catchy song over and over again when she had started dating Brandon. She hadn't understood how a kiss—or even the mere possibility of one—could leave someone breathless then and had forgotten it until this moment while she struggled to catch her own breath.

"I should have kissed you like that in high school," she said.

"If you'd kissed me like that in high school, I never would have left for boot camp, and the army would have thrown me into Leavenworth for going AWOL before I even started."

She smiled. "I guess you should thank me."

He finally let go of her, and they separated a few inches. "I guess I should. And I will, if you let me. I'll thank you in so, so many ways, if you'll let me."

"Ahem." The screen door squeaked open, and Lexi stood in the doorway while looking over her shoulder into the backyard. "I'm coming in, but I'm averting my eyes. Seth, Rob is carving meat and doing other manly things that require assistance."

"I'm on it, Lex." Seth leaned close to Frannie and whispered in her ear. "Steak at your house tomorrow?"

God, there should be a law against what that man could do with a whisper in her ear. "My next night off is Wednesday," she whispered back.

"Damn it. Okay. Wednesday, then. I'll bring dessert, too, but you're responsible for the appetizer." He winked at her as he slid off his chair and smiled at Lexi as he walked past her. "You can look, Lex. We're all dressed now."

"You are shameless, Seth Collins." She pushed the screen door closed behind him, and in a flash claimed the seat he had just left. "Were you two kissing?"

How many times over the years had they had a conversation like this? But those days were behind them. "We're not in high school anymore, Lex. We don't need to do a postmortem on every kiss."

"So there *was* a kiss! Will there be a date?"

Seth had said friends share things. Frannie hadn't exactly forgotten that, but she was out of practice.

"There will be a date. He's making steak for me. And bringing dessert."

Lexi arched one eye. "Oh, I'll just bet he is. Do you remember the safe-sex talk, or do you need a refresher?"

"Please, God, no."

Lexi hugged her, and this time it was more natural, like they remembered how friends should hug. "This is a good thing, Frannie. He's a good guy. And if he does you wrong, I'll have my husband kick his ass."

Frannie sighed. "Have you been listening to country music again? I warned you about that."

"Grab your glass and the wine bottle," Lexi said, picking up the empty glasses from the counter. "And then walk with me really slowly because I want to hear all about your intentions with Seth."

"No intentions." Frannie took a big gulp of her wine.

"You're still interested in him. Or maybe interested again? Like back in high school?"

"I never said I was interested in him back in high school," Frannie answered. It was the only secret she had kept from Lexi back when they were still best friends.

"You didn't have to. You could never hide things from me, Frannie Willets."

Maybe that had been true once upon a time. But luckily for both of them, the past five years had made her a much better liar.

AS FRANNIE STEPPED onto the sidewalk in front of Patty's Diner, she pressed her fingertips to her lips. She had just had a make-out session right across the street, parked in Seth's car on the main drag through town, like they were a couple of desperate teenagers with no place else to go.

"So that's what it could have been like at my locker," she said to herself.

The whole night was what it could have been like if their lives hadn't been so rudely interrupted. Two sets of best friends laughing, sharing memories, telling stories of days gone by, falling into it like it was a luxury they had shared for years.

Frannie was almost past the diner when she realized the lights were still on. Licking was an early dinner kind of town, so the staff usually had the place cleaned up and locked down by 10:00 p.m. The clock in Seth's car, when she had finally pulled herself out of his arms, had said it was 10:15.

She turned around to see that Seth was still watching to make sure she got to her apartment safely. She had agreed to let him drive her home from Lexi's since she had walked there, but they had both agreed—well, she had stated, and he had eventually conceded—that it wouldn't bode well for actually getting any sleep if he walked her to her door. She waved and pointed to the diner. He blew her a kiss but still waited until she had entered the well-lit restaurant before he pulled away from the curb to start his long and—Frannie hoped—lonely drive home, full of thoughts of her and the next time they would see each other.

She took another step into the diner. Oscar and Patrice stood outside the kitchen door, watching her.

"I was just…" She pointed to the now-empty street. The way they were staring at her, they probably knew what she had just been doing. But it shouldn't make them look so unhappy. Maybe not unhappy. More like worried. "Patrice, what is it?"

Patrice said something to Oscar, who frowned but nodded and went back into the kitchen. "Come sit down."

Frannie slid into a booth, and Patrice sat across from her. It didn't escape Frannie's notice that this was the same place she had sat across from Lexi not even two weeks ago. The slight lines on Patrice's face deepened as she stared down at her own hands clasped on the table in front of her, refusing to meet Frannie's eyes.

"You're firing me," Frannie said.

It shouldn't have bothered her so much. She had never wanted this damn job anyway. But it stung. And there was no cause to fire her. The staff liked her more than she wanted them to, and she already had her own regular customers. It couldn't possibly be because of that public display of affection, even in this small-minded, backwardly conservative place. And she had no place else to go, no other job waiting in the wings. Damn it.

"We were only kissing, Patrice. And it was Seth. You know Seth. You *like* him."

Patrice widened her eyes. "You were kissing Seth? That's the best news I've heard all day."

"Wait, are you firing me or not?"

"No one's getting fired, Frannie. And what you do on your personal time is your own business." Patrice shifted in her seat. She was uncomfortable.

In the two weeks they had known each other, Frannie hadn't seen Patrice anywhere close to uncomfortable.

"You want some pie?" Patrice asked. "We already wrapped it up for the night, but I can cut you a big slice of strawberry-rhubarb."

"No, thank you." Frannie flew right past uncomfortable and stopped somewhere around suffocating fear. "Tell me what's wrong."

Patrice took a deep breath and blew it out slowly. "I think we had an unexpected visitor tonight."

Frannie's hands went cold and clammy. "My mother?" For once, she hoped the answer to this question was yes.

Patrice shook her head.

"Wait, did you say you *think* you had a visitor? What does that mean?"

"When Beth left about an hour ago, she saw a man parked across the street, watching the diner. She called on her drive home to tell us. She said it looked like he was casing the joint."

"Casing the joint?" Frannie repeated.

Patrice held up her hands in front of her. "Beth's words, not mine. But after she called, I took a look for myself, and she wasn't wrong. The way he took off like a bat out of hell didn't ease my mind."

"Was he tall, fifty-ish, evil-looking as hell?"

At least, that was the way Jack Greene had looked the only time Frannie had seen him in person, when she had gone with Lexi to visit Brandon Greene and scope out the house for the burglary at a time when his father was not supposed to be home. But he had been. To this day, Frannie didn't know how Lexi had held it together while the two girls had made small talk with that man.

"He was in his car, and I didn't get a very good look at him," Patrice said. "Mostly just a silhouette. The car looked expensive. Something foreign. Sound like someone you know?"

"You know the guy I stole from was rich, right?" Frannie asked.

Patrice nodded. "You think he's sniffing around here?"

"Maybe. He's not the kind of man you should cross." Not if you wanted to protect people you loved and you weren't a complete idiot. Frannie had failed on that second point. "He's too smart to do something to you or anyone else here, even to me while I'm still on parole."

Greene had used his family name and inherited money to get into one dirty real estate development after another. And he was as savvy as he was shady. No need to make his move while she was still under the watchful eye of the state. Unless he suspected she was going to run.

"We should tell the sheriff," Patrice said.

The panic hit Frannie fast and hard. The cops would take Greene's side over the word of a parolee every day of the week. And if they asked too many questions Frannie couldn't answer honestly, they would start paying attention to her. "No police, please. There's nothing I can really tell them."

Patrice spent a silent minute watching Frannie then slowly nodded. "Okay, you don't have to talk to them. But I already did. I asked them to drive by a little more often, especially after dark and around closing time. And we're instituting some new rules around here."

"Rules?"

Patrice walked to the front door and flipped the dead bolt lock and ceiling and floor slide locks on the front door. "First rule, this door and the back one both get locked the minute we close. If there are still customers inside, we'll have to let them out when they're done. Second rule, no one leaves by themselves after dark. And by no one, I mean you. When you're ready to go, you'll tell Oscar or me or one of the line cooks, and we'll watch to make sure you get into your apartment."

No rule could protect her from Jack Greene if he was coming for her. Now, though, was not the time to mention that if Frannie hoped to keep the cops out of it. She would stick to the story that Greene was smarter than that and hope it was true.

"Okay." Frannie managed a smile that might even be convincing. "Now, if you don't mind watching over me, I'd like to go home."

Patrice narrowed her eyes and assessed Frannie, but if there was something else she wanted to say, she let it go. "Sure thing. You've had a long day." She smiled. "At least some of it sounds like a *good* day. Seth, huh? I do like that boy."

Small towns. Everyone talking. Everyone watching. Everyone knowing things Frannie didn't want them to know. But at least Patrice had changed the subject. Frannie hadn't thought she would live to see the day when Seth was her safe word. "Yeah, I think I like him too." She inclined her head toward the kitchen's back door. "I'm just going to let myself out."

Patrice followed and watched as Frannie crossed the gravel parking lot, hands down at her sides, eyes darting, nerves fraying. Frannie stayed on high alert for the mysterious car, but Main Street was empty. She climbed the outside staircase to her apartment, unlocked her front door, and flipped on the inside light. She turned and waved to Patrice, who was still watching her from the diner's back parking lot.

Alone inside her apartment, Frannie slid the dead bolt to lock herself in then laid her hand over her mouth to keep herself from screaming. Her lips were still sensitive from her stolen minutes with Seth. So few minutes. But despite her sure words to Patrice, Frannie wasn't really sure what Jack Greene was capable of doing in the name of revenge. Or worse, what he would do if he figured out Lexi had been involved in Frannie's crime. Danger was officially on her doorstep, and no one in her life was safe. Her time here was up.

CHAPTER NINE

Frannie punched out on the timeclock and leaned against the sweating tiles of the diner's kitchen wall while she waited for Oscar to finish her takeout order. Her feet were killing her, not so much from the Monday lunch shift, which had run long so that it was now halfway through the dinner shift, but from the twelve-hour Sunday double shift. She didn't remember waitressing being this hard when she was nineteen. Then again, when she was nineteen, she hadn't lost nights of sleep worrying about whether the man she had crossed was coming for her or, worse, someone close to her.

Her phone buzzed in her apron pocket. When she saw Lexi's number, she answered it.

"Frannie. I'm glad I caught you. How are you? Is everything okay?"

Frannie hadn't had a chance to ask Patrice whether she had said anything to Lexi about the Friday-night visitor. "I'm fine. Everyone here is fine."

Lexi dropped her voice. "Do you think it was him?"

"Why are you whispering? Is Bettina there?"

"She's drawing a picture of Max at the kitchen island," Lexi said.

Cooking sounds of pans rattling and food sizzling came through on the line. Frannie closed her eyes and rubbed the back of her neck. "It sounds like you're busy making dinner. Why don't we have this conversation another time?"

"No, now's fine. I just wondered how you're feeling about the thing that happened Friday night," Lexi said.

Frannie groaned. This coded conversation wasn't nearly as clever as the secret messages from her former cellmate, Maurie Stonefield, a white-collar criminal who continued to manage her criminal enterprise from prison. It was more like the phone calls Frannie and Lexi used to have about her dates when Lexi's mother was hovering too nearby. Frannie had never been able to get Lexi off the phone then. Of course, she'd had a vested interest in the friendship back then. That, and a better attitude. But she had no interest in continuing this discussion.

"Listen, we both know he's dangerous, and yes, it was probably him," Frannie told Lexi. "And we both know it would be better for everyone if we cut this little experiment short."

Just as Brandon Greene had probably known Lexi had been involved in the burglary with her best friend, his father must have suspected the same thing. Over the past few days, as Frannie had puzzled together the pieces of Jack Greene's recent behavior, she had only come up with one conclusion that made sense. He wasn't only coming after Frannie for his money. He was coming after Lexi too.

She had to proceed carefully. Lexi was still fragile, maybe more fragile than ever, and Frannie would have to take care of Jack Greene on her own. But she needed Lexi to be a little bit scared of what the man could do to her and her family, just enough so she would tell Frannie where the money was.

She lowered her voice to a whisper. "We both know he's after me because he figures I still have his money. Turn it over to me, and I'll leave town, draw him away from here. Away from you and your family."

"He's not going to come after you for the money," Lexi said. "Not yet. You said so yourself. Maybe there's some other reason he's spying on you."

"Sure. Maybe he wants to work on *his* relationship with me too."

"No need to be snarky," Lexi whispered.

Frannie clenched her teeth in exasperation. No one else wanted to believe just how big a threat Greene was, and she couldn't tell them enough to scare them appropriately without breaking confidences and risking Lexi's happiness. Lexi *should* understand, but maybe her contented life also depended on deluding herself about the man. Frannie would have to piece together what Lexi had done after the miscarriage, where she might have gone, and where she could have hidden the money. Then Frannie would have to go get it herself. If that turned out to be a bust, she would come up with a new plan.

"Lexi, my dinner's ready, and I'm desperate for a shower," Frannie said. "Please remember how dangerous Greene really is and think about what I said."

"Okay, but I called for another reason," Lexi said. "Meet me tomorrow morning for hot yoga."

"For what?"

"Hot yoga. There's an 8:00 a.m. class. I don't have to be at the day care until ten, and Rob's working from home in the morning, so he'll take Teeny... *Bettina* to school."

Frannie sighed. One of the many luxuries of freedom she no longer took for granted was the ability to sleep in late in the morning. "Pretty sure I won't be awake by eight."

"Come on. It will give you a good stretch and focus you. You'll leave the class feeling better, I promise."

Frannie's aching back cried out for a long soak in the tub and a morning in bed. "Maybe. Let me see how I feel in the morning, okay?"

"Okay. If you can make it, Patrice can give you directions to the studio when you stop at the diner for your morning coffee."

"Don't tell me she owns the yoga studio."

Lexi laughed. "It's not one of her businesses. But she does own the building and lease the space to them."

When Frannie hung up a minute later, Oscar tapped his spatula against a Styrofoam box. "Your dinner's ready. Now get out of here. You look exhausted."

She grinned, thanked him, and almost made it to the back door.

"Frannie, just a sec," her boss called.

"I've already punched out. If it's one of my regulars—"

"He's not a customer." Patrice was smiling instead of dialing 911, so it wasn't Friday's unannounced stalker. It wasn't hard to figure out who her mystery visitor was.

Frannie walked back to the dining room, instantly spotting Seth in the booth closest to the kitchen as she emerged through the kitchen door. He was halfway through a piece of pie and stopped with a forkful of golden apples and flaky crust halfway to his mouth. His lips twitched upward, tugging her heartstrings tight with them.

Hold it together, Frannie. He's just a guy. But her stupid grin was already deceiving her. He grinned back, dropped his fork, and slid out of the booth as she approached. He pulled her into a hug and placed a less-than-discreet kiss on her lips.

"Don't do that," she whispered as she slipped into the booth across from him. "This is where I work."

"Good to see you, too, Fearless. And I have it on good authority that you're off the clock."

She wanted to be angry at him, but when she glanced at the six or so tables full of customers and saw exactly zero of them watching her, she relaxed. In her years inside, she had learned you had to let the small things go. With Seth sitting across from her looking so damn tempting and tempted all at once, she decided she could apply that rule on the outside sometimes too.

He pointed to her hands. "Nice box."

"My dinner. Roasted chicken and salad."

"You should eat before it gets cold," he said.

"Don't you want something? Besides pie, I mean."

He shook his head. "We had a big lunch meeting. Plenty of calories. And then I couldn't resist one small piece of pie, so I'm done." He waved toward the box again. "Don't let that stop you, really. I'd be happy to sit here and watch you eat."

She leaned against the firm booth back. "I'd like to shower first."

He pushed his empty plate out of the way and leaned forward with his arms propped on the table, his eyes intense. "As happy as I'd be to watch you eat dinner, I'd be so much happier to watch you take a shower."

A wave of hot, focused desire washed over her like it so often did when she was within lusting distance of him. She meant to make a joke about a woman just out of prison, but her mouth was thick and dry. It wouldn't have been a funny joke, anyway, just something to fill the heavy space between them.

"Frannie, still with me?"

She blinked. "I'm here." As her pulse settled and her libido, well, didn't settle but revved back ever so slightly, she leaned toward him. "What are you doing here?"

"Eating pie. Hitting on a beautiful woman."

"Was it Patrice or Lexi?"

"What?" The way he leaned back and crossed his arms over his chest told her he knew exactly *what.*

"Who called you?"

She could almost see the conversation going on inside his head. Logic, the kind that would keep him from getting on her bad, unevolved side, won out. "It was Rob."

"Of course." The hell of it was, she couldn't blame Rob. His primal instinct was to protect his family. If reaching out to Seth helped him achieve that, it would be the first thing he would do. "So, he asked you to come here and check up on me again? Maybe find out what I know?"

"Something like that, originally."

That last word pricked the back of her neck. She wriggled and sat up straighter. "Originally. But then?"

"He asked me to give you a call. I could have called, but it's only Monday, and I'm not scheduled to make you dinner until Wednesday, and suddenly that seemed like a long time to wait to kiss you again."

She fidgeted with her Styrofoam. It squeaked and cracked until Seth laid his hand over hers. "Tell me what's going on inside that gorgeous head of yours, Frannie."

"How much do you know about Jack Greene?"

"Not a lot but enough to know it's odd that he's skulking around now, while you're on parole, scaring Beth and Patrice half to death."

Frannie shrugged one shoulder. "He scared Beth. No one scares Patrice."

"You'd be surprised. Why do you think he'd risk it?"

This was what she got for falling for a smart guy, a guy who knew how to read people—or, at least, how to read *her*—too well. And she didn't have the energy to lie to him. Which left her figuring out how to tell him that she feared Lexi was in real danger and what she planned to do about it.

"We can't talk here," she said as she slid out of the booth. "You'll have to come home with me."

CHAPTER TEN
July 2011

"Are you sure we can talk here?" Lexi asked Frannie.

They sat in a dark corner booth in the mid-scale Italian restaurant where Frannie worked. It was one of three jobs she held, the others being cocktail waitressing on weekend nights at a local bar and overseeing animal care all day Sundays for a local vet. On top of that, she spent three days a week at vet tech school. She had to be exhausted.

Lexi was worn out from three days a week of college classes and the hours of homework, plus fifteen hours a week at the campus bookstore. But it was just like Frannie to get on with it. Even now, when Lexi had shown up desperate and looking like hell, Frannie had just said a few words to her manager, led Lexi by the hand to the private corner, and proceeded to wrap silverware into napkins for the next day's lunch shift while she waited for Lexi to talk.

"I'm sorry," Lexi said for probably the tenth time since she had walked in the door. "I shouldn't have bothered you at work. I don't want to get you in trouble."

"Oh, please." Frannie shrugged a shoulder. "I'm the best server they have, and it's not like I make a habit of having friends visit me at work."

Lexi watched her face to see if she could read any bitterness or sorrow there. But Frannie, who had always been a master at hiding her hurt, was now more practiced at it than ever. Or maybe after so much time apart, Lexi had lost her ability to see Frannie hiding her pain under a perfect mask of disinterest.

"It must be important since you didn't just text or call," Frannie said.

"It is." It was the most important and awful and terrifying thing she would ever have to say. *Frannie will know what to do. Frannie will know—*

"Earth to Lexi." Frannie laid her warm, solid hand over Lexi's. "Geez, Lex, you're freezing. Are you all right? Are you sick?"

"I'm…" She shook her head. Two words. That was all she had to get out. But they were the hardest two words. "I'm…"

She squeezed Frannie's hand, willing strength into herself.

Frannie's brown eyes were round and intense. Her usually unruly, dyed-black hair was mostly confined in a tight knot on top of her head. Lexi missed Frannie's natural hair color, the pretty dark red. The shade the shiny girls in high school had loved. The one Frannie had hated because of it.

"Lexi, for God's sake, you're scaring me!"

Lexi jolted out of her thoughts and took the deepest breath she could. She exhaled. "I'm pregnant."

Frannie sat frozen. Lexi watched and waited. After a few minutes, panic clutched at her breath. "Now you're scaring me," Lexi choked out.

Frannie shook her head like she was coming out of a trance. "Sorry, I just didn't expect…" She shook her head again then squeezed Lexi's hand and leaned in over the table. "What did Brandon say? You told him, didn't you?"

"He doesn't know. He *can't* know."

"Okay." Frannie's voice was solid now, almost sharp.

Lexi sagged with relief. This was the Frannie she knew, loved, and needed.

"Okay, you don't have to tell him anything. So you've decided..." She stopped and took a breath. When she spoke again, her voice was low, the hard edges gone. "I know you, Lex. If you shut Brandon out of this, it will upset the balance of the universe or something. You'll never forgive yourself."

"He can't know," Lexi repeated, wishing Frannie could figure out the rest of it without Lexi saying it, but Frannie sat silently, waiting. "It's not his."

Frannie widened her eyes and sat back then wiped the shocked look off her face. "Okay," she said again, and it occurred to Lexi that she was trying to convince both of them that the disaster would be okay somehow, someday. "I didn't know you were seeing anyone else."

"I'm not." Lexi plowed ahead before she could chicken out again. "It wasn't my choice."

Frannie gasped. "You were raped? Oh, Lex." She moved out of her side of the booth and slid in beside Lexi, pulling her into a sideways hug.

"Please don't use that word. I just want... I need your help. I can't keep it, but I can't ask my parents for help, and I don't know what to do, where to start." Lexi's face was soaked with tears although she didn't remember starting to cry.

"It's okay. It's okay." Frannie rocked her gently. "Have you told anyone? The police? A counselor?"

"The police would be a joke. He's powerful and connected, and he'll blame me. I showed up there alone. I accepted a couple of drinks. I think it might have been spiked or..." She shook her head. "They won't believe any of it. I can't prove it."

"Powerful and connected," Frannie repeated.

Lexi prayed she would stop. She didn't want her friend to know his identity, and it wasn't like Lexi knew many untouchable men.

"Like a professor?" Frannie asked.

"No, not a professor. Just trust me, Brandon can never know."

"Oh my god." Frannie pulled slightly away and lightly held Lexi's shoulders, forcing their eyes to meet. "Lexi, was it Brandon's father?"

Her words knocked everything out of Lexi. Her breath, her strength, her resolve. She melted into a mess of confusion and tears and snot. Frannie handed her a pile of paper napkins and hugged her again, patting her back like they were mother and child.

Mother and child. Lexi always wanted to be a mother. But not like this. *Please, God, not like this.*

Lexi didn't know how much time had passed by the time she pulled herself together, but the lights were out in the adjoining dining room, and the restaurant was quiet. "Is everyone gone?"

Frannie nodded. "It's my night to close. The manager usually stays, but I think he sensed woman problems and hightailed it out of here."

Lexi gave a wry laugh as she scrubbed everything wet and sticky off her face with a rough paper napkin. "He was right. There aren't many woman problems bigger than this." She took a shaky breath. "I'm sorry to dump this on you. I'm such an awful friend. We've hardly even talked since Christmas, and I just show up—"

"Stop it, Lex. You did the right thing in coming here." Frannie held up her arm and shook the charm bracelet around her wrist, the one Lexi had given her the last summer before she had left for college two hours away from home. "Best friends forever, right? You're the one who made me swear."

"I swore it, too, and I meant it, Frannie. Thank you for listening. That's what I really needed."

Frannie shook her head. "That's just the beginning of what you need. It sounds to me like you've decided what to do about this. So, what's the plan? When? Where? Do you have enough money?"

"I... I don't know. I haven't gotten that far. But... god, it has to be soon. I'm almost twelve weeks along."

Frannie blinked fast, trying to look calm but not quite succeeding. "First things first. So, 'when' is pretty much immediately. Are you still planning to go on that spring-break trip with your roommates?"

Lexi swallowed a lump in her throat. Frannie had remembered that detail. The trip was the reason Lexi hadn't planned to see Frannie again until summer break. She nodded.

"That's when we'll have to do it." Frannie went back to her side of the table. She had the look on her face she always got when her mind was racing a thousand miles a minute. "If you want to keep this quiet, just between the two of us, you'll have to tell some lies. Big lies, like telling your parents and Brandon that you're still taking that trip. But your friends will have to cover for you, so you'll either have to tell them what we're doing or—"

"I can come up with a story for them too." Lexi wasn't great at lying, but she could do it if she had to. Probably not to Frannie, but to everyone else in her life. She could be devious. A terrible, hurtful, believable story leapt to mind. "Last year, we covered for Sarah when she spent a weekend with a guy she was cheating on her boyfriend with."

"That would be a good cover. It would explain why they can't ever say anything to Brandon or your parents." Frannie frowned. "I'm sorry. I'm sure that will be hard. But when it's all over, you can tell your friends it was a mistake and made you realize how right Brandon is for you. And it's not like you'll be hurting him. He'll never know about any of it."

Poor Brandon. Poor wonderful, amazing Brandon, the only man Lexi had ever fallen in love with. Maybe the only one she ever would. Lexi could never tell him the truth about this. He hated his father for so many reasons, so she wasn't afraid of ruining their relationship. But knowing his father had done such an awful thing to the woman he loved would be too much for any son to bear. And there was always the risk that it would break Brandon, cause him to snap and take it out on his father, possibly get himself into trouble.

"I'll tell my roommates tomorrow," Lexi said. "There's a cute guy in my psych 300 class who sometimes walks me to my next class. Sarah spotted us together once and thought there was something going on."

Frannie scowled. She had met Sarah exactly once and had told Lexi in no uncertain terms that she wasn't impressed. "Well, cheaters do love company, so there's that. Okay, so we've got the when and an alibi. Next, where. I'll do some research online when I get home tonight, but Indiana is basically stuck in the nineteenth century for women. I'm pretty sure we'll have to go out of state. And the money... How much do you have in your savings account?"

Oh god, the money. How much would she need? So many things she hadn't considered. Lexi has spent most of the last three months hiding, vomiting, making up excuses about having a terrible flu, and pretending none of it was happening. That hadn't left any energy for planning. "Not much," she answered. "I pay for my own books and expenses."

Frannie bit her lip. "I just paid for my tuition and my board exam coming up at the end of the summer. I'm flat broke. We can't ask your parents, and my mom's usually not much better off than me."

"Please don't tell your mom." Lexi knew, logically, that she had bigger problems than Crystal knowing the truth about her, but the shame of anyone else knowing would kill her. It would make it all too real.

"There's one way to get the money and some justice," Frannie said. She was frowning and pensive, and Lexi knew she wouldn't like where this was going. "This is Jack Greene's fault. He should pay for it."

Fear hit Lexi like an actual gut punch. She wrapped her arms around her middle. "Frannie, no. I can't ask him for money."

"That's not what I mean. We're not asking him anything. We're just taking his money. Remember that time last summer when Brandon came to visit you at your parents' place? We were all drinking one night, and he started bitching about his dad?"

Before that night, Frannie hadn't said a bad word about Brandon, but Lexi had known from reading Frannie's face that she had detested him. After that night, she had said she understood why he spent so much of his life acting like an asshole. Which Lexi argued he didn't. But that had been Frannie's way of saying she felt sorry for him, that there were worse things than never knowing your dad—like having a monster for one. "I remember."

"He talked about the shady stuff his dad does," Frannie continued. "Like keeping cash in his safe. Thousands of dollars of cash."

"You want to rob Jack Greene's safe?" Lexi whisper-shouted. "That's got to be a felony."

"Technically, it would be a burglary. But, yeah, a felony." She was way too calm about this. "We'll need to know his schedule and figure out when he'll be out of the house. Any chance he's taking a summer vacation?"

"Probably no time soon. He spent more than a month in London and just got back last week," Lexi said and realized too late that it sounded like she agreed with the plan. She did not.

"Then we'll have to get the timing just right. Is he still out every Tuesday night?"

"How do you recall so many details about Brandon's father?"

Frannie shrugged. "Evil people are interesting. More like characters in a book than people you meet in real life. Well, in *my* real life."

Lexi tried not to be hurt by the way Frannie was drawing a line between their lives.

"You'll have to get the code to unlock the safe," Frannie continued. "You said you saw it once when Brandon took out his mother's necklace for you to wear to the formal last fall."

Lexi leaned her elbows on the table and propped her head in her hands.

"Does their house have security cameras?" Frannie asked.

Lexi shook her head. "Brandon suspects his dad doesn't want his shady friends who come to visit to be caught on tape. But Frannie, we can't do this."

"*We* won't. All you have to do is find an excuse to make Brandon take something out of the safe and memorize the security code when he does it."

"No way will that ever work."

Frannie shrugged again. "Then I'll work on a plan B. But you have to try. Swear to me you'll try, Lexi." She held up her hand with her pinky extended.

Lexi wrapped her pinky around Frannie's. "Okay, I swear." It wasn't like Lexi really had to worry about it. It would never work. Even if she could think of a way to get Brandon to open the safe in front of her, he wasn't likely to be careless about putting in the code. But he *had* done it before.

"We just need a few thousand," Frannie said. "Maybe he won't even miss it."

"Or he'll blame Brandon for taking it."

Frannie frowned. "What will he do if he thinks it was Brandon?"

"Make him pay it back, I guess. Although he usually feels guilty enough about being a shit father to let things slide." Like the time, a couple of years before Lexi had met him, that Brandon had borrowed his father's Mercedes without asking and totaled it. Brandon said his father had alternated between sulking and swearing for days but hadn't even made his son pay the insurance deductible to buy a new car.

"Okay, worst-case scenario," Frannie said. "Greene figures out some money is missing. He blames Brandon. Brandon denies it.

Then what, they don't speak for a couple of months? Sounds like a win for Brandon."

Lexi couldn't help smiling. "You're good, Frannie. Making this sound like we'd be doing everyone a favor."

Frannie reached across the table and held Lexi's hand. "I don't care about everyone, Lex. I care about you."

Lexi sank deeper into the booth. "Okay, but you'll try to think of something else, right?"

"I will. But either way, I won't let this end badly for you."

Lexi sent a pleading mantra out into the universe. *Everything will be fine. Everything will be fine. Everything will be fine.* But as a wave of nausea hit her, she was gripped by a terrible suspicion the universe had stopped listening.

CHAPTER ELEVEN
2016

Frannie had left the blinds drawn when she had left the apartment, so it was cool and dark when she and Seth stepped inside. She scanned the combination kitchen and living room and sniffed the air, trying to experience it as Seth was. She had dusted a few days ago, leaving behind a stale lemon scent. It could be worse. And it was easy enough to keep things neat since she didn't have enough possessions to make a mess.

She flipped on the overhead light and set her mangled dinner box on the table. When she turned around, he was just inches from her. He pulled her against him and held her carefully in his arms, waiting for her to melt against him before he tightened his hold. Maybe she should at least make a half-hearted case for her virtue. Did anyone still do that? Had they ever really done that? Certainly not anyone who had been charmed by as fine a specimen of manhood as Seth Collins.

"How much trouble are you in, Frannie?" His voice was soft.

Oh yeah. They had come here to talk. Obviously, he wasn't as easily distracted as she was.

"I'm not in any trouble."

Seth kissed her neck, not playing fair. "Lexi never said exactly how much you took from that safe, but I'm guessing it was more than the ten thousand the papers reported, which you then returned to him."

With a frustrated sigh, Frannie pulled away from him. She led him to the couch, and they sat down with their bodies angled toward each other.

"It was never supposed to happen that way," Frannie said. "Brandon had mentioned that his dad kept five or ten grand on hand at their house, and I grabbed less than half of the stacks of bills. I'd never seen that much money, so I didn't know what a few thousand should look like, and I was in a pretty big hurry. I didn't even notice they were stacks of hundreds, not tens or twenties. Later, we discovered it was more than a few grand. A lot more."

Seth ran a hand through his hair. Frannie wanted to follow suit with her own hand, but he would only think she was hoping to distract him, which was part of her reason for wanting to do it but only a small part of it.

He took both her hands in his. "Why didn't you turn all of it over to him after you were arrested?"

"Everything happened so fast, and my public defender told me to keep my mouth shut while he worked out a plea deal. Greene was the one who said the money they'd found in my car plus the little bit I'd spent before they caught me was everything."

Seth frowned. "Meaning he didn't want the cops to know how much cash he'd had in his safe. So now he's come looking for the cash. But why take the risk when you'll be off parole soon? He's waited this long. What's another month?"

"He's probably afraid I'll disappear with it once the state stops watching me."

"I see," he said.

By the look on his face, she immediately knew Lexi hadn't told him Frannie was only here to get her money. All too quickly, he was putting that part of it together by himself. Smart guy, damn it. The hurt on his face was replaced by anger then by a calm smile.

"I don't care why you're here," he said. "I'm just glad you are. Now we have to figure out how to quietly return Greene's money to him."

We. He had said "we." There couldn't be a *we*. He was an army officer. There had to be rules against him getting mixed up with stolen property and the other laws Frannie would probably have to break before this was all over. Still, it felt good to have a partner in crime again, even if it was just for tonight while she worked on her plot.

She jumped to her feet. "How about a drink? I could use a drink."

He followed her to the kitchen. She pulled a new bottle of white wine out of the refrigerator and two glasses out of the cupboard and poured a portion for each of them.

She leaned against the counter, aware, like she always was when she was around him, of just how close he was and how much she wanted to touch him and how happy he would be if she did.

"I feel like I should make a toast, but I don't know to what." She rubbed her neck. "It's been a long day."

He lifted his glass and clinked it against hers. "To taking care of Jack Greene once and for all."

She took a sip of wine, weighing just how much of her nascent plan she should share with him. He trusted her so easily, maybe because he was so trustworthy himself. Lexi trusted him, but she trusted way too many people, even after everything that had happened to her. Rob trusted him, but they had been together on the battlefield. That had to come with its own special brand of loyalty.

Now Frannie racked her brain for a reason to distrust Seth, but she couldn't come up with anything that held up to scrutiny. They had come from the same broken-down place, grown up with the same people, and carried the scars of being poor kids in the richest country on earth. Goddammit, it was too late. She trusted the hell out of him. She wanted to tell him everything.

Soon. But not tonight.

He set down his glass and pulled her next to him again, leaving his arm wrapped around her waist. "So, Lexi has the money hidden somewhere, right?"

She nodded. "And she won't tell me where. Not yet."

Frannie didn't mention she wasn't going to wait for Lexi to reveal her secrets. She would have to find the money herself. To do that, she would have to learn the details of what Lexi had done after they had gone their separate ways the night of Lexi's first miscarriage. When she knew where her friend had gone after the hospital, she could start figuring out where Lexi had hidden the duffel bag full of cash.

"If you're in danger, Frannie, it's time for Lexi to talk," Brandon said. "We'll tell her we have to give back Greene's money before you get hurt."

Frannie's heart hammered while a little voice whispered that this was it, the time to tell him the truth. Not that her plan had always been to disappear with the cash, and not that—even though the calculus had changed and now she would have to return Greene's money—she still had to leave.

"I might not be the only one in danger," she said. "Greene showing up in Licking now that Lexi and I are both here feels like a warning. If he suspects she was involved, he'll be pissed she crossed him and hasn't paid for it."

"But he doesn't have proof, does he?" Seth asked.

"No." She leaned against him, fitting so well there. "And we can't give him any. I have to get my hands on the money and take it back to him—and make him believe I'm the one who was hiding it all along."

"How will we do that?"

She didn't miss his continuing use of *we*, but she didn't correct him. "I'm too tired to figure that out tonight. And first things first—I need to get my hands on the money. Do you think Rob knows Lexi's hiding place?"

Seth ran his fingers down her back. She closed her eyes and savored the feeling. "It doesn't matter if he does." Seth kissed her neck, and she shivered. "If Lexi doesn't want us to know where it is, we won't hear it from him."

"That's sweet—and annoying as hell," she said. "But at least it means he'll do what it takes to protect her."

"You mean when you're gone."

Frannie froze in place, unsure of whether to lie one more time or just come clean. There had to be something very broken in her that she couldn't bring herself to tell the truth to this trusting man holding her in his arms.

Seth pulled slightly away from her and held her lightly by the shoulders. "It doesn't have to be that way. You don't have to run. Once Greene has the rest of his money, he'll go away."

Frannie loved his version of the story, but it was a fantasy. That was not the way people like Jack Greene thought. Her former cellmate and white-collar-criminal-extraordinaire Maurie Stonefield had taught her that. "I'm the public face of the girl who got one over on Jack Greene, even if I did get caught. Do you really think he'll ever let that go?"

Seth ran a hand through her hair. "I hope so. He gets his money then puts out word on the street—or wherever the hell his shady business partners get their gossip—that you paid off your debt to him in full and threw yourself on his mercy, and everyone lives happily ever after."

"Not everyone gets a happily ever after."

"We'll come up with a way to work it out with him," Seth said.

The sincerity in his voice and the hope in his eyes was enough to give her pause, to let her pretend for a minute it was possible his version of the world could exist. A world where Jack Greene would leave them alone, where no one would be in ongoing danger because of

Frannie's stupid decision, where she still had something worthwhile to give to Lexi and Bettina and her mother and even Seth.

And maybe there was a way to pretend just a little longer.

She grasped his hand. "I need to take a shower."

"Of course. Go, shower, so you can get to your dinner."

She tugged his hand. "You said you wanted to watch. Unless you've changed your mind."

He stood perfectly still for a minute. She wasn't sure he was still breathing. She was about to speak again when he wrapped his arms around her waist and hoisted her onto the kitchen counter, stepping between her legs and pulling her against his chest. He wrapped his hands in her hair and kissed her. His mouth was sweet and teasing. His skin was hot. He was hard where he pressed against her when she wrapped her legs around his hips.

It had been so long since anyone had held her this way, she couldn't even remember when it had been. She had spent what should have been some of the best years of her life locked up, cloistered away from male company, deprived of sex. It had left her desperate, and she couldn't hide the desperation any longer. It wasn't love. She wouldn't lose herself in anything as deep and terrifying as that. But she would pretend she was normal, *they* were normal, for just a little while.

"I haven't changed my mind." He ran his tongue along the pulse in her throat.

"Hmm. That's good because I've made up mine. I've decided you should sleep over tonight."

CHAPTER TWELVE

On Wednesday night, Lexi pulled the vegetable tray out of the refrigerator and set it carefully on the kitchen island. Everything had to be perfect because Frannie had finally agreed to another friend date.

Lexi inventoried the evening's snacks. Blanched asparagus, raw broccoli, thinly julienned carrots, the cheap sour cream and onion dip she and Frannie used to save their nickels and dimes to buy at the convenience store on the way home from high school, Oreo cookies. Frannie's favorites, laid on pristine white serving trays. Was it too much? Did it come across as desperate?

Lexi rolled her shoulders, took calming breaths, and shook out her hands. She had to stop doing this. This was *Frannie*. Her Frannie. Well, maybe not so much hers anymore but still a close approximation. So what if she hadn't called yesterday to tell Lexi about Seth herself? And hadn't shown up for yoga yesterday morning? And hadn't called and might not have reached out at all if Lexi hadn't left a voicemail on her phone? So what if Lexi had to be the one to reach out for now, or for the next three years, or for the rest of their lives? It wasn't too much to do for a person who had given up four years of her own life to protect her best friend.

Teeny burst through the back door with grass stains on her jeans and beads of sweat along her hairline. She thrust her hand into the air in Lexi's general direction, revealing the pink-and-yellow friendship bracelet Lexi had made for her a few nights earlier. "Can you check this? I think it might be loose."

Lexi smiled as she tugged at the strings. The bracelet wasn't going anywhere, but she would check it as many times as Teeny—Bettina—needed to be reassured.

As Lexi inspected the bracelet, Bettina didn't take her eyes off the chip and dip bowl piled high with pita chips surrounding hummus.

"What makes you so sure Frannie likes pita chips?" Lexi asked Bettina, who was the one who had insisted they serve them.

Bettina shrugged as Lexi released her arm. "She told me."

It was possible. Every time they saw Frannie, the two of them managed to steal private minutes to whisper and giggle. Lexi rolled her shoulders again and pasted on a wider smile. "Since you know her taste, maybe you should test the chips and hummus before she comes. But wash your hands first."

Bettina's face lit up, and Lexi suspected the bracelet check wasn't the only thing that had drawn her stepdaughter away from Max and Rob in the backyard. As she moved toward the sink, Bettina paused for a split second by the refrigerator and touched the blue-and-yellow friendship bracelet pinned against the pseudo-stainless-steel door. It was the first friendship bracelet Lexi had ever made for a dog, and it had taken some near tearful conversations to convince Bettina it wouldn't stay on his leg, but the fridge door compromise was holding for now.

Rob came in from the backyard as Bettina finished piling a small plate to the edges with her snack. He raised his eyebrows but remained silent when Lexi gave him a slight nod.

"Hey, kiddo"—he ruffled Bettina's hair as she passed him—"no sharing people food with Max. And we have to finish math homework and get a bath in..." He checked his watch. "Fifteen minutes."

Bettina paused at the door. "One chip for Max?"

"Zero," Rob said.

"Thirty minutes?"

Rob sighed the sigh of a parent used to being defeated by a six-year-old. "Twenty."

Bettina squealed and ran into the backyard as Rob sidled up to Lexi and stood behind her, wrapping his arms around her waist.

She dipped a carrot into the dip and fed it to him over her shoulder. "You do know you'll have to draw a firmer line when it comes to things like driving and dating, right?"

"Yeah, but she'll hate us by then. It'll be easier."

Lexi started to turn around in his arms to kiss him but stopped when the doorbell rang. "That's Frannie." She ran a hand through her hair, checked that her blouse was tucked into her jeans, hurriedly remounded the hummus, and smoothed over the top of the dip.

"I'll let her in," Rob said.

"No." She pecked his cheek. "I'll do it."

As he headed to the backyard, Lexi dashed to the front door and put on her most welcoming expression as she pulled open the door to find Frannie about to ring the bell again. "Hi! Come on in."

"Hi. I was worried I'd gotten the night wrong."

Frannie's straight reddish hair was pulled back into a low ponytail, and her face was freshly scrubbed and makeupless. She could have been sixteen again, except she no longer hopped from one foot to the other while waiting to be invited into her best friend's house. Now she held out a bouquet of blue-and-white flowers—and shot Lexi a polite smile, and they were twenty-five and nearly strangers again.

When they got to the kitchen, Lexi offered Frannie a glass of wine, but she refused.

"I'm too tired. It would put me right to sleep." Frannie glanced around the room, her eyes lingering on the friendship bracelet on the fridge door, but she didn't comment or ask about it. "Where's the rest of the fam?"

"In the backyard."

"It's a nice evening for a picnic." Frannie pointed to the snack display. "Can I help carry this outside?"

"Actually, um..."

Lexi had planned for them to have adult friend time in the kitchen. But Bettina ran up the outside steps to the screen door and pressed her face against the mesh.

"Max!" Bettina called. "Frannie's here!"

"Sure, let's take everything outside," Lexi said.

She and Frannie loaded up their arms and headed outside to the picnic table. As soon as Frannie had set down the dishes, Bettina threw open her arms for a hug.

Lexi forced a smile. *This is a good thing.*

Frannie pulled a small, rumpled paper bag out of her jean jacket pocket. "I have something for you. Well, actually for Max."

Bettina clapped her hands together. "The eye-goop stuff?"

"Something that might help."

"I'll go tell him!"

Frannie laughed as Bettina darted to the corner of the yard where Rob and Max were sitting on a blanket, waiting for her return so they could continue reading *Goodnight Moon*.

Lexi glanced at Frannie. "When did Bettina tell you Max's eye medicine isn't working very well?"

Frannie shrugged. "One of the times she called me."

Lexi tried to ignore the tight pain of her stomach twisting. "How many times has she called you?"

Frannie looked at her now, understanding widening her eyes. "I figured you knew or even punched in my number for her. She called me Monday and then again yesterday."

"Oh." Lexi hadn't given Bettina Frannie's number and didn't know how the girl had found it. But it was okay. Better than okay. It was good. Exactly what she had wanted for Bettina and Frannie.

"It's homemade, homeopathic," Frannie continued. "It might not help him, but it won't hurt either."

"You should probably apply it now," Lexi said. "Bettina has to get ready for bed soon."

With a nod, Frannie left Lexi alone on the patio. Rob and Frannie said hi, then she must have suggested he leave before they treated Max because he got to his feet and joined Lexi.

"Hey, why so glum?" He bent and gave her a light kiss on the lips.

She squeezed his hand. "I'm not."

"I was just heading inside to set up Teeny's homework and pajamas, but I can sit with you for a few minutes if you want."

"No, I'm fine. While you get Teeny—*Bettina*—ready for bed, Frannie and I will have a chance to catch up."

As Rob headed for the house, she blinked fast so he wouldn't catch the tears forming in her eyes if he glanced back at her. She watched Bettina and Frannie, heads bent together over Max, whispering and giggling the way neither of them did with her. She should be sitting on the grass next to them, hearing their secrets and laughing with them. Bettina, now pointing to her friendship bracelet, should also point to one on Lexi's wrist because that second one had never been intended for a dog.

I am still an important part of their lives.

Her calming mantra was belied by the tangle of emotions that were always so close to the surface these days. A few minutes and several deep, cleansing breaths later, Lexi finally relaxed.

Frannie crossed the yard and sat on the patio chair next to her. "Max is fine. He didn't seem to mind the eye ointment, but he wants to spend a few minutes alone with Bettina to enjoy the sunset."

Lexi couldn't help smiling. "It seems to be one of his favorite things."

Frannie sighed. "It is a beautiful sunset. I try to appreciate them as often as I can."

A sharp knife of guilt stabbed at Lexi's heart. "Did you get to see any while you were…?"

Frannie shook her head. "But I knew I would, eventually." She angled herself toward Lexi. "What about you? Did you appreciate the sunsets for both of us while I was gone?"

The question caught Lexi so off guard, she didn't answer for a long, quiet minute. "Yes, I guess I did."

Across the yard, Bettina jumped to her feet and called for Max to follow her, which he did. She stopped to hug both women, Frannie first but Lexi longer. It wasn't a bad tradeoff.

"Sleep well, sweetie," Lexi said then kissed her cheek.

"Good night," Bettina said as she herded Max to the back door and into the house.

Now that they were alone, Lexi was dying to ask Frannie about her date with Seth, but she didn't want to sound too eager. Frannie spoke before Lexi could figure out the right way to bring up the subject.

"Hey, Lex, did you ever think about spending any of the money?"

The last thing in the world Lexi wanted to talk about was the stolen money. Well, almost the last thing. The reason they had stolen it was the last thing.

"I didn't want any of Jack Greene's money," Lexi said. "Let's talk about something happier. Like, I don't know, you and Seth."

Frannie picked an imaginary piece of lint off her jeans. "Seth is… Seth. You know how he is. Good guy. Great guy. Great kisser. I hope you didn't know that. But speaking of the money, I never really heard about how everything went down after I was gone. You've given me the big picture but not the details."

"You already know everything there is to know." Lexi rubbed her temples. This was not why she had invited her best friend over for the evening.

Frannie touched her hand. Just a light touch but a huge step forward for them.

"I'm not trying to upset you, Lex," Frannie said. "But I had to do all this counseling and other bullshit while I was inside, and one of the things they always talked about was closure. That you couldn't get past the things you'd done until you had closure. And these past few weeks have made me realize, I can't really have closure without knowing the other things, the details I wasn't there to see. Like what happened after I left you at the motel."

Frannie needed closure. That made sense. That was what Lexi wanted too. Maybe Lexi's punishment wasn't supposed to be Frannie's anger or blame. Maybe it was supposed to be reliving the details of those dark days one more time. She owed that to Frannie.

Lexi laid her hand over her belly. "I don't remember much about the ambulance ride or the first few hours in the hospital, but once I was a little better, I did the same thing we'd done at the clinic the day before when the bleeding had started—gave them a fake name and said I didn't have insurance. As soon as I felt better, they started asking more questions, so I left. I took a taxi to drop me off at the little gas station near the bus terminal where we'd left the money then walked the rest of the way there. I got the duffel bag and caught a bus to Lexington. I paid cash for everything, just like you told me to do."

"Lexington. Right." Frannie nodded. "Because Brandon was there for his internship. And then you stayed there with him?"

Brandon. God, Lexi didn't want to think about Brandon, with his sparkling hazel eyes and easy laugh. But this was for Frannie. For their friendship. For their future.

"No, we didn't stay there," Lexi said. "I called him from the bus station, and he picked me up. As soon as I got in the car, he asked me if I'd heard any news from home. I said no, and he told me about his dad's safe getting robbed and you getting arrested. I acted surprised, and we both acted like he believed me."

"Did you ever tell him the truth about being part of it or about how much money we took?"

Lexi shook her head. "And he never asked. He just said we would tell everyone we'd been together the whole time, just so no one would get the wrong idea."

Frannie touched her hand again. "And you never told him why we did it, what his father had done to you?"

"Never." A tear slipped onto Lexi's cheek, and she wiped it away. "We drove back to Indiana and spent a week at his family's cabin near the lake, and he took care of me while I slept fifteen hours a day and bled and cramped and... And he never asked any questions. Sometimes I wondered..."

Frannie sat quietly, not pushing her. The whole night went still around them.

"I wondered if he knew I was pregnant and thought it was his," she said.

Frannie reached out again, and this time she held on to Lexi's hand. "Maybe," she said, but she didn't sound convinced. "And after the cabin, he took you home?"

"He did," Lexi said. "I apologized to my parents for lying about the girls' trip. I told them I didn't think they'd approve of me going away with my boyfriend. They were sad about what had happened to you and were glad I was safe. I don't think they wanted to know any more than that, just like Brandon didn't want to know."

"They're all good people, and they love you." Frannie stared out at the nearly dark sky. Her face was impossible to read.

"Is that enough closure for one night?" Lexi asked.

"Maybe."

"Good." Lexi breathed out her relief at being able to segue back to the present. "Now you can tell me more about Seth."

Frannie smiled without showing teeth. "He stopped by the diner Monday night to see me. He'd heard about the Friday-night visitor.

I'm sure you know all that. And he was supposed to make dinner for me tonight, but he got stuck in an important meeting that ran late, so he'll call me later." Frannie furrowed her brow. "You know, there was one other thing I wondered about you hiding out with Brandon. Where was this cabin you went to after Lexington?"

Lexi wanted to scream. She couldn't stand any more of this discussion. But Frannie needed closure, and she needed to help Frannie.

"Somewhere north of Versailles State Park," Lexi said. Less than an hour from their hometown in one direction and from Jack Greene's house in the other. Yet she had felt safe in that cabin in the woods with Brandon.

"And he stayed with you the whole time? I mean, you were in bad shape. You could have hemorrhaged or something."

"He left a few times to get supplies," Lexi said, "but the nearby town was only twenty minutes away, and there was a hospital there. If something had happened while he was gone, I just had to dial 911."

"Which hospital?"

Lexi furrowed her brow. "I don't really remember. It was in Batesville, but that wasn't part of the name. Why does that matter?"

Frannie pulled at her ponytail. "It doesn't. I'm just glad you were near good medical care if you needed it."

Lexi grabbed a handful of her unruly curls at the nape of her neck and sighed to breathe out the negativity of all those old memories. "Can we please just talk about something else?"

The back door swung open, and Lexi jumped.

Rob came to her and laid his hands on her shoulders. "Frannie, fair warning. She knows Seth stayed at your place all night Monday night."

"Did he call you?" Frannie asked Rob.

"He didn't, and much to my wife's disappointment, I didn't call him to press for details. You have to remember you're in a small town.

He parks his pickup truck on Main Street all night, right across from your apartment, and people are going to put two and two together."

Frannie put her hand on her forehead. "Christ on toast. Does everybody in town know?"

Rob grinned. "I don't think the news has made it to Teeny's first-grade classroom, but pretty much everyone else has probably heard something by now."

"That's why the women I work with have been smiling at me so much," she said. "I was beginning to worry my waitressing skills were improving."

"And Lexi has questions," Rob said. "Lots of questions, many of them probably inappropriate, but you're her friend, and she wants to know inappropriate stuff about her friends." He squeezed Lexi's shoulders. "And you, sweetheart, need to pay more attention to what your friend is telling you. She missed a big, important chunk of your life, and now she wants to learn about it. This is what we call progress."

Lexi and Frannie glanced at each other, mirroring their wide eyes and o-shaped mouths.

Rob gave an exaggerated bow. "And now I will go oversee Bettina's bath and bedtime ritual and will leave the two of you to talk like girlfriends are supposed to talk. But first I'll mention that I'm a little disturbed that I'm better at this female bonding thing than you are. You really need to step up your game."

As he disappeared back into the house, Frannie grinned then laughed. It was contagious, and Lexi laughed so hard she was near tears.

"He's adorable," Frannie said when she caught her breath.

"That's why I keep him around. Well, that and his butt."

"He does have a nice butt," Frannie agreed. "And a good point. We're kind of bad at this."

"We'll get better." Lexi leaned back in her chair and picked out the first stars of the night. *Star light, star bright, first star I see tonight.*

"We're good, Lex. We really are," Frannie said.

Lexi couldn't speak for a minute. It was what she had been waiting to hear from Frannie since the day she had driven into town. Still, she would hold back, not spook her friend. "Good. Now you need to tell me something, *anything* about Monday night."

Frannie rolled her eyes. "Oh, all right. I guess I am kind of dying to tell someone. So, Seth came into the diner." She spent the next ten minutes telling Lexi a PG story about their night together, but Lexi got the gist of it.

"I'm glad you're finally giving the guy a chance," Lexi said.

"Me too." Frannie yawned then stretched. "But now I'm beat, so I think I'll head home."

Lexi grinned. "You mean back to the love nest?"

"It's not a love nest, and besides, it's empty tonight."

Lexi walked Frannie back into the house and to the front door. "Thanks for sharing with me. It was... It felt nice, didn't it?"

"It was nice."

It wasn't like old times, but they were one step closer. Maybe someday it could be better than old times. Maybe this time Lexi wouldn't be so needy, and Frannie wouldn't have to take care of her. If things went really well, maybe one day Lexi could return the favor and take care of Frannie.

CHAPTER THIRTEEN

At two in the morning, Frannie was startled awake by a strange sound from her cellmate. It took a few seconds to remember she was out of prison and narrow down the beeping to her phone announcing a text message. She grinned, ready to read a steamy message from Seth, even if he had sent it at an ungodly hour. But as her bleary eyes focused, she realized it was from Lexi.

At the emergency vet. Max is really sick. Doc looking at him now.

Frannie rolled out of bed, twisting in her sheets and landing on her butt with a thud. She sat on the floor in a puddle of bedclothes and thumbed a response.

What can I do? Tell me where you are. I'll be there ASAP.

Frannie disentangled herself and stumbled toward the dresser. She had pulled out jeans, a T-shirt, and a sweatshirt by the time Lexi responded.

No need to do that, but thanks. I didn't mean to wake you, but Bettina made me promise to text as soon as I got Max to the doctor.

Frannie remembered Lexi's hurt looks when Frannie and Bettina whispered and laughed together. She thought about Rob's description of a happier time between Lexi and her stepdaughter. Bettina had wanted Frannie to know right away. That didn't mean Lexi had wanted the same thing. Maybe Frannie inserting herself in this situation would only cause a bigger rift between the two. And what right did she have to do that, anyway, as a temporary adult in Bettina's life?

Please let me know if there's anything I can do. And send updates when you can. <3

It took another minute for Lexi's response. *Thanks. I will.*

After a minute, the phone screen went dark and stayed that way. Frannie laid her clothes on the dresser, threw her sheets and blankets back on the bed, and crawled into them. Sleep eluded her. All she could think about was that scruffy mess of a mutt and the sweet wisp of a girl who loved him with all her heart. She had made promises to Bettina that she had yet to keep.

With a groan, Frannie sat up in bed, picked up her phone, and began searching the Internet for dog trainers near Licking. Half an hour later, she had found a service that looked like a good fit, filled out their appointment form, and paid a deposit on the recommended three beginner training sessions. She copied the link and emailed it to Lexi with the subject line *A gift to Bettina and Max when he's recovered.* Lexi might hesitate to accept it for herself, but Frannie hoped she would be hard-pressed to deny a gift for her stepdaughter.

Frannie lay down again, this time relaxed enough to sleep, content that she might finally be making headway in leaving at least one part of Lexi and her family's lives better than she had found it.

SITTING IN THE DINER kitchen, wrapping flatware in large white paper napkins for the next day's breakfast shift, Frannie kept an eye on her phone lying on the stainless-steel prep table in front of her. She willed a text to appear there, a follow-up to Lexi's brief 6:00 a.m. message that had said Max would be fine and was going home soon. Since then, it had been radio silence. It was something Frannie would have sworn she had craved since her captivity in this stiflingly small town: a respite from Lexi's calls, texts, voicemails, and invitations.

But the silence from Lexi and Bettina was worse.

This was how it would be once she was gone. She wouldn't know about Max's future illnesses or his eventual death, which hopefully wouldn't come until he was a very old and happy good boy. She wouldn't be able to worry over Bettina's childhood skinned knees or teenaged heartbreak. If Lexi ever got sick or when her elderly parents died, Frannie wouldn't be there to help pick up the pieces, even if she did find a way to keep in touch with her mother and keep tabs on her friend's life. This was good practice for her future and a good thing for Lexi and Bettina. The healthiest thing for all of them.

They don't owe me anything. She didn't belong inside their closed circle any more than she had fit in with the shiny girls at school. When Lexi had gotten a chance to join them in high school and had taken Frannie to some of their parties, they had been polite, welcoming even. Then they had petted her like a zoo animal and treated her like the anomaly she had always been and would always be, while Lexi had fit right in.

When Frannie's phone dinged with a message, she grabbed it. The message wasn't from Lexi, but it lifted her spirits.

Hey, beautiful. Heard Max is sick. Any updates?

Exchanging flirty texts with Seth was a better way to pass the time than ruminating. It was actually a damn good way to get through the night.

Hey yourself, hottie. Nothing since 6:00 a.m. You?

The phone dinged again.

Nothing here either. Call me when you get home so I can hear your sexy voice.

She promised she would, and gladly. For the first time all day, she had something to look forward to. When the phone she still held in her hand rang, she jumped. The caller ID flashed Lexi's cell phone number.

Frannie answered the phone, skipping the niceties. "Is everything okay?" So much for that healthy detachment.

"It's fine now," Lexi said. "We're all just exhausted. But Frannie, a dog trainer? That was so sweet of you. Of course I'll reimburse you."

"Don't do that. It's a gift." Frannie stood, stretched, and paced along the tile wall, out of Oscar's earshot and his way. "So, last night. What happened?"

"Max swallowed a chicken bone, and it got stuck going into his stomach. We have a strict no-people-food rule for him, which apparently Teeny has been flouting pretty much since the day we brought him home. She'd shared some of her chicken dinner with him, and then he went looking for more in the trash. He probably would have done that regardless, but Bettina was convinced it was her fault."

"The poor kid must be a wreck."

"She feels terrible, but I think we've finally convinced her to stop giving him people food." Lexi's voice was soft, and Frannie suspected she was crying.

"You sound exhausted. Did you get any sleep?"

"Not much. I thought Max and I would get out of the ER around seven or eight, but it was closer to noon, and Teeny's school had early dismissal. Then Rob had to work late, so dinner got delayed and—I'm so tired I'm babbling. I wanted to give you an update. I really am sorry. I would have called from the vet's office if I'd had my wits about me."

"That's okay." Hearing about the barely controlled chaos of Lexi's domestic life was oddly soothing. All the worry of the past several hours fell away. "Tell Bettina how happy I am for her and Max, and then get some sleep."

"Meet me in the morning for yoga," Lexi said. "My back will never forgive me if I don't stretch it out after sitting in plastic waiting-room chairs all night. You still owe me for being a no-show Tuesday morning, even if Seth is really the one to blame."

Shit. Frannie knew she had forgotten something when Seth had distracted her.

"Okay, you, me, and the birds, 8:00 a.m. See you then." A strange feeling settled over her as she hung up the phone. Relief.

"Your dinner's almost ready," Oscar called to her.

"Thanks. You're my favorite, Oscar."

She headed for the time clock. Hearing footsteps from the dining room, she stretched out her arm, hoping to punch out before anyone could—

"Hey, Frannie. Customers are requesting you, hon." Beth smiled at her. "Oh, good. I caught you before you punched out for the night."

Frannie flashed her sweetest smile. "Let's just pretend you didn't."

"Nope. It won't take long. They just want dessert." Beth grabbed two sets of flatware and headed back to the dining room.

"What is it with this diner? I never get out of here on time," Frannie said, but no one was listening.

Frannie glanced longingly at the Styrofoam box full of her dinner, too tired to even remember what she had ordered but desperate for it, just the same.

"I'll keep it warm for you, doll," Oscar said.

"Thanks."

Despite the temporary interruption to her plans, she would still have a good night. Bettina and Max were fine, and Lexi would be, too, after a good night's sleep. A sexy man was waiting to whisper sweet nothings to her over the phone while she ate the dinner she had needed for the past couple of hours. If her luck held, maybe her customers would give her a big, fat tip for staying late. If Frannie's plan to find the money worked, she wouldn't be in town much longer. She would spend the time storing up enough good feelings to last a lonely lifetime.

The pot of decaf wasn't on the burner. Beth had taken it to Frannie's customers, the only ones left in the place. As Beth stepped away from the table, Frannie caught sight of the woman with grizzled blond hair and a too-broad smile speaking with Beth like they were old friends. Frannie's mother laughed at something Beth said then smiled at the man sitting across from her.

The man Frannie's mother had been dating. It had to be. She had hoped never to meet him, but maybe it was better this way. At least Frannie would have an image of and a feel for the person her mother could lean on when Frannie disappeared.

"They want two pieces of pecan pie," Beth told Frannie as she placed the pot of decaf back on its burner and disappeared into the kitchen.

Frannie placed two slices of pie onto dessert plates and started speaking as she approached the table. "Hey, Mom. This is a surprise."

"Hello, sweetie." Her mother threw her an air kiss. That was new. No doubt showing off for the date. "Frannie, there's a good reason for my surprise visit. There's someone special I want you to meet."

With a deep sigh and a forced smile, Frannie set down her mother's pie and turned to place the pie in front of her mother's *boy*friend, a terrible description for a middle-aged mother seducer.

She froze. Except for her shaking hand.

She hoped they wouldn't notice, but it was so bad, she couldn't place the plate on the table in front of him. His dark hair was shot through with more gray than it had been the last time she had seen him, across a crowded courtroom. His handsome, angular face, so much like his son's, was the same except for a gray shadow of a beard that seemed out of character for the way she remembered him. His one wholly unchanged feature was the flatness of his dark-blue eyes. They couldn't be more different from Brandon's.

When Lexi had first started dating Brandon, Lexi had told Frannie that it was his sparkling hazel eyes that had drawn her to him. Nearly two years later, Lexi had told Frannie it was Jack's cold blue eyes that haunted her nightmares.

"Let me help you with that, Frannie." Jack took the plate out of her hand and set it on the table. "I think I've spooked you."

Her mother grabbed Frannie's other hand. "Don't look so terrified, Frannie. Jack comes in peace. Don't you, Jack?"

Greene nodded his agreement, and Frannie realized she hadn't stopped staring at him. "Like I told you in court, no hard feelings. You've paid back your debt to me and to society."

It was a lie, and he and Frannie both knew it. He had come for a reckoning. Her mother was just a useful tool for him. Her mother, her unwitting, hapless mother, had brought the son of a bitch straight to Frannie. The last time he had been here, he'd had the decency to stalk her and spy on her colleagues from a distance. Now he strolled right into the heart of Lexi's town without batting an eye. He was bold. Sure of himself in the way only those who are above the law and know it can be.

From all accounts Frannie had heard and seen, Maurie Stonefield had behaved that way until she had ended up behind bars. If only such a fate awaited Lexi's rapist, but the years and circumstances had conspired to let him walk free. And now he was sitting in Patrice's diner, drinking the best coffee in the state, scaring the bejesus out of Frannie. And screwing her mother in every sense of the word.

Greene grinned at his date. How could her mother not see the monster behind those cruel, dead eyes? But her mother smiled back at him with a stupid, mooning look. Frannie stumbled backward a step, gobsmacked. Her mother looked like a woman in love.

"Oh, before I forget"—Frannie's mother let go of her hand—"how's Teeny? Lexi's mom stopped into the pharmacy today to pick up a prescription. She'd just talked to Lexi, who was in the vet's office with that poor mutt."

"She's... They're fine." Frannie could barely form words. This man was a rapist, Lexi's rapist. A monster. And Frannie's mother was discussing the details of Lexi's life right in front of him. *She doesn't know*, Frannie reminded herself. *She's not trying to be an ass. She just doesn't know.* She cleared her throat. "I don't think we should talk about that."

Greene held up his hand. "Frannie, it's fine. I hold no ill will toward my son's ex-girlfriend. I'm glad to hear she's doing well with her little family." He held Frannie's gaze. "Right here in this quaint little town."

Frannie barely heard his words over her pounding heart that echoed in her own ears.

"I'd like to get to know you better." Greene kept talking. "To get to know the Frannie your mother speaks so highly of." Greene flashed his toothy grin at her. Like a wolf with a cornered rabbit.

Frannie's head swam. "What do you want?"

She shouldn't have asked. This was not a conversation to have in front of her starstruck, hoodwinked mother. Greene exchanged a look with his date, and her mother nodded and slid out of the booth as though they had planned this.

"I have to wash my hands," she said. "I'll be right back. Be nice, Frannie."

Greene motioned to the seat her mother had just vacated. "Frannie, please join me."

She shook her head and backed into the table behind her then pulled out one of the metal-rimmed vinyl chairs and sat on it backward. It allowed her to prop her elbows on the chair back and hold her spinning head in her hands.

Frannie whisper-shouted. "We both know why you're here."

The edges of his smile turned down. "I really do think you misunderstand, Frannie. I like your mother. I'm sure I'd like you, too, if I got to know you."

He wouldn't mention the money, not here where they could be overheard. And neither would she. "That's not why you were sitting across the street casing last Friday night."

"Was I?"

Backing down wouldn't get her answers, so she dredged up the courage to glare at him.

He sighed. "I came here to see if you were working. I thought I should have the decency to tell you myself that I'm dating your mother, given the"—he spread his hands wide—"oddness of the situation."

"Normal people don't do that. A normal person would have come inside and asked for me."

"Perhaps," he said. "But my life is far from normal."

He had answers for everything, and Frannie didn't believe any of them.

"You're not here out of decency," she said.

He arched an eyebrow. "I can't force you to believe me, but it's true. For your mother's sake, I think you should acquiesce."

She didn't know whether the chill in her bones was from the veiled threat against her mother or the way he said that last word. Was that what he thought her unconscious best friend had done, that she had acquiesced to him? Frannie wanted to throw the rape in his face, but bringing it up would take them down a road she didn't dare travel, for the sake of Lexi and her secret, the one Frannie had gone to prison to protect.

"But someday," Greene continued, "I really would love to hear just how you pulled off your little escapade. I find it hard to believe you acted alone."

Frannie struggled to keep her face blank and hide the terror he struck in her.

"At first, I thought Brandon might have been part of it, but now I'm sure he wasn't." Greene pointed his fork in Frannie's direction. "That girlfriend of his though. Your best friend, if I'm not mistaken."

His pointed words confirmed her suspicions. He was after Lexi. She had been planning to run away with the money for weeks—years, really—as if it was in her control. But it wasn't.

"We can reach an agreement." Frannie forced steadiness into her voice. "Get away from my mother and *stay* away from her, stay away from Lexi and her family, and then I'll give you what you've come looking for. After that, I'll disappear for good. But only if my mother and Lexi stay out of it."

"We don't need an agreement, Frannie, just an understanding that your mother is important to me, and I don't want our past—the one with you or your friend—to interfere with my relationship." Greene slipped his grinning mask into place. "There she is," he said as Frannie's mother approached the table. He held out his hand to her. "Darling, let's have Frannie box up our dessert for us. It's so late, and I'm more tired than I realized. We can have this with a nice decaf espresso when we get to my house."

Frannie concentrated on maintaining her blank expression as she fetched a carry-out box for them. She packed up the pie and handed the box to her mother, who remained under Jack's spell and didn't even notice Frannie's stony silence. Her mother kissed Frannie's cheek and promised to call over the weekend.

Jack smiled and held out his hand to Frannie. "It was so pleasant to meet under these circumstances, wasn't it? And our chat was illuminating. I look forward to our next meeting."

When the front door clicked closed behind the smiling couple, Frannie nearly collapsed in the middle of the dining room. But she put one foot in front of the other and made it to the kitchen before hunching over with her hands on her knees. She wouldn't pass out, wouldn't curl into a ball, wouldn't let her mind shut down.

Just when she thought she was doing more good than harm, Jack Greene had showed up to remind her why she never should have come here in the first place. Frannie couldn't wait for Lexi to give her Greene's money. Frannie would have to find it and take it because she was out of time. She had made a very dangerous man a promise she couldn't afford to break.

CHAPTER FOURTEEN

As plans went, Frannie had come up with worse. Given that she had thrown it together in the day and a half since she had learned her mother was dating Lexi's rapist, it was damn near brilliant. Still, by the time she left the meeting with her parole officer Friday morning, she was already second-guessing herself. Maybe because she had gotten out of bed before the roosters to go to yoga class, her one last chance to make Lexi happy. Maybe because she had made the long drive to Madison and sat in a stifling waiting room with a few fellow criminals, some of them less concerned with hygiene than others. Maybe because she was about to do something that skated awfully close to another crime.

Most definitely because the last time she had thrown together a plan under duress, she had ended up with a four-year prison sentence. And like last time, she wasn't really skating close to a crime. She was committing one. Getting caught for trespassing or a B&E so close to the end of her sentence would not end well for her. And even if she pulled it off, disappearing with nearly a month left on her parole would still rebrand her as a wanted criminal. But the demon snapping at her heels kept her moving forward.

Frannie struggled to read the directions she had scratched on the back of a rumpled envelope, cursing the day she had become dependent on the GPS in her phone, which now lay abandoned on the nightstand beside her bed. Seriously, how many true crime shows did you have to see before you realized the cops always put the bad guys at the scene of the crime by reviewing their cell phone records?

At least that part of her plan still held up in the light of day, and she made it to the Ripley County courthouse after only three wrong turns and an extra half hour of driving.

Frannie tucked her hair up into a baseball cap and slid on her sunglasses, despite the overcast sky. She shrank into the corner when she got some side-eye from a few of her elevator companions then nearly turned tail and ran out of the Records office when the youngish woman with bug-eye glasses and short bright-pink hair asked for her ID.

"Just a driver's license," the woman said, smiling and cracking her chewing gum.

Frannie smiled back, trapped. She couldn't risk leaving behind proof she had been here, but she had no other way to find Greene's vacation cabin. "Sure. I have it right here."

She dug her wallet out of her purse and exchanged her driver's license and ten bucks for copies of the plats for his parcel and the surrounding properties. To her great relief, the clerk handed back her license without making a copy or writing down any information from it, and Frannie made it back to her car without evoking any more suspicious looks.

She sat in her car in the parking lot, poring over the land plats and comparing them to the county map she had picked up at a gas station earlier that morning. After scratching out another set of directions on the envelope, she pulled away from the courthouse and headed east, only taking off her cap and sunglasses after passing the town limits and making sure no one was following her. Not that she had done anything illegal yet. But the day was young.

As thick forest flew by on both sides of the long, straight road, part of Frannie's mind wandered to that day from a previous lifetime. All those stacks of bills in Jack Greene's safe. Frannie had been so stupid. She should have known something was off. Only later, when she had picked up Lexi in another town and they had headed east on the way toward New York state, to a place where no one knew them and where a second-trimester abortion was legal, had they counted the money. It was over a hundred thousand dollars.

"Holy shit," Frannie had said.

"What have we done?" Lexi had dropped the stack of bills she was holding like they were a ticking bomb. Which they were.

In that moment, Frannie had known Jack Greene was just as shady as the rumor mill had whispered he was for years—and probably just as dangerous to cross. She had just poked a stick into a pit full of rattlesnakes, and there would be no turning back.

They counted out ten grand to use for their expenses and stuffed it into Frannie's backpack, leaving the rest of the cash in her oversized gym bag. In the middle of the night, she had pulled into the shadows in a bus-station parking lot a mile off I-71. Lexi was already sick that first night, but Frannie made her memorize the locker number where she had stashed the bag and had made her friend stuff the locker key into her jeans pocket in case Frannie couldn't get back to retrieve it anytime soon. As soon as she had realized how much money she had stolen and what that much cash must mean, Frannie had known Greene would call in every favor he could from every crooked cop and bought-off politician he knew, and if she and Lexi didn't get far enough fast enough, they would get caught.

That was when she had come up with her backup plan—one she hadn't shared with Lexi—to make the world believe Frannie had committed the heist alone.

Lexi's harrowing miscarriage slowed them down, and they were bound to get caught. So once Lexi was safe in the hospital and the money was stashed in the bus-station locker, waiting for Lexi to return for it, Frannie had driven another hundred miles then turned herself in.

Frannie came to the end of a paved county road and hoped it was where Lexi had taken the money, in a stroke of genius hiding the stolen cash on Greene's own property. She turned onto a dirt road that—if she had read the plat maps correctly—would lead to a few hundred acres divided into six parcels, the largest of which had been in the Greene family for a couple of generations. Frannie turned onto another dirt road, this one narrower and disappearing under a thin film of weeds. She drove off to the right side of the cabin, into some dense brush, to camouflage her car in case a random hiker wandered past. It was an under-baked part of her plan, but desperate times...

She grabbed her bag of tools, containing a two-piece shovel, a spade, a sturdy army knife, some screwdrivers, and a heavy-duty flashlight, from her trunk and headed to the cabin. She stopped on the front porch and surveyed the overgrown yard, trying to put herself in Lexi's place, inside Lexi's fragile body and terrified twenty-year-old mind.

"You would have still been weak from all the blood loss. But you would have buried it here. You would have been too terrified to take it home and hide it there."

The cleared land was flat and uncluttered, providing no obvious hiding places. The tree line started too far away for a fragile Lexi to have hiked that far. That left the cabin itself.

Frannie started with the easy targets. First, the front porch, which was pretty low to the ground, with no loose boards and no easy way to pry off sideboards to stash a duffel bag under it. Frannie shone her flashlight through each seam just to be sure, finding nothing but dirt and some weeds and hundreds of scurrying insects. The side and back porches yielded the same disappointments. By the time she realized she would have to break into the cabin, it was late afternoon, and the sky was dark, darker than it should be, and she vaguely remembered a forecast about thunderstorms rolling across the state. She was not a fan.

"Well, why not, Mother Nature?" she muttered while she tried to pick the backdoor lock, only to run up against a dead bolt. "Just send a storm my way while I'm alone in the middle of nowhere, breaking into a creepy cabin."

Lightning streaked across the sky, and the wind whipped against her face. She gritted her teeth as she weighed her options and determined that she wouldn't be able to get inside without breaking some glass. She pulled the shovel handle out of the bag as another streak of lightning zigzagged its way to the ground in the forest to her right. The thunder boom shook the trees, and fat raindrops splatted onto the leaves.

She slammed the shovel handle into the glass above the lock on one of the back windows. It didn't even crack. She panicked. Leave it to Jack Greene to outfit his country cabin with reinforced glass. She shivered as the wind whipped around her again, this time pelting rain against her skin.

It wasn't like she could leave without trying everything. This was her last chance. There were no other options left on the table. She was going into that damn cabin if she had to march into the forest while darting between lightning bolts to haul out a tree branch sturdy enough to break the window. But first, she would take another shot with the shovel.

Her desperation bolstered her strength, and this time she made a hole in the glass then cleared away the jagged edges. She reached through the opening, unlocked the window, and slid up the sash. She climbed over the ledge, pulled the tool bag into the cabin, and closed and locked the window. She used the toe of her sneakers to push the glass fragments to the wall's edge then positioned the long navy drapes over both the hole and the broken glass. With any luck, by the time anyone showed up here and noticed the damage, Greene would have his money, she would be in the wind, and there would be no way to prove she was the one who had committed the B&E.

She was in the kitchen, which was almost as swanky as the one Frannie remembered in Greene's mansion, if half the size. No way

Lexi would have hidden the money anywhere easy to find, but Frannie still took the time to look in every cupboard and closet, check for loose floorboards and tiles, and tug at every surface, searching for a secret cubby behind it. She checked under furniture, behind curtains, and in dark corners on the main floor, which in addition to the kitchen had a full bathroom with fancy fixtures and a subway-tiled shower and an enormous great room with a soaring, thick-beamed ceiling and a floor-to-ceiling blue slate fireplace. She pulled over a dining room chair and stood on it to check every fireplace stone, even while realizing Lexi wouldn't have been well enough to manage such acrobatics when she had been here. She ducked to look up into the chimney, which was too small for any adult to fit inside.

Frannie repeated her actions in the three bedrooms and two full bathrooms on the upper floor, checking the obvious, not-so-obvious, and obscure possibilities, and still came up empty. She plopped down on the large bed in one of the rooms then jumped when another strike of lightning, followed a split-second later by thunder, shook the house. With her thoughts no longer laser-focused on the bag of money, she realized she was in the master bedroom, probably Jack Greene's room. Her stomach roiled, and she lurched into the hallway.

As the storm flashed and rattled and rain bounced off the large skylight in the ceiling over the staircase, Frannie huddled on the steps and wondered if she was too far away from civilization to hear the tornado sirens if they went off. When she was a kid at home alone and storms came through town, she would hide in a closet, wishing for a basement.

A basement.

The cabin could have one. She hadn't found an access door from inside the building, but maybe there was one on the outside. She hadn't checked the side of the cabin that didn't have a patio, but now she raced down the stairs, hoisted her tool bag onto her shoulder, and let herself out the back door. She was drenched and mucking through mud by the time she reached the side of the cabin, but she didn't give a damn because she spotted the basement doors. They were painted green to match the surrounding grass. She yanked on the handle, only to find it locked. There were only the tiniest slivers of windows, too small for her to squeeze through even if she broke one.

She howled into the wind. She was soaked, starving, and by now running late for dinner at Lexi's house. There was no way in hell she could go through all of this and walk away empty-handed. But if the money was in that basement, she was going to have to go home, teach herself how to become a master lockpicker, and come back another time.

To hell with that. There *was* no other time.

She stared at the nearest narrow basement window, shaking with cold and fury. She stepped closer and squatted down to peer into it. Close up, maybe it wasn't too small, after all, not for someone Frannie's size. A flash of lightning showed a terrifying view of shadows and spider webs, just for a split second. But as she had been telling herself all day, desperate times...

She opened her now-drenched duffel bag, pulled out the shovel, and bashed at the window over and over until she shattered the glass. She used the blade edge to smash and scrape away all the glass, exposing the full opening. Dropping the shovel and picking up her flashlight, she shimmied onto the ledge until her legs dangled into the room. She tried very hard to cast away any memories of horror movies where heroic idiots had their legs snatched and caught by the always-smarter monsters and gulped in a big breath of air and held it like she was about to plunge into a pool.

The drop was farther than she had estimated, and the impact jarred her feet and ankles. Worse, she lost her grip on the flashlight, and it slammed to the ground. The light blinked out.

"Perfect."

A few seconds later, another flash of lightning illuminated the space enough to reveal track lights on the ceiling and a bank of light switches a few feet away. Plunged back into darkness, she felt her way along the wall until she reached the switches and pushed them all into the up position. Brilliant light flooded the basement and rendered her temporarily blind, but as soon as her eyes adjusted, she smiled. It was about the least scary basement she could have imagined, with a narrow, empty bar and a few bar stools along the wall to her left, a small fireplace along the wall to her right, and a poker table and chairs and an old-style foosball table in the space between them. The floor was flagstone, with a large and probably expensive ornamental rug lying over most of it. Everything was covered in a substantial layer of dust, as if the caretaker rarely, if ever, made it down here. This had to be the place.

She picked up her flashlight and tapped it a few times, and the beam blinked on. Finally, things were going her way. She moved along the walls and floor, using her flashlight to observe every inch, looking for cracks or hidden panels. All solid. She checked under and behind the bar then the furniture. Her smile faded as she wondered what she had missed. Her gaze rested on the fireplace. Surely it was too narrow, like the one upstairs. Still, she stepped forward and angled the flashlight beam up into the dark interior. And groaned.

The space was ever so slightly deeper than the chimney upstairs, but it was enough. Lexi was taller than Frannie, but she was thin. And nearly four years ago, after weeks of stress, depression, and morning sickness, she had been even thinner.

"Yeah, perfect."

Frannie sat inside the fireplace with her torso and head engulfed by the chimney and her legs stretched out on the floor, glad for the small blessing that despite the black stains on the hearth, it was soot free. Half entombed, she jiggled her legs to maintain her sense of freedom as she swept the flashlight beam over the stones of the chimney interior, circling higher and higher. Then she spotted it. A black webbed strap. Exactly the kind of strap that had been on the gym bag she had stuffed full of Jack Greene's money.

Gripping the flashlight in her left hand with the beam focused on the prize, she wriggled her right arm to get it above her head and stretched as far as she could. Her fingers stopped inches from the strap.

"No. No, no, no, no, no!" Her voice echoed in the confined space.

She shifted again, this time getting her heels under her butt so she could lift her entire body the few necessary inches higher. It didn't help the fear that was barreling toward terror about getting trapped here. Alone. In the woods. Where a hapless caretaker probably wouldn't find her until an unbearable smell made its way up through the floorboards.

"Stop it!" she whisper-shouted. Her words echoed eerily around her.

She took long, even breaths. She needed one of Lexi's mantras right about now. What was the process? Repeat it three times.

"I will not die in this damn chimney. I will not die in this damn chimney. I will *not* die in this *damn chimney*!"

She pushed upward from her feet. The movement only gained her a few inches until her shoulders wedged into the narrowing channel, but that was all she needed to be able to wrap her fingers around the strap. She gave a squeal of joy, which quickly turned to frustration. The bag was stuck. She ran her hand along the edge of the strap and felt where it was caught in a crevice between two stones.

Swearing, sweating, and fighting off terror that caught in her throat and made her think more than once that she might suffocate, Frannie worked the strap, wiggling it back and forth, edging it out of its trap. Her shoulder went numb, and the paralysis worked its way up her arm. Just before it hit her fingers, the strap shifted and popped free. She barely had time to brace herself for the weight of the bag falling on her head.

The impact didn't come.

She wriggled herself out of the chimney with the strap clutched in her hand. Only the strap. The rest of the bag was gone. She scrambled forward on hands and knees and aimed the flashlight beam as high as it would go. No gym bag. She lay on her back and surveyed the entire height of the chimney, inch by inch. Nothing to see except row upon row of stone and mortar.

She inched out of the hearth and picked up the strap, clutching it to her chest. It had been here. The bag, the money. This was definitely where Lexi had hidden it. Frannie stared at the strap, turning it over in her hands. The small patches of dark-blue material at the ends of the strap weren't frayed or torn. The bag hadn't broken under the weight of its contents. It had been cut.

Someone had found Frannie's stolen money and had stolen it out from under her.

CHAPTER FIFTEEN

Two hours later, soaked to the skin, trembling with fear, Frannie stood on Lexi's front porch and stared at her friend.

"What am I going to do?" she asked Lexi. "I was going to give that money back to Jack Greene to get him out of our lives. But someone took it. Maybe Greene himself. If he already has it, if he found it in that chimney, he must realize you put it there." Which meant he had proof Lexi was Frannie's partner in crime. The same panic that had gripped her hours earlier when the walls of the chimney had been closing in on her now returned.

"He has it," Lexi whispered.

"Maybe."

Lexi looked terrified, which made Frannie feel like crap. She took her friend's warm hand in her ice-cold one. "Let's not panic, Lex. We don't know for sure who took it."

"We do. I do." Lexi met her gaze. "I know Jack Greene has the money because I sent it back to him."

"You... Are you crazy? Then he knows you're involved and—"

Lexi shook her head. "I did it anonymously, through someone else."

Black spots collected at the edge of Frannie's vision. "Seth?"

"No. Oh, Frannie, no. Seth wasn't even in the country then. And I didn't tell Rob about it at first." Lexi threw her arm around Frannie's shoulders and pulled her through the front door. "You're shaking so hard. Let's get you inside and dried off. You can borrow some of my clothes."

Frannie's instinct was to break free and run off into the night. But she was exhausted, numb, and out of ideas. Her best friend—her *ex*-best friend—had lied to her, had been lying to her since the first time they had talked after Frannie had been released on parole. And she had augmented the lie, used it to lure Frannie to this Podunk town and into her happy little family. And Frannie had fallen for it because she was pathetic. Because somewhere, deep down and buried until this minute, Frannie had wanted a best friend again.

The shock of betrayal wore off, but another one replaced it. Greene already had his money back. Which meant he was only coming for vengeance, this time against the one who hadn't paid for crossing him. This was all about coming for Lexi. And Frannie had no leverage to use against him.

"Please." Lexi pulled Frannie's hand. "Come inside. You're ice cold."

Rob was waiting inside the front door. Frannie must have looked worse than she realized because he strode across the living room and pulled a blanket off the sofa then returned and threw it around her shoulders. "I'll check on Bettina and Max in her room."

Frannie must look bad enough to scare small children and skittish pets.

He left just as Seth entered from the kitchen. Seth's wide smile disappeared the second he saw her. "Jesus, Frannie, what happened?"

He held her, and without even thinking about it, she pressed against him. He wasn't part of it, part of Lexi's lie, part of this whole mess. She needed so badly to trust someone. Maybe he was the one.

"You're like an ice cube." Over her head, he spoke to Lexi. "Maybe she can take a shower to warm up."

"Why didn't I think of that?" Lexi grabbed Frannie's hand and tugged her out of Seth's embrace. Frannie mourned the feel of him against her but followed Lexi upstairs toward promised hot water, with Seth following close behind.

"Everything you need is in the hall bathroom. Shampoo, soap. The purple towels are Bettina's, the pink ones are for guests. I'll bring you something to wear. Some yoga pants and a sweatshirt should work. And warm socks."

Lexi left her outside the bathroom and trotted toward the master bedroom.

Seth shooed Frannie into the bathroom. "Go on. I'll bring in the clothes when Lexi comes back with them."

So many things Frannie should say, so many things she should explain to Seth, but she couldn't feel her fingers or toes or face. She dropped her wet, dirty clothes on the bathroom floor, wondering what had happened to her muddy sneakers, vaguely remembering she had kicked them off inside the front door. What was happening to her mind?

She made the shower steaming hot and stepped into it. The water scalded at first, but she endured, washing her hair and scrubbing her skin until it was raw. The warmth seeped into her bones and chased away the chill, taking her anger with it. By the time she climbed out of the shower and wrapped herself in the fluffy pink towels that smelled like lavender and vanilla, her dirty clothes were gone and replaced with Lexi's clean ones, folded neatly on the vanity. And her fury at her friend's betrayal had settled to a dull ache.

Frannie should have seen it coming. *Would* have seen it if she hadn't been blinded by her own childish dream of a best friend forever. It was the most Lexi thing she could imagine. Return the money to Greene. Restore order to the universe. Protect Frannie and everyone else in her life from bad karma and Greene's wrath. Lexi always had been too naïve for her own good.

Frannie dressed and hung up the towels. Hearing Bettina's voice in the hall, she checked herself in the mirror to make sure whatever had worried all the adults wouldn't frighten the kid. She was pale as hell, with bloodshot eyes surrounded by dark circles. Scary, but she had looked worse. She pinched her cheeks and pasted on a smile. Scarier. She dialed it back to a small grin. It would have to do.

She found Seth and Bettina sitting at the top of the stairs.

Upon spotting Frannie, the kid leapt to her feet and ran to Frannie. "Max is all better. Lexi stayed at the vet all night the other night, but when I got home from school, he was all better."

Frannie sat on the carpeted floor. "I heard he recovered."

Bettina nodded. "I just took him to the backyard on his leash, and Daddy's cleaning off his muddy paws, but you'll get to see him. And he's so much better, he's not even afraid of the backyard grass anymore."

"I'm glad to hear it."

"He ate a chicken bone," Bettina whispered. "He's not supposed to do that. He knows now. And I'm not supposed to feed him from the table. He knows that now too."

Frannie nodded somberly. "I'm glad he's learned his lesson. It's a lesson for us all, I think."

Bettina laughed. "Were you gonna eat chicken bones too?"

"Not anymore," Frannie said.

Max padded up the stairs with Rob behind him. He wagged his tail and his entire back end when he saw Bettina, although maybe a little of his joy was for Frannie as well. She petted and congratulated him until Rob announced it was bedtime. Max immediately trotted off to Bettina's room.

"Wow, he's learning so many things." Frannie ruffled Bettina's hair. "You're doing a great job with him."

Bettina fought her smile but couldn't quite do it. She threw her arms around Frannie's neck. "Good night."

Frannie hugged her back. The girl's pajamas smelled like lavender and vanilla, like the towels. It was the scent of safety, the smell of home. As quickly as she had jumped into their hug, Bettina pulled out of it and took off after Max and her father.

As Frannie stood, Seth stared at her. "What?" she asked.

He smiled and held out his hand. "Just something I didn't expect." He inclined his head toward the stairs. "Lexi's not doing very well, but I think she'll understand if you can't talk to her right now. While you were in the shower, she and Rob told me about giving back Greene's money."

"I should have known that's what she would do." Frannie let Seth hold her hand as they walked down the stairs.

He stopped at the bottom of the staircase and pulled her into a hug. "It was a shitty thing to do. She gave the money back to her rapist then lied to you about it. What the hell kind of sense does that make?"

Frannie glanced toward the kitchen. Through the doorway, she watched Lexi wiping down counters that were no doubt spotless. "In Lexi's world, it probably makes perfect sense." She kissed Seth's jaw and pulled out of his embrace. "Give us a few minutes?"

In the kitchen, Frannie took the cleaning cloth from Lexi and tossed it in the sink. She guided Lexi to one of the barstools lining the kitchen island then took the seat beside her.

"I screwed up," Lexi said. "I lied to you. I'm sorry. It was selfish. I just wanted to see you again. I was going to tell you the truth that first day in the diner then ask you to stay. But when you got there, I knew right away you were going to turn around and leave, unless..."

"Unless you gave me a reason not to."

Lexi shook her head. "I didn't mean—"

"Lex, we have a bigger problem right now, and we need to figure out how to solve it," Frannie interrupted her.

Lexi took a shallow breath. "I thought I'd gotten rid of him. What does he want?"

Frannie glanced over her shoulder into the living room, where Seth stood against the wall. Rob had come downstairs and stood a few feet from his friend. Frannie inclined her head, and the men joined them in the kitchen.

Seth laid his hand on Frannie's shoulder, and the warmth and weight of it gave her courage. She caught Lexi's eye to make sure she had her full attention. "Greene came into the diner with my mother."

Frannie stopped and waited. Seth squeezed her shoulder in silent support.

Lexi tugged at her hair with one hand. "Oh no. No, no, no. He can't be the man she's dating."

Frannie nodded. "Yes. Remember I told you he saw her at the drugstore a few months ago? That's when it started. By that time, he had his money back, right?"

Lexi nodded. "I had Patrice's daughter, Patty, arrange it through a friend of hers from law school, a few months before our wedding. I couldn't start our family with that hanging over my head."

Frannie glanced over her shoulder at Seth and raised an eyebrow. He sighed in tacit understanding. Lexi believing she could set the universe to rights. Rob looped his arm around his wife's waist.

Frannie would rather have made her request without Rob there to judge her, but it was better for Lexi to have his support. "Lexi, I need to get her away from him. It's not going to be easy unless she knows the truth."

Lexi licked her lips. "About the money, you mean."

"No. About the rape."

CHAPTER SIXTEEN

May 2011

When Lexi pulled into the wide, curved driveway in front of Brandon's family home, she panicked. She had never been to her boyfriend's house without him. She had never had to make conversation with his dad alone. She should have cajoled one of her roommates into joining her or waited at her dorm for him to arrive later that night like they had planned.

But after two weeks apart while Brandon completed his senior research trip to Colorado, all she could think about was seeing him as soon as possible, and she texted his father with her stupid idea, only to nearly die of embarrassment after hitting send. But then Mr. Greene had texted back saying it was a sweet idea and she was welcome anytime. Now she sat in her car, watching the rising wind whip up the rain, and debated whether to turn around and drive back to campus.

A knock on the car window made her jump. The figure outside her car was shrouded in mist. The security lights above the garage created a reflective glow that made everything harder to see. But it had to be Brandon's dad. Who else would it be? She pressed the button to roll down the window and smiled.

"Hello, Mr. Greene."

"Brought you an umbrella," he said. "When I saw your car pull up but didn't hear you come to the door, I realized you might have left home without one."

Cold mist swirled around Lexi, and she shivered. "Yeah, the weather changed in the half hour it took to drive here."

Mr. Greene bent down, and Lexi stared into eyes that were dark blue, so dark they looked black in the misty light and watery from too much Scotch, which she could smell even though he was a good foot away from her. At fifty, he was still a handsome man, an older version of Brandon, but there were deep creases around his eyes, and he had jowls and, at the moment, bloodshot eyes. A part of her recoiled at the thought of Brandon growing to look like his father someday, but if she could keep him from developing his father's terrible habits of smoking stogies and sucking down Scotch like it was roadside lemonade on a hot day, it might be avoidable.

He nodded toward the front of the house as he pulled open her car door. "Come on inside where it's warm, darlin.'"

She shivered again as she stepped out of the car and took the umbrella Mr. Greene handed her. She kept a few feet between them as he led her to the house. She hated it when Brandon's father called her darlin'. Something about it was so... unbecoming for a man his age, as her mother would say.

She followed him up the steps to the wide wraparound veranda that greeted visitors to the stately old home. It was a family estate, passed down from the time of Mr. Greene's grandfather, who had made his fortune over a hundred years ago when he had opened the savings and loan that was the predecessor to the family's current financial institution. For years, there had been rumors about both the institution's solvency and Brandon's dad's never-diminishing wealth despite the severe shift of the business winds. Brandon had shrugged off her questions about it.

"I have no intention of joining the family business, so why should I care?" he had told her one night after four beers and had never said another word about it since then.

She often wondered if it had anything to do with his mother dying so young, but for the entire year they had been dating, Brandon had talked about leaving town for good as soon as he graduated from college. Only, the past few months, he had amended the timeline to when they had both graduated, which for Lexi wouldn't be for another year.

Mr. Greene held open the front door for her. Lights were on inside the house. So many lights that Lexi wondered if there were people in every room. But it was dead silent inside, except for the crackling of a fire. She stepped into the front hall—always an impressive sight with its soaring ceiling and winding staircase that looked like something out of *Gone with the Wind*—and thought she heard the click of a lock as Mr. Greene closed the front door.

"Come on in," he said. "You can set up your cake and balloons for Brandon in the—" He stopped and looked at her then smiled. "Well, I guess we'll get those out of your car when this rain calms down. In the meantime, let's get you warm. I was just relaxing in the great room."

The room lived up to its name. It had a ceiling as high as the entryway with a full wall of windows that looked out over the acres of property the family owned, acres of rolling farmland and dense trees. Lexi crossed to the windows, drawn to them as she had been the other few times she had visited the house. She stared out at the barely discernable shadows of the dark landscape and the starless sky. There was supposed to have been an almost-full moon that night, but the clouds and mist had obscured it. Lexi shivered again, sensing somehow that it was an omen. Magical thinking, Frannie would chastise. And maybe she would be right. Or maybe it was just that Lexi hated the thought of Brandon's plane landing in this weather. That was probably it.

Still, Lexi rubbed her charm bracelet, the one that matched the bracelet Lexi had given Frannie. Looking out the window for a sign from a star, any star, Lexi fingered each charm and silently recited a Robert Browning poem. Rhyming wielded some kind of protective power, despite what Frannie said.

Mr. Greene's voice interrupted her silent recitation just as she got to "I listened with heart fit to break." Another bad omen. "Here."

She whirled around. He stood close to her, much too close. He held out a thick rocks glass with whiskey in it. She wasn't sure what a proper portion of whiskey was, but this looked like way too much. She shook her head. "I don't drink."

"Come on now. Just to take the chill out of your bones." He pushed it closer to her. "Can't have you catching pneumonia on my watch."

Lexi wanted to point out that illness didn't work that way, that it was only an old wives' tale, but Mr. Greene was not the kind of man you argued with, especially if you were a twenty-year-old who was dating his son and hoping to stay in his good graces. The stinging, pungent smell of the alcohol burned her nose, but she didn't know what to do, with the window to her back and Mr. Greene so close, nearly pushing the drink into her chest. And she was cold. She shouldn't have worn the green jersey dress that ended just above the knees of her bare legs. Even with her long raincoat, the dress was too short. It left her too exposed. For the weather. For everything.

"Hand me your coat before you catch your death," Mr. Greene demanded, and she obeyed. "And take this." He pushed the glass into her hands.

Mr. Greene carried her coat to the front hall then returned and stood on the other side of the room, beside the great stone fireplace that climbed the wall all the way to the wooden rafters. He motioned to one of the two overstuffed chairs in front of the hearth.

"Come over here and get warm." Again, a demand.

Again, respect for her elders, especially for the father of the young man she loved, overrode the cautionary bell ringing in the back of her brain.

"That's it," he said. "You'll be all warmed up in no time, and when that rain slows down, I'll get your things out of the car for you, and you can set up a nice little welcome-home surprise for Brandon."

She took a seat as she had been told. Mr. Greene remained standing. He lifted his glass in a toast and took a gulp. She sipped her drink and winced as the spicy liquid hit her tongue, followed by a burn that chased its way down her throat and into her stomach.

Mr. Greene chuckled. "No need to baby it."

Lexi took a deep breath then sucked down half the contents of her glass. She caught her breath and drank the rest. Relieved, she cradled the empty glass between her palms and stared into the flames. It seemed like less than a minute had passed when the alcohol hit her bloodstream. She hadn't eaten much that day. She had picked at breakfast and had skipped lunch. And now the edges of her thoughts felt fuzzy and confused.

The glass disappeared from her hands then returned with more whiskey in it. Mr. Greene watched her expectantly. Dutifully, she worked her way through her second glass and held it up to him when it was empty.

"Please, no more. I'm warmed enough now."

He smiled at her. She smiled back then thought maybe she shouldn't have. But he was her boyfriend's father. Being rude to him wasn't an option.

"What time is..." Her tongue suddenly felt thick. She gripped the chair arms and looked at Mr. Greene. He rose and fell and floated. "When will Brandon..." Her heavy eyelids drifted shut, and she slumped forward.

"Whoa," Mr. Greene whispered in her ear. "You might have had a little too much. Stay with me, darlin.'"

She struggled to open her eyes and succeeded. She twisted to rise out of the chair and failed. She leaned forward and was propped against something. Against someone. Was it Brandon? No, not Brandon. He wasn't home yet.

"It's okay, babe. I've got you."

Brandon never called her that. "Brandon, what's happening?" She struggled to see his face. It was him. It had to be. But something was different. Wrong.

The chair shifted then reclined.

"Relax, babe. Just relax," Brandon-but-not-Brandon said.

He laid his weight on top of her. She was pressed between his heavy body and the chair. She struggled to breathe properly. "Please." She shook her head. "Please, no."

He didn't answer. Just tugged at the top of her dress. She wanted to roll away from him, but there was nowhere to go. It was never this way between her and Brandon, crass and rushed and embarrassing.

She raised her arms to cover herself. "Brandon, what are you... we can't, not here."

But his hands were all over her. Down her top and up her skirt, using his fingers, not waiting for her to be ready. She screamed. He muted the sound by grinding his mouth against hers and pushing his tongue between her lips. It was never like this. Brandon was never like this.

Then his fingers were gone, only to be replaced by *him*.

She hadn't agreed to this. But she must have. Brandon would never do this if she hadn't agreed. But the details were fuzzy. Her ears were ringing. His face was going in and out of focus.

"Brandon, please stop." She touched his cheek.

He didn't stop.

She cried, but either he didn't notice, or he didn't care about her tears or about the tenderness that had always made it special between them.

Then his weight was gone. Her dress was back in place, and a blanket covered her. She tried to force her eyes open to look at him, to see if he regretted what he had just done. But it was dark now, too dark to see his face.

"You just rest, darlin,'" he whispered in her ear. Dread turned to horror as Lexi realized the truth. Just before unconsciousness, he whispered to her again. "This will be our little secret."

SOMEONE GENTLY SHOOK Lexi's shoulder to wake her. Brandon smiled down at her. For a split second, she thought she had been wrong. It must have been him, after all. Or more likely, a nightmare.

"Hey, you got here early." Brandon pulled her into a hug. "My dad said you showed up a couple of hours ago to set up a surprise, but you were soaking wet and needed a stiff Scotch. Which he says you don't seem to hold very well."

Her head swam. Brandon hadn't been there. Whatever had happened, if something had happened, had to have been... Brandon held her tight as she shivered in his arms.

"God, Lexi, you're like ice."

"Where is he?" she whispered.

"Who? My dad? He had a Lion's Club meeting. Babe, you're shaking. Maybe you're getting sick or something."

She nodded. It seemed like the easiest lie to tell. "I need to... powder my nose."

He laughed, a soft, low grumble. "We've been dating a year. You can say 'pee' in front of me, you know. Here, I'll help you up. Do you need me to carry you?"

She shook her head as he helped her stand. She walked on unsteady legs to the main entry hall and made a sharp right turn and then a left into the half bath. She closed and locked the door then pressed her back against it as she sucked in air to catch her breath.

The gasping made her stomach clench. She leaned over the toilet just in time to vomit up the remnants of a glass of Scotch. Had there been more than a glass? Had it really just been whiskey, or had there been something else?

She had taken a drink from a man she thought she should trust, even though a warning bell had been clanging in her head. *Stupid, stupid, stupid.* What would Brandon say if he found out? It didn't matter. He would never find out.

Our little secret. Remembering the words made her retch all over again. It would remain their sick secret. All of it. What Mr. Greene had done to her, the evidence he had left inside her along with blood that had trickled out into her underwear and the bruises he had put on her thighs.

Lexi sat on the toilet, wrapped her arms around herself, and rocked. It was over. Done. She would be more careful in the future. She would never be alone with that man again. If she could help it, she would never even see him again. It wasn't like he and Brandon were close. As soon as Brandon graduated, she would drop out of college, and they would leave. She could finish her degree wherever they landed.

She stood, washed her hands, splashed cold water on her face, and checked her fake smile in the mirror. Frannie would have seen right through it, but no one else would. Not even Brandon. And for tonight, he was the only one she had to fool. She rubbed her lucky bracelet again, not blaming it for her terrible fate. This was her own fault. She hadn't been good, hadn't been careful. But she would be in the future. From here on out, she would do all the right things so she could get back to the happy life she was supposed to have.

CHAPTER SEVENTEEN
2016

Lexi jerked backward. "I'm not going to talk to your mother about him. Or about the incident. I've talked about it enough to last a lifetime."

"Have you though?" Frannie said.

Seth laid a hand on her shoulder. "Frannie," he said softly.

It was a warning but one she wasn't about to heed. "You lied to me, Lexi. You've been lying for weeks. That is not okay. Do you even understand that? Do you understand that this is not normal, this is not how you can treat people? You don't get a pass because you don't want to deal with what happened to you. Have you even gone to therapy in all these years?"

Lexi's shoulders shook, and her eyes filled with tears.

Rob wrapped his arm around his wife. "That's enough, Frannie."

"No, it is not enough, Rob," Frannie said through clenched teeth. "If it were enough, she would be able to call it what it was. Not an incident. Not the terrible thing that happened. Rape. That's what it was, Lexi. A rape. And you're never going to get past it if you lie and make up stories to create some fantasy life, and meanwhile you can't even say the fucking word. Rape!"

"Frannie, stop," Lexi sobbed.

"Only if you stop lying and hiding and faking. Say it, Lexi: Jack Greene raped you!"

"Enough!" Rob stepped in front of his wife. "Get out. Go home. You've done enough damage for one night."

"Oh, I've done damage?"

Seth stepped between her and Rob. "We're leaving." He turned and wrapped his arms around Frannie. "Come on. You're shaking. I need to take you home."

"Frannie," Lexi whimpered. "I'm sorry I lied."

"You don't owe her an apology," Rob said. "Not after that little performance." He glared at Frannie, and she leaned into Seth for strength. "Are you trying to destroy her?"

Frannie considered his angry accusation then slowly shook her head. She spoke softly as the fight went out of her. "No. No, I'm not." She looked past Rob, into the red, swollen face of her ex-best friend. "I think I'm trying to help you, Lex. And I'm doing a shit job of it, but I really do think you need help."

Frannie needed to say more, but she couldn't do it. She would have to deal with the fallout tomorrow, after she'd had some sleep and had gotten past the shocks of the day.

She collapsed against Seth, who picked her up in his arms. It felt good to let him be strong for her, just this once. No one spoke a word as he carried her to the front door, which Rob silently opened and then closed behind them.

Seth kissed her forehead as he carried her to the driveway. "We'll take my truck and get your car later."

She managed to open the passenger-side door, and he placed her on the seat. She laced her fingers in his. "I'm in over my head."

"Tell me," he said.

"Every minute since the day Lexi told me about the rape and the pregnancy, I've had a plan. Spirit her out of that Podunk town for an abortion. Steal the money to pay for it. Cover our tracks, keep her secret, survive prison. Get the stolen money so I can disappear." She leaned against him. "I never stopped long enough to make sure Lexi had a plan of her own."

Seth kissed her fingertips. "You weren't wrong, Frannie. Too harsh but not wrong. Lexi needs more help. Rob told me she was in a support group for a while. That's how she worked up the strength to tell him and to let him confide in me. But this is PTSD, and there's no quick fix for it."

Frannie nodded. "I think Lexi and I are both out of plans. Working without a net. I should be screaming into the void or curled up into a ball on the floor. But I'm just..."

"Numb." He pulled her against him. "When I was in Afghanistan, my mind was always on high alert. Even if we were in the green zone, even when we were off duty and goofing around, I always knew where my weapon, Kevlar, and gas mask were. I knew where every one of my men was, knew every exit out of the building, knew the first ten things I'd do if a bomb exploded or the chemical sensors beeped.

"Then I came home, and I didn't have to think like that anymore. I thought I'd feel relieved or happy. Or maybe I'd wake up in the middle of the night screaming. But I just went numb." He kissed her. "It goes away, for better and for worse."

"When?"

He shook his head. "I can't say. It'll be different for Lexi, different for you because it's different for everyone. But in the meantime, I've got your back."

That was different, possibly exhilarating. Probably terrifying. She wouldn't know for sure until the numbness wore off.

FRANNIE'S HAND TREMBLED as she tried to insert her key into the apartment door lock. Seth covered her hand with his and took the key, unlocking and opening the door in one graceful move.

"Can I make you a cup of tea?" he asked, rubbing her shoulders as she shivered. "Or maybe go to Patrice's packet store and buy you some whiskey?"

Without answering, she pressed her back against the closed front door and pulled him to her. She was freezing, and he was the only thing in the world that could warm her. When he slanted his head to kiss her, she shot up on her tiptoes and pressed her lips to his, gripping his shoulder then dropping her hands to the base of his T-shirt. He broke their hot, wet, deep kiss just long enough to pull the shirt over his head and do the same to hers.

She fumbled with his belt buckle, but her numb fingers didn't work properly. He stilled her hand with his, and she dreaded his rejection, worried he would tell her she needed hot tea and rest when the only thing she needed right now was this hot man. Instead, he wordlessly unbuckled his belt, unzipped his jeans, and pulled them and his boxer briefs down over his hips, stepping out of them as he kissed her again. His skin was so warm under her touch. It thawed her, ignited her, made her need him on her and in her and murmuring in her ear.

She shoved down the borrowed yoga pants and kicked them aside then anchored herself to his shoulders so she could wrap her legs around his waist. He held her back from him, and she sucked in a breath, waiting again for him to stop her.

"Protection," he whispered then bent to pull his wallet out of his jeans and a silver wrapper out of his wallet. He rolled on the condom then sat down on the sofa and pulled her onto his lap.

She wrapped her legs around his hips as he sank into her without admonishment, without judgment, without a word. His eyes held tenderness and something else. Pain.

From that look, she knew. Knew he had been here. Knew he understood. For a fleeting second, she was jealous of whatever warm body had melted his numbness and brought him back from the brink, but the jealousy evaporated as he held her so tightly to him.

For the first time she could ever remember, Frannie truly needed someone, and without a word, without a question, without any demands, Seth was there for her.

FRANNIE STARTLED AWAKE and struggled to place what had woken her. She turned onto her right side, toward Seth. His breathing was deep and undisturbed. On the nightstand, her phone vibrated, and she reached out to answer it before it woke him.

"Hello," she whispered as she rolled out of bed and padded to the bedroom door.

The person on the other end of the line didn't speak.

As the sleep fog cleared from her mind, she realized how stupid she had been to answer the phone without knowing who was calling. She checked the number. An Indiana area code but nothing else that she recognized. Shit.

Closing the bedroom door firmly behind her, she sagged against the living room wall. "Greene, is that you?"

Still silence.

"Goddamn it, I know it's you. You have your money, and I went to prison. This is between us, just you and me. Leave everyone else out of this, and tell me what you want from me."

He hung up without answering her.

"Just tell me what the hell you want," Frannie whispered to dead air.

She walked to the sofa and sank into the cushions then dropped her phone onto the coffee table and leaned forward with her elbows on her knees and her head in her hands. "No plan. No play. No next move. What the hell am I going to do?"

The numbness was wearing off. Raw fear was setting in.

"Did you say something, Frannie?" Seth stepped out of the bedroom, half asleep and completely adorable, with his hair spiked on his head and a pillow crease on his left cheek.

"No." She sat up and smiled, hoping it covered her desperation.

He moved toward the kitchen. "You want some water?"

"Sure."

A minute later, he handed her a full glass and sat beside her.

"Couldn't sleep?" he asked.

She nodded. She then took a long, slow sip of her drink and leaned her head on Seth's shoulder. "What do you think Greene will try to do to Lexi? I don't think there's any evidence that could send her to prison."

"I don't know. Maybe..."

"Maybe he'll retraumatize her," Frannie said.

He put his arm around her. "Maybe Rob and I should talk to him."

Frannie couldn't involve one more person she cared about in the mess she had created. "No one's talking to him. First, I need to get my mother away from him. Then I'll figure out the next step."

Which had to be to leave everyone behind. Maybe a public falling-out with Lexi, one that got back to Greene, would convince him Frannie had worked alone after all. Then she would disappear, and he would go back to blaming her and her alone. Like she had planned from the beginning. She glanced at Seth. Only now, that plan sucked.

Seth took her hand in his. "*We'll* deal with it. You're not alone, Frannie."

No, not this minute. But she would be again—and much too soon. She squeezed his hand. "Can you stay all weekend? I mean until Monday morning? Sundays are my long day at the diner, but I can ask Patrice to let me off as soon as the rush is over. And tomorrow—I guess that's tonight—I work the dinner shift, but I shouldn't be too late. And I should spend a couple of hours with Bettina and Max."

"Careful, Fearless. It sounds like you're building a life here."

God, it did sound that way. "I just... I mean, are you interested in seeing me in between all that? I guess that sounds pretty boring."

He shook his head. "You're worth the wait, and there are always things I can do in this town. But are you sure you want me here? Tuesday morning, you couldn't get me out of here fast enough."

"I was just trying to be discreet, for all the good it did. Everyone in town knew we'd spent the night together before they'd had their first cup of coffee."

"I don't know," he said. "Two and a half days together." He kissed her hand then pulled her to her feet. "Come back to bed and convince me."

She arched an eyebrow. "I really have to convince you?"

"No, but I thought we could pretend for the next hour or so."

She held tightly to his hand. "Sure, let's pretend."

She would pretend, for the next hour and the next couple days and every minute she could spend with him until she slipped away in the night and dropped off the face of the earth.

CHAPTER EIGHTEEN

Frannie put on her sunglasses and stepped onto the grassy expanse of the town park. She immediately recognized Sarah Marsh, dog trainer extraordinaire, from the picture on her website. The woman was pulling dog toys out of her large blue backpack emblazoned with the Down Dog company logo.

"Sarah, thanks for coming." Frannie stuck out her hand.

Sarah grinned as she shook Frannie's hand. "Miss Willets, nice to meet you."

"I'm glad you could fit Max in on such short notice."

"Saturdays are usually booked for a couple of weeks out, but we had a cancellation," Sarah said. "It must be kismet."

Kismet. Lexi and Sarah would get along just fine. She hoped Bettina and Max would like her too.

Frannie glanced at the parking lot. According to the clock tower across the street from the park, it was two minutes past noon. It wasn't like Lexi to be late. If she was still coming, after last night. Surely she wouldn't miss this. It was for Bettina.

Nervously, Frannie smiled at Sarah. "Max is a good dog. He's just very afraid, especially of strange people."

"From the intake form, it sounds like his anxiety leads to undesirable behaviors," Sarah said. "And then there are the issues with rules, like not feeding him people food, especially bones."

"Did I say all that?" Frannie didn't remember mentioning the chicken bone. Then again, she was functioning on a few hours of sleep.

"You gave a very detailed report, including Max's skin and membrane issues, and that you've been treating him with homeopathic remedies. I'm guessing you grew up with dogs."

"No. I grew up wanting dogs, and I worked at a vet's office for a while." Frannie didn't mention she was a vet tech school dropout.

"Really? Why'd you stop?"

"I had other things going on, and I couldn't do it anymore." Frannie didn't even have to lie, unless you believed in lies of omission.

"You could always go back to it." Sarah pulled out a treat bag from her backpack.

The door had closed on that dream and about a hundred others five years ago, and Frannie didn't want to talk about it. They stood in silence as minutes ticked past and the minivan still didn't appear.

"Is it possible they're not coming?" Sarah asked.

"I don't know. Bettina is desperate to get Max kid-friendly enough to show him off to her classmates." Frannie stared at the parking lot, willing the minivan to appear.

"Tell me a little more while we wait," Sarah said. "What are Max's unfriendly traits?"

"Unfriendly is such a judgmental word." Frannie crossed her arms over her chest. "Like I said, he's scared when he gets near other people."

"How does that manifest?"

Frannie quirked an eyebrow at the new-agey sound of the question. Sarah Marsh really could be the perfect fit for Lexi. "He runs away, tries to hide. Sometimes whines."

"Hmm." Sarah furrowed her brow.

"Is that a problem?"

"Let's hope not," Sarah answered. "But if he had a trauma when he was young—you said he's a year old now, so it definitely would have happened during a very formative time for him—that could be contributing to his anxiety."

Frannie spotted Lexi's minivan turning into the parking lot. "Here they are now."

Lexi parked then climbed out of the vehicle. She smoothed down the front of her perfectly pressed tan khakis, adjusted her long, curly hair over her shoulder, and opened the back door of the van to help Bettina climb down the small step to the ground.

"There might be other factors contributing to his anxiety," Frannie said.

Sarah followed the line of her gaze. "Anxious mother? That wouldn't help."

"Stepmother, actually." Frannie turned to the trainer and lowered her voice even though Lexi wasn't within earshot yet. "I think Max makes her nervous, like she doesn't quite trust him with the kid."

"Good to know." Sarah kept her eyes keenly trained on the dog and his two companions as Lexi led him out of the van and handed his leash to Bettina. "I'll work on that relationship first, build up the trust between them."

Frannie glanced between the approaching group and Sarah. "How long do you think that will take?"

After the last few days, Frannie needed a win and couldn't very well cross Bettina and Max off her to-do list as long as the dog was still an anxious, chicken-bone-swallowing mess.

"It'll take as long as it takes, but I promise to give it my utmost attention. If anyone can get quick results with Max and his pack, it's me."

"Frannie!" Bettina kept a firm hold on Max's leash while she trotted to Frannie's side and wrapped her arms around her waist. "What's Max's surprise?"

Frannie patted Bettina's back and smiled at Lexi, who for all her smoothing and preening looked as exhausted as Frannie felt. "Max's surprise, and yours, is Miss Sarah, owner and lead dog trainer of Down Dog."

Lexi shook Sarah's hand. "That's over in Linton, isn't it?"

"That's our main location. I have a smaller office just up Route 69. My husband and I bought an old farm out there a couple of months ago."

"The Miller property?" Lexi said. "Bettina's grandparents live out that way."

Bettina rolled forward on her toes. "Max and I have a goat we keep on their farm."

"A goat." Sarah raised her eyebrows. "Maybe your Max has a little bit of herder in him, then. Why don't you tell me a little more about him, about his daily routine, when he eats, when he walks, how much time he spends alone. And then you can show me how you play with him."

"Yes." Bettina grinned at Frannie. "Let's show her how we taught him to fetch, Frannie."

"Actually, I have to make a phone call." Frannie glanced at Lexi. "But I'll bet Max would love it if Lexi played with you."

"He would," Bettina said. "He wanted her to wear the bracelet I made for him since it kept falling off his paw."

Lexi held up her wrist, proudly displaying a blue-and-pink threaded band that matched the one on Bettina's arm. A woven friendship bracelet, the kind Lexi and Frannie had made for each other in third grade. *Best friends forever, best friends forever, best friends forever.*

Frannie swallowed the lump in her throat. "I'll be over there." She pointed to a green park bench positioned between the grass and the sand-covered lot with a huge wooden play fort.

"Give me a minute?" Lexi asked Sarah. She walked a short distance with Frannie then stood beside her while watching Bettina. "Thank you for this. I should have thought of it."

"You would have when things calmed down." Frannie pulled off her sunglasses. "Lex, about last night, the things I said were out of line. I'm sorry."

Lexi shook her head. "I'm sorry too. I shouldn't have lied. When you told me all you wanted from me was the money, I thought you'd never speak to me again if I told you I didn't have it. I panicked."

"How about a pact that we'll both do better?" Frannie held up her pinky. "Deal?"

Lexi hooked her pinky around Frannie's. "Deal. But can I add a condition?"

Frannie hesitated. "That depends on the condition."

"Don't run away. Not yet. Pinky swear it?"

Frannie sighed then tightened her pinky around Lexi's. "Not yet. But that's the most I can promise."

CHAPTER NINETEEN

That night, Frannie could hardly believe she was sitting at the small, square kitchen table in her own apartment. Seth had covered it with a snow-white table cloth and sparkling silver cutlery, oversized wine goblets, and silver-rimmed white plates that shimmered in the candlelight. After her long shift at the diner and her soak in the hot bath he had drawn for her, Frannie was finally getting the steak dinner he had promised her weeks earlier.

She had pulled her hair up into a twist and dressed in a shimmery, silky pale-blue dress that she had bought somewhere in the years between high school graduation and incarceration. The thin slip of material held his rapt attention all through dinner and light-hearted chitchat. When they finished eating, Seth cleared their dirty dishes, poured the last of the red wine into their glasses, and sat down across from her again, not bothering to conceal the fact that he was ogling her. It was a date, an honest-to-god date, the kind that normal people got to have. She couldn't have asked for anything more perfect from him, even if she needed to tell him it was their last weekend together.

He held up his glass to toast her yet again. "To the amazing woman sitting across from me, who manages to look more beautiful every time I see her."

They clinked glasses and sipped their wine. It was full and rich and made her mouth pucker just a bit. She had never thought of herself as a red wine drinker, but then again, she hadn't had much time to think of herself as much of anything in particular. Normally she was okay with that, but tonight it left her with an emptiness she couldn't quite shake, even when Seth smiled at her the way he was now.

He slid back his chair and tugged on her hand. "Come over here."

She climbed onto his lap. He wrapped his arms around her and rubbed her neck. "You're exhausted, Fearless. You never got back to sleep last night, did you?"

"No." She kissed his neck. "Not for lack of you trying to wipe me out."

He grinned. "Strictly for your own good." He kissed her, slowly and gently, holding her steady and safe while her weary body melted against him. When the kiss ended, he pushed a stray strand of hair behind her ear and frowned. "Have you come up with a new plan yet?"

She waved her hand in the air, playing it off like it was no big deal, even though it was the biggest deal in her life right now. "I'll figure out something."

"Another way to leave?" Now she understood his frown. "I know that was your plan when you came here, but I'd hoped things had changed."

"Things have changed." Damn it, sitting here in his arms, it felt like *everything* could change. "But Jack Greene is still a threat to Lexi and my mother."

"I've been thinking about that." Seth traced his fingers down the side of her neck, making it much harder for her to think. "And checking into him."

Frannie sat up straight. "I told you not to get involved in this."

"Don't get involved in this? *This* is your life, Frannie. I'm involved. But I think he's just playing head games. The good news is, despite how shady his businesses seem to be, he's not mobbed up, and he doesn't hire thugs to do his dirty work."

She climbed off his lap. "No, he can do that himself. Just ask Lexi."

Seth grabbed her hand and kissed her fingers. "I'm not saying he's a mensch or that you should ever be alone with him. I'm just saying you don't have to run from him. If you don't feel safe here, come stay with me. There are lots of guys with guns there, and most of them are my friends."

Stay with him. The way girlfriends stayed with boyfriends all the time. She had never had the chance to do that. She smiled despite her best efforts not to. She wanted to give in to Seth. If Greene was only playing head games with her, she might actually stay for a while, have a few more date nights with Seth, and spend a few more afternoons watching Max's training in the park. But Greene was looking for a way to get to Lexi. His intent hummed along her prison-honed senses at a frequency only she could receive. She couldn't ignore it, and she couldn't be the instrument of Lexi's destruction.

But she couldn't explain it to Seth, even if she could make him believe her. She couldn't give him any opportunity to try to stop her. She took his fingers lightly in her hand. "This is the part of the date where I invite you to stay over."

He raised an eyebrow. "Is it? I thought you'd already invited me."

"Yes, but staying over is code for coming to bed with me. Right now."

He stood and pulled her against him then gave her another spine-melting kiss. "Or I could serve dessert. Chocolate mousse. I used Lexi's mom's recipe."

Frannie's mouth watered at the mention of it.

"And we could continue our conversation."

Her mouth went dry. "I don't know what else there is to say. This is where I live, and the diner next door is where I work, and holding a job is a condition of my parole. I can't just hang out all day at your fancy abode with armed guards. And armed guards aren't a great selling point for me, by the way."

He winced. "I'm sorry. I wasn't thinking. I don't actually live inside a guarded perimeter. I rent a small house just outside of the base."

She was overcome with a sudden urge to see it, to see where he ate his dinner and made his morning coffee. To see the bed where he slept. To imagine herself there with him.

"The point is, nothing's going to change before my parole is up," she said.

Seth wanted her to stay. Lexi wanted her to stay. But Greene wanted something else, and the more she thought about the conversation with him at the diner, the more she realized he aimed to hurt Lexi in order to punish Frannie.

Which meant she was about to disappoint the people who were asking her not to run. But she wouldn't ruin this night by telling Seth the truth.

He opened his arms, and she stepped into the circle of them. He swayed with her to the soft background music. "There's nothing to stop you from thinking about what you want to do with the rest of your life. If you could do anything—no strings, no past, no worries—what would you do?"

She laid her head on his shoulder and closed her eyes. "What's the point of that? There are always strings and my past and my worries." She tried to sound unaffected by the question, but her heart pounded from just considering it. She had no idea what she would do if she could ever be that free.

"Didn't you want to be a vet?" Seth asked. "You're great with animals, at least with that pile of fur that Bettina swears is a dog."

She pressed closer to him. "Max is definitely a dog. He's a great dog. But I couldn't be a vet. Love animals, hate science. Besides, I was really only interested in it for the TV show."

He pulled back and held her by the shoulders. "What TV show?"

"The one I imagined I'd be doing with all my exotic animals."

He smiled and pulled her close again.

She inhaled the spicy scent of him. "Umm. That's better. Stay here, stay close."

He kissed the top of her head. "Yes, ma'am. Maybe you really want to be a zookeeper."

"Right now, all I want to be is seduced." She kissed along the base of his throat. "Or the seducer. I'm good either way."

He shivered as she kissed her way along his jawline. "You're trying to distract me."

"Is it working?"

He lifted her up to settle her legs around his hips. "What do you think?"

And then he stopped talking and kissed her, and she didn't have to tell him any more lies.

FRANNIE PULLED ON HER favorite soft blue T-shirt and a pair of cutoff sweatpants and followed the scent of cooking bacon. She stopped in the doorway between the bedroom and the rest of her small apartment and took a minute to enjoy the sight of Seth there, in faded jeans and an olive-green T-shirt with US Army printed on it, his dark hair still tousled from the night in her bed, his feet bare and tan against the pale fake-wood floorboards.

He stopped flipping the bacon and held the spatula in midair. She glanced at his face to find him staring at her with his lopsided grin, so blatantly enjoying her enjoying him. Like a punch to the gut, it hit her. This was not an easy thing they had, not a casual affair to flame out as fast as it had ignited, or to walk—or run—away from without regret.

"Good morning, sunshine." His simple utterance made her heart hammer, damn it.

She smiled and headed for the full coffeepot. "Good morning yourself." She pulled mugs out of the cupboard and grabbed the milk from the refrigerator, which now contained an impressive array of cooking ingredients like eggs and cheese and something green and leafy.

"If making me dinner includes making me breakfast, too, I should let you do it more often."

Dammit. She didn't mean that. She couldn't mean that. Yet the words had come out of *her* mouth, she was pretty sure.

As he scooped eggs and bacon onto plates, his grin broadened to a full-on smile with dimples and eye creases and so much beauty she just wanted to sit utterly still and drink him in. *It's because it's our last morning together. Nothing more. Definitely* not *attachment.* Tomorrow he would be up at oh dark thirty, as he called it, to start his long drive back to the army base and his job and his real life.

"It could be my weekly gig, our Saturday night thing." He winked at her as he set their plates on the table then retrieved another plate with extra bacon from the stove.

This time, she stopped her blabbermouth before she could agree to another promise she would never keep.

"This looks amazing." She stopped with a forkful of eggs partway to her mouth. "But there's something green in mine."

"Eggs Florentine."

"I don't know what that is."

He nudged her hand to move it closer to her lips. "It's spinach. Trust me, you'll like it."

"Ah, the green leafy stuff. Are you trying to wean me off diner grease and on to health food?" She put the eggs in her mouth then moaned as the eggs and spinach and cheese and some sort of spice coated her tongue. "Because I think I might be okay with that."

He laughed. "That's not what you were going to say. But yes, that's my diabolical plan. Although you'll get no complaints from me about what diner food does for *you*. But you might have to cut back on the caffeine before you wear me out."

His flirting was going to kill her. To get on firmer ground, she spent the rest of the meal and her second cup of coffee—half caff, he informed her—talking about safer subjects, like Max's trainer, the yoga class she had finally taken with Lexi, the high school classmates they wouldn't want to see again, nuclear disarmament.

Seth dropped the last piece of extra bacon onto her plate and cleared the other dishes, stacking them into her ancient dishwasher with wordless efficiency as she sipped her coffee and wondered if all soldiers were as domesticated as he was. He quirked an eyebrow at her when he caught her staring at him then slid into his seat and took her hand.

"So, I told Rob I'd swing by their place this afternoon and help him fix a bookshelf in Bettina's room. Sort of a peace offering."

"Are you two okay, after Friday night?"

He nodded. "I think something good came out of it. He said Lexi's talking to him. Not details about the rape, but her feelings. So, about dinner. I can be back here in plenty of time to throw something together. Maybe some cold chicken on a salad, and I'll pick up fresh bread at the bakery."

She hesitated, wanting it too much, wanting his time and attention and thrown-together meals more than she had any right to want. Or have. "Lexi will want to feed you while you're there, so I can just grab something before I leave work. I don't want you to go to any more trouble than you already have."

"It's no trouble. And I was thinking you could return the favor." He kissed her fingers. "Come to my place one night this week. Tuesday, Wednesday, Thursday. Whatever night you have off. I'll show you around base, take you out for a nice dinner. Or, if you'd rather stay in, you can cook something for me."

She shook her head. Tonight would be their last night together. It had to be. Even one more night with him would make it damn near impossible to leave. And she knew that one day very soon, she had to leave, before Greene could make another move.

"You wouldn't want me to cook," she said.

"I wasn't really inviting you over for your cooking. Like I said, dinner out, dinner in, cold cereal, and I'll pour the milk." He kissed her fingers again then opened her hand and kissed her palm. "I just want you to come to my place and spend the night in my bed."

Now she didn't just feel her heartbeat in her chest. It was in her throat, her fingertips, her toes, the deep pit of her belly. *God yes.* "Seth, I can't."

She withdrew her hand from his to create physical distance, picking up the piece of bacon as an excuse. Then she set it down and screwed up her courage with a deep intake of breath. "I think we need to slow things down. It's great. *You're* great, but we should keep this casual." She said it all in one long, painful exhalation.

The hopeful light in his eyes dimmed. His open, boyish grin hardened into something distant and cold. "Of course. My mistake."

He rose from the table and disappeared into the bedroom.

She stood and followed him. "Seth, I'm sorry. It's not… I didn't mean it the way it sounded." But she did mean it. She had to mean it.

With the same military precision he had used to clean up the breakfast dishes, he packed the few belongings he had brought with him into his duffel bag and slung it over his shoulder.

Letting him go was what she had to do, what she needed to do. Breaking it off wouldn't get easier with more dates or laughs or tumbles in bed. Still, she couldn't help herself. She reached out and touched his arm as he stepped past her. "Where are you going?" she asked.

He stopped, kissed her cheek, then pulled away and stalked to the front door.

"Seth, please."

He shook his head. "Just keeping it casual, per the lady's request." He opened the door then turned to take a long, slow look at her. The way he lingered on the details of her like he was memorizing every inch told her he knew he wasn't leaving her. He knew *she* was leaving *him*. "Take care of yourself, Fearless."

The words landed like the second gut punch of the day, and then he was gone.

CHAPTER TWENTY

Frannie spent the afternoon shift at the diner vacillating between being glad for the distraction of work and overwhelmed by the need to curl into a ball and dissolve into tears. Seth was gone.

He was *gone*.

It had only been a few hours. She should be able to convince herself this wasn't any different from spending days apart, living their lives in separate towns. Yeah, her heart wasn't buying that bullshit. For the first time in her life, she had gotten close enough to a man for him to break it. Then she had pushed him away, practically packed his bag and shoved him out the door. She had been careless and stupid. Again.

"Hey, Frannie." Beth, who had been oddly unobtrusive about Frannie's mood, laid a hand on her shoulder. "Mr. Connor just sat down at the counter."

"On a Sunday?" Another man who couldn't stand her was the last thing she needed today.

"He won't make it in tomorrow because his nephew's taking him to a baseball game." Beth shot Frannie a sympathetic look. She might not be asking about what was wrong, but Frannie must be telegraphing the hell out of it. "Do you want me to take care of him today?"

Frannie shook her head. She wasn't so pathetic that she couldn't pour a cup of coffee and cut a slice of pie for a cranky old man. "We have peach pie today, so his grunts will be less hostile. I'd hate to miss out on all that love."

Beth grinned as she headed for the kitchen, and Frannie picked up the coffeepot and carried it to Mr. Connor.

"Good timing, Mr. Connor. We just brewed a fresh pot."

He grunted in acknowledgment.

She retreated to the other end of the counter to wrap clean flatware in napkins for the next shift and wait for him to ask for his refill and pie. She wondered what he would think next week when he came to the diner and discovered she was no longer here. Would he notice or care? Maybe be relieved the no-good ex-con was purged from his cozy small-town existence? Some part of her didn't want to let his opinion of her stand, not that she could really do anything to change it. But at least she would leave on a friendly note.

When she brought him his piece of peach pie and refilled his coffee before he requested it, she gave him a smile that was almost genuine, the best she could muster given her aching heart. She floundered about what to say to connect to him. Something about baseball, maybe, but she didn't even know where the nearest team played or what it was called.

"Beth told me your nephew's taking you to a ball game tomorrow," she tried.

No response.

She nodded anyway. "Well, I hope your team wins."

He glanced at her and made full eye contact before looking back down at his newspaper. As she stepped away from him, he spoke. "My late wife used to make peach pie."

Frannie froze for a minute, afraid to move and scare him off. She wondered what it must be like to love someone for years, decades, not just weeks, and then have them disappear from your life.

She turned gently and smiled, this time for real. "I bet they were wonderful."

He nodded and lifted his fork, this time not looking at her. "Even better than this."

"I'm sure they were." She blinked back tears as she left him to his pie and newspaper, slipping into the safety of the kitchen where she could hide from the old man and his still-broken heart.

Somehow, their heartbreaks, despite being so different, had allowed a sweet and human moment to pass between them. Progress. Serious progress. It was almost a shame she couldn't stay long enough to really win him over.

FRANNIE DIDN'T QUESTION it when Patrice hung the closed sign on the diner door fifteen minutes early. She screwed the lid onto the last of the refilled salt shakers and sighed in relief. The last customers had left half an hour earlier, and no one was likely to show up now. The only thing worse than a crazy-busy night at a restaurant was a painfully slow one.

"The good news is, you got all your side work done, so you're free to go." Patrice fake fanned herself with a paper napkin. "In case you have a hot date or something."

Frannie turned in a circle to make sure everything looked in order for the morning shift, giving herself a chance to blink back tears while Patrice couldn't see her face. "I'm on my own tonight." She was proud of how unconcerned she sounded about it.

"Oh. That's too bad. Well, then get some dinner before Oscar scrapes down the grill."

"Patrice, before I go, I have a favor to ask."

Frannie rubbed her palms on her apron. She had meant to ask as soon as Patrice had arrived during the dinner shift. She'd had plenty of opportunities during the slow evening as her boss had sent the other waitresses home one by one. Now it was time for Frannie to leave, too, but she still struggled to make the request. It would solidify her plan. It was completely necessary. And it was so final.

Patrice stood leaning against the breakfast counter, one eyebrow raised, waiting.

"I'm scheduled for the breakfast shift Friday. I was hoping I could have that whole day off, like last week." Not that *that* had gone well. That horrible day had shifted everything into warp speed, and she still hadn't caught her breath from it.

"Is everything all right, Frannie?"

Frannie pasted on her fake smile and adopted her light, lilting, nothing-to-see-here voice again. "Everything's fine. I just have something I have to do."

Patrice stood silently, one brow arching, waiting again. The woman should consider a career in law enforcement. That look could make anyone confess.

Frannie cleared her throat. "It's my mother. I have something important to discuss with her."

"Something you can't do over the phone?"

She should have gone with a lie about her parole officer. She cleared her throat. "I'd rather not. Like I said, it's important, and she's not going to like it." As she spoke the words, Frannie knew they were true. She had told herself that after she left, Greene would drop her mother. But what if he didn't? She had to make sure her mother dumped him, but she didn't know how she could do that without Lexi's help.

"Is this about her new beau? I get the feeling you don't like this mystery man."

"That's an understatement." Especially now that his identity was no longer a mystery. "There are some things I've learned about him that I have to tell her. She won't appreciate my meddling, and she'll probably be disappointed in me all over again."

Patrice narrowed her eyes and studied Frannie's face long enough to make Frannie wonder if her mask of composure had slipped.

Patrice shooed Frannie toward a table. "Sit. Oscar said you haven't eaten since you got here. You need some cheesecake."

Frannie tried to protest as Patrice cut a generous piece of dessert for her. She had never gotten up the nerve to try it. The graham cracker crust and cherry sauce on top didn't give her pause, but she couldn't make peace with the idea of cream cheese in a pie.

"How about some coffee? There's only decaf left."

Frannie jumped up from her seat. "Actually, I was going to make some herbal tea."

That made Patrice smile. "Lexi's getting to you, I see. Next, she'll have you making homemade candles for your morning meditation."

"She'd rather get me back to that morning torture she calls a yoga class." Frannie reached for a tea bag of blue cohosh, Lexi's current favorite, hung it on a cup, and streamed hot water from the dispenser behind the counter.

When she sat down again, Patrice had taken the seat across from hers and was stirring cream into her decaf. Frannie tore open two blue packets of sweetener and dumped them into her tea.

"Try a bite of cheesecake," Patrice cajoled as Frannie wrinkled her nose. "Just one bite. If you don't like it, I'll throw it away myself."

"Fine." Frannie took a small corner that was mostly crust and cherries, with just a hint of the suspect cheese. It was almost as good as the eggs Seth had made her that morning. Just twelve hours earlier. Before they had said goodbye for good. She nodded as she stared down at her plate until the threat of tears passed. "That's good. How have I missed out on this all these years?" She took another bite, a full-size one this time, just to show her sincerity.

Patrice took a swig of coffee then set down her cup and clasped her hands on the table in front of her. "Now, about what you said earlier, why do you think your mama is disappointed in you?"

Frannie raised her eyebrows while she finished another bite. "Are you kidding? I mean, you've been really cool about this ex-con thing, and I appreciate it." She paused as the depth of just how much it meant to her hit her. "I really, truly appreciate it." She shook off the sentimentality that had threatened to consume her all day. It was a ridiculous and useless emotion. "But I went to prison. Not exactly the kind of thing that makes a mother proud."

"But disappointed is a strong word. Did Crystal say that to you?"

Frannie sipped her tea as she considered it. Her mother had said she was sad. She had said that a lot. She had said she was sorry and overwhelmed and that she would visit every week. And she had, except for the few times Frannie just wasn't up for company from the outside world and the one time her mother had gone to the ER with a cellulitis infection on visiting day.

"I can't remember her ever using that word," Frannie said.

"That's my point. We mothers don't normally hesitate to call attention to our disappointment. If anything, she would have been drowning in guilt, except that she knew you did it for a good reason, for Lexi."

Frannie stopped with the last forkful of cheesecake halfway to her mouth. By Lexi's account, Patrice had engaged Patty's help to return Jack's money, but the women hadn't had a clue how Lexi had come by Frannie's crime spoils in the first place. "What did Lexi tell you?"

"Not much. But I was able to put the pieces together. Point is, if my daughter had made such a bad life choice but it was for a really good reason, I'd be able to sleep a little better at night. Still with a lot of guilt, but better."

Frannie nodded along to Patrice's observations. They made a kind of sense, except... except. "My mother doesn't know any of that. I made Lexi swear she wouldn't tell my mother or her parents or anyone in that suffocating, backwater town. Rob, she met later, of course. And then they told Seth, but he was long gone from Smithton by then."

Her voice trailed off as she realized Patrice was staring at her, wide-eyed. "So, let me make sure I understand this, Miss Frannie."

Uh-oh.

"Your mother does not know a blessed thing about why you stole Jack Greene's money. He's a shady character, but you saw fit to cross him, to break into his house, then into his safe, and Miss Crystal has no idea there was possibly a good reason for it."

Frannie swiped her fork across her empty plate. "Well, when you put it that way, it sounds mean not to have told her. Kind of stupid. Selfish."

"Keep going."

"It's not like I broke down the door with an axe, by the way," Frannie said, hoping Patrice would look less disappointed in Frannie if she knew Frannie had made a careful plan. "I memorized the security codes of the front door and the safe and lifted the spare key when I was at Greene's house with Lexi and Brandon. I wore gloves and a hoodie."

Patrice's eyes were even wider now, if that was possible.

Frannie set down her fork and picked up her cup. "Not that any of that makes it better. But there was a plan, and the first half of it worked, and then things happened, and the second half went off the rails."

That wasn't exactly true. The second half had gone according to a plan too. It's just that it was an alternative plan, made on the fly, while she had thought her best friend might bleed to death.

"What does your mother think happened? Why does she think you turned to a life of crime?"

Frannie shrugged. Her mother had never come right out and asked, and Frannie had never volunteered an explanation.

"If you had to guess," Patrice insisted.

Frannie set down her empty cup and stared into it. A few tea leaves had escaped the bag. Not enough to read her future, but she didn't need tea leaves or guesses or Lexi's kind of magic to know what it would be.

"She probably thought I was selfish and stupid and trying to run away from my life," Frannie said.

"You could ease her mind a little bit if you told her the truth." Patrice finished her coffee and got to her feet. "At least a little part of it. The part where you sound like a good, if misguided, friend and not like a spoiled, selfish daughter. Because raising a daughter like *that*, now that would cause guilt. And maybe some disappointment too."

This day just kept spiraling further down the tubes.

"Hey, Patrice?" Courage failed her when her boss looked at her with those kind eyes. "Do you mind if I take home some of that cheesecake?"

"It's not much of a dinner, but help yourself." She turned back toward the kitchen.

"And Patrice?"

She looked at Frannie again.

"Thank you. Really. Thank you for everything."

CHAPTER TWENTY-ONE

At the end of her Monday night shift, Frannie stepped out of the back door of the diner and walked down the wooden steps to the parking lot. Oscar followed her, locking the door behind them.

"You look dead on your feet, Frannie. Need a ride?"

She grinned. "It's tempting, but I think I can walk fifty yards."

Although that might be as far as she got. While Sunday night had been painfully slow for business and had given her far too much time to think about the week ahead, and worse, the weeks after that, tonight the place had been packed nonstop. On the upside, she hadn't had time to dwell on Seth or her mother or Lexi or Bettina until now.

Oscar's cell phone rang. Frannie glanced over her shoulder. He was leaning against his car, frowning. "Suzie again." One of the kids was sick, and his wife had been calling for the past hour.

Seeing him with his phone made Frannie check for hers. "Oscar, I have to go back inside for my phone." She saw the pained look on his face. "But go now, please. I'll be fine."

He shook his head. "Patrice said—"

"It's a two-minute walk. I'll keep my cell phone in my hand with 911 on speed dial."

Oscar scowled but gave one curt nod. "Just this once. But go straight to your apartment and lock the door behind you."

"Yes, sir." She smiled and waved then unlocked the back door with her set of keys. A minute later, she relocked the same door, and true to her word, kept her cell phone clutched in her hand.

She stepped onto the sidewalk that ran in front of the apartment building. In the dozens of times she had walked this route over the past weeks, she had memorized each dip in the cement and every crack in the pavement between the diner's back door and her building's outdoor staircase, to the point that she could have walked it blindfolded. Tonight, she also could have found her way by following the sound of Mrs. Beale's overtaxed air conditioner on the ground floor, the noise of it whirring steadily against the soft hum of traffic out on Route 231 as motorists drove right past the green sign pointing the way to Licking.

"If only I'd had the choice to keep driving," she said out loud as she climbed the stairs, but her heart was barely in it.

An out-of-place sound made her stop halfway up the staircase. For a minute, she only heard the traffic and the air conditioner. Then it came again, the squeak of an animal or the creak of a metal post. Neither of those explained the breath-hitching, palm-sweating terror the intrusive sound caused. The third time, the sound was clearer, closer. It was a whistle, a very human whistle. Something stirred the hedges lining the dark and deserted parking lot of the office building across the street. A shadow separated itself from the bushes and took the form of a tall, wiry, dark-clad man.

Patrice and Oscar had warned her. She had promised them both she would be careful. What had she just said to Oscar? 911 on speed dial. Except she hadn't counted on every muscle in her body freezing. She stood alone in the world, facing the man she knew was out to destroy her and her ex-best friend and possibly her mother, despite what everyone else believed.

He waved his arm, beckoning her.

Please let me be asleep. Please let me be asleep. Please let me be asleep. But adopting a mantra like Lexi would do Frannie no good. She was much too wide awake and nauseated for this to be a bad dream. Like in every half-baked dream and horror-movie cliché, when the terrified, isolated girl's muscles finally responded to her command to move, she moved toward her monster instead of showing the most rudimentary common sense and running the hell away. What choice did she have? The monster knew where she lived, where she worked, and how to get to her through her mother.

She stopped on her side of the street, able to see Jack Greene clearly from this vantage point. She breathed a sigh of relief when a beige sedan drove down the strip between them. It wasn't even ten o'clock. There would still be cars driving past and people awake and the possibility that someone would hear her scream over the sound of Mrs. Beale's air conditioner, if it came to that. And the sheriff's office had promised Patrice they would loop around once every fifteen or twenty minutes. For all Frannie knew, that would be any minute.

Grasping onto a small sliver of bravado, bolstered by standing in full view of potential witnesses that could show up any minute, she crossed her arms over her chest in defiance. He wanted to scare her, and she couldn't stop him from succeeding. But she would be damned if she gave him more ground. "Why are you here?"

"Come over here. I hardly want to yell back and forth across the street." His voice wasn't a yell at all. It wasn't even menacing.

Still, her nearly empty stomach clenched and curdled, and she fought not to vomit from fear. "I'm not coming one step closer."

"Fine." He held up his hands. "I really don't want to argue with you, so if you want to talk across the street, that's what we'll do."

Her stomach unclenched, but her muscles remained coiled. She had no idea why he was being so conciliatory, and she didn't much care. She just wanted to get whatever this was over with. "Why are you here?" she repeated.

"Because I care about your mother, and us being at odds is breaking her heart."

That shocked Frannie into silence. She had expected him to mention the larceny, implicate Lexi, threaten all of them. But... "You didn't seriously come here because of my mother."

"I did." He shoved his hands into his pants pockets and slouched. His change in stance aged him ten years. For the first time ever, Frannie thought he looked old. And something else. Broken, maybe. Sad, definitely. "She's important to me."

"I don't believe you." Frannie wrapped her arms around her shoulders, steadying herself.

He looked away from her, off into the darkness. "Do you know where my son lives?"

Frannie furrowed her brow. "Brandon? Isn't he in Colorado?"

He turned to face her again. "He visits for a couple of days over Christmas and comes home for a long weekend every once in a while. He's my only child. After my wife died, it was just the two of us for all those years, and now I hardly see him. Your mother and I understand each other that way."

Her mother never would have won a parent-of-the-year award, but Greene comparing himself to her made bile rise in Frannie's throat. And it made her brave. Maybe stupidly so. "The situations are nothing alike. She would never do the terrible things you've done. Brandon leaving the state and staying away is all on you. The things you did..." She choked back tears. She would not cry and show weakness in front of this asshole.

He stood up straight and hardened his glare. The monster was back. "I want to do this the easy way, Frannie. The right way, with you and me on the same side, for your mother's sake. But if you won't cooperate, that's your problem. I'm not leaving her because you can't get over the indiscretion I had with your friend. Crystal is too important to me. "

"Indiscretion?" Frannie clenched her fists at her sides. "You nearly ruined her life! She could have—" She just barely stopped herself from revealing Lexi's pregnancy and near-fatal miscarriage. That was one secret Jack Greene would never know, damn him.

"Lexi and I both made bad choices. I was so lonely, and she was so drunk. We both were. And then..." He frowned. "And then you made your own bad choice. The minute you got caught with my money, I knew Lexi had told you about our night together and you blamed me for it. But she and I were both to blame. Your mother understands that. Maybe when you and Lexi grow up, you'll understand it as well." He headed for his fancy car then stopped and turned to her with a shrug. "Either way, I'm here to stay in your mother's life."

He drove away without another word.

The air was still. The night was quiet except for the unrelenting groan of Mrs. Beale's air conditioner. It was like her conversation with Greene had never happened, like he had been a figment of her imagination. A bad dream. A waking nightmare.

Frannie dislodged her feet from the ground and lurched toward the stairs. She was nearly to the second floor when she realized she was drenched in sweat. She fumbled with her keys, gulping down sobs as she struggled to unlock her apartment door. He blamed Lexi for the rape. He had said it was just a bad choice. Lexi had gone through a living hell and then had nearly died. Now he had rewritten history to claim it wasn't his fault. He had fed those lies to Frannie's mother, and now her mother believed him. And she always would. She would never take Frannie's word as truth.

Frannie fell into her apartment and slammed the door behind her. She jammed both dead bolts into place and slid to the floor with her back propped against the door. She needed to call someone, to hear another voice, to make someone aware of what had happened to her. Not her mother. Christ on toast, her mother might actually be in love with the man. Or at least the man she thought Jack Greene was.

She couldn't call Lexi. No way could she break the news that Jack Greene planned to stay in her mother's life, and therefore in all their lives, over the phone. Patrice would be asleep by now. Seth would be... She didn't know what Seth would be. She hadn't had enough time to learn what Seth would be doing in his own house, far away from her, at that hour. The night she had needed him and he had stayed with her had been a fluke, just as she had suspected. Thinking he would be here when she needed him again had been a childish dream.

She wrapped her arms around herself and lay down on the fake-wood floor. This was the way her life had once been. The way it would be again. Frannie was destined to spend the rest of her life alone.

CHAPTER TWENTY-TWO
July 2009

Frannie and Lexi's lives were about to diverge for the first time in ten years, and Lexi was running late. She hated herself for agreeing to grab coffee with two of her three college roommates when she had already scheduled a date with her best friend.

But Lexi was going to spend the next nine months sharing a tiny, two-bedroom suite with these new people, so it had sounded reasonable when Regan suggested hanging out for a while to get to know each other. Sarah had begged off, but Ashleigh had immediately agreed with Regan, and together they had stared at Lexi, waiting for her decision. She'd had a feeling the choice she made would set the tone for her relationship with them, and they seemed like nice, smart, cool girls. She didn't want to ruin her chance at a friendship with them.

She arrived at Frannie's place—her mom's small rental house, which wouldn't be Frannie's home much longer—at nearly eleven at night. It was dark except for the dim glow seeping through the dirty glass of the lamp pole in the front yard. She texted Frannie and waited. It took a few minutes for a light to come on in her bedroom, so Lexi must have woken her, which made Lexi feel even shittier.

BRT, Frannie texted back, and a minute later she greeted Lexi at the front door.

"Sorry if I woke you," Lexi whispered.

"No need to whisper. My mom's out on a hot date."

"On a Tuesday night?" Hot date meant all-nighter, usually with a guy she hadn't known long. Frannie's mom never seemed to know—or date—guys for very long. But she used to confine her dating escapades to the weekends.

"Does it matter?" Frannie sounded annoyed, so Lexi dropped it.

Lexi followed her to her room. "Wow. It's so different."

Everything important to Frannie—her favorite books from the middle shelf of her bookcase, her jewelry box with the windup ballerina and containing not much more than a couple of pairs of earrings and the friendship bracelet she had outgrown years ago, a handful of framed pictures of her with her mom and grandma, a poster of Cat Power, and the tassel from her graduation cap—were missing. Probably packed into the small cardboard box by the door. One large suitcase, presumably stuffed with the clothes from her now-empty closet, stood under the window. On the opposite wall, her single bed still had sheets and her sleeping pillow on it but no comforter or stuffed animals or throw pillows.

Lexi knew every inch of this room as well as she knew her own. Or she had. But in the three days she had spent at college orientation a couple hours away, Frannie's childhood—*their* childhood—had disappeared.

"Lex, don't cry." Frannie hugged her, and long black hairs that had come loose from her ponytail tickled Lexi's nose.

She wiped away tears and hugged Frannie back. "I'm not crying. Not much."

Frannie pulled away and pointed to the light-green saucer chair where Lexi always sat cross-legged, opposite from Frannie on her bed, while they shared their deepest secrets. But now they were silent. Lexi didn't know what to say. It was like all the meaningful things they had to tell each other had disappeared along with Frannie's mementos. Lexi's chest tightened as she wondered whether this was how it would be, now that she was going in one direction to her mid-sized college and Frannie was going an hour the other way—to a bigger town where she had already secured two part-time jobs so she could start saving for vet tech school.

Frannie was the smartest person Lexi knew and had graduated near the top of their ninety-nine-person class, but she wasn't college bound. Up through junior year, they had taken it for granted Frannie would qualify for academic scholarships, but when it came down to it, the offers she received weren't enough to make up for her shortfall. Her mother couldn't take out a second mortgage because she had never had a first one. Frannie had spent months last spring doing the math until she couldn't deny it anymore. A four-year college was out of her reach.

Lexi's mom kept telling her not to feel guilty. Frannie was smart and talented, and she would find her place in the world. It was easy to believe that advice when Lexi was on campus or with her new roommates. Pretty damned hard when she sat across from Frannie in her shabby, packed-up bedroom.

Frannie's face brightened, and Lexi sat up straighter, ready to hear whatever she wanted to share. "I'll pick up my car tomorrow morning. The mechanic had to change out the brake pads, but everything else passed inspection."

"That's great. Your first car. So, you'll be all ready to go next Tuesday."

Frannie shrugged. "Or tomorrow. My lease started today, so I can go whenever. Mom's going to be a wreck no matter when I leave. There's not really any reason to stay."

A lump formed in Lexi's throat. Frannie had been in bed, probably asleep, and planned to get up and leave in the morning. "I almost missed you."

Frannie smiled, but it was small and tight, and she stared down at her short, chewed-down fingernails. "It's okay. We've said goodbye like a million times this past week."

Lexi nodded. "Sure, but this is different."

Frannie's eyes shone with tears, but she covered with another fake smile. "I'm probably coming to see you in October."

"At Halloween. That's almost two months away." Lexi's brain caught up to Frannie's words. "What do you mean probably?"

"I'll be the new person at my jobs. I don't know how many weekends I'll get off."

Lexi's cheeks were wet again, but this time she didn't bother wiping them. "That's not fair. We planned it." Even as she said it, she knew it was childish, but she couldn't help it.

Frannie huffed and leaned back against the wall with her arms crossed over her chest. "We planned it to accommodate your schedule. Excuse me for having a life too."

"That's not what I meant, and you know it."

They were silent again for a few minutes, then Frannie sighed. "I told the garage I'd pick up my car at eight, so..." She glanced at her bedroom door in a not-so-subtle hint.

Lexi had known things were going to change, but not like this. "Frannie, I'm sorry I got here a little late."

"Two hours late."

Lexi nodded. "I know. I'm a total shit. I'm sorry. But please, I don't want to fight on our last night."

Frannie frowned and blinked fast. "I don't want to fight either."

Lexi's chest loosened. "Good. Then close your eyes."

"What?"

"Don't ask questions," Lexi answered. "Just close your eyes."

She did, and Lexi pulled a tiny box out of her purse and opened the hinged lid. She slowly extricated the silver charm bracelet. "Now hold out your right hand." She hovered the bracelet above Frannie's wrist. "Best friends forever. Best friends forever." She draped the bracelet on Frannie's wrist and snapped the clasp. "Best friends forever."

Frannie opened her eyes and stared down at the gift. "Lexi, it's beautiful."

Lexi smiled. "You won't outgrow this one."

Frannie fingered each charm. A star, a moon, a BFF, a dog, and a heart. "One of these things is not like the others," she said as she laid her finger on the tiny schnauzer.

"Well, you always wanted a dog, but I wasn't sure your landlord or your roommates would appreciate a real one."

"Oh, Lex." Frannie threw her arms around Lexi's neck.

Lexi had never been so happy about giving a gift. They felt like themselves again.

Lexi sank down onto the bed beside Frannie and leaned against the wall. "I guess we shouldn't watch a murder channel marathon since it's so late," she said, referring to the true crime network they had been addicted to since middle school.

"Probably not." Frannie pulled a plastic grocery bag out from under her bed. "But then I'll have to eat these all by myself." She dropped the bag onto the bed between them. It held three types of Oreos: regular, double stuffed, and mint.

"God, I hate the mint ones," Lexi said.

Frannie grabbed the remote from her nightstand and clicked on the small TV sitting on a stand near the window. "Who said they were for you?" She snatched them away from Lexi and settled the bag on her lap.

Lexi took the bag of double-stuffed cookies for herself and scooted over to share the pillow propped behind Frannie. She didn't stop smiling for the next three hours as they watched detectives solve cold murder cases and stuffed themselves sick with cookies.

Some things, even most things, might change, but Frannie and Lexi would always have each other.

CHAPTER TWENTY-THREE
2016

Something was different about Frannie. When she had called Friday morning with an invitation to a girls' night at her apartment, Lexi could barely contain her excitement. All week, Frannie had begged off all the get-togethers Lexi had proposed. Lexi had started to panic. But then the out-of-the-blue, short-notice invitation. Lexi had rearranged her schedule, offered to bring the lasagna Frannie loved, and left work fifteen minutes early so she could defrost the food and put on makeup and still be on time.

Now Frannie was smiling and chattering, but she still managed to be weirdly subdued. She had something on her mind. Lexi was beginning to suspect her friend had an agenda.

"Thanks again for bringing dinner, Lex," Frannie said. She sat at the table, slicing peppers for their salad while Lexi peeled carrots at the sink. "I swear I didn't invite you here expecting you to cook for me."

"Happy to do it." Lexi grinned. "I always make a couple of lasagnas at one time so I can freeze one. Really, all I had to do was defrost it and partially heat it while I put on some fresh makeup." She hoped she sounded casual, nonchalant. She wanted to come across as less desperate and emotionally needy than she felt.

Frannie smiled as she worked, but Lexi thought it looked forced. She knew she should ask what was on Frannie's mind, but she wasn't sure she wanted to know. This was real progress. Lexi didn't want to jinx it.

A knock at the door surprised her. She glanced over her shoulder. "Expecting someone? Or maybe it's Seth coming to make up with you. If you want me to invent an excuse to leave—"

"No, it's not him." Frannie widened her eyes. "I just remembered... I can't believe I forgot I invited her."

Frannie was good at pretending, hiding, and acting like she didn't care about much of anyone or anything, but she was surprisingly bad at outright lying, at least to Lexi. "What's going on?" Lexi asked.

Frannie walked the few steps to the door without further explanation. She pulled open the door and smiled. "Hi, Mom. Thanks for coming." She shot a pleading look over her shoulder at Lexi as if asking for forgiveness.

Lexi tried to remain expressionless.

For her part, Crystal looked like she had spent the afternoon preparing for this dinner date. She wore a yellow flowered dress and white jacket with matching high-heeled sandals. She wore her hair in an almost-elegant bun. She cradled a Tupperware container in one arm and threw her free arm around Frannie's shoulders.

"Did we agree to dress up for dinner?" Frannie asked as she took the plastic container and stepped aside to let her mother into the apartment. She glanced down at her own jeans and blue T-shirt then at Lexi's red patterned dress. "I feel like I'm the one who didn't get the memo."

Lexi shot her a tight smile. "How could there have been a memo when I didn't realize there were going to be three of us?" She realized how rude that sounded the minute the words came out of her mouth. "I'm sorry, Crystal. I didn't mean anything by that."

"No offense taken. You're a surprise to me too. A pleasant one, of course." Crystal set her Tupperware box on the counter and gave

Lexi a hug. She wore a light scent, possibly an expensive perfume. Probably a gift from Jack Greene. "You look wonderful as always, Lexi. And look at our Frannie." She beamed at her daughter. "Frannie, you've gotten some sun and some color in your cheeks."

"Would you like a glass of wine, Mom?" Frannie asked, ignoring her mother's compliments.

"I'll wait until dinner." Crystal glanced around the apartment. "Is it just the three of us? Or is your mom coming, Lexi?"

"No, just the three of us." She glanced at Frannie. "I think." Lexi laid her hand over her stomach, suddenly not feeling well. She hoped her friend didn't have any more surprises for them.

"Well," Crystal said, "I just need a minute in the powder room. That's a long drive without a rest stop for a woman my age."

"Yeah, forty-four is ancient, Mom." Frannie led her mother to the bathroom as if she could get lost choosing between the only two interior doors in the apartment.

"No need to get smart, young lady," Crystal said, but she was smiling.

When they were alone again, Lexi wiped her hands on a dish towel and propped her hands on her hips. "What's up, Frannie?"

Frannie shrugged. "I agreed to have dinner with my mom, and then I invited you, and..." She cracked open the Tupperware container. "She brought cookies. Oatmeal raisin with chocolate chips. My grandmother's recipe that you love."

Suspicion washed over Lexi, making her feel light-headed. This was a setup; she could feel it in her bones. The only reason she could think of that Frannie would lie about inviting her mother had to be...

The oven timer dinged, thankfully giving her something to do. She turned away from Frannie before she could snap at her friend and insist on the truth. She pulled open the oven door and inspected the lasagna then put on oven mitts and pulled the pan out of the oven. She set it on the trivet on the kitchen table. "It needs to rest for ten minutes, then you can cut it." She pulled her purse off the back of a kitchen chair and turned toward the front door.

"Where are you going?" Frannie asked.

Lexi spun on her heel and glared at Frannie. She had spent so much time over the past few weeks trying to get into Frannie's good graces, she had forgotten how it felt to be angry with her friend. The depth of fury she felt shocked her.

"You're lying to me," Lexi said. "I thought you wanted to have a friends' night, but this whole thing was a setup to bring your mother and me together."

Frannie reached for her hand. "Lex, don't. It's just dinner. My mom would love to catch up with you."

"This is about *him*, right?" Lexi watched Frannie's face. "Unless Crystal is done with him by now. Please tell me that's the case. She never stays with any of them long."

"Jesus, Lex. That's rough."

Lexi blinked back tears. "I'm sorry. You're right. She really stepped up for you while you were in prison. I'll be nice to her. I owe her that."

The bathroom door swung open, and Frannie's mother was already talking. "Lexi, Frannie tells me you and Rob got Teeny a dog." She pulled plates from Frannie's cupboard and set them on the table as she spoke then went for the silverware drawer.

"Bettina," Frannie said reflexively, but she didn't put any heat into it.

Crystal didn't acknowledge the interruption. "Frannie said his name is Max. Bettina must love him. How's she doing in school?"

Crystal's lighthearted prattle set the tone for the rest of the dinner. Lexi relaxed into the conversation, and the tension slowly eased out of her body. She really could see the good in Frannie's mother despite the woman's many flaws. But by the end of dinner, Frannie's smile seemed tight. She was restless, shifting in her seat. That set Lexi on edge all over again.

"Don't forget about the goat," Frannie said as she scooped up the salad bowl and carried it to the sink. Crystal and Lexi stopped clearing dishes and stared at her. "We've covered everyone else we know. I wouldn't want the goat at Bettina's grandparents' farm to feel left out."

Lexi narrowed her eyes, but Frannie's mother smiled sweetly. "We've left out someone else," Crystal said.

Now Lexi smiled too. "Seth."

Frannie shot a pleading look at Lexi.

Lexi lowered her voice. "They had a lovers' spat."

"Aw, that's a shame." Crystal patted Frannie's hand. "Is he still such a polite boy?"

Frannie scowled at her mother. "He's twenty-seven. He hasn't been a boy in years." She gave Lexi a withering look. "And I never said anything about a spat."

Lexi ignored Frannie's discomfort. After all, she was the one who had brought the three of them together. She should have expected Seth would come up in conversation with her best friend and her mother.

Lexi spoke to Crystal while they resumed clearing the table. "She almost never says anything about him. But he always has good things to say about her. Until this week. Rob says he's gone radio silent on the matter."

"Enough about that because there's nothing to tell." Frannie turned to face both women and leaned against the sink. "But since we're all here, maybe we should take the opportunity to discuss another important matter."

Lexi's gut twisted. *No. No, no, no!* That sounded like a segue into the one topic Lexi would not tolerate. She set the half-empty lasagna pan on the counter. "Actually, I have to call it a night. I promised Bettina I'd be home in time to tuck her in."

"Lex, just ten minutes." Frannie laid her hand on Lexi's shoulder.

Lexi stepped away from her and gave Frannie's mother a quick hug. "Let's do this again when my mom can join us."

"That would be great," Frannie's mom said.

"Please, Lex, stay. Mom brought cookies." Frannie flashed puppy-dog eyes at her.

Lexi refused to fall for it. She would not indulge Frannie. She would not discuss Jack Greene with Crystal. "Gotta run. Don't forget the dog park tomorrow morning." She grabbed her purse and headed for the front door. "And I'll pick up my pan next week."

Frannie followed her, catching up with her at the top of the outside staircase. "Lex, come on. Don't run away like this."

Lexi whirled around to face her. Anger rushed through her like a flash flood. "Don't ambush me. I told you I cannot have this discussion with—" Lexi stopped talking when Crystal popped up behind Frannie. Lexi smiled and waved to her. "Goodnight, Crystal."

Frannie's mother waved from the doorway, and Lexi hurried down the stairs. By the time she reached the minivan, she was crying. A minute into the drive, she pulled off the road, sobbing. How could her best friend have done that to her? How dare she try to force Lexi into a confrontation with Crystal? Did she really expect Lexi to share her deepest, darkest secret with the woman who was dating her rapist?

"DAMN IT," FRANNIE MUTTERED as Lexi drove away.

A small part of her flinched, understanding that the ambush, as Lexi had called it, had cracked something between her and Lexi, something fragile that had just begun healing. But dealing with that would have to wait for another day. She couldn't let this night end until she finished what she had started when she had invited Lexi and Crystal to dinner.

She herded her mother back into the apartment and motioned for her to sit down at the table. "You'll stay for tea and cookies, right?"

Her mother remained standing. "I think I should go too. I have the hour-and-a-half drive home."

"Mom, it's eight o'clock. One cup of tea. You'll still be home by ten."

She popped open the Tupperware container and took a cookie. When she bit into it, the taste of childhood triumphs and failures filled her mouth. The time she had gotten the highest grade on the algebra final. The night she had come home from her disastrous first date with the star of the baseball team, a boy she had worshipped from afar for months before he had finally asked her out then had made it clear he had only wanted one thing from the pathetically smitten girl with freckles and untamable red hair. The time she had won the third-grade spelling bee, beating out Jayde, the shiny girl who was supposed to have won. The weekend after she had walked herself home alone from kindergarten, bringing hell down on her mother's head and her own.

"I might not go straight home." Her mother smiled slowly. "I might stop in Indianapolis on the way."

Indianapolis. Where Jack Greene lived.

Frannie dropped the cookie onto the counter and struggled to swallow the large bite she had taken. Her mother was being nice. Maybe even motherly. And Frannie had to break her heart.

Her mother took her hand. "Frannie, you look upset. Is this about Seth?"

Frannie picked up her water glass and took a big swig to wash down the cookie. Then she slid into a kitchen chair. Her mother sat across from her. "It's about the truth, Mom. I've never told you the truth about the burglary."

"You've told me everything I need to know."

"There was a good reason I took the money. It was for Lexi."

"For Lexi." Her mother shook her head. "That doesn't make any sense. You were across state lines, running away. Lexi was with Brandon. She was with Jack's son while you broke into his safe." Her mother wrinkled her brow.

Put the pieces together. Put the pieces together. Put the pieces together. If ever she had needed Lexi's magical thinking to work, now was the time.

But her mother shook her head, not getting it. "Lexi didn't need the money. Her parents were paying her tuition. And there was no reason for her to run away. She had friends and a boyfriend."

Unlike you, her mother didn't need to add. But Frannie had still had a friend, her best friend, and she had given up four years of her life to save her. And her mother was going to face the truth about Jack Greene if it damn near killed all of them.

"And an unwanted pregnancy," Frannie said. "Lexi was pregnant."

"Pregnant. And just twenty years old." Her mother took a deep breath and exhaled slowly. "I understand how scared she was. I understand it completely. But I was alone when I was pregnant with you. She had Brandon. They could have made it work."

"No, they couldn't." This was it, the moment of truth. Or more precisely, the moment of the lie, when the promise she had made to keep Lexi's secret crumbled to dust. "It wasn't Brandon's."

"Someone else? Lexi?"

"Not by choice."

Frannie hesitated, let it hang in the air for her mother to decipher. But that was exactly what Lexi had done all these years, and look what had happened: Jack Greene had gotten off scot-free while

Frannie had languished in prison, so he had never been forced out of their lives. That had to change.

"Lexi was raped, Mom, by Jack Greene."

"Oh, Frannie." Her mother laid her hand over Frannie's. Her face softened. "That's why you called him a monster? It was a mistake. They made a mistake, and I don't doubt Lexi felt awful about it, the way she loved Brandon. And if she was pregnant, that must have been terrible for her, and I can understand why she hid it—and even why you stole the money to help her." Her mother squeezed her fingers and smiled.

Just as Patrice had predicted, Frannie's mother understood and sympathized with what her daughter had done. The relief had to be the reason for her serene expression, given she had just learned the man she was dating, a man she obviously had feelings for, had raped her daughter's best friend.

"So, you understand why you need to stay away from him. He's dangerous. He's a rapist."

Her mother furrowed her brow. "Frannie, they made a mistake."

She had used that word twice now. Frannie shook her head.

"Jack regrets it," her mother continued. "Doing that with his own son's girlfriend. But it doesn't make Lexi or Jack a monster."

Frannie's breath came too fast and shallow. "No, Mother, it was not a mistake. He raped her. Are you listening to me? Do you understand? Rape!"

Her mother pulled back her hand and stood. "That's ridiculous. He told me about it himself, Frannie. Not the pregnancy. He didn't know, did he?"

Frannie shook her head as her fingers and toes went numb.

"But he told me how it happened. A stormy night, alone in his house, drinking Scotch, him so lonely, her intrigued by an older man."

"Oh my god." Frannie collapsed forward onto the table. "He made it sound like a romance novel. I was wrong when I called him a monster. I should have called him a *sick, fucking* monster because he raped her!"

"This is ridiculous." Her mother picked up her handbag and stomped to the front door. "I'm not going to stay here and listen to this nonsense. In your desperate need to hate the man who forgave you, you've twisted Lexi's words." Her mother stopped with her hand on the doorknob. "Is this why she ran out of here? Did you ask her to go along with this lie of yours to break up Jack and me?"

"She ran out of here because the memory still overwhelms her. She's sickened and disgusted by it." She shook her head, remembering how pale and sallow Lexi had looked, sitting across from Frannie at the Italian restaurant. The scent of tomato, garlic, and basil had hung in the air there too. The shadows under her eyes. The way she jumped at every little sound and glanced over her shoulder like she was being hunted. "You should have seen her after, Mom. You should have seen the damage."

Frannie was still shaking, but the fury was fading, leaving behind the familiar wake of helplessness.

"She has a good life, Frannie. A happy family. A job she loves. From where I'm standing, she's not the one who's damaged."

Frannie struggled to find words. Her mother opened the front door to leave. Frannie grabbed her arm.

"Mom, please do one thing for me the next time you talk to Jack Greene. Tell him Lexi and I are fighting. Not about what, but just that we're fighting and that we've been fighting since I came here." The wheels were spinning faster now, careening out of control. "Lie to him. Tell him Lexi never forgave me for stealing the money and blames me for her and Brandon breaking up. Then never speak to Jack Greene again. Promise me you'll do this for me."

Her mother snatched away her arm. "Frannie, what the hell has gotten into you? Maybe we both need a break. I'll call to check on you next week."

Her mother walked out the door and closed it quietly behind her without saying goodbye. Like all of this was Frannie's fault, when she was the only one dealing with the truth and trying to protect them all.

CHAPTER TWENTY-FOUR

A few minutes after ten the next morning, Frannie stepped through the dog-park gate, carrying a drink tray. She spotted Bettina and Sandra working on commands with Max. He responded almost immediately to Sandra's entreaty to heel, which made Bettina jump and clap her hands. That in turn made Max forget to heel and run in front of his favorite person. Sandra gave them both a patient smile and started again.

Lexi was capturing all of it on her phone from her spot on the park bench a few yards away. Frannie had been sending Lexi text messages since her mother had hung up on her at six that morning. She had tried every iteration of apology she could think of and had begged Lexi to call her. Lexi hadn't answered her. Frannie stared down at the drink tray. A large cup of Patrice's famous coffee for Frannie and a large cup of a peppermint-infused herbal tea for Lexi. It was supposed to be good for calming emotions. Frannie had googled it. The scent was pleasant enough, but it wasn't doing a lot to soothe Frannie. Still she held out hope that drinking it would put Lexi in a more accepting frame of mind.

"Hi, Frannie." Sandra had sneaked up on her with Max at her side, just as Frannie had been steeling herself to make an apology.

Bettina, just a few feet behind Max and Sandra, was so excited she hopped from one foot to the other. "Your turn!" Bettina announced as Sandra held out the leash.

"This is a harder command for Bettina to master," Sandra explained, "and I think Max needs an adult to work with him too."

Frannie glanced at the drink tray in her hand then at Lexi.

"You can leave those on the bench," Sandra said.

"Shouldn't Lexi be the adult working with Max though?" Frannie asked.

"Lexi is making good progress." Sandra frowned. "But she and Max need to focus on their mutual trust issues. He already trusts you."

Great. One more reason for Lexi to be pissed at her. But the kid was grinning from ear to ear, and wasn't that what this dog training was all about?

Frannie crossed the grass and stopped at the bench. "Good morning."

Lexi nodded but didn't make eye contact.

"I brought you tea," Frannie said. "Peppermint." She set the carry-out tray on the bench beside Lexi and dropped her oversized purse on the ground. "I'll leave this here, if that's okay."

Lexi remained silent.

"I'll be back shortly. Then we can talk. Lex, I'm sorry."

Still no comment from Lexi. This would take longer than Frannie had hoped. She couldn't remember Lexi ever staying mad at her for more than a few hours. Then again, Frannie had never before ambushed her friend.

Frannie joined Sandra, Bettina, and Max. The three humans spent a few minutes keeping step with Max while Sandra gave the verbal commands. She then turned over the responsibility to Frannie. After a few minutes of mixed results, Sandra laid a hand on Bettina's shoulder.

"Let's let Frannie and Max spend a few minutes working on it alone."

"Sure. You can do it, Francesca." Bettina gave Frannie's hand an encouraging squeeze.

Even from yards away, Frannie saw Lexi flinch. She was the one who had wanted Frannie in Bettina's life, but now she was hurt every time she saw them together. Frannie fumed. When was Lexi going to stop being so damn stubborn and be satisfied with what she had? A devoted husband and a hopeful kid and a mess of a dog and an imperfectly wonderful family. And a friend who really was sorry for what had happened last night.

"Frannie, he's waiting," Sandra prompted.

"Can I walk him over to Lexi?" Frannie asked.

"Sure. Remember, make him heel as you walk, and when you get there, command him to sit."

Frannie did as Sandra instructed, stopping a few feet in front of Lexi and telling Max to sit. He obeyed. Frannie looked over her shoulder to see Bettina giving her a thumbs-up. Frannie held up a finger, asking them for a minute, then sat down beside Lexi. Max tugged at the leash.

"Sit, Max. I need a minute," she said without looking at him. "Listen, Lex, can we just move past this? My mom needed to know the truth, but you're right. I shouldn't have ambushed you like that. If we could just talk—"

"You told her?"

Frannie nodded.

"No." Lexi switched off her phone and threw it into her purse. "Then I'm officially not speaking to you."

Max tugged at the leash.

"Please, Max, sit. Lexi, if you could just accept my apology, we could schedule a time to talk."

Lexi shook her head. "Not everything is about you, Frannie. Today is about Bettina. And Max."

"Max!" Bettina called.

Out of her peripheral vision, Frannie saw Bettina and Sandra running in their direction. Lexi jumped to her feet. Frannie turned slowly toward the dog, trying to make sense of the chaos erupting around her, and saw Max's head buried in her purse.

Her purse.

She jumped to her feet and tugged at the leash. "Max, no! Sit, Max."

Sandra reached them and pulled at Max's collar to get him out of Frannie's bag. Shards of a plastic wrapper hung out of his mouth.

"Was there food in there?" Sandra asked.

Frannie nodded, horror dawning on her. "Cookies."

"What kind?" Sandra asked. "How many?"

Frannie swallowed. "Oreos. An unopened sleeve of them." She glanced at Lexi. The look on her friend's face made it clear that the horror was dawning on her as well. "I didn't have time for breakfast, and I just grabbed them, and—"

"Is he all right?" Bettina asked, panting as she caught up to Sandra. "Did he eat something bad again?"

"Yes, he did," Sandra answered. "Chocolate is very bad for dogs." She glanced at Lexi. "Let's get him into my car. The emergency vet is only ten minutes away."

"Vet?" Bettina clenched her fists at her sides and glared at Frannie. "What did you do to Max? What did you feed my dog?"

"It was an accident." Frannie knelt on one knee in front of the girl. "I swear, I didn't mean for this to happen."

Bettina crossed her arms over her chest. "You were supposed to be watching him."

Sandra picked up Max in her arms, and Lexi grabbed Bettina's hand. "Come on, sweetie. He'll be fine. We just need to get him to the vet's office."

"I'll come too." Frannie jumped to her feet and gathered her purse and the drink tray.

"No!" Lexi and Bettina said together.

Lexi clicked her key fob and unlocked the minivan from a distance. "Bettina, help Sandra get Max settled. I'm right behind you." She turned to Frannie and dropped her voice. "You've done enough damage for the day. And the week and... Just stay away, Frannie. Like I said, this is *not* about you!"

Frannie nodded as she blinked back tears, but no one saw her. They were all hurrying away from her, rallying around Max. As much as Frannie wanted to help them, Lexi was right. Frannie had screwed up six ways from Sunday over this past week. She threw the untouched drinks into a trash can and sank down on the bench and watched Lexi and company drive away. The way she had driven Lexi away last night, and then Crystal. And Seth last weekend.

She had only meant to help them. All of them. But it was like 2011 all over again, and she was ruining everything and everyone she touched. *The best-laid fucking plans...*

IT WAS LATE, WELL PAST Bettina's bedtime, and the kid was struggling to keep her eyes open. Frannie knelt beside her bed, eternally grateful to Rob for opening the door. He probably wouldn't have if Lexi had been home, but he told Frannie she had gone to pick up Max from his all-day stint at the vet.

"I'm so sorry, Bettina. I swear, it was an accident."

Bettina rolled onto her side, away from Frannie. "You're the adult. You're supposed to do better."

"I know that. And I will do better. I promise." Frannie closed her eyes and silently cursed herself. What the hell was she doing, making promises she couldn't keep? She always meant to do better, yet she so rarely succeeded. She opened her eyes and tried again. "Your dad said Max will be fine. And he'll be home soon. That will be great, right?"

"I think you should go," Bettina said. "I don't think Max will want to see you."

The lump in Frannie's throat tightened. She sucked in a breath, catching the scent of lavender and vanilla and home on the sheets. She patted Bettina's shoulder then lurched to her feet. "Of course. I don't want to upset Max more than I already have. But could you tell him I'm sorry—really, really sorry, from the bottom of my heart?"

Bettina closed her eyes and didn't answer.

"Okay. Well, call me soon. Whenever you're ready. Let me know how Max is doing."

Frannie slipped out of the room just as Rob reached the top of the stairs. "Hey, someone is here."

Frannie's heart hammered. "Is Lexi home already?"

He shook his head. "Listen, Lexi told me what happened last night. And for the record, I understand why you did it, but Jesus, Frannie, that was unfair."

"I know." Frannie followed Rob down the stairs, speaking to his back as they went. Speaking to people's backs seemed to be her new normal. "And I'm sorry. I screwed up."

Rob halted at the foot of the stairs. "Lexi also told me Greene paid you a visit. You should have told us right away. That guy is dangerous."

"There's nothing anyone can do," Frannie said, stepping off the bottom stair and into the foyer.

"Isn't there?"

Frannie turned toward the man who had just emerged from the dining room and spoken.

"Seth."

Frannie's eyes met his for a brief moment, and she waited for him to greet her or at least smile in her direction. Instead, he held out a manual to Rob.

"Okay, I've got the cameras set up all around the perimeter," Seth said to Rob. "I've loaded the software, but you'll want to read the manual to understand how to back up the data. All that video footage will take up a lot of memory, so you should burn it to an external hard drive."

Frannie stood still and silent. She should say something, but she didn't know what. Ever the outcast.

"Well," she said to no one in particular, "I should..." She took a step toward the front door.

Rob moved into her path. "You can't go home alone, Frannie. Not until we secure your place too. Greene already showed up there once."

"Which you failed to mention to anyone at the time." Seth bent over his small duffle bag that was on the table, still not meeting her eyes.

"I told Lexi I'd seen him and what he said. And it wasn't about her. It was about my mother."

"It affects us all," Rob said. "And we all need to be more careful."

Frannie nodded. "It looks like you're covered here."

"And what about you?" Rob asked.

Frannie told herself she didn't care that it wasn't Seth asking the question and worrying about her safety. "I won't walk home from the diner alone after dark anymore. And I'll keep the dead bolts locked."

Seth sighed and finally looked at her. "The back door doesn't have a dead bolt. Just a chain lock."

Now Frannie crossed her arms over her chest and tried to match Rob's annoyed expression. "That door leads to a tiny balcony with no stairs to the ground. It's basically a fire escape."

Seth swung the duffle bag over his shoulder. "You're on the second floor. Hardly a difficult climb for someone who's motivated. You'll need security cameras on both the doors."

Rob leaned against the front door, making it clear Frannie was stuck here until these two alpha males agreed on what was necessary to keep the little lady safe. "You already put up cameras at the diner, didn't you?" Rob asked.

Seth nodded. "Patrice asked me to do it about a month ago."

Frannie's heart stuck in her throat as she remembered exactly when that was. The day she and Seth had met. Well, had met again, after years and worlds and lifetimes apart.

"I'll take Frannie home and take inventory of what needs to be done at the apartment building," Rob said.

"No. Stay here and take care of your family." Seth glanced at Frannie. "We're adults. We can set aside our differences for the sake of safety. Right, Frannie?"

She was pretty damn sure she didn't agree. She had no intention of setting aside their differences. She wasn't the one who had stormed out of the apartment and hadn't bothered to call or text. Okay, so she hadn't called or texted him, either, but that wasn't on her because she wasn't the one who had left. Those were the rules of dating. Or breaking up or whatever they were doing.

"Frannie, you're okay with that?" Rob touched her shoulder.

She was exhausted from the day and overwhelmed by the testosterone in the room. Still, she deferred to a lesson Lexi had tried to teach her countless times, something about catching more flies with honey.

She dropped her shoulders and raised her eyebrows and tried to look pathetic, which couldn't be too hard in her current state. "Can't this wait? Jack Greene's after my mother, not me."

Seth pulled his keys out of his pocket and made a noise that was somewhere between a grunt and a sigh. "You have no goddamn idea what he might be after. It's late, I'm tired, and I have a long drive home tonight, so if you could get over yourself, let's get this done."

Frannie's jaw dropped as her mind raced to find something suitably cutting to say.

Rob stepped between her and Seth. "Frannie, I know this is a pain in the ass, but please, do it for me. And for Lexi and Bettina. You're important to them. To this family."

After the last two days, Frannie wasn't so sure any of them would really care if something happened to her. But both men were right. Jack Greene was a wild card—and a dangerous one. Hours from now, when she was alone in her bed, hearing noises she couldn't identify, she had to be able to stay calm and maybe even get some sleep, knowing Jack Greene couldn't get to her. And she would have Rob's insistence to thank for it.

"Fine," she agreed. "Let's make this quick, Collins."

Seth glared at her. "Right behind you, Willets."

Frannie said good night to Rob as she walked past him. Seth followed her to her car. He bumped against her shoulder when she slowed her walk to dig her keys out of her jeans pocket, and her heart sped up in the weird little triplet beat it only played when he got too close to her. When she watched her climb into her car, she stared back at him like an idiot until he broke the gaze and climbed into the driver's side of his pickup truck.

Get it together. He's only coming home with you to set up security. But the look in his eyes told her he had been thinking the same thing she had: there could be worse things than being alone together at her apartment.

CHAPTER TWENTY-FIVE
February 2007

Lexi realized long before Frannie did that Frannie was in love with Seth Collins. Like ten years before. Although if it hadn't been for Clarissa James and her slumber party in the tenth grade, Lexi might have missed it.

It wasn't the first time Frannie and Lexi had been invited to one of the parties of the shiny girls, as they called Clarissa's four-girl clique. They had even attended some of them, usually the afternoon birthday parties where they had arrived with a joint gift, occasionally the pool parties at Jen Dartmoor's house. Frannie always rolled her eyes and said it was Lexi's fault they were invited because everyone loved Lexi. Lexi knew the parties bored Frannie to tears, and Frannie only went to them to make her best friend happy.

But at that slumber party, the first time they had agreed to stay overnight somewhere other than each other's houses, Lexi started to wonder whether they had both been wrong all along. About the reason for being invited, not Frannie's general boredom with the whole idea of group hangouts. While Lexi was sure Frannie's apathy toward normal teenage events was often a cover for her hurt feelings over being excluded, when it came to shiny-girl parties, Frannie was definitely not interested.

Now Lexi sat at Clarissa's dressing table with a mirror, in which she could see Frannie on the opposite side of the room, on a cushioned window seat, where she had taken up residence with a book. It was her well-worn copy of *Wuthering Heights*, which they wouldn't be required to read for English class until next year. Clarissa stood behind Lexi with a brush in one hand and hair clips in the other as she tried to wrangle Lexi's frizzy curls into a sleek updo. Clarissa's own light-brown hair was smooth and well-behaved in the chignon Jen had given her.

"More product," Jen suggested from her spot on the floor, where she sat in a triangle with Bradee and Jayde.

Clarissa reached over Lexi's shoulder for the bottle of defrizzer. "How many books does Willets read in, like, a month?" she asked in a low voice.

Lexi met her eyes in the mirror, not sure how to interpret her question. She didn't know exactly, and sometimes Frannie reread books or didn't finish ones that sucked. Lexi guessed it was at least twenty a month, but she wasn't sure if that was something Clarissa would hold against Frannie. "I'm not sure."

"She's smart, but not in a stuck-up way like Madison Berger," Clarissa said.

A knot Lexi had just noticed in her stomach eased.

"And she could be really pretty," Clarissa continued. "Do you think she'd let me show her how to put on some makeup?"

No. No, she did not think Frannie would allow that, unless maybe Lexi begged her.

Clarissa was grinning as she tugged at the ends of Lexi's hair. Lexi narrowed her eyes. "Why are you so anxious to put makeup on Frannie?"

Clarissa glanced in the mirror at Frannie, still reading, happily oblivious to what the shiny girls were doing or planning. "I'll tell you in private," Clarissa whispered. Louder, she said, "This is going to take some heavy-duty product. My mom has some stuff in her bathroom."

Clarissa grabbed Lexi's hand and tugged her out of the chair. She led Lexi down the hall, through her parents' bedroom, and into a large, white-tiled bathroom that was as big as Lexi's bedroom and about twice as big as Frannie's. She closed and locked the door behind them then whirled to face Lexi with what her dad would call a shit-eating grin on her face. Which was totally gross but totally fit Clarissa's wide smile.

"Someone has a huge crush on Frannie," she said.

"What? Who? How do you know?" Lexi wasn't surprised. She knew how amazing Frannie truly was. But how could a guy have been interested in Frannie without her best friend knowing? It was like Lexi had failed Frannie somehow.

Clarissa threw back her shoulders, enjoying the moment and the secret knowledge she held over Lexi. Lexi hated her a little bit just then.

"Seth Collins," Clarissa whispered even though no one could hear them.

"No way." Lexi shook her head. She would have believed one of the Jonas Brothers had driven through Indiana, spotted Frannie on the side of the road, and fallen hopelessly in love with her at first sight before she bought Seth Collins liking her. "She hates Seth Collins. It's mutual." Or so Lexi had thought. Maybe. But maybe not.

Clarissa knelt down to rummage through the cabinet under her mother's sink. "I saw it with my own eyes."

"Saw what?" Lexi knelt down to be level with her.

Clarissa pulled out a gray bottle of something and motioned to Lexi to sit on the closed toilet. "Saw him hitting on her at her locker."

"Hitting on her?" Lexi twisted around to look Clarissa in the eye to see if she was lying.

Clarissa turned Lexi's face forward and massaged thick cream into her hair. "Well, flirting with her at least. I overheard him invite her to Tom's party."

"Tom's party was last night. Frannie didn't go." She'd had dinner at Lexi's house, like she had almost every Friday night for years, since her mother had gotten promoted to assistant weekend manager at the drugstore.

"I didn't say she took him up on the offer," Clarissa said. "But she didn't look totally icked out about it either." Clarissa ran a brush through Lexi's hair, which was now surprisingly tamed. "But there were sparks flying between them, trust me. I know about these things."

Clarissa *had* had a lot of boyfriends.

"Wait." Another knot formed in Lexi's gut. "Didn't you date Seth for a while?"

Clarissa rolled her eyes. "For, like, five minutes last year. I mean, I was only in ninth grade." She made it sound like last year was a lifetime ago. "He's not really my type. He's hot and all that but kind of serious. He's like Frannie that way. Now Sam…" She arched her eyebrows and grinned at Lexi in the mirror.

"You like Sam Collins?"

She shrugged one shoulder. "A little bit. He's kind of immature sometimes, but he's a lot of fun. When he's a senior like Seth is now, he might be dating material."

Wow. Two years from now. As high school dating went, that was playing the long game.

Clarissa turned Lexi toward the bathroom mirror and twisted and tugged at her hair again, this time with better results.

"But wait," Lexi said again, playing over the conversation in her head. "If Seth already likes Frannie, why does she need makeup? It sounds like he needs to make her like *him*." Assuming she didn't already, if Clarissa was right about the sparks.

"Didn't you ever see *Grease*?" Clarissa asked.

"Oh god, my mother loves that movie."

"Mine too," Clarissa said. "This is like the scene at the end of the movie when Olivia Newton-John's friends do her hair and makeup and sew her into those black pants. Danny already has a crush on her, but when he sees her like that, he can't be cool anymore. He totally loses it."

"Okay, so the plan is to make Seth totally lose it."

"Yeah. I'm like a fairy godmother and matchmaker all in one." Clarissa pushed a couple of hairpins into place. "There!" she said, holding out her hands to present Lexi to herself in the mirror. "I'm a miracle worker. First you, next Frannie."

Lexi followed her back down the hall, wondering the whole time what she should tell Frannie about all this. Then again, Frannie was the one Seth had flirted with, and she hadn't mentioned anything about it, leaving Lexi to find out from Clarissa. Lexi hated Frannie a little bit just then too.

Back in Clarissa's bedroom, the other three shiny girls had some-how gotten Frannie to join them on the floor. She was smiling at something Jen was saying, but when she caught Lexi's eye, she raised her eyebrows ever so slightly to convey that she was mildly horrified to be the center of attention.

"Frannie's next," Clarissa announced, which made Frannie's expression of mild distress morph into a look of *hell no*.

Lexi smiled and shook her head at Frannie to assure her there was nothing to worry about. Frannie flashed back a genuine smile, the kind she saved just for Lexi, her true best friend, and whatever jealousy Lexi had felt over Clarissa knowing a secret she had learned from eavesdropping disappeared.

"But it's going to require sustenance," Clarissa said. "Jen, help me raid the kitchen. Frannie"—she motioned to the chair in front of the makeup table—"make yourself comfortable. When I return, I shall perform more magic." She frowned as she leaned close to the top of Frannie's head. "Although in this case it will be more of a miracle."

The other shiny girls tittered with laughter while Frannie, who was an expert at keeping her emotion-hiding mask in place at all times, went pink along the edges of her cheeks. This called for a defense from Frannie's best friend in the world. But instead, Lexi feigned interest in the New Direction poster on Clarissa's wall and kept her mouth shut.

Clarissa and Jen headed to the kitchen while Bradee and Jayde continued whatever conversation Frannie had been pretending to enjoy. Lexi patted the makeup chair, and Frannie scowled but sat down in it. She stared down at her fingernails, refusing to look at Lexi again.

"You know how Clarissa is." Lexi squeezed Frannie's shoulders. "She just says things to create drama."

And pain. Lexi knew that about her, knew that about all the shiny girls, yet she had dragged Frannie to this slumber party. But why did it have to be so hard? Why couldn't Frannie lighten up a little bit and enjoy being invited by the cool kids for one night? A white-hot anger flashed through Lexi.

"I wouldn't do this for anyone but you," Frannie said, still staring down at her hands.

Lexi didn't know if she meant submitting to Clarissa's makeover or coming to the party in the first place. Either way, it was the truth. Lexi's anger deflated. "I know. Well, me and maybe Seth Collins?"

"I wondered what Clarissa had overheard," she said. That was Frannie, never missing a thing. She grabbed Lexi's hand and met her eyes in the mirror. "I didn't tell you about it because there's nothing to tell, by the way." She hadn't missed Lexi's hurt feelings either.

The hollow place left behind by Lexi's anger filled back up with guilt. In that moment, she understood that they—or at least Frannie—were there to be a sideshow for the shiny girls to enjoy. "Clarissa's not going to believe you."

"I don't care what Clarissa believes," Frannie said. "Just you. But I'm not looking forward to whatever she has planned for my hair."

Lexi grimaced. "And your face."

Before Frannie could escape from the makeup chair, Clarissa and Jen returned, weighted down with boxes and bags of treats. Jen tossed an ice-cream sandwich—the kind Frannie ate at the end of school lunch a couple times a week—in Frannie's direction, and she caught it.

"Thanks," she said.

Lexi waited for her to protest when Clarissa stood behind her and assessed her, but Frannie transformed her face into the blank slate it usually was around people other than Lexi and bit through chocolate and ice cream.

"We'll do your hair last," Clarissa said. "It's so pretty, I think we'll just do some ribbon curls, don't you think, Jen?" Clarissa ran her hands through Frannie's red locks like she was a professional stylist looking for inspiration. "Such a gorgeous color. Promise me you'll never change it."

Clarissa didn't seem to mind that Frannie remained silent, and no one else seemed to notice that Frannie smiled to herself. If Lexi had to guess, she would have said Frannie's plan to dye her hair had moved up on her list of priorities. Clarissa should enjoy the red color now because by Monday, it would probably be gone. Lexi's mom always said actions spoke louder than words, and right now, the look on Frannie's face told Lexi her reaction to Clarissa's primping would be a silent roar.

As she watched Clarissa fuss and Frannie scheme, Lexi wondered if Seth Collins would like Frannie as a jet-black brunette as much as he liked her as a redhead.

CHAPTER TWENTY-SIX
2016

Seth stepped into Frannie's apartment before her. She followed him and closed the door behind them. She waited by the door while he checked her bedroom and closet then her bathroom. It all seemed very dramatic and a little over the top, especially since her run-in with Greene had been nearly a week ago, but she couldn't deny that it felt nice to have someone make a fuss over her.

Seth walked down the small hallway between the bedroom and bathroom that led to the back door. He opened it and looked out over the backyard then closed and locked it.

"It's a sturdy chain lock but not enough." He walked to the main room and picked up one of the straight-back kitchen chairs. Carrying it to the back door, he jammed the back under the doorknob. "Surprisingly effective. It'll do for tonight. Rob will come by tomorrow to install a dead bolt."

"Thank you." Frannie rolled her shoulders, realizing she'd had them hunched up almost to her ears for most of the day. She moved toward the refrigerator. "Can I get you something to drink?"

He shook his head. "I saw some of your neighbors' lights still on. I want to talk to them before it gets too late, ask them to be on the lookout for anything out of the ordinary. I'll be back shortly. Can you boot up your laptop while I'm gone? I'll need to install the camera software."

"Oh, okay. I'll just—"

But he was already out the door.

Frannie pulled a half bottle of white wine out of the refrigerator and two glasses out of the cupboard, despite what Seth had said. She poured herself a small glass and took a sip to calm her nerves then grabbed her laptop off the coffee table and sat at the kitchen table while it whirred to life.

Seth returned before she expected him, knocking gently before entering. "I spoke to the neighbors on each side of you. They'll keep an eye on things. I told them to call 911 if anything worries them." He glanced at her. "You should do the same. I mean it. Fearless as you are, err on the side of caution."

She nodded, rendered silent by his use of her now-favorite nickname, and mesmerized by his cool, focused efficiency. She couldn't remember ever seeing anything so fascinating, so virile. So utterly sexy.

"And your neighbor downstairs who cranks her air conditioner up to the max."

"Mrs. Beale."

He nodded. "Her lights were off, so talk to her in the morning if you can. And I'll talk to Patrice about getting a quieter air conditioner installed as soon as possible."

"I'll talk to Patrice."

He shook his head. "I'll let her know it's for security reasons and give her some options."

So. Damn. Sexy.

He leaned close to her to see the computer screen. He navigated to a website and downloaded a program then checked his phone for a code that he punched into her laptop.

She leaned closer to him, drawn by the muscles of his arms and the clean scent of him.

"Please don't," he said quietly without looking at her.

The regret she heard in his voice made her lean back in her seat and turn away from him.

A minute later, he stepped away from the table and reached into his backpack. "I'm going to do a quick-and-dirty installation of these cameras tonight. Rob will put them on brackets when he comes by to install the new lock."

Half an hour later, he had installed cameras and trained one on each of her doors. He pulled out one of the kitchen chairs and moved it a foot farther from her, typed something into her computer, then turned the screen toward her.

"These are the camera feeds. That's your front door on the left, the back door on the right."

"Wow." The images were black and white and slightly grainy, but even with almost no light, she could see the doors and balconies clearly.

"They're night vision," he explained. "Keep the computer by your bed during the night. If you hear anything, check the feeds. If you don't hear anything but you just get a bad feeling, check the feeds. And if you see something..." He glanced at her.

"Call 911."

He nodded his approval then got to his feet.

"Seth, wait." She stood and took a step toward him and laid her hand on his chest.

He didn't touch her, but he didn't step away from her either.

She ran her hand up his chest to rest on his shoulder. "Could you stop being angry at me for a minute?"

"I can't do this right now, Frannie."

She put her other hand on his other shoulder. "Stay." She stated it, but they both knew she was asking. Begging.

He pulled her hands off his shoulders and pressed them to his lips. "Has anything changed?"

"Everything's changed." She took a step toward him and pressed her body against his. He was heat and hard muscle and raw desire. "I know Jack Greene is dating my mother at least in part to harass me. Maybe also because he's old and lonely. But he's made it clear he's not going away, so I have to get my mother away from him."

"And then what?" He met her gaze. "Will you stay?"

Her mouth went dry. All she had to say was yes. She didn't have to mean it. She just had to say it. But she couldn't lie to him. And she wasn't sure she was really wanted here in Licking, in Lexi's life, so how could she promise to stay?

"Your silence says it all." He stepped back from her.

She grabbed his hand and kissed his palm. "That doesn't mean you have to leave. Just stay tonight."

He pulled away from her. "Stop it, Frannie. Stop trying to fuck me into compliance."

"That's not what I'm doing."

"Isn't it? Because it sure looks like that from where I'm standing." He slung his backpack over his shoulder.

"No, wait." She reached for him again. "I just haven't figured things out yet."

"I get that," he said, moving to the door. "But that doesn't work for me."

"Seth—"

"Goddamnit, Frannie, we're through here. Lock the door behind me." He looked at her with a heartbreaking coldness in his eyes. "Take care of yourself." He slammed the door behind him.

The pain cut deep and hard. She doubled over and fought to catch her breath. But what had she expected? She couldn't do this. She couldn't curl into a ball on the floor and wait for the next shoe to drop. She took deep yoga breaths that would make Lexi proud. If Lexi knew. If Lexi would ever deign to speak to her again.

When the sharp ache in her belly subsided, Frannie straightened herself. She stared at her laptop, her mind doing what it always did when trouble came for her: building a plan. But she had learned a few new tricks since she had first run up against Jack Greene, not the least of which was that one plan is never enough. Always bring a backup. And with Greene, maybe a backup for the backup. She sat down, typed Greene's full name and address into the search bar, and started chasing him down rabbit holes all across the Internet.

ON WEDNESDAY NIGHT, the dinner rush at the diner died down by seven. Frannie took advantage of the slow pace and told Beth she was going on a break. She slid into one of the chairs at the small table in the corner of the kitchen, just outside Patrice's office, and checked her phone. Nothing. Not a single text message or voicemail or missed call. Other than her parole officer calling on Monday, no one had tried to contact Frannie since last Friday, the day everything she had planned had started blowing up in her face.

Lexi, Bettina, and Max were all fine. In this Podunk town, Frannie would have heard if they hadn't been. Plus she had caught a few glimpses of them at the park. Seth was no doubt fine as well. He had built a great life for himself before Frannie had crashed back into it. He would move on and soon probably wouldn't even miss her. For all she knew, he might be over her already.

This was the plan. The original, primary, one-to-rule-them-all plan. Make sure everyone was happy and living their best lives without Frannie so she could slip off into the night. The only one who wasn't fine was Frannie. The nonstop pain in her belly and the perpetual lump in her throat hadn't been part of the deal, but they wouldn't go away.

Then again, she wasn't 100 percent sure everyone was safe and happy. Her mother hadn't returned a single call or text since she had hung up on Frannie Saturday morning. It was probably just Crystal drama, but Frannie would feel better if she heard it straight from her mother. Maybe she should drive to her mother's house. Or maybe...

Frannie thumbed through her phone's contact list and tapped on the number of the pharmacy her mother managed. After a few rings, she got the voicemail system. She tapped zero until she was routed to a person. She recognized the voice of the woman who answered.

"Hi, Marianne. This is Frannie."

"Frannie, how are you, darlin'? You haven't stopped by the store in forever. But your mama mentioned you're living a few hours away now."

Frannie smiled in the hopes of making her voice pleasant and re-laxed. "I am. And speaking of my mother, I've been trying to call her, but I think something might be wrong with her cell phone. Could you get her for me?"

"Oh." Marianne's voice changed. "She's not here tonight."

Frannie furrowed her brow. Was Marianne, a kind, good Christian woman Frannie had known since childhood, lying to her? "But she always works on Wednesday nights."

"She does, darlin', but she took a few vacation days. Left yester-day."

"Wait, she left, like she's actually taking a vacation?" Frannie could count on one hand the number of times her mother had left Smithton for a vacation. "Did she go with someone? Maybe her boyfriend?"

"Listen, Frannie, if Crystal didn't discuss this with you, I'm not comfortable—"

"Marianne, please." Frannie rubbed her sore neck and threw back her shoulders. If a little white lie or two was what it took to find her mother, it was worth it. "I'm sorry to involve you in this, but the truth is my mom and I had an argument, and she's ignoring my calls." Frannie leaned forward and dropped her voice. "And here's the thing: I have to get ahold of her. I'm in some trouble, and I really need her help."

"Oh, Frannie. What happened? Is there anything I can do?"

She had Marianne on the hook like she knew was necessary, but she didn't feel good about it. She would come clean and apologize later. After she was sure her mother was safe. "I just need to talk to my mom. And to know where she is. Did you say she went with someone?"

"I'm pretty sure she went alone," Marianne said. She dropped her voice to a near whisper as well now that she and Frannie were co-conspirators. "The truth is, I think she might have had a big fight with Jack. She said she needed to cut loose and get a little wild."

Shit. "Wild" and Frannie's mother did not go well together. But could Frannie dare to hope her mother was on a bender because Jack Greene was out of the picture? "Do you know where she went?"

"Louisville."

Kentucky. Across state lines. Her mother might as well be on the moon as far as Frannie was concerned.

"Marianne, could you do me a huge favor? Like I said, I hate to put you in the middle of this, but I really need my mom to call me. She's more likely to answer if you call her from the store."

Marianne hesitated then sighed. "What do you want me to tell her?"

"Let her know I'm in trouble, and ask her to call me right away."

"Okay, I'll call right now. You take care of yourself, Frannie."

Frannie stared down at her phone as minutes ticked past, waiting for it to ring in her hand. When Patrice stepped out of her office, Frannie looked up.

"Dinner rush is over," Frannie said. "I needed a break."

"That's fine," Patrice said then frowned. "You look worried. What's wrong?"

Frannie shook her head. "Just waiting for a call back from my mother." When Patrice didn't walk away, Frannie frowned too. "She hasn't been returning my calls, and now I found out she went to Kentucky to cut loose." Her phone rang for the first time in days. "I have to take this."

"I'm sure she's fine." Patrice patted Frannie's shoulder then headed for the dining room.

Frannie answered the call. "Mom, you worried me."

"Frannie, are you all right? Marianne said you're in trouble. Is it something about your parole? Do you need bail money?"

"No, Mom. I'm okay. There's nothing wrong." Other than the fact that her own mother heard "trouble" in association with her daughter's name and instantly thought *criminal*. "I've been texting and calling you for days and haven't heard a word from you."

"Sweetie, I'm fine. Just needed a little break from that dingy old house. It's too quiet. It's lonely. " She slurred as she spoke. Which meant she wouldn't be able to drive herself home anytime soon.

"Are you really in Louisville? Did you go alone or with someone?"

"Of course I'm alone. It's not like I have anyone to go with me."

Frannie took a calming breath. Alone wasn't great, but it was a damn sight better than being with Jack Greene. "Where are you staying?"

"What does that matter?"

"Mom, I want to know where to find you."

Her mother grunted. "Do you plan to join me? I'm across state lines, Frannie."

Frannie sighed. "I'm guessing that was part of the appeal of Louisville. How about this: promise me you'll head to bed now, get some good sleep, and when you're awake and sober, you'll drive to my place. I have the day off tomorrow. We'll do something together. Get a mani-pedi or something. Just you and me."

"That's sweet, Frannie. You miss your old mom. But how long is that going to last, huh?"

"What do you mean?"

"I mean, I know you're going to run. I suspected it, but Jack confirmed it. He said you're going to do what Brandon did. I know I disappointed you...." Her mother's voice shook, and her words trailed off.

Frannie winced. "Don't listen to him. You and I have had our problems, but I want to bring you home. Just tell me where you are."

"Don't you worry about me. I'm making new friends. I was having drinks at a place called the Blue Rooster, and I got invited to an after-hours... I can't remember. He wrote it down for me."

Frannie jotted down Blue Rooster on her palm. "He, who? Someone you know?"

"Bob, I think. Or Bill. Ben?"

It didn't matter that her mother couldn't remember the loser's name because he had probably given her a fake one.

"Don't go anywhere with that guy, okay?" Frannie said.

"I already told you, he's taking me to a party tonight. But I'll follow your advice about getting some rest first."

"Mom, please."

"Stop worrying. Everything is fine. I have to go now, but I'll call you on Friday."

Frannie wanted to agree. She wanted everything to be okay. But she had a really bad feeling about her mother gallivanting around at after-hours parties with Bob or Bill or Ben. Her mother never dealt well with breakups, and if that's what had happened between her and Jack, who knew what self-destructive thing her mother might do.

"I'm really tired," her mother said.

"Mom, I'm going to—" The line went silent. "Seriously, you just hung up on me?"

Frannie dropped her head into her hands and groaned. She ran through the few options she had. None were good, but leaving her mother to her own devices in her current state was the worst of the bunch. She left the kitchen and joined Patrice behind the counter. Thankfully, only one small party had arrived since Frannie had gone on break, and Beth was taking care of them.

"Patrice, I was supposed to close tonight, but is there any chance I can leave now?"

Patrice arched an eyebrow. "Emergency?"

"Kind of."

"Should I be worried about you? Maybe concerned that you'll do something stupid like drive out of the state just a couple of weeks shy of being off parole?"

Frannie rubbed the back of her neck. "I'll try to call my mother back and talk her into sobering up and coming home. But if I can't..."

Patrice emptied a coffeepot then nodded toward the kitchen. Frannie followed her.

"What about Seth? Can you send him? Or Rob?"

Frannie shook her head. She couldn't ask this favor. Even if any of them were speaking to her, it wouldn't do any good. "I don't know where she's staying. She mentioned a bar, but that's all I have to go on. And if I do find her, my odds of dragging her back here before she gets into trouble are slim. Anyone else's will be zero."

Patrice stopped by the back door. "Two things: One, I'm going to keep an eye on you until I see you go into your apartment; and two, if anything happens and you only get one phone call, you call me. I'll leave my cell phone on overnight. My daughter knows some of the best defense attorneys in the state, and a lot of them owe her favors."

A cold dread settled in the pit of Frannie's belly. Something clattered in the kitchen, and she had a flash of a steel cell door clanging closed behind her. "God, I hope it doesn't come to that. But if it does, I'll call you."

Who else would she call anyway? Frannie Willets was on her own.

CHAPTER TWENTY-SEVEN

Back at her apartment and freshly showered, Frannie tucked her black button-down blouse into her black jeans and glanced in the mirror. All she needed was her blue apron and she would look like she was on her way back to the diner for another shift. As she twisted her hair into a ponytail and secured it with a hair band, there was a knock at her front door.

"Shit." The list of who could be visiting her was short. In fact, it was nonexistent.

The knocking didn't stop. Frannie cracked open the front door before Mrs. Beale started yelling about the racket. Since her quieter air conditioner had been delivered a few days earlier, the old bird could hear every sound within a five-mile radius.

Lexi stood on the other side of the door. She didn't take a hint from the narrow crack and pushed her way into the apartment.

"Come in." Frannie scowled as she closed the front door. She took one look at Lexi's all-black outfit and shook her head. "No."

"No, what? I haven't even said anything."

"You don't have to. We look like twins." Frannie glanced down at her much-shorter body then at Lexi's black knit hat with her hair tucked under it. "Kind of. But despite your good taste in criminal attire, you are not coming with me."

"Oh, you're going somewhere?" Lexi crossed her arms over her chest and gave Frannie her best bossy teacher look. "Because I hadn't heard you were going anywhere, at least not from you."

"I thought we weren't speaking to each other."

"It was an argument, Frannie, not a breakup. You can't make a run for the border without telling me or letting me have your back."

"News travels fast. Patrice?"

Lexi didn't answer.

Frannie rubbed the back of her neck. "I'm not leaving the country, just going to Louisville to bring my mother home before she gets herself into trouble. And you are not getting caught helping an ex-con violate parole."

"I want to help Crystal too. I meant what I said about owing her. And I brought a gift for you. For luck." She pulled something out of her pocket.

"The luck of not getting caught? Do you hear how risky this is?" Frannie refused to look at what Lexi held out to her. "Fine. Whatever it is, I'll take it with me. Just leave it there." She pointed to the kitchen table, but Lexi stepped past Frannie into the living room.

"Come over here where the light's better, and hold out your arm."

Frannie sighed loudly and rolled her eyes. "Fine, but then you leave."

Lexi fastened something around her wrist, and Frannie looked down at it. Five charms dangled from a delicate silver chain: a sun, a moon, a dog, a heart, and a #BFF. Tears welled in her eyes. "Is this—?"

Lexi nodded. "Your mom let me take it with me when I visited her a few years ago." She handed an identical bracelet to Frannie. "Here, you have to put mine on me." She grinned. "Otherwise, the magic won't work."

The magic. Frannie smiled, too, as she secured the bracelet on Lexi's wrist. They had whispered schoolgirl incantations about unending friendship and undying love when they had woven their first friendship bracelets in the third grade. Lexi had bought the silver replacements and given Frannie hers on their last night together before they went their separate ways, Lexi off to college and Frannie off to a bigger town where she could work enough jobs to earn the money for vet tech school.

"Star light, star bright, first star I see tonight," Frannie whispered.

Lexi's look grew serious. "I wish I may, I wish I might, have the wish I make tonight."

They hugged then clasped left hands and pressed their bracelets together.

"We should have worn these the night we ran away. Things would have gone differently," Lexi said.

"I wish a lot of things had gone differently, then and now. I'm sorry about Friday night. And then Saturday with Max."

"Max was an accident." Lexi smiled as she shook her head. "The dog is a walking accident waiting to happen every minute of every day. As for Friday..." She fingered the bracelet on her wrist. "We're good, Frannie." She glanced up at her friend. "I mean it."

Frannie nodded because she didn't trust herself to speak without bursting into tears. Those were the same words Frannie had said to Lexi a few weeks earlier. When Lexi said them now, it sounded like she really meant them, just as Frannie had. She touched her own bracelet and hoped the charms would keep her safe tonight.

It was a schoolgirl fantasy, always had been, but god, how Frannie wanted to believe in the magical protective power of the bracelets. She and Lexi used to swear the magic in their thread bracelets had kept them safe from shiny girls, thoughtless boys, and overbearing parents. Then they had outgrown their talismans, cut the too-tight threads off their wrists, and everything between and around them had begun to change. But maybe that was just how growing up happened.

Another knock at the door startled Frannie out of her reverie.

"I'll get it," Lexi said, and with her long strides, she beat Frannie to the door. She opened it wide to let in Rob, who was loaded down with a large thermos and a plastic grocery bag.

"No." Frannie crossed her arms over her chest.

Rob grinned. "Nice to see you too." He glanced at both women. "You two look ready for a covert op."

Frannie looked him up and down, with his hooded sweatshirt, jeans, and sneakers, all in black. "So do you, which is odd since you're not going anywhere other than back to your own house. With your wife."

He held the thermos in the air, ignoring her. "Nectar of the gods, also known as Patrice's coffee. Patrice asked me to remind you to keep it down at this dinner party so she doesn't get complaints." He set the thermos on the table.

"Dinner party? That's not much of a cover story," Frannie said in a quiet voice. "But I appreciate the coffee."

Patrice's coffee had its own kind of magic, not the least of which was the ability to keep Frannie awake all night. It couldn't hurt to take it with her when she made the two-hour drive then traipsed around Louisville for god knows how long in search of her mother. *Alone.* Because if Frannie got caught, she was not taking anyone else down with her.

Lexi kissed Rob on the lips. "When will Patrice get here?"

"Patrice?" Frannie shook her head. "Y'all have lost your damn minds. None of you are going with me."

"Of course not Patrice," Rob said. "She's our babysitter. Come on, sweetie," he called over his shoulder. "We're letting all the cold air out of Frannie's apartment."

A few seconds later, Bettina appeared in the doorway, with Max on his pink leash trotting right behind her. Bettina slid off her pink backpack and handed it to her dad, who unzipped it and fished around, pulling out a folded piece of pink construction paper, which he handed to his daughter.

Frannie gripped the back of a kitchen chair, ready to demand they all leave. She just needed a minute to steady herself for the withering gaze the kid would shoot her way. As far as Bettina was concerned, none of Frannie's other crimes—past or future—came close to what she had done to Max. Now the girl took the paper from her dad and marched right toward Frannie, who braced herself.

Bettina held out the paper. "Max made this for you."

Frannie took the offering and unfolded it. On the left side of the paper, there was a picture of a yellow-haired girl, a larger red-haired girl, and a black swirl with a pink line coming off it. She glanced at Bettina, who watched her with wide eyes. "Is this the three of us?" Frannie glanced at the dog. "Thank you, Max. It's beautiful."

"I had to draw it for him. And I had to write this for him too." Bettina pointed to the oversized, uneven letters on the right side of the paper.

I'm sorry. Thank you. From Max (and B)

"My teacher checked the spelling for me," Bettina continued. "Max is sorry for eating your cookies and then getting mad. And he's grateful to you for finding Sarah."

Lexi laid a hand on Bettina's shoulder, and the girl took a deep breath.

"And me too," Bettina. "I'm sorry, and thank you."

Bettina held out her hand. Frannie shook it then swallowed the hard and painful lump that had risen in her throat. Damn it, this evening was going nothing like she had planned.

Bettina glanced around at the adults. "Francesca, why are you dressed like Lexi?"

"Actually, Lexi is dressed like *me*."

That seemed to be enough information for the kid. She nodded. "May I watch the Cartoon Network on your TV, please?"

Frannie didn't bother looking at Lexi and Rob for approval. If they were going to take over her apartment, she felt perfectly justified in making TV choices for their kid. "You may."

"And may Max sit on the sofa with me?"

Frannie looked at the much-improved mutt, recovering nicely from his most recent run-in with toxic substances. His weepy-eyed, mangy-furred days were long behind him, but his paws were filthy. "He may not."

Bettina settled herself on the sofa with the remote control. Without missing a beat, Max jumped up beside her and flopped against his best friend.

Frannie looked at Lexi, who mouthed an apology.

"I have a better idea, kiddo," Rob said. He pulled a small screen and headphones out of Bettina's backpack and set her up with a movie. "Makes it easier for the adults to talk," he said as he rejoined Lexi and Frannie.

"There's nothing for the adults to talk about. You should go home." Frannie glanced at the living room. "Or you can make yourselves comfortable on my muddy sofa. I'll be back around dawn, give or take."

"Not without this." Rob held up a printout of a satellite-image map of Louisville. "You'll need to go old school because you can't take your phone with you."

"I know that. I'm not an idiot," Frannie said. "I have a separate GPS."

Rob nodded. "Well, that sounds like a great plan, unless your parole officer or someone else can link the GPS to you."

"How would they do that?" Frannie asked, but the mere suggestion made her uneasy.

Rob shrugged. "It's just a possibility. And it's as trackable as your phone if someone wants to prove you violated parole by crossing state lines."

Frannie reached for the printouts, but Rob held them away from her.

"We can be useful," Lexi said. "We've got your back."

Frannie's throat tightened as the familiar grip of too much emotion closed around it, that same tightness that always came when anyone got too close. And yet, she wanted to fight it this time. She remembered those days spent making cookies with her mother, when a hug was always just a wish away. And those first heady days of Lexi's friendship, when someone had suddenly switched on the sun in Frannie's world. The closeness hadn't choked her back then. It had embraced her.

Rob laid the printouts flat on the table. "Patrice said Crystal gave you the name of a bar. I'll look it up on my phone." He glanced at Frannie. "Let's keep all incriminating evidence off your devices. Then we can draw a circle around the club on the printouts and start looking for hotels and motels within that radius."

Frannie snatched up the printouts. "Thank you for these. They'll be very helpful to me."

"To all of us." Lexi snatched them back from her.

"Look, Bonnie and Clyde, I appreciate your offer, but we all know it's best if I do this alone." Frannie glanced at the sofa. "You have more important things to think about. You can't go around aiding and abetting a parole violation."

Lexi grinned. "Then I guess we'd better not get caught."

Another knock on the door made them all freeze.

"Do you think Patrice got out earlier than she expected?" Frannie asked.

Rob shook his head. "Half an hour was her best-case estimate."

Frannie arched an eyebrow and stared down Lexi. "You didn't."

Lexi shook her head. "Patrice did. He's the one who called us."

"Shit."

Frannie pulled open the door. Despite her lack of surprise at finding him there, she sucked in her breath at the sight of Seth.

This. This was a man who knew how to carry off all black. She dropped her gaze to his long-sleeved T-shirt with three buttons at the top, all undone to reveal a sprinkling of chest hair. The shirt clung tight to the muscles of his chest and arms and even managed to show off his abs. It looked like his narrow hips and long legs had been poured into those black Levi's, and unlike the sneakers the rest of them wore, soldier Seth wore combat boots. Black, mid-calf, laced-up-the-front, combat boots.

"See anything you like?"

That quiet, husky voice of his—not a whisper so much as an invitation—drew her attention back up to his face with his wolfish grin and hella-thick five o'clock shadow.

Frannie sighed. "Well, hell."

"On wheels." He winked at her. He glanced over her shoulder. "Looks like you're having a party. Aren't you going to invite me in?"

"That depends." She crossed her arms over her chest and leaned against the doorjamb, buying herself time to figure out how to get rid of this tall, dark, sexy drink of water when she was so damned thirsty. "Everyone else brought a hostess gift. What did you bring for me?"

She knew the second his smile widened that she had fallen into the deep end. He spread his empty hands wide. "I'm open to suggestions."

"Frannie, what's going on over there?" Lexi called. "You're letting in all the hot air. Invite the man inside."

Frannie took a step toward Seth, causing them both to be more out of the apartment than in it. "Listen, after the last time we saw each other, I don't think—"

"I'm not here to argue with you, Frannie. I'm here to help. Maybe we can't have what I'd hoped"—he shrugged one shoulder—"but I'm not going to let you down at a time like this. No man left behind. It's one of those army oaths they make us take. And I know a thing or two about accomplishing a mission."

Damn, he made a good point. A much better point than anyone else currently crowding around her small kitchen table. "Okay. I call a truce."

"Likewise." He squeezed past her, not bothering to keep from brushing the length of his body against hers, sending a shockwave of desire through her. "But I didn't say I'd play fair," he whispered.

He kissed Lexi on the cheek and patted Rob on the back, settling into their little group like the last puzzle piece snapping into place. She should have seen it coming, should have seen *him* coming. She should have seen all of them coming and stopped them. Or maybe she had seen it and hadn't really wanted to deter them.

If she had any sense, she would bolt right now while none of them were watching her.

But that was a lie.

If she really had any sense, she would stay right where she was, surrounded by these people who had shown up for her, who had her back, as Lexi had said. That light, effervescent feeling of sunshine and warm hugs enveloped her. She was about to risk the one thing she never thought she could do without again: her *freedom*, her escape from anyone who might ever depend on her again. But nothing had ever felt more right than this night.

Seth slid a large backpack off his shoulder because, despite his empty hands, of course he had come with gifts of his own. He pulled out binoculars, electronic devices she couldn't name, and finally, a cell phone, which he tossed to her.

"It's a burner. You've got one. I've got another." Seth glanced at Rob and Lexi. "Everyone knows we have to leave our phones here, right?"

Rob and Lexi nodded. Frannie arched an eyebrow to convey the ridiculousness of him even needing to ask.

Seth grinned, and Frannie nearly swallowed her tongue.

"That's what I figured," he said, and Frannie wondered if they were still discussing cell phones.

Frannie cleared her throat and returned to being all business. "So, Lex."

Her friend, her first true friend but no longer her only one, looked ready to argue with whatever came out of Frannie's mouth.

"Can you get us some coffee mugs from the cupboard? I think we could all use some caffeine to help us focus." She stepped over to the table. "And Rob, could you get some pens and markers out of that drawer over there then start searching for motels inside our circle?"

Seth leaned into her, pressing his bicep against her shoulder. He smelled like fresh air and a slice of heaven and spoke in that irresistible, quiet voice again. "Anything I can do for you? Maybe teach you how to use some of my equipment?"

"You talk like we've moved from a truce to a conspiracy," she whispered. "I'm surprised, after all the things we said." Things *he* had said, but she wouldn't nitpick. Not tonight.

"Yeah, I screwed that up."

Frannie grinned. "You mean you should have stayed?"

"I mean I should have made you beg me to stay, and then I should have talked you out of leaving." He grinned back at her, the big bad wolf once again. "I won't make that mistake again, and I can be very convincing." He nodded toward the pile of things on the table. "And I do travel with excellent equipment."

God, had it only been a little over a week since they had been like this with each other? So much had happened in that short time, it was like she had been missing him for months.

"Testing your equipment will have to wait until later," she said. "Right now, we need to make a plan."

Rob slid a pile of pens to the center of the table while Lexi carried over full coffee mugs, and Seth slid his burner phone back into his backpack and offered to do the motel search while Frannie spread out Rob's printouts on the table.

With the background sound of Bettina laughing at something happening in her movie, Frannie looked at the crew huddled around her table. They were *her* crew, her friends, and now her partners in crime. Literally. But what was aiding and abetting a parolee in crossing state lines compared to bringing her mother home safe and sound?

Frannie touched the charm bracelet Lexi had given her then took a deep breath. "Okay, I think she'll be in a motel because they tend to be cheaper. We'll start with the ones closest to the Blue Rooster."

CHAPTER TWENTY-EIGHT
November 1999

Lexi was worried Frannie wouldn't believe her about needing to do something special to seal their friendship. So Lexi didn't tell her. Instead, she offered to show her new friend how to make a cool bracelet, and Frannie answered, "I guess that's okay," in that chill, calm way she had of speaking, but she smiled when she said it.

It was the second Saturday since they had met, and they sat across from each other at the craft table in Lexi's basement, surrounded by beads, sparkles, and little paint pots. But they were ignoring all of that. Lexi fidgeted with the pale-pink, blue, and yellow thread while Frannie practiced putting knots in hers, the way Lexi had taught her. Lexi had made friendship bracelets before, but Frannie's smaller fingers were better suited to weaving them together.

"Thanks for coming over today," Lexi said as she held out her partially finished work for Frannie to inspect.

"Thanks for inviting me." Frannie laid her half-made bracelet on the table in front of her and stared down at it. "I was surprised you didn't invite Clarissa and her friends. They want you in their group. I can tell."

"I would never invite Clarissa James to my house, and I'd especially never make a friendship bracelet with her." Lexi resumed weaving the threads together, but they only tangled. "I swear I've done this before. I don't know why it looks so bad this time."

"Here, let me help." Frannie took it from her and tightened each thread one by one, until it actually started to look like something more than a jumbled mess. "So you don't like Clarissa?"

"Who could like her? Except that stupid Jen and Bradee and Jayde." Lexi bit her lip. Her mom always warned her not to talk about people, especially not behind their backs. "Sorry, that was impolite."

Frannie raised her eyebrows. "I guess it is. But it's also true."

They giggled at that, and suddenly Lexi's shoulders relaxed, and her fingers were looser, and they changed the subject to talk about the Goosebumps books, whether they would ever be made into movies, and who they would want to cast in them. The conversation turned to the Power Puff Girls (loved them), the Spice Girls (hated them, except for Ginger because she could definitely kick Clarissa's butt), and which boys at their school might someday be cute. Lexi wasn't about to admit that she thought fifth-grader Seth Collins and his annoying brother Sam, who was in their class, were already cute because Frannie hated them.

When they finished their bracelets, Frannie held up both of them. "Not too bad. Yours came out fine. Now what?"

Lexi reverently took back the bracelet she had woven. "Hold out your left arm. Come on, just do it." She tied the bracelet onto Frannie's wrist then held out her own left arm. "Now you tie the one you made onto my wrist."

Frannie did as Lexi asked. Lexi toyed with ideas about what to say next. She didn't want Frannie to think she was weird, but she had to tell her about the incantation. It was a new word she had learned, and she hoped it would impress Frannie. Lexi had said an incantation to make her parents stay together, and it had worked. And then on the first day of school, she had said another one while she had wished for a new best friend.

Now that Lexi had found her, Frannie needed her to go along with the magic. Without it, they couldn't be sure their friendship would last. Lexi decided directness would be best. If she pretended she knew what she was doing, Frannie might believe her. "Now we have to say the incantation."

Frannie wrinkled her nose. "Is that the thing in church?"

"Church?" Lexi pondered that. She had used parts of the Lord's Prayer in her first spell, but it didn't seem related. "I think that's the invocation. Incantation means spell. We have to wrap the magic around the bracelets so they'll work."

Frannie ran her fingers over her bracelet. "Okay. But what are the bracelets supposed to do?"

"They keep us safe and guarantee we'll always be friends."

Frannie looked up at Lexi. "Always? Like forever? BFFs?"

Lexi nodded solemnly. "Best friends, always and forever. As long as we say the magic words."

"Okay."

Frannie looked earnest and sincere, and that was when Lexi knew how much Frannie wanted to be her best friend too. "So... what are the magic words?" she asked, and they both laughed.

"Sorry, I guess I forgot to tell you," Lexi said when she could keep a straight face. She took a deep breath. She had memorized a new poem because this was important.

Frannie watched her with an intensity that proved she understood the gravity of it.

"Repeat after me," Lexi said. "Oh, first we have to hold each other's left hands and press our bracelets. Right. Now, repeat after me. Ready?"

"Ready."

Lexi started. "A friend is like a heart that goes strong until the end."

"A friend is like a heart that goes strong until the end."

"Where would we be in this world..."

"Where would we be in this world..."

"If we didn't have a friend."

"If we didn't have a friend." Frannie blinked fast, and Lexi thought she might have seen tears in her eyes, which was strange because she was sure Frannie Willets did not cry. Frannie cleared her throat. "Is that it?"

"Almost. Do you know Star Light, Star Bright?"

Frannie nodded.

"We have to say that together. Ready?"

"Ready."

They spoke in unison. "Star light, star bright, first star I see tonight. I wish I may, I wish I might, have this wish I make tonight."

Lexi held their arms up in the air, triumphantly displaying their magical bracelets. "We did it, Frannie. Best friends forever!"

"We did it!" Frannie's smile faded. "But I think there's one more thing."

They dropped hands, and Lexi leaned forward, wondering what she could have forgotten, suddenly afraid that the magic wouldn't work. "What is it?"

"I'm pretty sure we have to say Star Light, Star Bright when we see the first star."

Lexi wasn't sure that was necessary for the magic to work, but Frannie was frowning, looking genuinely worried, and Lexi wasn't willing to take a chance.

"Okay, I know what to do."

Lexi ran upstairs to the kitchen, checked with her mom to make sure her plans were allowed, and raced back down the stairs. "It's all set. You're staying for dinner. My mom's going to call your mom. And she said we can sit outside to watch the sunset. Then we'll be able to see the first star."

"And then we'll be BFFs."

"BFFs."

They hugged and jumped around the basement.

Lexi knew it was going to be true not just because of the bracelets and the magic but because Frannie believed in the magic. Frannie believed in Lexi. That would keep them together, best friends forever.

CHAPTER TWENTY-NINE
2016

As they crossed the state line into Kentucky and into the border city of Louisville, Lexi didn't turn around to glance at Frannie in the back seat. She worried that might jinx them somehow. Instead, she glanced at her husband behind the wheel of their minivan. So solid. So kind. So strong. Her glance turned into a stare as she recounted all the good things he had brought into her life. He glanced at her and winked then retrained his eyes on the road. No one spoke. None of them had said a word since they had left the Licking town limits.

When they passed the Blue Rooster at the heart of the city, Lexi finally shifted in her seat to see her friend. Frannie and Seth were staring straight ahead, looking out through the windshield. They sat on opposite sides of the back seat, but their hands met in the middle, their fingers just touching. *Just hold her hand!* Lexi wanted to tell Seth. But their relationship or mess or whatever was between them was their business, not hers.

"Are you ready?" Lexi asked Frannie, mostly because she wasn't sure what else to say.

Frannie nodded. "The first motel on our list is in this block, on the right. You can pull up in front of the office, and I'll—"

"Security cameras," Seth said quietly.

"You need to stay in the car, Frannie," Rob said. "I'll go in to ask about Crystal."

Frannie pressed her lips together like she was trying not to say what she thought of their input then spoke anyway. "That should go over well: big, scary-looking guy dressed in black asking about a single woman traveling alone."

Rob glanced at her through the rearview mirror. "I'm a small-town dad. I'm not scary-looking." He glanced at Lexi. "I'm not, am I?"

Lexi shrugged. "You could be, if someone didn't know you. I mean, Frannie has a good point about some random guy asking about a woman who's alone." She looked at Frannie. "So I'll go."

Frannie sighed loudly and didn't look much happier about that idea, but she gave one small nod of concession.

Rob parked in a shadowy corner of the parking lot, and Lexi climbed out of the van and hurried into the motel office. She asked a few quick questions and used her phone to show Crystal's picture to the man behind the counter. He said no one by that name or description was a guest. She went back to the minivan, and they drove to the next place a half a block away and then the third, with the same results.

"Maybe they're lying because they're not supposed to talk about guests," Frannie said. She was fidgeting and frowning like she always did when things didn't go as planned.

"I don't think so," Lexi said. "They'd probably just tell me that. Here, Rob, this is number four on the list."

At the fourth motel, a young woman, maybe college age, sat behind the counter. When Lexi approached, the woman looked up from the textbook she was reading and set down her yellow highlighter. She stood and smiled.

"Hi, can I help you?" She stepped behind the computer. "Checking in?"

Lexi glanced at the woman's name tag. "Actually, Erika, I'm looking for someone who might be a guest here."

Erika's smile faded. "I'm sorry, ma'am, but I can't give out information about guests."

That was the best lead they'd had so far. Lexi pulled out her phone. "I understand, but it's kind of an emergency. This woman is"—she showed Crystal's picture to Erika while she decided on the best lie to use—"well, she's my mother. She's going through a tough time. A divorce. My dad's being an asshole and... I'm sorry to dump all this on you. I'm just worried about her."

The young woman frowned down at the phone. "My dad was the same way when my parents went through a divorce." She sighed then gave a resolute nod. "To be honest, I've been a little worried about your mom myself."

Jackpot. Lexi's heart pounded.

"I've warned her away from some of the bars around here, especially ones with after-hours parties," Erika continued. "Some of those guys start drinking and, you know..."

Lexi's stomach clenched. She nodded. Yes, she did know. "Do you know if she's in her room right now?"

Erika shook her head. "I couldn't say."

Lexi slipped her phone into her pocket and leaned over the counter. She dropped her voice to a whisper. "Could you say what her room number is?"

Erika furrowed her brow and chewed on her lip. Lexi feared a no was coming.

"Please, Erika. I need to find her before anything bad happens to her."

Erika leaned closer to the counter. "You did not hear this from me," she whispered. She inclined her head to the right, indicating that side of the complex. "Room 317. I can't give you a key though."

Lexi nodded. "That's okay. I'll take it from here. Thank you so, so much."

"Hey, good luck," the woman called as Lexi walked away. "With your parents and their divorce."

The kindness in the face of Lexi's white lie should make her feel guilty. But it didn't. Her fib was for a greater good. Lexi was being strong for Frannie. Useful. She was prepared to do whatever it took to help her best friend. She glanced back at Erika. "Thanks."

She exited the office and headed for the minivan. She spoke as she climbed into the passenger seat. "Room 317. Frannie, I'll go with you."

"I think we should all go," Rob said. "It's not safe for the two of you to wander around here alone in the dark."

"No," Frannie said. "Lexi's right. She's going to feel ambushed enough as it is, even without the cavalry backing me up."

Seth scowled. "How about a compromise. We'll walk you up to the third floor and wait by the stairs while you talk to her." He frowned and glanced at the row of bars across the street. "If she's here."

The four of them climbed out of the minivan. Rob kissed Lexi, and Seth squeezed Frannie's shoulder. Frannie led the way up the metal-and-cement staircase, followed by Lexi, then Rob and Seth. When they reached the third floor, Lexi linked her arm in Frannie's, and the men stood sentry at the top of the stairs.

"She's going to fight us on this," Frannie said, "so... whatever it takes, right?" She echoed Lexi's earlier thought. Frannie knocked on the door.

There was shuffling inside the room. Frannie and Lexi breathed a sigh of relief in unison.

"Who is it?" Crystal's voice was rough, like she had been on a bender for days.

"Mom, open the door."

"Frannie?" The chain lock scraped, and Crystal cracked open the door. Her face was flushed, and her curly blond hair was tangled. She blinked like they had woken her. "What are you doing here?"

"Looking for you." Frannie tried to peer past her mother into the darkened room. "Can we come in?"

"I was just on my way out."

Frannie glanced at Crystal's hair.

Crystal raked her hand through it. "Getting ready to go out."

"Mom, we're coming in." Small-but-mighty Frannie leaned on the door and moved it a few more inches.

Crystal threw up her hands and stepped back, allowing them inside. The sheets on the double bed were crumpled. Clothes were slung over Crystal's large black suitcase and scattered on the floor. A row of full whiskey bottles was lined up on top of the dresser, in front of the TV.

Frannie stopped in front of the bottles. "Having a party?"

"Don't make accusations, young lady." Crystal stepped past Frannie and picked up a wide-toothed comb. "I took some distillery tours and bought those to take home. It's not like I'm breaking..." She stopped with her comb in midair. "Frannie, what the hell are you doing in Kentucky? You're violating parole."

Lexi stepped forward and touched Crystal's arm. "Let's not say that too loudly." She glanced at the walls, which she suspected were paper-thin.

"And you, Lexi. You let her come here? I expect better sense from you."

Frannie flinched like she had been slapped, but she didn't respond to her mother's provocation.

White-hot anger flashed through Lexi. "She's here for you, against her better judgment and mine. You can at least be decent about it."

Crystal widened her eyes and took a step back from Lexi. "I'm worried about her. Frannie, I'm just worried. Why are you here?"

Frannie bent and grabbed a pile of clothes off the floor, opened the suitcase, and dropped them into it. "We're taking you home."

Crystal's phone dinged. She snatched it up from the nightstand and read a message, then frowned and glared at Frannie. "I'm on vacation until Friday."

"You can relax at home." Frannie opened the drawers, checking to make sure each was empty. "You're not in a good frame of mind, you're drinking too much, and you're planning on meeting a stranger at some dive-bar party."

The phone dinged again. Crystal glanced at the message. She shook her head. "I'm already late, and I need to get ready. And you need to get your ass back to Indiana before you end up in jail." Crystal's phone dinged a third time.

"Mom, you need to listen to reason."

Crystal stared down at her phone.

Frannie's face turned red. "Mom, are you listening?"

Lexi stepped closer to her friend, ready to lay a calming hand on her shoulder. Crystal started typing. Frannie grabbed the phone out of her hand. Crystal lunged for it.

Lexi stepped between them. "Let's take it down a notch." Lexi used the soothing tone she had been taught in her teacher symposiums, the one that worked for adults and children alike. "Crystal, please hear us out."

"What the hell?" Frannie said.

Lexi turned toward her. "Let's all stay calm, okay?"

Frannie held up the phone. "Is this the guy you're meeting? This asshole who called you a bitch because you're running late?"

Crystal shook her head. "You're taking it out of context. I promised I'd be there fifteen minutes ago."

Lexi had only witnessed Crystal's follies with men from a safe distance, but Frannie'd had a front-row seat to the mess for years. She had watched her mother pick losers, heard her defend their crappy behavior, listened while her mother cried over them when they eventually left her.

"He's trash, Mother!"

Lexi estimated that it was probably the hundredth time Frannie had told her mother that about one of her men.

"Maybe trash is all I can get!" Crystal shouted back. "Jack Greene wasn't trash, but now he won't speak to me."

"Wait," Lexi said. "He dumped you, not the other way around, after what Frannie told you?"

Crystal sobbed and dropped onto the bed. "I don't know if I'm dumped or not. He won't call or text me back."

Frannie took a deep breath and dropped to one knee beside her mother. "That's not a bad thing because he's not a good guy."

"I told him what you said," Crystal said between sobs. "I just wanted to hear his side of it. But it hurt his feelings, and now he's mad, and..." She sucked in gulps of air.

Lexi's stomach clenched. She wanted to vomit. Crystal was talking about Lexi's rape. She wanted to hear the rapist's side of the attack. It was sick. Disgusting. She wanted to shake Crystal by the shoulders and scream until the ridiculous woman understood.

Frannie shot Lexi a sad look. She mouthed, "Sorry."

Lexi nodded. It wasn't her friend's fault. Hell, it wasn't really Crystal's fault either. The woman needed help. Their help. *Whatever it takes.*

Lexi sat down beside Crystal and took her hand. She inclined her head to the suitcase, indicating to Frannie to keep packing. Her friend read the signal and went back to checking drawers.

"Crystal," Lexi said, using her upset-child-soothing tone, "I'm sorry about all that's happened to you. I'm sure Jack Greene can be charming." She didn't believe that, but this was for her friend. "But Frannie is right. He's not a good guy. I know you have your doubts about what she told you. So maybe it would help if you heard it from me. It's time to tell my story, and I need you to hear it."

Frannie turned toward Lexi with raised eyebrows. Beside her on the bed, Crystal went still and quiet.

Lexi frowned and squeezed Crystal's hand. "After it happened, I thought about all the things I'd done wrong, all the red flags I'd ignored, all the warning bells in my own head that I overrode because I needed to be polite and respectful. I was in love with Brandon, and this was his father. I couldn't be rude, could I? Women are not supposed to be rude or hurt men's feelings, are we?"

Frannie zipped Crystal's suitcase and slid down to the floor with her back to the dresser. There were tears in her eyes as she watched Lexi.

"So when he offered me whiskey, I felt like I couldn't say no, even though I didn't drink, and he knew that. By the time I drank it, it was probably too late. I had way too much, but also"—she glanced at Frannie—"we talked about this. The way I blacked out and the way I felt later—and for days—we're pretty sure it was spiked with something."

"Like a date-rape drug," Frannie said.

Tears spilled onto Crystal's cheeks, but she didn't speak. At least she wasn't defending him anymore.

Lexi continued. "When he pushed me down on a reclining chair and lay on top of me, I couldn't fight him off. I probably couldn't have anyway. He's not a small guy. But I couldn't even lift my hand to slap his face or to try to push him away."

Crystal gripped Lexi's hand. She was listening, thank God. Lexi hoped she was also believing, because it was tearing out a piece of Lexi's soul to put the memories into words.

"I managed to say no. I begged him to stop. He was rough, and I was crying. He hurt me. I did not consent to that. Even if I'd been too far gone to say no, that wouldn't have been consent. He took what he wanted from me, and he didn't give a damn that he killed a piece of me to do it." She took a shaky breath.

Frannie sat on Lexi's other side and held her hand. "You don't have to go on."

"I do have to." She didn't want to, but she needed to—and not just for Crystal's sake. "Afterward, when I woke up, Jack was gone, and Brandon was there. I tried to tell myself it was some kind of nightmare, but it didn't work. And I was so ashamed. I felt so dirty. I went to the bathroom, and I had bruises. I was bleeding. He hadn't used protection and..." She couldn't put words to that detail.

"Lexi, I had no idea," Crystal said. "I never would have..."

"Mom," Frannie said softly. "Go on, Lex. Or do you want me to?"

Lexi shook her head. She had begun telling her story, and she was going to finish it. "Brandon and I were meticulous about protection, so when I realized I was pregnant, I knew it wasn't his."

Crystal sucked in her breath. "Pregnant? That's so hard at that age. And then under those circumstances." She had a faraway look in her eyes, as if she was thinking about a different time and place.

Something clicked inside Lexi, and she knew with a certainty that Crystal wasn't empathizing with Lexi's plight; she was sympathizing. Sometime, somewhere, with some monster of a man, Crystal Willets had been raped. The pity and kindness she had never been able to feel for her best friend's mother now filled her to overflowing. She leaned over and hugged Crystal. She whispered to her. "If you ever need to talk..."

Crystal nodded as she pulled away and wiped her eyes with her sleeve. She wasn't going to speak of it at this moment. Maybe she couldn't do it in front of Frannie. Maybe she would never broach the subject again. But Lexi would make sure Crystal understood she could turn to Lexi if and when she was ready.

"After what he did to you," Crystal said, bringing them back to Lexi's story, "Frannie decided to steal from him."

"She did it for me," Lexi said. "To pay for the trip out of state and the second-term abortion. And then I miscarried. It was bad. Dangerous. And we were about to get caught." Lexi leaned into Frannie, crying so hard now she could barely get the words out. "And she knew I was broken, and she didn't want anything else to happen to me, so she took the blame. All by herself. She did that for me."

The three of them sobbed and held each other, but with every passing minute, Lexi felt lighter. Less damaged. More sure that she had needed this release for a very long time.

Finally, she took a deep, cleansing breath. "So, Crystal, please believe us when we tell you Jack Greene is not a good man, and you deserve so much better than him."

"I already have better." Crystal gripped Lexi's hand and reached past her to take Frannie's hand as well. "Come on, girls. Let's go home."

IN THE WEE HOURS OF the morning, Frannie and her crew, with Rob driving the minivan and Lexi driving Crystal's car with Crystal passed out in the back seat, arrived back in Licking. Rob dropped off Seth and Frannie in front of her apartment. They stood beside each other without speaking until the taillights of the minivan disappeared around the corner, two streets up Main.

"Nice of them to let your mom sleep it off at their place," Seth said.

"Maybe I should have insisted she stay here. I could have put her on the bed while I slept on the sofa."

"She'll be fine."

Frannie wrapped her arms around herself, taking it all in. They had done it. They had brought her mother home and kept Frannie out of prison. Actually, Lexi had done it. Frannie had willingly taken the rap for her friend five years earlier, and Lexi hadn't owed her a thing for that. But if she had, what she had done tonight to save Frannie's mother from a terrible mistake would have paid everything back, with interest.

"I have to tell you what Lexi did to get my mother to come home with us," she said. "I didn't want to say it in front of Rob because Lexi will want to share it with him."

She quickly recounted Lexi's bravery, without sharing the details. Those were Lexi's and Lexi's alone to share when and how she needed. Frannie tried to put into words what it had meant to her, although words couldn't do justice to describing what an incredible gift it had been.

"She's so brave," Seth said. He wrapped his arm around Frannie. He was solid and warm and wonderful. "She learned that from you."

Frannie shook her head. "I think we learned it from each other."

"You're shivering," Seth said. "Let's get you inside."

Frannie arched an eyebrow. "Are you tucking me in?"

"More like checking the perimeter."

"Okay." She tried not to sound disappointed. Two minutes later, while Seth locked and relocked the dead bolt on the back door and checked the night-vision camera feeds, Frannie poured herself a large glass of cold white wine and gulped it down. "Can I get something for you?"

Seth shook his head. "I have my water bottle in the truck."

She braced herself. Lexi had been so brave earlier. Now it was Frannie's turn. "I'm sorry for the way we left things. I didn't want you to leave last Sunday. Or this past Saturday." She took another gulp of wine. "I don't want you to leave tonight. And I swear, I am not trying to fuck you into compliance."

He grimaced. "That was a little harsh, wasn't it?" He stood beside her and leaned against the countertop. He tucked a strand of her hair behind her ear. "Thank you for apologizing. I accept. But as for staying over... Sixteen days, right?"

She didn't have to ask for clarification. She had been counting down the days since they had stood at nearly 300. "Yep. Sixteen days until I'm free. It will be a Saturday, so it might not be official until the following Monday, but—"

He cut her off with a kiss, one of those where he tucked one arm around her waist and threaded his other hand through her hair and melted her insides.

"After your parole is up and you've decided what you're doing with all that freedom, we'll have a long talk." He pulled away from her and kissed her temple. "Assuming your decision means you're still here. Lock the door behind me, and give me a call if you need anything." He walked to the front door then turned toward her and smiled. "You're safe here, Frannie. I promise."

Then he was gone. Again. But this time loneliness didn't swallow her. She smiled, really smiled. Two weeks felt like forever, but it was nothing compared to the four years she had served at the state pen and the five years Lexi had waited for justice. The next sixteen days would give Frannie time to be sure she wasn't promising anything she couldn't deliver. And it gave her more than two weeks to set her backup plan, the one that might keep Jack Greene at bay.

She reached into her back jeans pocket and pulled out the burner phone. Seth would know how to get rid of it. But first, she would make good use of it. She punched in a number she had committed to memory a little less than a year ago because it hadn't been safe to write it down. Even though it was well past midnight, someone picked up after the first ring.

"Hello," a man said.

That surprised Frannie. Then again, anything would have surprised her because she hadn't known what to expect. "I'm trying to get in touch with someone." She hesitated. Could she say the name? Was there a code word or something she had forgotten? "A woman."

"I know who you're trying to reach," he said, cutting her off. "You calling from a secure line?"

"Yes."

"Hold tight." He hung up.

Well, that had proven useless. Frannie let out a string of oaths the likes of which she hadn't muttered since she had reentered society. Before she could finish what was turning out to be a rather elegant way to repeatedly mutter "fuck," the phone in her hand rang.

She answered. "Hello?"

"Who is this?" The voice on the other end was cigarette raspy and annoyed and unmistakable.

She grinned. "Hi, Maurie. It's Frannie."

CHAPTER THIRTY

For the next two weeks, Frannie took Seth up on his offer that she could call him if she needed anything. As it turned out, she could think of something she needed almost every day, from an answer to a question about the security cameras to his advice on a new computer to a recommendation about marinating steak. True to his word, Seth answered every time. So when she called him three days before her big day of freedom, she wasn't surprised that he not only answered, but sounded in great spirits.

"Miss Willets, what a shock to see you blowing up my phone again. What can I do for you this time?" he practically purred.

"That tone of voice gives me all sorts of ideas, but I'm still at work," she said.

"That is a shame. Hey, if you're calling from work, is there really something wrong?"

"No. In fact, it's something good. I just talked to Lexi. She's going to call Brandon tomorrow."

"Her ex-boyfriend, Brandon? Does this mean she's going to tell him about the rape?"

"She is." Frannie smiled. "I don't know if you've seen her lately—she and Rob have gone mum on all things Seth Collins—but she's doing amazingly well. Stronger than I've ever seen her."

"I've only been in Licking once, to watch a game with Rob. Other than that, he's come here alone a few times to have a beer. Same thing on my end. They're not mentioning Frannie Willets to me."

"Staying out of our business," Frannie said. "Very diplomatic and unlike our friends."

"Yeah, it's weird. Is there something I can do for Lexi?" He dropped his voice to a sexy whisper. "Or for you?"

Frannie fanned herself then pulled her mind out of the gutter. "I'm hoping you'll reconsider your moratorium on coming here. Lexi plans to call Brandon from here at the diner tomorrow. She's asked Rob not to be here, which he doesn't love. But afterward, she's inviting my mom and her parents to join us at her house for dinner, around six."

"And you need an escort?" The way he lingered on the last word made it sound lurid. She liked it.

"Need is a strong word." And accurate about so many, many things when she thought about Seth. "But in addition to wanting an escort for the evening, Lexi would love to have you there. But she wanted to leave it up to me."

"I'd love to come, Frannie." His voice was soft and serious now. There were so many sides to this man, and Frannie adored them all. "I'll be there at six sharp."

"Actually, could you come a little early? Maybe swing by and pick me up? There's something I need to discuss with you."

"I thought the plan was to talk next week."

She grinned. "Plans can change. Loosen up a little. You might enjoy yourself."

"I know I'll enjoy myself. That's the problem."

She chewed her lip, wondering how much she should say over the phone when she wanted to tell him everything in person. "Meet me behind Patrice's at 5:30. I promise you won't regret it."

"An offer I can't refuse from the woman I can't forget." Seth sighed. "I'll be there for you, Frannie. But then, I think you already knew that."

LEXI ARRIVED AT THE diner at 4:00 p.m. sharp on Thursday. She was wearing the same floral-print dress she had worn the day she and Frannie had reunited, five and a half weeks and a lifetime ago.

"You're early," Frannie said. She wiped her hands on her apron then hugged her friend. "Day care let out early?"

Lexi shook her head and pulled off her sunglasses. "I asked one of the other teachers to cover my class for the last hour. Can we sit?"

"Sure." Frannie led her to a booth in the back corner and slid into the seat across from Lexi. "Have you changed your mind? Because that's okay. You don't have to do this, not today, not—"

Lexi grabbed Frannie's hand. "I'm doing this. And I'm doing it today." She pressed her lips together and stared out the diner window. "You know why, right?"

Frannie squeezed Lexi's hand. "Five years ago today. That's the day Jack Greene raped you."

Lexi nodded. "And now everyone important to me knows what happened, except Brandon. It seems unfair. He deserves to know the truth about his father and about why I broke up with him."

"Not at the expense of yourself though," Frannie said. "If you're not ready..."

"I'm ready," Lexi said. "Just nervous. Too nervous to wait until five, like we planned." She looked at Frannie. "I'm ready to do it right now."

"Should I give you some privacy for the call?"

Lexi nodded then spoke so quietly, Frannie nearly missed it. "Thank you, Frannie. I never would have gotten to this point without you."

"I don't know about that. You're stronger than any of us ever gave you credit for. But I'm here for backup."

For the next ten minutes, Frannie busied herself with wiping down tables and checking the levels in ketchup bottles and allowing herself the occasional errant thought about Seth, while across the room Lexi spoke into her phone and wiped away tears. But Lexi didn't wave her hand or catch Frannie's eye in distress. Frannie finally gave up hope of distracting herself with work and joined Patrice at the counter.

Patrice poured a cup of coffee and slid it in front of Frannie. "It's all working out. After today, she can put all of this behind her, start enjoying the happy life she's building."

In the corner booth, Lexi set down her phone and stared out the window. Not smiling but no longer crying either. Progress. More than Frannie could have imagined they would make when she had first arrived here. She had spent most of the time since then thinking about how the hell to get out of town, with or without Greene's money. Now she had the chance to leave with something else—peace of mind.

But tonight she would tell everyone what she had known for the past two weeks. Frannie Willets wasn't going anywhere.

FRANNIE WALKED DOWN the alley between her apartment building and the diner and found Seth leaning against his truck in Patrice's parking lot. He jolted to attention when he saw her approach, and his jaw dropped. She was wearing the same silky, pale-blue dress she had worn the first time he had made her dinner, and the reaction she was getting from him was exactly the one she had been dreaming of for the past two weeks.

"Wow!" Seth whistled. "Just when I thought you couldn't look any sexier than you did in your all-black, Johnny-Cash-wannabe outfit. I thought I was meeting you back here because you'd just be getting off work."

She shook her head. "I wanted us to have some privacy, but I thought it would be overstepping to invite you to my apartment." By the time she reached Seth's side, she was sweating. It was partly the hot, late-May sun, although there was some cloud cover and a nice breeze, so maybe it was more the nearness of him.

Seth shoved his hands into the pockets of his dark jeans. Frannie hoped it was because he didn't trust himself to keep his hands off her. His stance showed off his muscled chest and arms under his light-blue button-down shirt with the top three buttons open.

Seth gave her a cockeyed grin. "You look like you *need* something, Frannie."

Frannie pulled her hair up off her neck and fanned herself with her small clutch purse.

That got Seth's attention. He stared at her throat then raked his eyes down and back up her body. By the time he met her eyes, he didn't bother hiding his desire for her. "Christ, I've missed you. I tried not to."

"It's not your fault. I have that effect on people."

He took one of her hands and tugged her closer to him. "Maybe, but you have a very specific effect on me." He caught a tendril of her hair that the wind blew into her face and tucked it behind her ear. Then he kissed the edge of her ear.

"Not fair," she whispered.

"I warned you two weeks ago, I won't play fair." He bent to whisper into her ear. "I'll do everything in my power to convince you to stay."

She traced her finger along the skin exposed by his undone buttons. "Speaking of playing..." She grinned at him.

"Yeah, you don't play fair either." He pressed her hand flat against his chest.

She took a step closer to him. His cologne was a light, fresh scent on the breeze, the same scent he left on her pillows when he spent the night in her bed. "So, about that talk we were going to have next week. I know you wanted me to be totally free, to have all my options on the table before I announced a decision about staying or going."

He nodded. "That was my intent. But here we are, a few days early."

His heartbeat thrummed under her fingertips. She looked up at him. "I don't need any more time or any more options. I'm staying."

"Staying, staying? Past your parole? Past next week?"

She nodded. "Past next year."

He whooped and pulled her against him, whirling her around in a circle. "Not that I ever doubted it," he said as he slid her back down onto her feet. "How could you resist me?"

"Oh, is that what these past couple of weeks have been about? Giving me a chance to resist you?"

"More like time to miss me." He traced her lower lip with his thumb. "And now all I can think about is picking you up Saturday and driving you across the state line to have my way with you."

She kissed the tip of his thumb. "Which state?"

He shook his head. "Doesn't matter. And just for the record, in case you're free later tonight, I do just fine within state borders too."

She stepped closer, pressing the length of her body against his. "About that. I have a plan."

"Oh, I'll bet you do."

"This one involves making up for lost time."

"Oh, I like this plan," he said. "Especially if making up for lost time means what I think it means. But you know, more time is always passing, and you have to keep up with that *and* make up for lost time."

"Hmm." She furrowed her brow. "You're right. Maybe you don't have the endurance for this mission."

He pulled her tightly against him. "Don't you worry about my endurance."

He backed her against the truck, and she wound her arms around his neck as he bent his head and kissed her. All the plans in her mind went quiet as she sank into the strength of his arms and the softness of his lips.

"I think we better get out of here before we get arrested," he whispered in her ear.

"Ooh, you're going to do things to me that could get us arrested?"

He patted her bottom. "You should be a little less excited about breaking the law."

She cocked an eyebrow at him.

"On second thought, forget I said that. I don't want you any less excited, ever. In fact, I'd like to take you over to your apartment right now and let you get excited to your heart's content."

She laughed. "Nope. It's Lexi's big night, and we can't be late."

"I almost forgot. There are other people in the world." He winked at her.

"Oh, speaking of Lexi, Rob is throwing her a birthday party two weeks from Saturday, and I told him I'd help decorate the diner, so clear your schedule because we'll need you here that weekend. All weekend."

He grinned as he helped her into the passenger side of the truck then climbed into the driver's seat.

Frannie snapped on her seat belt and leaned over to kiss him. "On the drive, I think we should discuss your fitness routine to make sure we're maximizing your endurance. For instance, I hope you ate your Wheaties and took your vitamins this morning."

He snapped on his own seat belt and leaned over for another kiss. "I'll hook myself up to an IV vitamin drip, if that's what it takes to keep up with you."

CHAPTER THIRTY-ONE

Two weeks later, on Saturday afternoon, Frannie sat in the passenger seat of Seth's pickup truck as they took the exit off Route 244 and drove into Licking.

"I know you like having me stay at your place when I don't have a shift at the diner," she said, "but I knew we should have stayed here last night. Now we're half an hour late for Lexi's birthday party." She grinned. "Lucky for me, Lexi will blame you."

"Nah. She knows I can't help being irresistible." He parked across the street from Patty's Diner and leaned over for a kiss.

"Hold that thought," she said as she unlatched her seat belt. She hopped down to the sidewalk as Bettina and another kid her size, with a very clean and dapper-looking Max on his pink leash between them, emerged from the alley between the diner and her apartment building.

"Hi, Aunt Francesca. Lexi says you're late." Bettina eyed Frannie then Seth, who joined them and took Frannie's hand. "But she said it's probably Uncle Seth's fault."

Frannie covered a snort while Seth frowned and did his best to look indignant.

Bettina took her friend's hand. "Jenny, you remember Francesca. She's not my real aunt, but I call her that now because she's Lexi's best friend, kind of like a sister."

Jenny smiled. "Like us."

Damn. Two cute kids and a dog were enough to melt her down into a puddle. If Seth hadn't squeezed Frannie's hand just then, she would probably have collapsed from adorableness overload.

Jenny held a hand over her mouth and whispered something to Bettina, who smiled.

"Right," Bettina said and addressed Frannie and Seth. "You should go inside now. We'll be in soon."

Frannie grinned as the girls walked away with Max. "She's getting to be as bossy as her stepmother."

"Speaking of her stepmother, Lexi won't be mad because we're not really late." Seth took her hand and pushed open the diner door.

"What does that—"

"Surprise!"

Frannie stepped inside the familiar space, which had been transformed for the party. Most of the tables and chairs had been removed, replaced by throngs of people—maybe not the whole town but a sizeable chunk of the residents Frannie knew. The decorations she and Seth had helped Rob hang last night, including streamers and clusters of balloons, were still there, but the Happy Birthday banner hanging over the breakfast counter had been replaced by one that read Happy Freedom Day.

Lexi pulled Frannie into the diner while Seth held her up with a hand on her back.

"I don't understand," Frannie whispered. But she blinked back tears because she was beginning to get it. "This isn't for your birthday?"

"My birthday isn't for another week," Lexi said. "And it will be something nice and quiet, in our backyard. Today is all for you."

Frannie laughed. "You made me decorate for my own party?"

Lexi gave her a side hug. "It was just to keep you busy while we planned the rest of it."

Patrice hugged Frannie and introduced her to her daughter, Patty. Frannie's mother, Lexi's parents, and Bettina's grandparents were next in line, followed by dozens of Frannie's regulars, who were thrilled she would be staying; Jenny's mom, who wanted to engage Frannie's services for grooming her springer spaniels; and at least twenty people Frannie had never met.

"Frannie will chat with all of you outside where it's cooler," Patrice said. "And besides, all the food and my special-made iced coffee are out there, so scoot."

"The main party is in the empty field behind the parking lot," Lexi said as the crowd followed Patrice's orders. Seth, Lexi, and Frannie also headed outdoors but more slowly.

Frannie turned to Seth. "And you knew about this."

"I was sworn to secrecy." He kissed her and almost made her forget he had kept the secret from her.

"All right, break it up, Collins," Lexi said as they stepped outside. "Rob and Oscar are grilling. Go help them with manly things. And no, not the kind that involve my friend."

"One quick thing before I get sent to Manberia," Seth said. "You should both know that my brother Sam is here. He called last week to say he'd be nearby, and when he heard you were both here... I couldn't say no."

"Sam's not so bad, now that he's stopped throwing spitballs," Lexi said. "He has stopped that, right?"

Seth grinned. "He has. But he hasn't stopped dating Clarissa James, so she's here too. But she grows on you, I promise."

"Like fungus?"

Lexi nudged her shoulder. "We can be nice for the afternoon. Right, Frannie?"

Frannie crossed her arms over her chest. "Fine. We'll be nice. Even say hello to them. But if she goes for my hair, I won't be responsible for my actions."

Seth arched an eyebrow. "Sounds like a story for another time."

"It's really not."

He kissed her again. "Then we're agreed. You'll tell me all about it tonight." He flashed a wolfish grin. "In bed."

As Seth walked away, someone beside Frannie cleared his throat, and she jumped and turned around.

"New waitress." Mr. Connor held two cups of punch. "One for you."

"Thank you, Mr. Connor."

He tapped her cup with his, and they each took a drink.

"I hear you might be sticking around this town," he said.

She nodded. "Do you have a problem with that?"

"Hmm. Depends. You plan on causing trouble?"

"No, sir."

"You plan to keep working at the diner?"

"Yes, sir. At least for a while." Until she could finish training for her new career, but that was no one else's business just yet.

"And when you no longer work at the diner, will you stop by every now and then to have a piece of pie with me?"

Frannie swallowed the lump in her throat. She hadn't seen that one coming. She nodded.

Mr. Connor clinked his cup against hers again. "In that case, Frannie Willets, welcome to Licking, Indiana, population 2,433. Now go on, mingle with the other youngsters. I'm going to have a seat over there, help Miss Patrice serve up those pies."

"Speaking of mingling"—Lexi took Frannie's arm—"over there are my yoga teacher and some of the ladies from class. Let's say hi."

Frannie groaned. "They'll want me to join the class so they can torture me with sun salutations at dawn." Frannie turned toward Lexi and lowered her voice. "How about I tell you a secret instead?"

"That depends. Is this about Seth? Remember, I think of him like a brother."

Frannie shook her head. "Nothing like that. This is about Jack Greene."

Lexi didn't even flinch at the sound of his name. "Okay. Go on."

"The night we brought my mother home, when you told us the details about what he'd done to you, I wanted so badly for him to be punished. To spend the rest of his life in prison. But I knew that will probably never happen."

Lexi frowned. "Frannie, what did you do?"

"I paid back a favor." Frannie glanced around to make sure no one was near them then whispered, "Maurie Stonefield once told me she was serving so little time because she had information that was useful to the feds. I thought if I told her a little something about Jack Greene, she could have someone look into him, dig up serious dirt, and point the feds in his direction." Frannie shrugged. "She wins. We win. Greene loses."

"As much as I like the sound of that, Maurie Stonefield is a criminal too."

Frannie nodded. "But she's not a rapist."

Lexi pulled Frannie into a hug. "Thank you for doing that. But please be careful. I worry about you."

The backyard gate behind the apartment building opened, and Bettina and Jenny emerged with Max between them.

Lexi smiled. "At least I can worry a little less about Max. It's good he's gotten so much better with people because those girls are determined to introduce him to everyone at the party. Look at the two of them, thick as thieves. Like someone else I know."

"Hey, the thieving thing is behind us. Now we just jump parole."

"Not as of today," Lexi said. "Now we're so well-behaved, we're almost boring."

"Hey, Lex, aren't the girls missing something?" Frannie held up her wrist with the silver charm bracelet that matched Lexi's. "But maybe another set of thread ones." She touched the thread bracelet on Lexi's other arm. "Max shouldn't be the only one who gets a Bettina friendship bracelet."

"Good idea," Lexi said, "but we'll have to teach them how. If they don't do it themselves, the magic won't work."

"Oh, Lex, there's magic, all right. But it was never in the bracelets."

It was in their hearts, the hearts of best friends forever.

CHAPTER THIRTY-TWO
September 1999

Lexi stepped into the Parker Elementary School cafeteria, clutching her green lunch tray. Now she would find out what kind of impression she had made on her new classmates based on whether she was invited to sit with anyone. But there was only one invitation that really mattered to her.

Frannie Willets was the most interesting girl—the most interesting *person*—in the whole school. She hadn't spoken or fidgeted or even so much as coughed the entire morning, until Mrs. Jackson had called on her with a question about one of the books the third graders had been assigned to read over the summer. Frannie had answered it easily, completely, and without looking at anyone in the room except Mrs. Jackson. It drew Lexi's attention and everyone else's like a magnet.

"Don't think about sitting with her." Clarissa James, the coolest girl in the third-grade class from what Lexi could tell, had appeared beside her. "She's weird. She never even wears dresses. I don't think she owns any. You can sit with us." Clarissa nodded to the end of the table where three other girls already sat. "And you can tell us where you got that adorable skirt. And those shoes!"

Lexi glanced down at her white miniskirt with the tiny purple flowers that perfectly matched her purple tank top showing through the loose knit of her white sweater. Her mom had warned her against wearing her wedge sandals, but Lexi had insisted, and her mom had given in. Which told Lexi that her mom was nervous for Lexi's first day in a new school. "It's a fresh start for our family," her mom had said when she tucked Lexi in last night. "I know you miss your friends, but you'll make so many new ones. I just know it!"

And now Lexi had an invitation to sit with the popular girls on her very first day. She hated to let her mom down, but she wanted to say no. "I forgot to get milk," she said instead.

Clarissa smiled. "We'll hold your seat."

Lexi turned back to the kitchen and asked one of the lunch ladies for a carton of white milk. The woman frowned, but in a school so small that there was only one third grade, it must have been obvious Lexi was the new kid. The lunch lady handed Lexi a carton and told her to try to remember to pick up her milk while she was still in line. Lexi thanked her politely, which would have made her mom proud.

When Lexi returned to the wide-open cafeteria furnished with two rectangular tables for each grade, she glanced at Frannie again. Frannie shot her a look over the top of her book then dropped her eyes quickly, like she hoped Lexi hadn't noticed.

Lexi walked along the wall, getting closer to the girls' table with Frannie on one end and Clarissa and her friends on the other. A hard tug on her ponytail stopped her. "Ow!" She whirled around to see Sam Collins, who had been moved to a desk at the front of the room before ten o'clock that morning for throwing spitballs at Clarissa.

"Back off, Sammy." That firm, steady voice that had answered Mrs. Jackson's question about *Stellaluna* came from right beside Lexi.

"What's it to you, Frannie Pantsless?" Sam asked.

That made Lexi glance at Frannie's jeans, remembering what Clarissa had said about Frannie not owning dresses and wondering what Sam's stupid name meant. And Lexi noticed Frannie's wedge sandals, a lot like her own, only more scuffed. They had two things in common: their taste in shoes and their dislike for Sam Collins.

Friendships happened with fewer shared interests than that all the time. Lexi put a wish out into the universe, just like she had last spring when her parents had almost divorced and she had lit candles and said chants and willed them back together. *A best friend forever, a best friend forever, a best friend forever.*

Frannie crossed her arms in front of her and sighed like Sam was boring her, and he backed up a step. He ran right into a boy who looked a lot like him but was a head taller and had a dazzling, white-toothed grin.

"You're not causing trouble, are you, Sam?" the older boy asked.

"Just being a jerk like his older brother," Frannie answered. "No need for you to get your jerk-self involved, Seth."

Seth only grinned wider, and Lexi couldn't help thinking how much cuter he was than Sam. Or maybe it was just that he was older, or that he didn't seem like the type to shoot spitballs at girls and pull their hair.

"Find a seat far away from the girls," Seth told his brother, who scowled but obeyed. "Sorry about that, Frannie. And new girl."

Frannie sighed again, loudly. "Her name is Lexi, not that it's any of your business."

Mrs. Jackson, who was on lunch duty, walked over to join them. "Everything okay here, Seth?"

He nodded. "Just came over to say hi to my brother and meet Lexi." He glanced at Frannie as he spoke, but she focused on Mrs. Jackson and managed to look both attentive and still bored.

"Good," Mrs. Jackson said. "Lexi, why don't you sit with Frannie? You two have a lot in common." She looked at Frannie. "Lexi is the only other third-grader who read more than twelve books this summer."

Mrs. Jackson's attention got pulled away by some flying French fries at the fourth-grade boys' table.

It was now or never. If Lexi wanted to learn more about Frannie Willets, this might be the only opening she ever got. "Do you mind if I sit with you?"

Frannie shrugged a shoulder. "It's a free country."

Lexi followed her to the table and sat down across from her.

Frannie picked up her book but didn't look at it. "Did you really read more than twelve books this summer?"

Lexi nodded. "Fourteen."

Frannie narrowed her eyes. "Were they chapter books or books with pictures like the ones we had to read for Mrs. Jackson's class?"

"Both kinds." Lexi sat up straighter. "One of the chapter books I read was the first Harry Potter." Lexi wanted to impress Frannie, but she couldn't lie to her. She was pretty sure Frannie would know if she did. "It took a while, and my mom helped me a little."

Frannie arched an eyebrow again, no longer looking disinterested. "I've read all three by myself. I'm on the library waiting list to read them again."

"Wow."

If Frannie checked them out from the library, she must have read them fast to finish them before they were due. That meant she didn't own them, so she couldn't go back and reread her favorite parts anytime she wanted, like on a rainy Saturday afternoon or a hot summer day when your brain is too tired to read something new.

"I have them," Lexi said as she squeezed ketchup onto her fries. "The Harry Potter books. If you ever want to borrow them."

Frannie narrowed her eyes at Lexi again, like she didn't quite believe it. Or maybe she just didn't trust someone being nice to her. Lexi glanced toward Clarissa's end of the table. The popular girls were watching them, but they looked away and started chattering when Lexi caught them. If Frannie didn't trust Lexi, it was probably Clarissa's fault for talking to Lexi like she was one of those girls. But she wasn't. She didn't want to chatter and giggle and talk about skirts. She wanted to talk about Harry Potter and Goosebumps and how Frannie found it so easy to stand up to the Collins boys, even the one who seemed like he was being nice.

And Lexi had an in with Frannie just like Mrs. Jackson had suspected. She lowered her voice to a whisper. "Do the other girls in this school even read books when they don't have to?"

Frannie shrugged, but she smiled. Lexi couldn't help smiling back.

"Probably," Frannie said. "But they probably wouldn't talk about it. It's..."

"Weird," Lexi finished for her. "Like talking about skirts and shoes is more important than talking about books."

"Yeah, I guess weird is the word for it." Frannie glanced down at the book in her hand. "Have you read any of the Baby-Sitters Club books?"

Lexi nodded. "A couple of them."

Frannie sat up straighter and chomped on a carrot. She pointed the half-eaten stick at Lexi. "You have to read the ones from back in the '80s. That's when the original author wrote them. They're the best. I have a bunch at home, if you ever want to borrow them."

Lexi hadn't been that interested in the ones she had read, but they had been from the past couple of years. If Frannie said the ones from the '80s were good, Lexi would try them. "Maybe we could do a trade," she said.

Frannie nodded and continued eating her carrots.

Unnerved by the silence and worried they had already run out of things to say, and even more worried she would bore Frannie as much as everyone else seemed to, Lexi rushed ahead, talking fast. "You could come to my house on Saturday. You can bring some books, and you can look at the ones I have. We can figure out how many of the same ones we've both read and trade ones we haven't."

Frannie raised both eyebrows at her then glanced down at her book. Lexi could almost hear the debate going on inside her head. She watched the emotions on Frannie's face as she considered whether it was worth it, whether Lexi was worth taking a chance and Frannie maybe getting hurt. That was when Lexi realized why Frannie was so good at showing she didn't care. She had to make it look that way to protect herself because Frannie Willets did care. About people, about other kids, about what they thought of her. About what *Lexi* thought of her. Maybe more than any other person in that whole school cared.

"We could make brownies," Lexi offered, going for broke, hoping a love of brownies was one more thing they had in common, searching for something that would make Frannie say yes.

Frannie nodded slowly. "I can ask my mom. She works on Saturdays, so I don't know..."

"My mom and I could pick you up."

Frannie frowned, and Lexi worried she had pushed too far.

"Or your mom can just drop you off on her way to work, and you can stay for as long as she's there."

Frannie nodded again, not as slowly this time. "Okay. She'll want to call your mom to talk to her first."

Lexi's mom would want the same thing. Lexi was glad she hadn't had to say it because she didn't know if it would have made her sound like a baby. "I'll give you my phone number."

"Okay." Frannie stared down at her lunch tray, and for the first time all day, seemed kind of nervous. "Thanks," she said so softly, Lexi almost asked her to repeat it.

But she didn't. Instead, she smiled and asked Frannie what her favorite thing was about the Baby-Sitters Club books. She thought maybe her mom had been right all along. This move would be a good thing for all of them. Her parents would stay together. Their new jobs would give them more time together as a family. And Frannie

Willets, the most interesting person at Parker Elementary School, maybe even in the whole state, would be her new best friend.

Best friends forever, best friends forever, best friends forever, Lexi put out into the universe again. And she prayed the universe was listening.

Acknowledgments

In my life as an author, I've discovered that every book I write requires a village to support its creation. Often, that support comes in (literal and figurative) care and feeding of the author. With every book, I depend on my core team of supporters, and this time was no exception.

Once again, thank you to my family. Particularly, Augusta Christensen, thank you for your unwavering belief in my dream of being an author for over twenty years. To my friends, many of whom are also writers, thank you for laughs and drinks and hugs—virtual and IRL—that keep me going through every unpredictable twist and turn of a writing career. Special thanks to Amy, Joan, and Sheila, who have cheered unflaggingly for Frannie and Lexi's story to see the light of day.

With every new book, I've also had the great good fortune to add to my support circle. This time, I owe heartfelt gratitude to Lana Storey for supporting the early development of the manuscript and to Sheila Athens for guidance and support throughout the rest of the writing journey. Special thanks to the Red Adept team, including Lynn McNamee, Angie Gallion, Darlene Gardner, Erica Lucke Dean, and the team at Street Light Graphics for believing in this book and carrying it across the finish line.

Last but never least, thank you, reader. It thrills and amazes me every time a reader invests time and emotion into a story that once just lived inside my head. I hope Frannie and Lexi's story will continue to live inside your heart.

About the Author

Nancy Yeager spent her early years longing to be an English countryside vet, thanks to James Herriot's *All Creatures Great and Small* book series, and dreaming of being an adventurous archaeologist like George Lucas's Indiana Jones. After studying veterinary pre-med and earning an anthropology degree, she realized her true passion was story in all its forms.

Nancy now writes in multiple fiction genres. When she's not reading, writing, or binge-watching stories, she's often pursuing a physical challenge, like training for a triathlon or aspiring to achieve the perfect crow pose. She also spends her time drinking too much coffee, not enough red wine, and just the right amount of bourbon. She lives in Maryland with her fabulous family, which includes her demanding overlords, collectively known as The Cats.

Read more at https://nancyyeagerbooks.com.

About the Publisher

Dear Reader,

We hope you enjoyed this book. Please consider leaving a review on your favorite book site.

Visit https://RedAdeptPublishing.com to see our entire catalogue.

Check out our app for short stories, articles, and interviews. You'll also be notified of future releases and special sales.

www.ingramcontent.com/pod-product-compliance
Lightning Source LLC
Chambersburg PA
CBHW061103190726
48286CB00006B/1865